MAURIN THE ILLUSTRIOUS

MAURIN
THE ILLUSTRIOUS
A TRANSLATION FROM THE FRENCH OF JEAN AICARD BY ALFRED ALLINSON, M.A.

WILDSIDE PRESS

WILLIAM BRENDON AND SON, LTD., PRINTERS, PLYMOUTH

CONTENTS

CONTENTS

CONTENTS

CHAPTER XXXVI

CHAPTER XXXVII

CHAPTER XXXVIII

CHAPTER XXXIX

CHAPTER XL

CHAPTER XLI

CHAPTER XLII

CHAPTER XLIII

CHAPTER XLIV

x

CONTENTS

CONTENTS

MAURIN THE ILLUSTRIOUS

: : MAURIN : :
THE ILLUSTRIOUS

CHAPTER I

In which Pastouré plays the part of the Classic chorus, and informs
the public of such events as it concerns us to know.

PASTOURÉ, otherwise known as Parlo-Soulet, being alone,
in bed at his brother's house at the *Cabanes Vieilles*, was
talking to himself, as his way was, in a loud, clear voice :
" Yes, yes, I always said Maurin wasn't dead. Yet it's
true enough that villain the charcoal-burner, that smutty-
faced black devil of a Grondard, attacked him in the
middle of the night while Maurin was squatted in his hut
of boughs—I have the story from his own mouth—on the
look-out for wild-boar. Yes, he was on the look-out, was
Maurin, and when a man's like that—I know it of my
own experience—his ears are precious wide open and he
can catch the faintest sounds ; but then, you're never
sure of yourself, because all the tiny, tiny little noises of
the woods seem to kick up a regular uproar in your head.
A pine-cone dropping makes you jump, and a fellow says to
himself, ' They're coming, the wild-boar ; there's several
of 'em—a whole herd ! ' and there's never any boar at
all. . . . Or else, just the opposite, you hear 'em kicking
up the ground, and you think, ' Oh ! it's nothing—just a
squirrel's knocked down a fir-cone ! ' Yes, it's mighty
easy, at night, in the woods, for things to cheat you—the

soughing of the wind, the flickering of the shadows, anything and everything. Well, Maurin, who had heard the
undergrowth rustling a bit near him, just thought like
that, ' Oh ! it's nothing ! ' But all the while it was that
black-faced blackguard Grondard—he had been spying
round to make sure he was there—creeping up with his
gun. . . . *Noum dé pas Dioû!* I think I can see the scoundrel ! . . . He'd be sidling up cautiously, cautiously—
a step forward, and then a stop for a good five minutes !
Then suddenly he pops the muzzle of his gun in between
the branches. But Maurin knows what's in the wind now
. . . and in an instant he grips the barrel and turns the
weapon aside ; it goes off—and misses him ! . . .

" That's where Maurin showed his artfulness ; he gave
a great bellow, a terrible cry like a man mortally wounded,
to make Grondard think he had accomplished the foul
deed he had come to do. So the villain, feeling convinced
his bullet had reached its billet, made off at a gallop, he
did—and precious glad, no doubt, he'd managed so well !
. . . They say Maurin, when he was attacked, had just
fired off his two barrels at the wild-boar ; but Lord ! they
only show their ignorance. No, it's not true—how could
it be, because the boars must have scented Grondard or
heard him, if they had been anywhere about. . . . Now,
how else could Maurin defend his life, all entangled as he
was among the branches, if not by the trick he tried,
dropping with his agonised cry of ' Mother, mother ! I'm
killed ' ? He came out presently, gun in hand, when he
heard his enemy racing off through the woods ; . . . but
racing, no, that's not the word—I'd just like to see a man
racing, at midnight too, through the thick heather ! Why,
the thing's impossible in broad daylight. . . . However,
all's well that ends well ; the unrighteous don't always
prevail, and Maurin's safe and sound this time. . . .

" But, all the same, he makes over many enemies.
First there's Grondard ; he firmly believes Maurin killed
his father—a vile dog everybody knew was good for
nothing. Then Sandri, whose girl Tonia he has taken

from him. Then Orsini, Tonia's father, who'd rather have
his daughter marry the gendarme. Then that rich hunks
Caboufigue, whom he's baulking of being Deputy. Then
Tonia herself, who's a Corsican and has a pretty grim
way of her own of loving a man, as the women have there ;
and if he makes her jealous, she'll as like as not, one of
these fine mornings, let him have the point of her Corsican
needle !... He's not careful enough of women, isn't
Maurin ; that's where he makes a mistake. He loves 'em
all, and he's a fool for his pains ;... they'll play him a
scurvy trick yet ... and it's Parlo-Soulet says so !

" Luckily, just for a bit, his friends seem to have the
upper hand. That M. Rinal—and he's Maurin's great
admirer—has very fine acquaintances, to be sure, and
friends in the Government. The other day, when the
Minister came to see him at Bormes, he up and asked him
to save Maurin from his scrape—and Maurin deserves it
too ! So all these confounded plaguy difficulties, all these
procès-barbaux they make against him every time he takes
sides for justice, real justice, against knaves and fools, all
this is to be clean forgot, all to be as if it had never been,
never been seen or heard of ! And Maurin's enemies,
Grondard and Sandri and all, will pull a face, mes beaux
anges de Dieu ! as long as from here to Les Martigues.
Later on, never fear, he'll bring down more of 'em on
himself, more procès-barbaux, because it's his nature to,
pechère ! and he can't help it ; anyway, for a while he'll
have a breathing space ! But not a very long while, it's
certain sure, because it's his nature, I say, to attract
procès-barbaux, the same as cypresses, folk say, attract
the lightning.

" Why, what can you expect of a man who will have
nothing but real justice, just justice in the world ? Yes,
he's one—I see that plain enough—who'll always have the
fools against him ; and the fools are a mighty army, I tell
you ; all the world's in its ranks !

" What d'you expect of a man who goes and forces a
chap like Caboufigue to sign him a paper promising he'll

never so much as try to be Deputy—and he a millionaire !
It's putting against him a citizen who's more powerful
than the Almighty in this world of ours, for money, my
lads, money is the King of all Republics.

"And that day Verdoulet killed Grondard (it was
Verdoulet, I know, for a fact ; his wife's a chatterbox, and
let out the whole story at last), why did Maurin, who saw
him do it, why on earth did Maurin tell him, 'I'll never
give you away'? No, he ought to have said, 'I'll never
give you away, Verdoulet, unless I'm accused myself of
doing it.' But, there, he has promised not to say a word;
and, having promised, he'll keep his word, the fellow !

"Yet this is the worst charge so far of all I've heard
of against him, for, after all, it's a man's life is concerned—
if you can call Grondard a man ! He was a devil, really ;
but he had a face on him like you or me—and that was
cruel unfair !

"And why, I ask you, does Maurin let 'em say he did
it, when he knows who fired the shot? This Grondard
was a bad lot, and the folks called him the *Besti* (the
Brute) ; the Ogre was another name he had, because he
used to chivy the children he came across in the woods.
The day he met his death he was chasing a little girl
who was carrying her father his dinner one noon in the
woods. Verdoulet saw him from a distance almost in the
act of doing his villainy, and up with his gun and shot
him like a mad dog. All Maurin had to do was not to
show himself and slip away at once. But not he ; he must
come forward forsooth, and tell Verdoulet, 'Well done !
I'll never say one word !' Then what happens ? Why,
Verdoulet, when they accuse Maurin before his face, as
they do at times, just lets 'em talk away and think, like
the rest of the world, that Maurin did it. . . . And a good
deed too, it was, a fine stroke of business ! It rid the
country of an odious ruffian, a thief, a dangerous robber, a
bad citizen and a bad neighbour, a scamp and a scoundrel ! . . . But make the world see things in the light of
true justice—not you ! . . . It needs a Maurin to conceive

such a thing as possible at all ; and he'll pay the piper for his folly in the end, *pechère !* And what can I do, pray, but just look on and cry my eyes out ; for he won't hear me speak, and whatever he wishes, that I shall always do."

Having thus expounded matters to himself at great length and indulged in manifold comments, only some of which we have reproduced, Pastouré turned over in bed on to his right side and fell asleep, grumbling and growling.

CHAPTER II

Saulnier, the stonebreaker, gives the Don Juan of the woods a piece
of not unpleasant news.

MAURIN was marching cheerfully along the high road that
runs from Le Don to La Molle. His heart was light, for
M. Rinal's efforts had been crowned with success, and now
everything was arranged, all difficulties smoothed away
and offences forgotten, by special favour.

Hercules had just announced in a fashion there was no
mistaking the presence of partridges in the near neighbourhood. The dog stopped dead and pointed, his tail
stuck out stiff as a ramrod, just as any well-trained animal
should ; but then—a thing which a well-trained dog
should *not* do—after each point he would turn his head
and look back at his master and flick his tail, as if tipping
him a wink !

" I understand," laughed Maurin ; " yes, they're partridges, but partridges of a special sort . . . they're Saulnier's partridges, eh ? Now you drop your tail and lie
flat, do you ? . . . That's because you've recognised
Saulnier's fox. . . . And the weasel, you've nothing to
say to her ; you don't think her worth your notice ? "

Things were, in fact, just as Hercules announced.

Soon Maurin caught sight of the partridges scuffling
along the dusty road, their little legs striding fast, while
their wings were half open and flapping the air. Away
they went to find covert between the fox's paws. *She*
was lying full length on a long heap of stones, on one end
of which Saulnier was seated, lifting and dropping his
heavy hammer, breaking between his legs the big pebbles
from the neighbouring mountain-stream. He cut a strange

8

figure, did the stonebreaker, with his big, round wired goggles that protected and hid his eyes.

"And the weasel?" asked Maurin.

"She put herself in a safe place," Saulnier said, "under my fox's bushy tail, as her way is, directly she heard your step."

"Good day, all! good day!" cried Maurin heartily; "you're all well and hearty, I can see.

"Chè novo?"

"Oh! there's something new afoot for you," said Saulnier; "your friends are hunting for you everywhere. They've not seen you anywhere, neither the conductor of the diligence, nor the foresters, nor Grondard, nor the innkeeper at Les Campaux, nor the folks at Le Don, nor anybody, in fact."

"My old mother was a bit out of sorts," said Maurin, "and I've been looking after her. . . ."

"They tell me," Saulnier went on, "there's no more complaints out against you now, and the gendarmes aren't after you any more?"

"And it's true enough; but you said my friends were looking for me. Why's that?"

"At Bormes, at M. Rinal's, there's news waiting for you."

"Good news?"

"Neither good nor bad. Something to do with politics."

"Very well, I'll go and hear it," said Maurin.

"That's not all," added the other, getting up and dropping his hammer to lift his cap with one hand while he wiped his forehead with the back of the other. . . . Then, after a pause, he looked slyly at Maurin, clapping a finger underneath one of his spectacled eyes, and said:

"There's something else too."

"And what's that? You're not so close-lipped usually."

"If there's any special hurry, I can go faster," drawled Saulnier. . . . "And maybe this *is* a bit urgent; but there, it's not so urgent as all that neither, I reckon."

"Stop your joking, Saulnier, and have done now,"

cried Maurin ; but at the same time he pretended to be in no particular hurry to hear the news. He knew there were times when the old fellow loved to have a bit of talk, and that it was his way occasionally to make his communications drag out as long as ever he could on purpose to exasperate his hearers. And then the more impatient you got, the longer old Saulnier kept you waiting—though you might make sure of this, he only did so if the delay involved no real risk or danger for you.

But now Saulnier once more came to a dead stop. His eyes were dancing with malicious joy. The crow's-feet on his temples wrinkled like the sea dimpling before a breeze ; while the lines about his nose and mouth laughed an odd laugh. The mysterious, inexpressible inner life of the man came out in every feature of his face in eloquent hieroglyphics that spoke plainly enough what his lips still refused to say.

"And so you've got no more to say ? " suggested Maurin, with the impassive calm of an Arab sheikh.

"Why, I've told you nothing yet ! " declared Saulnier.

Maurin quietly took a seat on the heap of stones, his gun between his knees.

"There," resumed Saulnier, "there you have a gun may yet get you into trouble these days—and you may well be sick of *procès-verbaux*, mate, by this time ! Close time began again *yesterday*, you know."

"Yes," retorted Maurin ; " and can't you see I'm carrying my gun home, like a good, sensible man ? "

Both burst out laughing, each looking as knowing as the other.

"And then," Maurin explained further, " you know very well it's eagles I shoot ! and that's not game, so you can kill it any time. Fox the same."

"Don't you abuse foxes," laughed Saulnier ; "and remember this, eagles don't need you to take a dog with you!"

"There I beg your pardon," protested Maurin ; "I can prove conclusively a dog is the best bait for luring eagles."

At this allusion, which recalled the incident of Secour-

geon's eagle and his subsequent misadventures, the pair
guffawed so uproariously that Saulnier could hardly stand,
and doubled up with a hand on either knee to finish out his
laugh comfortably. Otherwise he would have been forced
to sit down to it, his paroxysms of mirth shaking him as
a *mistral* shakes a plum tree and brings the plums rattling
down.

"And now for what you've got to tell me?" put in
Maurin.

"Ah!" grinned Saulnier, taking a long breath, "I
haven't had such a good laugh, not since I was a boy, I
haven't! The thought of old Secourgeon will set me laughing any day—any day till I get my retirement."

"You'll have a retirement pension, eh?"

"Everybody ends with one of sorts. Some get one
paid in money; all get one in the shape of some ugly infirmity or other. . . . But to come at last to what I really
have to tell you, Maurin, it's along of you and Tonia. I tell
you she's in love with you; every day she leaves her
father Orsini's house, and every day, ever since you escaped out of Sandri's hands, she goes to the *cantine* at
Le Don to see if you've been there again. When she believed you were dead, just think, she was so unhappy she
was like to die. At first hearing, she dropped in a dead
faint, and they had all the trouble in the world to bring her
round. And since that day, she has been seen in tears over
and over again, and she's getting as thin as a wolf in winter!
What's betwixt you is your concern, but to see a pretty girl
crying, that's enough to melt a stone! . . . And she is
pretty, is Tonia. . . . So just think it over, as you go along
to Bormes, my lad, and consider what you'd best do. . . .
And so, a good journey to you; I knew you'd be in a hurry
to be off directly I told you my tale. Go your ways, and
let me get on with my work. Work's a fine thing, though
mine is a bit too hard and too monotonous; still, it warms
a man up as well as a glass of *aiguarden*."

Maurin groped in his bag and pulled out his flask, which
he held out to Saulnier.

"There's no refusing a good offer. . . . To your good health ! "

He lifted his elbow, smacked his lips, wiped his mouth with his sleeve, and said, " *Gracias !* "

Maurin put back his flask, shook Saulnier by the hand, got to his feet and marched off, followed by Hercules ; the dog seemed loath to leave the old fellow's tame fox, which hardly reciprocated the compliment.

Saulnier sat down again, resumed his goggles, and picking up his hammer fell to cracking the stones between his outstretched legs.

One by one the partridges ventured out from between the fox's paws, and went back to the dusty middle of the road.

Finally, the weasel crept out from under her protector's bushy tail, while the latter laid her sharp-pointed nose luxuriously on her crossed paws.

CHAPTER III

Caboufigue fails ignominiously at once as a financier and as a
sportsman.

ANXIOUS to study so perfect an example of his peculiar
type, Cabissol had assured Caboufigue that on all occasions
he would find him ready to help him with his advice and
assistance. The opportunity was not long in occurring.

A dreadful financial scandal had just shaken the whole
country, scattering confusion and disaster broadcast like
some hideous infernal machine. A million anarchist
bombs crammed with the most powerful explosives would
not have spread such havoc as this catastrophe on the
money market. The little savings of the poor were swept
away, and the cheerful blaze extinguished on a thousand
hearths. In the broad plains of France and in the woods
of the Maures dejected-looking peasants might be seen,
sitting on their plough-tail, or on the ground beside their
half-famished cow browsing on their neighbour's grass,
and busy reading and re-reading with a dismal eagerness
the halfpenny journal that announced their ruin. Maurin
came across one of these poor fellows who was shedding
tears of rage and biting his nails in impotent fury.

" What are you crying for ? " Maurin asked him.

" I'm crying because I'm ruined. I had ten thousand
francs, and the scoundrels have robbed me of my money."

" And why," asked Maurin, " did you put your money
in their hands, if not in hopes it would bring you in ten
times as much as the fair interest it does in the savings
bank ? "

" That's very true," sighed the fellow.

" And supposing all the rest were ruined," said Maurin,

13

" and your ten thousand francs had brought *you* in, and only you, a hundred thousand ? "

" I don't care a d——n for the others ! " declared the man.

" Then you may cry yourself into a fit, my boy," retorted Maurin, " for all I care ; your plight only makes me laugh. You're only a half-baked bourgeois after all. Poor France ! "

Under M. Rinal's tuition it was not Maurin's son only that was learning lessons. The father, too, retained something from the old savant's lessons ; and his mind, which had always been open to generous impressions, found new windows revealing the broad and gloomy horizon of the realities of social life and human selfishness.

" Poor France ! " was an exclamation frequently to be heard nowadays from Maurin's lips. It is a favourite phrase with the Provençal countryman. He says *Pauvre moi !* to express his own grief ; *Pechère !* in sympathy with the individual hardships of his fellow-men. But it is always *Pauvre France !* to bewail the evils that appear to him to impair the vitality of the country as a whole.

Caboufigue was compromised in these shady speculations. His name was a mark for the most violent abuse in the daily press. He had corrupted others, and himself been deteriorated in the process. His broad, red face that once beamed with perpetual satisfaction lost its cheerfulness. The dread of alarming possibilities and responsibilities robbed him of sleep. In a few days he lost flesh amazingly, and lamented ruefully, " The skin hangs loose about my poor legs like a pair of trousers ! " What conscience cannot do in such cases—for such men have no conscience—fear did with him. He had terrible fits of remorse ; of nights he was a prey to appalling nightmares. From a grotesque he had become a tragic figure. He lived in constant terror, expecting every moment to see his door open to admit the gendarmes ; he was going to be arrested, he thought ; he was going the way so many other fellows had gone before him. The electric bell at his front door left him trembling every time the postman mounted the magnificent *perron* and set it ringing. He was on an island, and he had a wholesome fear of the mainland. He would climb up to his tower, armed with a long ship's telescope, to watch the approach of the tiniest boat, trying at long range to make out who its occupants were. At sight of a sunshade across a lady passenger's knees, he thought it was a Police Commissary come for him, girt with his tricolour sash. Poor Caboufigue was every day losing a little more in weight. " I'm melting, melting away," he groaned ; and it was true, he was dissolving like pewter on a red-hot shovel. In this parlous state he sent in sheer desperation a friend to M. Cabissol to beseech his aid. He could not, and durst not, write to anyone. He longed to talk things over, and asked for a personal interview. *Verba volant.* He begged M. Cabissol to arrange for him to meet Maurin, whose influence seemed to him altogether supernatural ever since he had obtained the cross for him. M. Cabissol replied :

" Be at Hyères on such a day, at such an hour. I have had Maurin informed ; we will join him by carriage. The pretext must be a shooting-party. Come in shooting rig ; this will serve to distract your thoughts, for the papers lead me to guess the cause of your anxieties."

Caboufigue was punctual to the minute. From Hyères he drove off with M. Cabissol to join Maurin in the out-skirts of La Venerie, not far from Bormes. Maurin was waiting their arrival.

" We have marked the lie of a number of badger earths, and taken the dogs we want to work them ! The carriage will wait for you at the inn, near here."

The three sportsmen, Maurin, Cabissol, and Caboufigue, set off to walk to the scene of action.

" We shall find Pastouré there before us ; he's busy with a *vibou* (billhook) clearing the ground of scrub round the earths."

" M. Caboufigue," began Cabissol, " wishes to have a

talk with you, Maurin ; he is very anxious, and he has his reasons . . ."—and M. Cabissol repeated, not without a sarcastic ring in his voice, the confidences Caboufigue had made him during their drive.

"But what," Maurin demanded, "can I do in the matter ? "

"I should like," stammered Caboufigue, his cheeks pale and his hands shaking, "I should like—you know, the individual by whose help you got me the cross—I should like you to write again to the same individual . . ."

"To give it back ? " put in Maurin.

"To see me safe from harm," whined Caboufigue miserably.

"But if facts cry out against you, what can she do ? "

"Write all the same. It may be a word . . . possibly a word. . . . The fact is, I don't know," faltered the poor man, half frantic.

"What are you afraid of, Caboufigue ? "

"Nothing—and everything."

"What harm have you done ? "

"The same as all the others ; but they haven't got my name in writing anywhere. If one man holds his tongue, I am saved."

"And who is the man ? "

"Why, who should it be ? " cried Caboufigue ; "it's the individual's husband. . . ."

"But, to tell you the truth," said Maurin, "your fate does not move my pity much. What call have we, what interest have we, we honest folks, to render you a service of the sort ? How will it serve the ends of justice—the very smallest, tiniest bit ? "

"You have the same interest as you had before," replied Caboufigue, simply and frankly ; "if my name is mixed up publicly in this business, I'll offer myself as a candidate for the Chamber, in spite of the promise I gave you, and if it cost me the half of my fortune, I mean to carry the day against everybody."

"Oh, ho ! " laughed Maurin derisively ; "so here we

have a pig turning on the dogs just like a wild-boar. . . .
But, to say nothing of the undertaking you gave us not to
stand, are you so sure that, compromised as you are, you
wouldn't be doing for yourself altogether by appealing
to the judgment of the electors? They might, likely
enough, instead of sending you to the Palais Bourbon, send
you to the hulks, my boy!"

"I shall never be compromised deep enough for that.
I've never done any very dreadful things, I swear to that,"
protested Caboufigue. "I've only done like everybody
else—petty pilferings, you know . . . but I've nothing so
serious against me as to justify extreme measures. It's
my cross I'm most afraid of losing."

"And do you really and truly imagine," said Maurin,
"that in the pickle you're in, they'd elect you Deputy,
even though you poured out gold like water? And what
about the opposition I shall raise against you, to begin
with?"

"Your opposition will be honest and straightforward,
at least," groaned Caboufigue; "I know you, you're a
good fellow and a fine fellow at bottom."

"I see what you are," said Maurin; "you're one of
those chaps who hide their bits of roguery and petty
thefts and self-seeking intrigues under the cloak of great
sounding words and a whole heap of humbug. You shout
for anyone who will hear, 'It's for my country! for France!
Let's do one thing or the other! We must have this war
or that! For the honour of the flag!' But all the while
you're after doing some dirty little job! . . . Don't
count on me for help; you sicken me! As for your
standing, you have given up all idea of that, remember.
That's sufficient, so there's no need for other reasons.
That was why I got you your decoration! It's enough—
because it's already too much. Have you no shame,
deuce take it?"

"M. Caboufigue is right enough from his point of view,"
observed M. Cabissol slyly. "The Chamber would re-
habilitate his reputation."

c

"Think it over, Maurin," insisted Caboufigue; "we'll talk about it again to-night."

"I *have* thought it over," declared Maurin roundly

"No, no," urged the persistent Caboufigue; "you've not said your last word. About my candidature, yes, I know you're against me; but still, you'll write a word to the lady, won't you? That will cost you nothing."

"Bah! you're a fine beggar!" sneered Maurin, looking slightingly at Caboufigue; "I've no further answer to give you. Now I don't want to lose my one or two badger skins. You'll come with me and see 'em drawn, if it amuses you, and you can go back in your carriage afterwards."

So Caboufigue went on with the party, hoping that before the end of the day he would manage to touch the heart of this old friend of his boyhood.

"You know, Caboufigue, badgers, it's of their hair we make shaving-brushes, so we shall be working for you after all."

Meantime Pastouré was cutting the scrub close, and having cleared the badger earths on the slope of the hill, he was now holding in the dogs and telling them in loud tones:

"We shall have 'em! There's two of 'em, I can hear 'em scratching. He's a long while, is Maurin, bringing along his man, who, by what he says, is no great shakes with all his money, and not a very lucky one either, *pechère!* . . . There, I'm pitying the chap again! The whole blessed thing seems to me for the best, and the ruin of all those idiots who think you can kill six hares all at once with one shot. Everything's worth paying for, mates, even a good lesson. . . . Ah! here comes the *messiés* (gentlemen). . . . 'Pon my word, yes, he looks, with his double pig-skin, a very fine specimen of a swine! . . . But there, the main thing to-day is to kill the *rabà* (badger)."

Maurin posted Caboufigue and M. Cabissol, explaining:

"When the little dog has gone in by this hole, the *rabà*

won't be long in showing at the other one yonder. Then
aim at his nose, before he bolts, and he's a dead badger.
Else he slips out, the little varmint, and then rolls himself
up into a ball and puffs himself out, and then the lead
won't pierce his thick skin, and so he'll roll right away
down the hill and into the brushwood like an indiarubber
ball. Look out! the dog's at work."

After a wait in dead silence, the *rabà* suddenly showed
his nose.

" Your shot, sir! " said Maurin politely to M. Cabissol—
and that gentleman's gun roused the echoes in the hills.

The dog dragged out the *rabà* from his hole half dead.
Then another badger poked his nose from the earth.

"Now you, Caboufigue! " whispered Maurin.

But Caboufigue's nerves, since he had been the victim
of such intense and chronic terror, had been in a sadly
jangled state. He aimed carefully, took his time, and
pulled the trigger ; but the condition of distress he was in
made him clumsy and absent-minded ; he had clean forgotten to load, and both barrels were empty ! The cock
fell with the impotent click of a missfire ; but the noise
was sufficient to frighten the badger out of its seven senses,
and coiling itself up into a ball, it rolled rapidly down to the
bottom of the ravine, without anybody even thinking of
a second shot, so instantaneous and irresistible was the
laugh that shook the sportsmen's sides—all except Caboufigue, who was covered with confusion.

"You blundering beggar! " ejaculated Maurin on the
spur of the moment. Then, after a hearty laugh :

" Yes, you're always the same, you great hog! " he
declared. " If your chances for the Chamber weren't dead
already, my man, I tell you you'd have killed 'em by that
silly trick."

" Joke away, joke away ! but hear what I've got to say,"
growled Caboufigue presently, " and do what I ask you
to do."

" When you've a shot right in front of your nose, you
clumsy brute, you go and miss your chance ! I've only

got to tell the story without a word more," Maurin wound up, "and you'll be the laughing-stock for ever of all the countryside of the Var and all my kingdom of the Maures."

"Oh! by the Lord!" cried Caboufigue impatiently. "We're all liable to make mistakes. Take your own case; do you suppose people would approve your doings, if they knew how you got my cross for me and by whose instrumentality?"

The monstrous ingratitude of such a speech and its veiled threat was too much for Maurin! Caboufigue, who had profited by his recommendation, now called the whole affair scandalous, and like to bring him, Maurin, into danger! the man actually seemed prepared, if it served his purpose, to denounce him as an object of public scorn! A sudden gust of anger carried away the King of the Maures, and Caboufigue received a resounding box on the ear.

"You shall pay me for that!" cried Caboufigue haughtily. "I have a son!"

He said so much quietly enough, but then fell into a fury, and walked off, adding:

"Come, let's go back to my carriage, M. Cabissol."

"Look here, M. Caboufigue," said Cabissol, who had much ado not to burst out laughing; "look here, between old friends, old friends of boyhood, that's nothing, you know; you must kiss and make up."

But Caboufigue would not hear a word, but marched off the ground, followed by Cabissol, wearing a polite but amused air.

CHAPTER IV

Maurin pays two visits, both of a highly agreeable character.

MAURIN was now aware from old Saulnier's indiscreet chatter that he held a higher place in Tonia's affections than he had supposed. He gloated over the pleasant news for a week, and ended by making his way one fine morning to the Forester's lodge. . . . He had come to a resolution that surprised himself.

" Great heaven ! " cried Tonia at sight of Maurin; " to think I believed you were dead ! . . . All the same, it's as well my father's not in ! "

" Oh ! " said Maurin coolly, " now I've nothing to fear from the Law, why should I be afraid of your father ? "

She stepped up to Maurin, put a hand on each of his shoulders, and gazed into his eyes. Being much shorter than her lover, she had to crane back her head, and as she looked up at him towering above her, the girl's bosom rose and fell at a fine rate with love and excitement !

Her eyes were full of yearning, and looked liquid and almost tearful.

" You're crying ? " he asked. " Why, I thought you'd be so happy ! "

" Happiness makes women cry sometimes," she told him. " Yes, I love you, Maurin, I know that now. . . . Will you have something to eat and drink ? . . . And if my father comes in, you must have an explanation together."

" No," he said, " I'm neither hungry nor thirsty. But tell me, how are things going with you ? "

" We've had words with Sandri, because of you; but he has sent to tell us he'll come back at the first word, and

21

let bygones be bygones. I laughed at him so for letting you escape that he rather lost his temper. Why, Maurin, only to think of you as a prisoner, to know you in confinement, I should have fallen ill, I should have gone mad! You are a fine creature of the woods, my gallant Maurin! you would die yourself, if they kept you in gaol!"

He kissed her long and lovingly on cheeks and eyes and mouth, and every part of her pretty face. But she kept repeating :

"But all the same, Maurin, my father mustn't see you ; so go now."

"Yes, if you wish . . . but in that case, come and see me for a bit at the *cantine* of Le Don."

"To be sure I will," she assented, "if you go now. We shall be freer there."

So he went, and she followed him presently, so happy to see him and be with him she had no thought of asking anything else, of demanding that he should marry her, or even be faithful to her. No, she only stood silent and still awhile in his arms. All her scruples were gone, because she loved him! She was so happy she would have left her father's house that minute, if Maurin had said to her, "Come!" She would have followed her wild wolf of the woods wherever he chose, though she must die for it!

They talked long together.

"For all one night I believed you dead, my brave Maurin! . . . I should have killed Grondard, if Grondard had killed you!"

"And you would have done very wrong," declared Maurin.

"Wrong!" she exclaimed; "you don't understand then what vengeance means? You don't intend, if you have a chance, to empty your gun into the brute?"

"In self-defence, yes, I will, if I must," said Maurin; "but as for killing him in return for his shot of the other night, no, I shall never do that."

Tonia made a face.

"Bah! you are only a Frenchman," she laughed. "I

can't expect a mainlander to have the blood of our island folk."

" A man's life," said Maurin, " is a thing you can't bring back again ; so one must think twice before destroying it. Grondard is a brute beast, and that's his best excuse—*but* he'll do well not to attack me face to face ! "

As he said the words, the gallant fellow showed such a fine flame in his angry eyes that Tonia suddenly threw her arms about his neck, crying, ' I love you, oh ! I love you ! "

" And," he asked, " when shall we see each other again this cold time of year ? "

" Here, sometimes, if you will," she said, " in this little room where passing customers don't come, and from which I can see through the windows, by pushing the curtain a bit on one side, if my father's coming to disturb us. . . . Then, if needful, you have the door the other side opening on the woods."

" The *rabà* (badger)," he said, " always has two holes to his earth."

Next he went to see M. Rinal. He marched boldly into the village, his gun unloaded, his dog at his heels, the passers-by greeting him here and there as he went along.

The house-door at M. Rinal's was open, as usual, and stepping into the corridor, he tapped discreetly at the door of the small parlour where he could hear the master of the house talking.

" Come in ! " said the pleasant, hospitable voice.

Maurin's boy was bending in deep attention over his copy-book spread open on the table before him, and had his back to the door. His eyes never left the paper. He did not look round or make the slightest movement, not having heard the door open.

Maurin did not venture to reclose it. M. Rinal, glancing over the child's head, signed to the father to take a seat without a word.

" H'sh ! " he said mutely, finger on lip.

Softly Maurin pushed to the door ; he had already by a wave of the hand ordered his dog to stay outside in the garden, and the good beast lay down to keep guard over the gun and game-bag his master had deposited at the foot of a tree.

In perfect silence Maurin sat down, his hat between his hands and his hands between his knees.

Once more M. Rinal signed to him not to speak. Then, aloud, the old savant began, addressing the lad :

" Now you have read the chapter and I have explained it to you, repeat me all the things it says, as you have understood them."

Then the boy, lifting his eyes from his book, recited slowly :

" In the beginning, man was a savage. He was naked. He made himself rude weapons out of sticks and stones. He lived in caves ; he came out of them to go hunting, and he went hunting to feed his wife and his little ones, who stayed at home in the cave meanwhile. Whenever he encountered other men out hunting, he was angry, because they were chasing the same beast that he wanted to have himself to feed his family. And sometimes, when two men met thus, they fought one against the other to dispute the prey.

" One day, however. against a savage animal that was stronger than he, a man asked the help of another man. And helping each other, they were, the two of them, stronger than the beast.

" And thereupon they thought that instead of fighting, one man with another, each to have his prey all to himself, they would find it a much better plan to share it between them, and to remain united so as to be always the stronger against all the wild beasts.

" And this was the first association or society of men.

" Next, these two men allied themselves with a third, a fourth, and so on, till it came to founding villages, and presently towns.

" And all those who had formed alliance owed to each other mutual help and assistance, and paid one another by dividing the product of their labour.

" This compact remains in force. Each man owes his work to all men, and all men are bound to work for the safety and well-being of each. It is thus we come to have rights and duties.

" This compact binds together everybody, for each individual understands that if he refused to work for everybody, justice would demand that such a one should be put back, naked and alone in the savage state in which the first man was; and no one would consent to such a thing.

" For the most wretched of mankind is still highly favoured that there are houses all ready built, and wheat sown, and flour, and bread, and fires burning, and light.

" And if anyone dies of hunger without its being his own fault, everybody is blameworthy, for each individual has the right to live, and the laws must be altered which allow a man to die of hunger for lack of work.

" And the laws will be altered, if the people, well taught at school, know their own best interest and learn to choose wisely those whom they send to make the laws.

" So long as the laws are not altered, we must obey them, because they represent the deliberate and intelligent will of the people themselves, as opposed to their instincts and passions as savages.

" But if an individual refuses society his share of work, he is unworthy and a worse traitor than the open enemies of the city, for society has the right to rely on those who are bound together by the compact of rights and duties.

" Country is a great association, which embraces many cities, villages, provinces.

" Humanity has duties and rights which are common to all countries, and which are far greater and nobler.

" We must be strong, because a man must be the stronger, to defend the right of the weaker.

" We must search, before everything, in all countries, after justice, which is the best guarantee of our interests, and have in our hearts the love of mankind, which is greater even than justice itself, inasmuch as it includes it."

The child stopped, and for the first time saw his father, but he still sat good and quiet at his book.

" He is learning all that," said M. Rinal, " from a little copy-book I have arranged for him ; it also teaches him that true justice is an ideal, a realisable idea, but the realisation of which is long of coming, for many men are wicked and false and violent, and these forget that if all have obligations to each, it is on condition that each works for all to the best of his powers. And if the shares are unequal, it is because goodwill is not equal in all men, nor intelligence either. And it can never be brought about that they shall be. It is to be wished, therefore, in the interests of all, that the best men and the most intelligent should guide all the rest ; government must belong to experience and knowledge. The beasts themselves choose their leaders in conformity with this law."

When M. Rinal, who had been addressing the child, looked up at Maurin, he saw that, with steadfast eyes and unwinking lids, the man was weeping quietly.

Suddenly springing up and dropping on his knees beside his son, Maurin threw his arms about the lad, pressed him to his breast and kissed him, saying :

" Yes, yes, you'll grow up to be a *man*. Work hard, youngster, work ; for ' work is freedom ' ! "

And before the old savant could prevent him, Maurin had clasped one of his delicate, wrinkled hands which hung in its muslin ruffle over the arm of his armchair and, despite M. Rinal's efforts, kissed it hard, without there being anything humiliating in this act of enthusiasm and affection.

When his fit of excitement was over :

" If I could talk like that," Maurin declared, " I'd care mighty little for anybody ; I should be a man, a man indeed. No doubt, to know one's duty does not always hinder a man from doing wrong . . . I see that ; but then, even in doing wrong, one is at least acting for the best."

He paused a moment ; then, shaking off his agitation :
" You have something to tell me, M. Rinal ? " he asked
in his everyday voice.

" We wanted to have a talk with you about the approaching elections. Any day you like best. M. Cabissol
will come. He has found it impossible to refuse M. Labarterie an opportunity of meeting you."

" Labarterie," queried Maurin, " is that the man with
the pretty wife, eh ? "

" So it seems," assented M. Rinal.

" And the man I explained the art of blackbirding to ? "

" So M. Cabissol told me."

" And he hasn't had enough of my blackbirds yet ? So
now he wants thrushes, eh, the exorbitant fellow ? Well,
he won't get much out of me "—and he laughed gaily.

" Well, then," concluded M. Rinal, " that's understood ;
we shall meet here at Bormes. We'll arrange a dinner at
Halbran's, to celebrate your reconciliation with the bench
and the police ! "

" That's all right," Maurin agreed, and the day for the
gathering was settled there and then.

" Ah ! by the by," added M. Rinal next moment, " I
have also heard from M. Cabissol that M. Caboufigue
wishes to see you."

" Father or son ? " asked Maurin, with a wink.

" I don't know which."

" Well, he'd better come the same day as the others, to
your meeting of the clans."

" I will write to M. Cabissol," said M. Rinal at once, " to
arrange it all."

CHAPTER V

The township of Bormes, mindful of its Roman origin, decrees Maurin the honours of a triumph; and to make things complete, the hero of the day engages in single combat with a Roman Baron.

On the appointed day the first to arrive, at an early hour in the forenoon, were M. Cabissol, M. Labarterie, accompanied by his wife, and a friend invited by M. Cigalous, a wealthy physician from Paris, then rusticating at Cavalière, M. Noblet by name.

At the entrance of the *Place* at Bormes the Parisians were surprised to find themselves passing under an arch of greenery, bearing across the top an imposing inscription between two tricolour streamers :

LONG LIVE MAURIN OF THE MAURES.

The Mayor, M. Cigalous, explained the reasons that had made him wish to accord a public welcome to the King of the Maures—a monarch popular with all classes of the population under his administration. "Maurin," he assured them, "is a good citizen ; and we are telling him so in our own way."

"*Té !* " exclaimed Maurin the moment he clapped eyes on Labarterie, who was not wearing his hunting-cap, "so you've got a hat on to-day ? "

It was his fashion of saying "good morning."

Pastouré, taciturn as usual, and two or three friends belonging to Bormes, electors of importance, formed a group round Maurin. They were François Marlusse (coming originally from Bandol), Novarre Pierre, and Benoni or Benoît Soufflarès.

M. Rinal hardly ever went into society, but he had promised to be at the dinner at Halbran's.

"And Caboufigue, father or son, isn't come yet?" asked Maurin.

"I wrote to them, as you wished," said Cabissol, "to say they would find us here to-day, if they cared to come."

The group was now standing in the *Place* of Bormes— a sort of shelf as it were, hanging on the hill-side, and over the new balustrade could be seen the plains of Bataillier, and further away the wooded hills of La Favière and Bénat, with the semaphore rising from the highest point. Away to the left hand the isle of Le Levant, an emerald ringed with lapis lazuli, and beyond the broad Mediterranean.

The guests already assembled were soon joined by two more, friends of Cigalous—Mascurel and Lacroustade.

Each of these worthies possessed a peculiar trick of his own that caused amusement to their friends.

Mascurel had a most quaint and original way of talking. If he spoke in Provençal, he always translated his sentence into French immediately afterwards; if in French, he instantly translated into Provençal. He would say, for instance : "*Bounjou, bon jour*" (good day); and then, "*Ça va bien aujourd'hui ?*" followed directly by, "*Va ben, ueï ?*" (all well to-day?), "*Jugariou qué fera beoù,*" then next moment, "*Je parierais qu'il fera beau*" (I'd wager it'll be a fine day). "*Je suis content de vous voir,*" then "*Siou countent dé vous véire*" (I am glad to see you), and so on, and so on.

As for Lacroustade, he had a mania for repetitions and inversions. He would say : "To see you gives me great pleasure, sir; it gives me great pleasure to see you. It's a bad day for snipe-shooting; for snipe-shooting it's a bad day. I've been married, married I've been; but, *pechère*, my poor wife died quite young; but quite young, *pechère*, she died, my poor wife."

Another thing that made the climax of comicality when he talked was his laugh; he laughed like a duck ! Men laugh in every tone and on every vowel; his laugh was a quack! quack! quack! This ridiculous quack! quack!

capped each of his repetitions, as if he himself saw the irresistible drollery of his favourite trick of inversion and
repetitions. When he was there, sometimes everybody
present would start laughing out of sheer sympathy and
nothing else, and involuntarily imitating his quack!
quack! quack!—so that any company of persons among
whom he figured might very readily be mistaken for a
flock of ducks.

"Everybody is come, M. le Maire," a *garde* came up to
announce to M. Cigalous.

"Then, gentlemen, come along."

"Where to, my good Cigalous ? "

And the latter added with an air of some mystery :

"To the great hall of the Maison Commune. The rest
of the guests are waiting for us there."

Thither they at once proceeded, to find a group presided
over apparently by M. Rinal.

The Mayor made the introductions :

"MM. Tombemousque, Escartefigue, Terrassebœuf,
Arrachequesne. . . ."

It sounded somehow as if he were calling the roster of
a team of athletes by their nicknames, and appreciating
the comicality of the thing he smiled merrily. No doubt,
in the first instance, these tremendous names were given
in jest, and our fathers' fun is thus handed down to us
through the ages.

Tombemousque and Terrassebœuf smiled benignantly ;
both these personages with the terrifying names had gentle
eyes that gazed out amiably from good-natured faces.
The most formidable of the pair, Terrassebœuf, had a
coal-black beard that looked for all the world like a false
one and began literally under his very eyes. Easy-going
and peaceable as the man was, he always carried a brace
of revolvers in his belt, under his tightly buttoned jacket,
and when he was asked :

"Why do you always go about armed like that, Terrassebœuf ? "

"*Qué sias couyoun !* " (how silly you are !), he would

answer with his tranquil smile. " You know quite well
I represent a famous firm of gunmakers. If I didn't carry
my revolvers about with me, *pechère !* I could never sell
them ! . . . That's easy enough to understand, come. . . ."

" Gentlemen," said Cigalous, " let me also introduce
MM. Lacornude and Pignatel. Hearing that Bormes was
to have the honour of welcoming Maurin of the Maures to-
day, they informed me of their intention of coming to pay
him their compliments, each in the name of his Commune.
MM. Pignatel and Lacornude are here to represent Gonfaron and Le Plan-de-la-Tour. Their presence effaces
even the thought of the little misunderstanding that once
arose between Maurin and the natives of their respective
towns."

These delegates from Gonfaron and Le Plan-de-la-Tour
came and pressed Maurin's hand. Pignatel spoke first,
and addressing the hero of the day :

" In what you said to our small boys of Gonfaron recalling the old joke of the flying donkey, there was nothing to
make anybody turn a hair, *pechère !* It was a pity we were
not there ; then all that ridiculous affair would never
have happened. The Mayor, as you will remember, only
made matters worse. He did not know you, and took you
for a stranger and outsider, one of the sort whose fun gets
on our nerves, because they do it in an unfriendly spirit.
With you it's different altogether ; you can say what you
please, for we know you ! But the Mayor did not, and
when you stood out against him, he lost his head. He
gave in to a lot of lads who only wanted an excuse for
throwing stones, and old wives who don't know what
they're saying, and a few old dotards out of the Ark. . . .
That's why, when M. Rinal got the *procès-verbaux* torn up
that hindered you moving freely about your kingdom, all
Gonfaron signed a petition in your favour, and as our
Mayor would not forgive and forget, they forced him to
give in his resignation. Folks who can't take a *galégeade*,
what's the good of them ? Those who understand a joke
best are the most intelligent in serious matters. . . . If

there are any Parisians 'here, they've only to open their
ears. . . . The ass of Gonfaron is not an eagle, that's very
sure, but nevertheless he'll not let any man of the North
take liberties with him. . . . So long live Maurin of the
Maures, say I ! "

The crowd which had gathered under the windows of
the Maison Commune heard the appeal and echoed with
one voice the cry :

" Long live Maurin of the Maures ! "

After Pignatel, Lacornude, the representative of Le
Plan-de-la-Tour, took up his parable.

He declared that as a result of Maurin's memorable
intervention on the Feast of St. Martin, the Municipal
Council had decided that on the day of their Patron Saint,
no poor man *should ever shiver again in their Commune !*
He wound up his speech with the words :

" And this result alone is an eloquent testimony in favour
of our gallant friend Maurin. Long live Maurin of the
Maures ! "

When the Mayor's guests left the Mairie, the whole town
was assembled in the *Place* awaiting them, and followed
them with acclamations. Then, just as the cortège reached
the triumphal arch erected in Maurin's honour, bang !
bang ! bang ! went the saluting mortars, giving three
grand salvos of artillery one after the other. There was
endless clapping of hands, and the church bells rang a
rousing peal, by the Curé's orders—yes, actually by the
Curé's orders—while the pretty girls threw branches of
flowering mimosa at Maurin, who laughed . . . and felt
a little inclined to cry at the same time.

" Long live ! long live the King of the Maures ! "

" It's beyond belief ! What extraordinary ways of doing
things ! " muttered M. Labarterie to his wife.

Cigalous overheard him.

" Sir," he broke out with some heat, " don't express
your opinion of my countrymen quite so loud ; they
might hear you, and they would not like it. You are a
Northerner, are you not ? "

MAURIN THE ILLUSTRIOUS 33

"Oh! no," said Labarterie; "I was born at Lyons."

"That's just what I said; you are from the North. The real South begins, or ends if you prefer it, at Valence. Well, let me tell you this; you and your Parisians, you know nothing whatever of our temperament, and, upon my word, it's a pity! The Capital should make a thorough study of the spirit of each of her provinces if she wants to resume them all in herself. Instead of deeming herself a queen-city, a sovereign-city of right divine, a thing apart, with a unique glory of her own, she should be proud of all the races that make her what she is. . . . For what they are, these Parisians, we all know—a crowd of Provincials who forswear their province to make mischief."

"Well hit!" cried Maurin.

"Instead of that, you make fun of us, you play the contemptuous tyrant, you forget it is we who send you our best intellects, which you have only to polish."

"Bravo!" put in Pastouré.

"You are just as readily gulled, just as garrulous, just as fond of idle gossip, as we are—and perhaps more. Then why behave as if everything you do is well done, and whatever we do, ridiculous? Since railways came in we have ceased to be so far from Paris that we can be treated like Kanakas!"

"Well done, Cigalous!" cried Maurin.

"Let him go on, Maurin," said M. Rinal; "he talks like an angel."

"You shout 'Oho, Marius!' derisively, and you call our accent 'too awfully funny'—but the mincing drawl of your Paris cockney never strikes you as unpleasant! Yet his way of speaking smacks of the gutter, ours of the sea and the sea-wrack, of the ocean and the denizens of the ocean!"

"*Aganto!*" applauded Maurin.

"I am convinced," Cigalous resumed, more and more excited, "I feel convinced the tyranny and pride of a capital may be just as insupportable and just as harmful to the country as the tyranny of a man. The French

D

Revolution was not made to benefit Paris solely. And
who began that same Revolution ? Why, M. de Mirabeau,
qu'éro d'Azaï—who was from Aix—and it's not for nothing
the *Marseillaise* is called that and not the *Parisienne !* "

" Just one word ! " M. Labarterie begged, altogether
disconcerted and hardly knowing what he meant to say.

" No, not a word ; I've not done yet," Cigalous went on
imperturbably. ". . . Well, then, we do honour to our
friends, the fellow-citizens we admire, in our own way, the
way we choose. We cannot march them under the Arc de
Triomphe—seeing it's in the Place de l'Étoile at the top of
the Champs Élysées, as everybody knows—and besides,
these fellow-citizens of ours are humble fellows, and the
only wreaths we can offer them are of the green leaves of
our native woods—but what do you see so ludicrous in all
this ? Our homage is not proportioned to their merit ?
But what have *you* to say to that ? Why, pray, should we
not raise triumphal arches in their honour of olive leaves
and pine branches ? Is it not just and right ? Are we not
doing an act of sincere and legitimate respect ? We cannot
give them a concert beneath their windows of M. Parès'
music—who was *chef d'orchestre* at Toulon, by the by,
before he went to Paris—but our native *tambourinaïres*
are all they want ; they whack the asses' skin for them,
and all the asses in the world are not at Gonfaron. I don't
say so for you personally, but for the folks who never give
poor ' Marius ' his deserts, though but for him, *pechère !*
France would have no more song and laughter, for lack of
ever a ray of bottled sunshine ! For my part, I can see
nothing grotesque in the friendly gathering we have invited you to see. Let me tell you, Bormes, on days such
as this, has set her drums beating, her mortars roaring,
and her flutes, come all the way from La Garde, making
sweet accord, in honour of the great and good Reyer, our
honoured guest, again for the worthy Jean d'Auriol, and
last but not least for our old doctor and friend, Rafaëli.
Yes, and there was one of your Paris journals that, like you,
dubbed our habits *grotesque !* To love one's friends and

tell them so before they leave us, to honour those who
work well and do their country honour, what is there so
strange, so singular in that ? What *would* be strange, yea,
and grievous too, would rather be for us *not* to do these
things ! Yes, I am sorry for lands that fail in the performance of this duty !

"One time, look you, in this very Square, the time we
fêted Jean d'Auriol, as we are now doing to Maurin—I
made them put up a little cabin all of greenery and flowering boughs to compliment a worthy dame who for thirty
years had kept a stall on the spot to sell cakes and sugar-
candy and gingerbread to our little lads and lasses. The
tears ran down her face, she was so proud and happy, and
the sight warmed our hearts. Think you the civic crowns
of a village must needs be ridiculous, because they are
poor and unpretending, or only when they are conferred
on humble recipients ? Well, *we* say in our homely, provincial way, *All mouths are sisters*, and what is good for
the great man, is delicious for his lowly neighbour."

"One word . . ," M. Labarterie tried to interrupt again.

"No, not yet, not just yet," Cigalous swept on in the
torrent of his eloquence ; "for many a day you Parisians
have exasperated our nerves ! Because they laugh at us,
is that the reason ? Not a bit, for it was our own selves,
and nobody else, taught them the trick of it. No, they
try our tempers because they never laugh laughingly,
because they take it all in deadly earnest, because they
misunderstand our kindly hearts and the best and brightest
characteristics of our temperament—qualities without which
France would be a mighty dull place, *Noum dé Diou !* You
likely know enough Parisians to repeat what I say to a
good many ? Very well, tell them this : there are times
when they make us long to be Provençaux again rather
than Frenchmen, and have our laugh out *without* 'em !
Yes, there's a time for everything, egad !—and when a
man's temper's roused, he leaves off joking ! That's a
thing it's well to realise a bit ahead of events. . . .

"Do you want really to understand ? Then look at our

friend Terrassebœuf here. He has a ridiculous name, and
he is as ready to laugh at it as anybody. He looks fierce,
but he is perfectly good-natured. People think he is a red-
hot Revolutionist, ready to resort to bloodshed on the
slightest provocation. He sells as many revolvers as ever
he can, and wears these terrible weapons dangling at his
belt. . . . Well, sir, don't you judge by appearances ;
the man's neither ridiculous nor ferocious . . . but he can
be either, if occasion demands. Do I make myself plain ?

"Not that our worthy Terrassebœuf is the inventor of
this way of selling firearms. We all of us knew, in '71,
a *fédéré* who had got himself named *Commissaire Spécial*
at the Marseilles railway station ; he, too, carried weapons
in his belt, never loaded, by the by, which he sold at the
best price possible, for he had a swarm of children to feed.
A lieutenant, who had been given orders to dislodge the
disturbers of the peace from the station, told his men to
lay hands on him and clap him with his back to the wall.
The poor devil was no more a Communard than you or I
are. But he was a Republican, and had only done what
he could to give his brats bread.

"'Come, stand there ! back to the wall, I say !'

"'Back to the wall ? Why ?'

"'Don't play the injured innocent ! . . . to the wall,
sir, you're to be shot !'

"'Oh ! come now, come ; you're joking, eh ?'

"'To the wall !'

"'What, what ! do you mean it seriously ?' stammered
'Marius,' whose face had gone very white. . . .

"Look here, M. Labarterie, we Provençaux are slow to
believe in extreme measures—our sky is too blue, our cli-
mate too bright—but once started, we can match the most
energetic.

"'If you are really in earnest,' said the poor fellow
gravely, 'give me leave at all events to say good-bye to
my son.'

"'Where is he ?'

"'In my office—the *Commissaire Spécial's* office.'

" They fetched his eldest boy, a lad of twenty, from whose own lips I have heard the story of his father's heroic end.

" ' My boy,' he said, when the youth appeared, ' this is a bad business ; they're going to shoot me, it seems. At first I thought it was all a *galégeade*, you know, but it's deadly earnest. . . . So kiss me . . . and here's my watch to remember me by. . . . *Vive la République !* fire ! '

" . . . And the man fell, shot through and through.

" He only wanted to live, and he knew how to die—that's all. Look you, M. Labarterie, there's a time for every-thing."

" Sir," said Labarterie, not without feeling, " I beg your pardon ; I take your meaning."

Maurin was furtively wiping his eyes.

" *Va la ben éspliqua ! bougramen ben !*—he's given him a good lesson, a confounded good lesson ! " declared Mascurel.

" Yes, he's given him a confounded good lesson ; a con-founded good lesson has he given him ! " echoed Lacrou-stade. " If the Parisians make fun of us, we can return the compliment ; we can return the compliment, we can, if the Parisians make fun of us ! quack ! quack ! "

" *Té !* " exclaimed Maurin suddenly, " I see a fine carriage coming ! It must be one of our *damagas* (shrikes), Caboufigue, father or son."

" *Es uno voituro dé gro moussu !* It's a stout gentle-man's carriage," observed Mascurel. " It strikes me I know the person who's riding in it ; *mi semblo qué lou counouissi, aquèou qu'ès dédins.*"

" All spick and span the carriage is," added Lacroustade ; "the carriage is all spick and span. Truly you might see your face in every panel of it ; in every panel you might see your face, truly you might . . . quack ! quack ! quack ! "—and the whole assembly, already forgetful of Cigalous' impressive address to M. Labarterie, roared with delight and broke into an uproarious imitation of Lacroustade's nasal laugh.

In the *Place* were gathered here and there—it was a

Sunday—little groups playing at bowls, who one and all
left their game to watch the arrival of this splendid equi-
page. The village girls, in all their holiday bunting, to use
Maurin's expression, were promenading arm in arm under
the mimosas and pepper trees. They ran up to lean on
the balustrade that overlooks the terrace immediately
below, and gazed down at the approaching vehicle with
equal curiosity. It was now nearly noon.

"It is Caboufigue junior," said Maurin.

"*V'aviès pas dit qu'èr' ùn darnagas?* didn't you say he
was a *darnagas* (shrike)?" remarked Mascurel.

"A *darnagas*, you said he was ; you said he was a *darnagas*," insisted Lacroustade, laughing his quack! quack!
quack! as usual.

At the corner of the *Place* and Halbran's inn the landau
pulled up. Caboufigue the younger, Baron de la Canestelle,
loudly dressed, a white collar worn over a coloured shirt,
a startling tie, a malacca cane in his hand, leapt from the
carriage almost before it stopped, and made for the group
amongst whom he saw Maurin standing.

"A thousand pardons, gentlemen," he began in his fine
Parisian accent, a brand-new article he rarely used;
"you know perhaps what brings me here?"

The gentlemen addressed bowed a polite negative.

Only Cabissol answered with a touch of irony in his
voice :

"*I* do, perhaps."

"Yes, the fact is, sir," the young man proceeded, "my
father has informed me that before a witness—yourself, no
doubt—M. Maurin treated him with a brutality and insolence, I will not say beyond, but below all expression in
words. . . . And I have come to demand, in my father's
name, and before everybody, M. Maurin's apologies!"

"*Ooù!*" broke in Maurin, "if that's why you've put
yourself about, you've done foolishly, little Baron ; why,
if I were to squeeze your nose, I could make the milk run
out like from a rotten fig!

"So you don't know that your father and I are old

schoolfellows ! *Voui*, yes, we were brought up together, we were in the school of poverty, with holes in our breeches, and we were giving one another shrewd knocks on the side o' the head when you weren't so much as thought of yet ! "

Caboufigue the younger, excited by the unexpected presence of a pretty and elegantly dressed woman, quite lost his temper, and in reply to this vulgar abuse, answered in the high-flown phrases dear to the angry bourgeois :

" I forbid you to speak to me in that tone. You must remember we are in France and not in the South Sea Islands, and that for lack of proper laws to protect us under a government of licence and disorder, gentlemen have sons to take up arms in their defence. The only vexation is that a man of birth cannot fight a cad like you (that's what I wanted to tell you before everybody), and that, being unable to meet you with the sword, one is ashamed to use the stick—the only weapon fit for you and such as you ! "

Maurin, too, was stimulated by Mme. Labarterie's smiles and the sympathy of the assembled village, where he was looked upon as a king, the King of the Maures.

" *Ooù, collèguo !* " he retorted. " You'd have done better, my lad, to-day to keep under your father's wing, who is a great fat goose, as everybody knows. If I understand you right, you seem to think you're the only fellow in all the world can wield a long knitting-pin, eh ?

" *Eh bé ! té !* then, parry, young 'un, parry that ! "

Maurin had suddenly snatched Cabissol's walking-cane out of his hand, and, throwing himself into a correct fencing attitude, now attacked the young man with such vigour that the latter instinctively assumed a posture of defence.

Cleverly enough the Baron de la Canestelle parried the first blow. This was precisely what Maurin wished. The return stroke followed and instantly provoked a reply. A ring began quickly to form, and next moment young Caboufigue found himself too hotly engaged to be able to withdraw without loss of self-respect. So he set to work

with a will, determined to show his prowess. . . . Maurin
kept him hard at it.

"Parry *carte !* parry *tierce !* " he kept shouting, bounding to and fro, as the Italian swordsmen do. He thoroughly
enjoyed the game, and he also wanted the joke to produce
its full comic effect.

His adversary broke ground persistently at every lunge
the terrible fellow made at him.

"*Aquelo, voui, qué m'agràdo !* it's fine, I like it fine ! "
vociferated Mascurel.

"It's a pleasure to see such sport ! to see such sport,
it's a pleasure indeed ! quack ! quack ! quack ! " went
Lacroustade.

The whole village came trooping up, to form a wide
circle round the duellists.

Cigalous, Cabissol, Arrachequesne, Escartefigue, Tombemousque, Pignatel, Lacornude, all were laughing heartily,
and Terrassebœuf louder than any, while even M. Rinal
smiled.

Maurin, stamping his foot again and again noisily, was
addressing his adversary :

"Hold your sword lower, man ! You're exposing yourself. . . . Close up, close up, my good fellow. Ah ! but
you want a teacher ! Well, here's one ready-made for you.
. . . Lower, I say ! that's right ! and now the point a bit
higher ! . . . Ah, ha ! touched, my little Baron. . . . The
first blood, eh ? You didn't expect that one, did you,
youngster ? Pretty, very pretty, to defend his father, dear
boy ! it proves a fellow has one ! Why was he so annoyed,
your dad, eh ?

"All's fair, mind you, betwixt two old comrades like him
and me ! You should have remembered that. . . . Come,
higher, now ! . . . I didn't want to see your seconds, but
you know the reason why, eh ? Why, because we've got
enough already, for sure—the whole village of Bormes—to
look on ! Ha ! touched again ! . . . You give ground
overmuch. Your wrist's not very firm either. . . . Your
pretty boots hurt you, maybe ? . . . Come, come, that's

not such a bad one now ; I'll make something of you yet.
. . . If I get you one right over the heart, I shall consider
you dead, so I warn you. Look, I see M. Rinal over there
laughing ; so there's a doctor all ready for me ; you shall
have the other, who comes from Paris, eh ? my fine Parisian.
. . . Don't be afraid, my lad ! Your mother won't have
to cry for you this time. I'm a good-hearted prince, my
kiddy. I don't eat small game—tomtits and suchlike, not
I ! that's only for young ladies. You're getting warm, are
you ? Yes, it's capital good exercise ! So you've grown
into a nobleman, have you, all of a sudden ? That doesn't
help a chap from dying, *pechère !* Soon as you're dead,
we'll have breakfast. *Aï ! Aï !* do remember the post office
is just behind you, and if they were to open the door, you'd
tumble right in back first, if you go drawing off any more.
. . . Eh ! eh ! touched, touched again. . . . *Té !* I have
an idea ; I'm going to post you ! I flatten you out like a
letter, and pop ! I clap a stamp on you ! There, I've
jammed it right over your heart. . . . Dead ! dead as
a door-nail ! "

Maurin lowered his weapon, while his opponent stood
dumbfounded, wiping his dripping forehead.

"And now," said Maurin, "seeing the custom's so
amongst you gentlemen in such cases, you'll come and dine
with me. Else, where *would* you dine ? "

Cabissol stepped up to the young man and talked a
moment or two with him in an undertone—"the whole
business was ridiculous. It would be best hushed up this
way. The spectators must think it was just a joke. . . .
Where could he dine, besides ?

"There's only one inn," he went on ; "then make one
table of it. Shake hands with the King of the Maures, and
do it with a laugh. You are only a child beside him. The
crowd will suppose it was all a bit of fun . . . and, all said
and done, what else was it ? "

Young Caboufigue saw there was nothing better to do,
showing more good sense than he had hitherto displayed.

"Shake hands, Maurin," he said. "You are an old

friend of my father's, I know that. . . . I allow I'm dead
—and I'm precious hungry. So let's to breakfast.".

It was well spoken, and good-humouredly. The young
fellow had suddenly thought—if those sticks had been
swords, he would here and now be in no condition to eat
his breakfast. He was not a bad fellow at heart, and behaved as an honourable gentleman should who is beaten ;
he gave his hand frankly to a generous adversary.

"*In your place*," M. Rinal told him with a serious face,
but a twinkling eye, "I should have acted like you."

When the crowd saw them talking and laughing together,
and then trooping amicably into Halbran's, they concluded
it was only a *galégeade* after all, and dispersed to their
several homes for the midday meal.

Bormes remembers to this day this memorable and
mirthful duel, where Maurin proved that in our century
the clown's cudgel is sometimes every whit as effective a
weapon as the gentleman's sword.

"*Oòuriòu pas douna ma plàço*—I wouldn't have given
up my place—*per un còou dé canoun*, not if they'd brought
cannon to bear ! " cried Mascurel, enthusiastically.

"Ay, it was a duel, such as we shan't see the like of
again ; the like of it we shan't see again, such a duel as
this, we shan't ! " roared Lacroustade, laughing like a
lunatic, his note more than ever resembling a duck's quack !
quack ! quack !

As for Pastouré, he contented himself, when Maurin got
in his final lunge, with holding out his great fist with thumb
uplifted, as his way was, but never said one word, this
characteristic gesture expressing a climax of delight and
admiration far transcending the power of speech.

CHAPTER VI

Maurin, master of the situation, makes his arrangements in view of
the forthcoming elections.

IN honour of so distinguished a gathering, Maurin had
done a bit of smartening up. He wore his least dilapidated
jacket, which really looked almost new. His unstarched
shirt was scrupulously clean, and his "company" shoes
had been blacked with his own hands. Through his dark
beard, which was naturally sparse, short and curly, the
eye could follow the fine contour of chin and cheeks. His
hands, which for years had handled scarcely any tool but
the gun, were sinewy, but by no means clumsy. His
general appearance, his well-knit figure, his frank, intelligent eye, were much to the taste of the Parisian, Mme.
Labarterie, a great reader in books of gallantry. . . . It
would not be the first time Princesses had stooped to love
shepherd swains. . . . Maurin, whose experience taught
him how the land lay, sat near her at table, and made no
scruple about casting some very ardent glances her way.

"The first toast to Maurin!" cried Cigalous, raising his
glass.

"No, the first toast always to the ladies!" corrected
Maurin.

The company drank to one another from time to time,
bowing and sipping their San-Clar.

Halbran, his apron tucked in his belt and his cap pulled
over his forehead, looking stout and rubicund, had agreed
for once to pocket his clay pipe, an old favourite he had
been fifteen years colouring, and was himself handing
round the dishes he had cooked. The genial fellow had a
pleasant, friendly word for every guest.

In due course the conversation turned on the coming elections. Above everything they must beware of Poisse, who had a sly finger in the opposition pie. Before very long there was to be a general meeting, to which all the Communes would send their delegates. This caucus would finally decide whether they should run a single candidate or more than one. One would be best, but how prevent a number coming forward and offering themselves ? Not one of the delegates would ever agree to give up his particular candidate, each and all of them believing, or pretending to believe, in accordance with his own individual interest, his candidate to be the best. This granted, what were the respective chances of the candidates ? Vérignon, by common consent, stood a very likely chance. As for M. Siblas, his candidature would prevent the reactionary votes further increasing M. Poisse's prospects. Caboufigue had promised not to seek election ; they had his word to that effect. Caboufigue junior pretended not to hear what was said under this last head, while Maurin looked askance at the poor young fellow.

There remained M. Labarterie, who, for all the high qualities he was credited with out of politeness, had not the ghost of a chance. He was unanimously recommended to retire.

" You see," Maurin told him, " in our part of the country Parisians are hardly wanted, no matter how famous. We want local men to represent us ; men like Vérignon. More than that, they must be known in a special way, known in our villages and country districts. Vérignon has written in the local papers and the Marseilles journals, the papers folks read of evenings, and he writes his stuff in a way that everybody can understand. Sometimes he pokes fun at the Government in our native patois, and that helps the worthy fellow—for a worthy man he is—more than any-thing else."

" Well said, Maurin ! " Cigalous seconded the speaker.

M. Labarterie announced that he would think it over, but refused to pledge himself.

Then, by way of helping her husband's chances, Mme. Labarterie showed more and more complacence towards Maurin ; he was enchanted, but thought to himself, " I'd have no objection to the wife, but the husband, no, I can't stomach him. Ah ! I see now why he wore such a tall cap at the boar-hunt. It hides his horns ! "

He smiled at his conceit, and a maze of wrinkles showed at the corners of his eyes, though without detracting from his characteristic look of youthfulness.

" Well, what do you say to that, Noblet ? " asked M. Rinal.

" I *had* thought of standing myself," replied M. Noblet ; " but M. Cigalous—I had a talk with him the other day at Cavalière, where a friend introduced me—told me exactly the same as you, M. Maurin, have just expressed so well."

" You are," said M. Rinal to the Parisian savant, " one of the greatest scientific names in France, an eminent author, and a philanthropist all love and admire. You have made marvellous discoveries, which have made you famous in Europe and America. You are the energetic champion of a principle fraught with the greatest possible good to humanity, that of arbitration between Nations, which will make war a rarity, a difficulty, if not an impossibility. It would be an honour to the Department to have you as its Representative. . . ."

M. Noblet bowed :

" If I were elected," he declared, " I would devote myself to the interests of the Republic, while regretfully renouncing, at least for a time, the scientific studies I love so well, and I might perhaps be of some service in the Chamber in furtherance of the cause of arbitration. It needs representatives having the ear of the powers that be . . . but I quite understand the objection you have stated . . . and I am afraid . . ."

" Your pardon, sir, excuse me if I interrupt you," broke in Maurin ; " you have reason to be afraid. Do not go out of your way to make enemies. People here, you see, don't know you. . . ."

" Are you sure of that ? " asked M. Rinal.

" I can prove it," declared Maurin.

" How ? "

" By the fact that I, who am in every sense a local man, I don't know him ! and I do know Vérignon. I can hardly read, it's true ; still, there are times, and not so seldom, when they read the papers to me, and then one has talks of evenings. . . . Well, I never heard of you, M. Noblet. . . . And, seeing you are the great man M. Rinal says, I reckon it would be a pity to have a merely contemptible poll recorded against you ; nor would that be very creditable to my people either, I imagine."

" Quite right ! " insisted Cigalous. " That's exactly and precisely what I told you, M. Noblet."

" And that is why I have withdrawn my name. We have just verified the correctness of the resolutions you had already half formed. I came here on purpose to hear the truth, and, as I often spend some time in the South, to help you as a good comrade, if I cannot join in the fight as a candidate."

" There, Maurin," remarked Cigalous, " you see all *bourgeois* are not what you are sometimes disposed to think they are. Here's one of the wealthiest and best of them. Yes, here we have the good breed, Maurin—the sort that our countrymen should take as models, don't you think so ? "

" I know very well," said Maurin, " there are such men, but I've never had much opportunity of seeing them hitherto. . . . And," he added courteously, " I shall be delighted to see more of them, if they will.

" And to that end, M. le Maire, will you ask them if some day they'll join me in a shooting expedition ; I'll see they find good sport—rabbit or hare or what not—and I shall have the benefit, I hope, of hearing something of their talk."

" Oh ! yes," cried Mme. Labarterie excitedly ; " do let us arrange a shooting-party ! "

" The season is over," remarked the Mayor.

" Next season then," insisted M. Labarterie, who was always eager to gratify his wife.

" Let's agree for the opening day then," urged Maurin, " if you like—everybody now present to come."

" It's a bargain," declared Cigalous.

The compact was sealed with glasses round ; after which the Mayor resumed :

" And last but not least, to return to politics, there's something you all ought to know, and you, Maurin, in particular. M. Noblet, while withdrawing from the struggle, offers to help our more favoured candidate, Vérignon, who is not a rich man, by paying half his election expenses ! "

" M. Noblet," said Maurin with dignity, and rising to his feet, " one *bourgeois* makes up for another. And I've seen others in my time—I wish I hadn't ! . . . but *motus !* Peace to their ashes ! . . . I saw a nobleman, too, the other day it did me good to look at and listen to—and that's the Comte de Siblas. He knows he will be beaten, but inasmuch as by standing he will be helping Vérignon (because he'll catch the reactionary votes Poisse would otherwise secure), M. de Siblas still offers himself. ' If my own political friends don't get in, at any rate I want to see men of character succeed,' that's what M. de Siblas told me, and *I* tell you what his sentiments are."

" Well," hazarded M. Rinal, " let's drink to M. de Siblas' very good health, eh ? "

" Take care, Maurin," laughed Cigalous, " take care ; they'll be saying you're compounding with the aristos ! "

" Ho ! ho ! " laughed Maurin, " I've no fear of that ; they know me too well. . . . And now, Halbran," he added, " make us some good coffee, good strong stuff to waken the dead ! "

" And bring in your oldest liqueurs. . . . Time enough for politics to-morrow," cried Cigalous genially ; " and you, Maurin, tell us one of your *galégeades.*"

" Well," began Maurin, " this is a good one . . . " ; but there he stopped.

" The fact is . . ." he stammered, " before ladies . . ."

" My wife," said Labarterie, " is a married woman."

" So we should suppose," grinned Maurin.

" Besides," went on M. Labarterie imperturbably, " she is a sportswoman, and a funny story over dessert won't scare her."

" So give me a cigarette," said Mme. Labarterie, " and light your pipes, gentlemen. Candidates' wives must show some intrepidity."

" Without his pipe," Maurin remarked judiciously, " Cigalous would die. But for my part, at times like this a cigarette's enough. When I have a cigarette betwixt my lips, or a glass of *cassie* in front of me, 'pon my word ! I feel like sweet seventeen ! "

The fact is, he did not produce his pipe with the idea of pleasing the lady. Soon all were drinking and smoking, and the conversation became general. Pastouré sat staring silently at Maurin, who had just begun to laugh out loud, without uttering a word.

" I can see by your face," said one of the Bormes men— a certain François Marlusse, coming originally from Bandol —" you want to tell your story, Maurin. Is it the tale of the diving-dress perhaps ? "

" Precisely ! " said Maurin ; " that's the very one I was thinking of telling."

" The diving-dress, eh ? the diving-dress ! " cried Caboufigue, who had been rather silent so far.

" The diving-dress ! bravo, the diving-dress ! " laughed Mme. Labarterie, pouting her pretty red lips to puff away the smoke of her cigarette.

Then all the company shouted in an eager, excited chorus :

" Yes, yes, the diving-dress ! the diving-dress ! "

" *Aï ben dîna* ! I have dined excellently ! " announced Mascurel.

" A better dinner no man could have ; no man could have a better dinner," echoed Lacroustade—and he broke out into a resounding quack ! quack ! quack !

Exhilarated by the good wines of San-Clar, one and all, intentionally or no, fell to mimicking a flock of ducks, a bird that only loves water. . . . Soon the very window-panes were trembling with the aquatic chorus. . . . When at last the merry uproar subsided, Maurin cleared his throat to begin the promised story.

E

CHAPTER VII

Maurin tells two of his tales, to wit: *The Diving-dress* and *The Bishop's Arrival at Saint-Tropez*, whereof the second, being a true story, is obviously truer than the first, which the King of the Maures invented out of his own head.

" I WILL tell you two of them, two of my stories," Maurin announced, " on one condition ; that you, Marlusse, relate your visit to the Paris Exhibition."

" Yes, yes ! " echoed Cigalous, " he'll do so, never fear. . . . It's all in the programme. . . . Now, Maurin, go ahead ; I don't know your diving-dress one."

" Oh, it's a very short story, this one," explained Maurin. " It won't keep you a couple of minutes."

" We're all listening, Maurin."

" It was in the days when I served the State," began Maurin, " as a bluejacket. Off the mouth of the gulf of Saint-Tropez, a torpedo-boat coming from Saint-Raphaël and making for Sainte-Maxime, kept a bit too close in shore and struck on a big rock. She had sunk in barely four fathoms of water, and they fetched two divers from Toulon in a tug. With the rest of the crew I was employed on the salving operations. From shore you could see quite well all that went on on board, and similarly, from on board, anything that happened on the beach. One of the divers had a pretty wife, who had accompanied him from Toulon, and used to go with him to Sainte-Maxime to spend the night there, when work was done. Of course, she was never allowed aboard the tug, and sometimes she would cook her man's dinner there on the sands, between a couple of boulders. One fine day when I had landed to go an errand to Sainte-Maxime, I came

upon the woman at the water's edge ; she had just been
bathing, and was only half dressed. The diver was under
water, examining the wreck, and the hand whose business
it was aboard the tug to turn the wheel of the pump to
supply him with air, had his back to us. I kissed the
woman, who made no very strenuous objections, and I liked
it so well I never thought of looking towards the ship.
When I did look, *nom de nom !* there was the diver climbing
his ladder, and half out of water already ; he was glaring
through the crossed bars of his helmet, and his eyes were
fixed on us. The man's head looked like a great balloon.
He was really terrifying. He stared and stared, and I was
so startled I clean forgot to let go his wife. He kept lifting
his arms to his helmet, which they began to unscrew, but
they could not manage this just at first.

" ' Oh, Lord ! ' his wife said to me at this, ' he'll have to
keep it on. He's going to be like that always ! *Leïs bànos
l'an poussa dins l'aïgo !* ' "

" Which means ? " queried Mme. Labarterie.

" Oh ! nothing much," said M. Rinal, ". . . well, it
means : ' There are some branches grow under water.' "

" Upon my word ! I don't understand," declared M.
Labarterie.

" There are branches *and* branches," explained M. Rinal ;
" we are talking now of the sort that grow on a stag's head,
and stop him running in the woods."

" Ah ! *I* understand ! " cried the pretty Parisian.

" You are very fortunate ! " muttered her husband. . . .
Then suddenly, " Ah ! I understand, too," he cried, clapping
his hands to his head.

The action put the climax on the story, and provoked
a universal shout of laughter.

" And that's all ! " concluded Maurin, giving the lady
an arch look.

" You promised us another," said Cigalous.

" You shall have it," said Maurin ; " and it's a true
story ; truer, even, than the last."

" What do you mean by *truer even ?* "

" I mean it's quite, quite true. The first isn't so entirely
true. It's merely a story I fancied might possibly happen.
One day I saw the diver's wife on the beach, and the diver
coming out of the water. ' Why, look ! ' I said to myself,
' just look ! to see the helmet on the chap's head, you'd
think *he had 'em* underneath ! ' ''

" Oh ! you Southerners ! " said Labarterie. " What
imaginations you have ! "

" Kind of you to say so ! " Maurin sneered inwardly.

" The other story ! now the other story ! "

" It will show you how, common sailor as I was, I set
a whole town ringing its church-bells and beating its drums
and hoisting its best bunting. . . .''

" Well, but . . . it's only what you have done to-day."

" Ah ! but," laughed Maurin, " I'm a different man to-
day ; I'm a king now ! . . . Well, I'll tell you all about it.
We were returning from Agay, on board our torpedo-craft,
and in devilment we had cut endless branches of oleander
as we came down the river ; then, with the captain's leave,
we had lashed these all sticking straight up round the
bulwarks. It turned our vessel into a little flowery isle,
and away we went in that trim for Saint-Tropez.

" It was late in June, just before the date of the great
fêtes and merry-makings of the town. We were out
in the middle of the bay, steaming this way and that,
rounding to and wheeling about, darting to and fro like
a porpoise at play, showing off our paces before entering
port, when suddenly we see a little smack, under easy sail,
close under our quarter. She was steered by a fisherman
of Saint-Tropez—a man I knew.

" ' Good-day to you, Maurin ! ' he hails ; ' you're rigged
out very fine to-day.'

" Just by way of joke, and without thinking what I
was saying, I shouted back :

" ' You see, we're bringing the Bishop with us ! '

" Well, it so happened at that very time Saint-Tropez
was expecting the arrival any day of the Bishop of Fréjus,
and, seeing our vessel coming in, all decked in flowers and

greenery, the idlers on the Quay were already asking one another the question, ' Can it be the Bishop's aboard ? ' But, of course, I knew nothing about that.

" An hour later, as we hauled into Saint-Tropez, we could see the whole population lining the Quay, all along in front of the Bailli de Suffren's statue ; the men were waving their hats, and the girls their sunshades and hand-kerchiefs. And the shouts ! and cheers ! and bands of music ! The Curé and all his satellites, in full fig, were just marching out of the church with their banners. Our Captain was highly flattered ; ' Very polite of them, I'm sure ! very polite ! ' he purred. Flags were hoisted, and every window decorated. The women were all in gala dress. The children were dancing in the streets. The Mayor had donned his scarf. Well, we tied up to the pier, and the Captain stepped ashore.

" ' Where is the Bishop ? ' was the very first question.

" ' The Bishop ! What Bishop ? '

" I was obliged to explain matters. The Captain only laughed ; but the Curé could not see the joke of having brought out his best wooden Saint and the great Cross, and the church banner—all for a pack of sailormen.

" So that's how I—I, Maurin—once before to-day, set a whole town pealing bells and beating drums and hoisting flags, and the Mayor and Council coming out in State. But I'm not a bit proud of the achievement. . . . Your turn, Marlusse ! "

" We've got to expect a more piquant sort of stories from you, Monsieur Maurin," sneered M. Labarterie.

" Oh ! I know *your* sort ! " retorted Maurin smartly. " You must always have something funny ! The one I've just told you is a good story, and a pretty story, only because it brings up before one's mind's eye the vessel sailing in like an island of flowers and the town decking itself with flags and blossoms and beauty to welcome her. If you can't see it all as if you'd been there, well, my story means nothing to you, that's all . . . Lord ! you must *see* the picture, it's all in that. . . ."

" Maurin has an artist's eye," said M. Rinal.

" That's the way with us all—us Southerners," declared Maurin.

Then, turning to M. Labarterie :

" I see *you're* the kind always wants yarns like the tale of Captain Cougourdan of the port of Les Martigues, and nothing else. Out at sea one day, he was studying his chart, this Captain Cougourdan, and, having verified the position of his ship, which was running free before a spanking breeze, and heading right for the bottom of his chart, where there was nothing more but the blank edge of the sheet with no drawing or writing on it at all : ' 'Bout ship ! ' he yelled, ' hard-a-port, hard-a-port, for God's sake ! . . . or we shall all go slap off the chart ! '

" Yes, I see it's to your liking, that last one, eh ? " pursued Maurin. " And we perfectly understand the reason why ! It's because it gives you an opportunity of ridiculing us, and persuading yourselves we're one and all a set of Cougourdans, and nothing else. You're fools enough, you see—and that's where you make your great mistake—to imagine, because a Southerner chooses to play the part occasionally, that he's really . . ."

" Really what ? " asked M. Labarterie.

" An ass ! " said the laconic Pastouré, who was never afraid of plain speaking, when necessary.

CHAPTER VIII

Marlusse, of Bormes, but originally from Bandol, tells *his* story of
the *Plan of the Paris Exposition.*

At this moment M. Cigalous, looking out of window,
caught sight of the Brigadier Cantoni, of the Bormes
Gendarmerie.

"Halbran, go and tell the Brigadier, who is walking on
the terrace yonder, to come in for a bit, as I want to speak
to him," and the innkeeper went out to carry the message.

"Cantoni," said M. Cigalous, "is the pick of the real,
good, right sort of gendarmes, a public servant beyond
compare." Then, when the man appeared :

"Take a seat and give us your company for a few
minutes, Cantoni. I want to introduce you to these
gentlemen. I have told them how highly you deserve
their esteem, and I have only spoken the plain truth."

Polite greetings were exchanged, glass in hand.

"Ah ! so you are there, Monsieur Maurin ? " observed
Cantoni, in a pleasant voice.

"Yes, here I am," replied Maurin heartily. "It's some
while now since I've quite dared to show up like this."

"Ah ! " laughed Cantoni. . . . "Yes, I know, I know.
. . . We have our orders, to be sure, at times, and we're
bound to obey 'em ; but everybody knows there's nothing
serious to be said against you. Quite the opposite, indeed !
for here you are to-day received with all the honours—
as you should be. True justice always has the upper hand
in the long run. . . . I congratulate you, Maurin. . . the
law has no quarrel with you now. I was on leave, by the
by, when you had that man-hunt, at which you got one
of your fellows killed. . . ."

55

" He's not the first, neither, you've seen ! " returned
Maurin cordially ; " and you've more than once given and
taken some ugly knocks in arresting scamps."

" What I meant to say," proceeded Cantoni, " was that
you did *rather* annoy the gendarmes that time, by what
I've heard say, and you joked them a *bit* over and above. . . .
A man who's posted on the look-out for wild-boar at a
battue can only stop the brute if he goes by him within
shot, and not away out of sight and near the other guns."

" But," said Maurin, in a fine conciliatory tone, " do you
imagine, Brigadier, I have a grudge against the gendarmes ?
There's a matter betwixt Alessandri and me, but it's
something betwixt man and man, and if the other gendarmes think it touches them, they're mistaken."

" You must know, Maurin, that in going after you
when they have orders to, they're only doing their duty."

" Granted ! " agreed Maurin ; " but then, I'm only doing
mine by escaping 'em, when I can and how I can.   It's not
being caught by them I'm afraid of, but being kept in gaol
by others.   My grandfather used to tell me that if he
were accused of having stolen Coudon and Faron, the two
mountains by Toulon, he would be loath, though all the
world could see the two hills still standing where they
always had, he would be very loath to have to prove his
innocence before a Court of Justice."

" It's an open secret to everybody," remarked Cigalous,
who was anxious to convince Cantoni of Maurin's innocence ; " it's an open secret by now that Maurin was
accused of murder—neither more nor less ! "

Mme. Labarterie gave a little shiver.   M. Cigalous
continued :

" Yes, accused of murder by Alessandri, on the word
of a fellow like Grondard.   The Grondards are brutes of the
lowest type, and whoever killed the father has delivered
the countryside of a perfect scourge.   That's what Alessandri should have told himself, and just left Maurin alone.
But Alessandri is a lover and a jealous man, and poor
Maurin paid dear for a few ill-considered jests.   For my

own part, I never dreamt of accusing Maurin when they found Grondard dead in the woods with a bullet in his carcase. But even had he been the author of the scoundrel's death, I should feel justified, as an honest man and a good Mayor, in applauding the deed, knowing as I do things about old Grondard to make your hair stand on end.

" And young Grondard ; didn't he, only a few days ago, try to kill Maurin ? But that happened with no one by, at night-time ; and when you can't prove a thing, why, it's best to hold your tongue ! . . .

" And my conclusion is, that before launching their warrant of arrest, the judges would often be well advised to examine into things a bit deeper, and feel the pulse of public opinion more carefully."

" I only learnt," said Cabissol, " when everybody else did, of the charge brought by young Grondard, and I think with the Mayor. I could tell some strange tales about your Grondard, and I will, whenever it's needful."

" But," affirmed M. Rinal, " there's this into the bargain : Maurin never did this act they charge him with, meritorious as it may have been. . . . Come, come, we're vexing him with our ill-considered chatter. We have something better to do than remind him of times of suffering."

" Oh ! as for that," broke in Maurin, " there was only one time I really suffered, and that was when I had my hands tied. . . . No, I didn't like that ! . . . But there, you're in the right, let's talk of something else. The word's with you, Marlusse ! "

Cigalous, meantime, had got into a separate conversation with M. Rinal :

" Oh ! come," the latter was saying ; " I tell you it is precisely as I say. Oh ! if you think everything's for the best in this best of all possible Republics ! There are some bits of red-tape have never had any common sense, and have less than ever in these days. Yes, sir ; I'm supposing a murder is committed here by a highwayman. Well, he takes the road from Cogolin to Draguignan. Do you imagine I, the Mayor, can telegraph to Cogolin ? Not a

bit of it. The murderer makes off east ; I must telegraph
west, that is to the officials for prosecution at Toulon.
That's what I am compelled to do in these days of railways,
motor-cars, and bicycles ! You now see how easy a
matter it is to police our country districts ! . . . But
enough of these absurdities . . . Now, Marlusse ! "

And the company, which had fallen silent to listen to the
Mayor, echoed with one voice, " Now Marlusse, your
story ! "

" Oh ! yes," protested the man, making a gesture of
elbowing away the demand, as if it were a hand laid on
his arm ; " oh ! hang it ! you are always asking me for that
story, till I'm just sick of it ! You only do it to poke fun
at me ! "

" Now, Marlusse, your turn ! " boomed Pastouré's
double-bass.

" Pastouré has spoken," cried Novarre ; " wonders will
never cease ! "

" Come, Marlusse," begged Benoni Soufflarès, " tell us
the story without so much pressing. You're ready enough,
most days, to din it in our ears ; but now, with everybody
praying and beseeching you, you won't hold back, will you ?
Come, out with it, *bestiasse !* "

" Come, you'll tell us that story ? *la diras, aquell' his-
toiro ?* " urged Mascurel.

" Oh, he'll tell it, his story ; his story, he'll tell it, never
fear ! " insisted Lacroustade.

Marlusse was a man of fifty, and his temples showed a
maze of crowsfeet and wrinkles that indicated a fine fund
of drollery and high spirits. He wore an immense imitation
panama in summer, and in winter a broad-brimmed felt
of similar proportions. Dropping the fore rim down over
his nose, like the peak of a cap, and turning up the back
behind his neck, he looked like a conspirator in front and
a musketeer from the rear. Before or behind, he had the
air of making fun of everybody and everything, till his
pipe with its reed stem seemed somehow to be prolonging
his irony into space in the shape of tobacco smoke !

Marlusse was a master cork-cutter, and had the comfortable looks of a man well pleased with himself and with life generally.

" Well, then," he began, " I'll tell you my tale, since I must ; but it's not one like the *Diver*, seeing it really happened. It's the story of our jaunt to Paris, where we went to see the *Essposition Universel*. I ought to tell you that for some time we had been putting our brass o' one side, like so many misers, M. le Maire there, Novarre, Soufflarès and I, with the notion of going to the *Essposition*, to keep the anniversary of glorious Eighty-nine, and to prove our good Republican principles, as everybody ought ! "

Here Marlusse broke off for the moment ; Novarre, Soufflarès, and M. Cigalous were looking at him, and he was returning their look, with the air of four augurs who know the inmost secrets of things. All four faces were wrinkled with a smile of common understanding. Evidently they shared between them some exorbitant mystery, some tremendous secret, something excruciatingly funny . . . something unfathomable by the *profanum vulgus*. Clearly what was *un*spoken was the most mirth-provoking part.

Then, after a pause, Marlusse resumed, in a plaintive voice, expressive of acute exasperation :

" How *can* they be so unfeeling ! Just look, ladies and gentlemen, they're all on the laugh already, my three travelling companions there, and they do it on purpose to annoy me. It's not my story at all makes them so merry, but because they know I never can tell it properly. . . . However, I'll just do my best, out of respect for the company."

Marlusse gave a comforting puff at his pipe, and continued :

" Well, the *Exposition* opens, . . . and off we go one day. . . . We settle down in the four corners of a comfortable third-class coach. . . ."

Here the narrator's face assumed a look of extreme

satisfaction, as of one enjoying the bliss of a veritable terrestrial paradise.

" We light up our pipes—and *jai tira, Mariu !* . . . It was an excursion train, you know. We go by Marseilles, naturally, and reach Paris in due time."

Here, seeing his audience laughing, Marlusse broke off afresh :

" If you're laughing at me already, Monsieur le Maire, I simply can't go on. Shall just have to give it up ! Come, now, Novarre, *don't* look at me like that. Give me a chance, Soufflarès, *do !* "

" Go ahead, Marlusse, lad, the Parisians are all ears."

" The first idea struck us at Paris was : ' Why, it's a town just like any other, only a little bigger, not a bit finer. It's all houses, same as at Bormes ; all the difference is, there's a trifle more traffic ! . . . To make a long story short, we went to stop at an inn, corner of the Rue Notre-Dame - des - Victoires and the Place Notre - Dame - des-Victoires, both at once . . . like this, look ! "

Marlusse deposited his pipe on a corner of the table, brought together his two extended forefingers, and, the middle finger of the right hand overlapping the forefinger and guiding it, he succeeded in giving his audience a visual representation of the angle of the Place Notre-Dame-des-Victoires, and the street of the same name in Paris.

Everybody looked on with an amused smile.

" The hotel is there, there, d'ye see ? " Marlusse kept saying.

" I can see it," declared M. Rinal.

" Good ! " resumed Marlusse, picking up his pipe again. " They say we folks of the Midi gesticulate ; but it's as clear as daylight the habit helps make things plain, eh ? "

" Yes, we can *see* the hotel," said Labarterie, finding Marlusse's eyes fixed on him.

" Well, we settled down there, and next morning off we went to their *Exposition*. . . . What a day it was ! . . . In we march, and what do I see ? Just shops—and more shops ; there were jewellers, and silk-mercers, with their

goods there behind the glass. ' *Té !* ' says I, ' have we
come so far to see the old Cannebière or the Rue Saint-
Ferréol ? ' All the same, I turn about, and twist about,
and stare my eyes out, as we'd come for that. Suddenly :
' *Vé !* ' says I to myself, ' I've lost my bearings ! Where's
the Mayor ? Where are the others got to ? ' And it was
true ; I had missed 'em, I had . . . *coquin de bon sort !* So
I start off to look for them, and I search, search for a good
three or four hours, I do. I twist and I turn till at last I
says to myself : ' Well, you know the hotel, anyway ;
best go back there.' So out I goes, my pretty lady and
gentlemen all—and *eh, bé !* would you believe it, I found
I'd been going round and round on the same spot for the
last four hours, *pauvre moi !* I had been wandering in and
out quite close to the same gate all the time—the one I'd
come in by and now went out at, *couyoun coumo la luno*—
looking as silly as the moon, if I may say it without
offence. But then I says to myself : ' Marlusse,' I says,
' this must never happen again. Not to lose your way
any more, you must buy yourself . . .' "

Here Marlusse came to a sudden full stop once more.
He cast a look of ineffable slyness at his three travelling
companions, who were laughing again uproariously, and
declared :

" There we are ! you can see for yourselves they're
making fun of me ! Didn't I tell you so, Madame ? The
point of the joke is not my story at all, but th'ir nasty way
of turning it into ridicule. It's only for that they make
me tell it ! It's not listening to me you care for, but just
watching *their* faces ! "

At this Soufflarès and Novarre could hold themselves no
longer ; each lifted a protesting arm to heaven, and
dropped his fist with a resounding slap on his thigh, with
cries of " Oh, that fellow ! that Marlusse ! "

" *D'acquéou Marlusso !* " translated Mascurel instantly.

" He's *too* funny, that Marlusse ! that Marlusse, he's
just *too* funny ! "—and Lacroustade's quack ! quack !
quack ! drowned everybody else's laugh.

The Mayor was smiling archly, amused at the Parisians' utter inability to make anything whatever out of it all. He merely remarked :

" There, you see ; the *mocos* are the only fellows know how to make merry at their own expense, as I told you."

Marlusse resumed :

" Oh ! laugh away, mates, laugh away ; never fear. I know what I'm going to say ! . . . I've not forgotten this time, and you'll be finely caught ! . . . I've marked it down, stamped it on my memory, the important word . . . it's engraved in my brain. . . . I've got it fast "—and he tapped his forehead with a look of genial triumph.

Then he continued, after a momentary pause employed in a scornful contemplation of his three friends :

" Not to be tedious—next morning I wake up betimes, and while my comrades are still snoring, I put on my trousers and jacket, I dress and wash my hands and face, and so on, same as I do every morning, and then I sally forth. . . . '*Té !*' I tell myself in the street, ' you're not going to lose yourself any more at the *Exposition,* so you must go right away and buy . . ."

Here Soufflarès, Novarre, and the Mayor burst into a great shout of laughter, while Lacroustade went quack ! quack ! quack ! frantically.

Marlusse gave them a furious glance ; after which he assumed a look of deep thought and profound intro-spection, as if absorbed in the pursuit of some subtle, elusive recollection. Finally, he burst out, in dire distress :

" *Noum dé pas Dioû !* I've forgot it again ! . . . *Eh, bé !* didn't I tell you so, gentlemen ? This is the cream of my story for those rascals ! That's why they make me tell it at every dinner we go to, just to make mock of me at their ease. The fact is—it's perfectly true ! —every blessed time I tell the story, I forget one word, the all-important word, too ! No matter how well I know it before I begin, no matter how often I say it over at table in the day and abed at night, I always end by forgetting it again ! It's a sort of infirmity, and they make fun of it !

. . . Come, a little good-nature for once, M. le Maire ; you know quite well what I want to say. . . . *Diga-vo mi !* Tell me, Novarre . . . or you, Soufflarès ! . . . *As féni, Lacroustádo, dé faïré lou canar ?* have you done your quack-quacking, Lacroustade ? your quack-quacking have you done ? Let me tell you in plain English, Mascurel, you're an ass, and then I'll put it into good Provençal for you : *siès qu'un couyoun !* *Zou,* just whisper it in my ear, Soufflarés . . . a, a . . . what I meant to buy, because I wanted it so badly . . . a thing, a what d'ye call 'em, a thingumbob . . . I've got it on the tip o' my tongue ! . . . and they *won't* tell me, because all they care for, Madame, is to watch me hunting for the confounded word . . . a paper, you know, a sheet, a prospectus, a . . . "

Suddenly his countenance, contorted in the grievous effort, the long-drawn agony of the fruitless search, relaxed ; his features beamed with satisfaction, like a shipwrecked mariner finding a harbour of refuge at last, and softly, softly, in the intoxication of a well-deserved victory :

" A *plan* of the *Exposition,*" he murmured. " Thank you for not telling me, gentlemen ; now I've found it for myself ; not a bit too soon ! . . . Well, to cut it short, there was a bookseller's shop in the same street as our hotel, and the man was just taking down his shutters. . . . I step up with a ' Good morning ! ' and he says ' Good morning, sir ! anything you want to buy ? ' And I tells him, I says to him, I says, I says, says I : ' I want . . . h'm, h'm ! I want to buy . . . h'm, h'm, h'm ! . . . Now I have it ! Just give me, if you please, Mr. Bookseller, just give me a . . . ' "

The blood rushed to the man's face, and his eyes seemed ready to jump out of his head. A passion of anger seized him. He gave his friends a look of positive hatred, and dashing his fist down on the table till the glasses rang again :

" *Noum dé pas Dioû !* " he shouted in stentorian tones ; " believe it or no, I've forgot the word again ! "

The Mayor, Novarre, Soufflarès were choking with laughter. Everybody was highly diverted. Cantoni could not contain himself.

It was his turn now to lift a hand and slap it down forcibly on his thigh—the recognised token for everybody and, above all, for a gendarme, of uncontrollable delight at some superlative joke. The gesture means as plain as speech : " Well, if ever I saw the like ! I'd never have believed it possible ! "

Lacroustade's merriment was like a whole flock of ducks quacking all together.

Marlusse appeared to calm down, and announced with a smile and a look round the company :

" All the same, if I'm asked for the tale again, I simply won't tell it, never ! I make myself too ridiculous. Now isn't it ludicrous, always to forget that word, such a simple word too ; isn't it just ludicrous ? I can say it well enough now—a plan of the *Exposition*, two plans, three plans, a hundred plans of the blessed *Exposition*. . . . I could go on saying it from now till to-morrow, without once missing —a plan, two plans, a thousand plans ! plan, plan, plan ! ran tan plan ! rataplan ! plan, plan, plan ! "

" Finish your story, Marlusse ! "

" So I tell the bookseller : ' I should like a . . . plan of the *Exposition*.' The man answers me back : ' Oh ! there's more than one there ; take your choice.' There was a pile of them in fact. . . . I take one, then two, then a dozen, and examine them one after the other."

Here Marlusse burst out laughing himself, and slapping his thigh as the others had done :

" *Oh ! coquin de sort !* but they were every one the same ! "

" The same edition ! " said Labarterie, in a bland, ex-planatory tone.

" When I'd taken plenty of time to choose, I just pick up the first that comes, and I says like this to the book-seller, ' How much ? ' and he tells me, ' It's so much.' I put my hand in my pocket and I give him what he asked."

Marlusse, as he spoke, made as if taking money out of his purse and counting it carefully into the shopkeeper's hand.

"And as I'm paying him, the fellow looks me up and down, and says he suddenly, just like this :

"'Why, *you're* from Bandol!' says he.

"*Noum dé pas Dioû!* but I *was* amazed"—and Marlusse, his fingers extended as if to make a long nose, stuck the thumb under his chin. This was to mimic the crook of a cod's head, when suddenly, to his intense surprise, he is whipped out from his native element by a Newfoundland fisherman.

"So I says to him, 'How ever did you know?'

"But he only began to laugh.

"'*Vé!*' I says to him—and Marlusse stuck the tip of his forefinger in his right eye, and pulled down the lower lid, which, all the world over, is understood to mean : "D'ye see any green? You'll not get over *me* in a hurry!"

"'*Vé!*' I says to him, 'either Novarre, or the Mayor, or Soufflarès, one or the other, is here, hid in your shop, and he's told you to say that to me. You *couldn't* have guessed it!'

"Then, gentlemen, I set to work to search for my friends, and turned his whole place upside down, while he kept laughing like a lunatic. . . . Well . . . there was nobody hid there at all. . . . Then I says to him, like this :

"'Oh! *tron de l'air!* how *could* you know I am from Bandol? For I do come from there! I've lived at Bormes since I was a babe in arms, but Bandol it was saw me born.'

"What d'ye think he answered? He just says like this in a quiet way, with his Parisian accent :

"'Oh! part by your coat, part by your hat, I guessed you were from some place midway between Toulon and Marseilles!'

"And I took home with me from Paris and always kept the—the——"

F

" The plan," Labarterie very kindly prompted.

" Thank you, sir, thank you," exclaimed Marlusse, with a great show of gratitude ; " but that wasn't just what I meant to say. What I took back home from Paris, more than all the rest, was the memory of that man's words. You see, they're for ever repeating, *Essposition Universel!* *Essposition Universel!* . . . They can talk of nothing else. Well and good, as much as ever you like ; but *Essposition* or no *Essposition*, Paris, mind you—I found out from that bookseller that Paris is indeed the capital, the queen, the shining light of cities ! . . . A city, my lad, where you've only to walk into the first shop you come to and they'll tell you anything and everything—down to what country you hail from, right away ! No, that's a thing I've never forgot ! So, let 'em make another of their *Esspositions*, and I'll go again. I've kept the plan ! "

CHAPTER IX

Pastouré, who can be long-winded enough in great emergencies,
   expatiates on the unwisdom of Maurin's present behaviour, while
   the latter is talking with his enemy Sandri.

In order to meet Tonia, who was waiting for him at the
cantine of Le Don, Maurin one fine morning had left Pastouré to shoot by himself in the marshes of the Almanarre
at Hyères. All the latter had brought down was a cormorant for a Russian Prince who was making a collection
of all the wild birds that can be killed in the Department
of the Var. Maurin had taken Pastouré into partnership
in this task, as he did in all his sporting enterprises, and
that worthy continued pushing his miry way through
the cane-brakes and furze-bushes. As he floundered on
he talked away to himself with much explanatory gesticu-
lation :

"Yes, a sort of shooting I can't bear ; I don't like it
at all, I don't. You want heavy boots. And it's cold this
morning. No chance of getting warm here by running.
The mud's that sticky it glues your feet to the road. It's
wretched work ! And why does he go and leave a chap
all alone in such a mess ? Egad ! because he's for visiting
his doxy. He's just going after sorrow, *I* reckon, like
everybody else ; but when love leads the way, no more
to be said ! If 'twere the itch they were playing for, they'd
be mad to win the game. . . . We're all made like that,
one as much as the other, we all run and run and run to
catch the flying prize, and all we do catch is a cold i' the
head. Where's he going ? To see his doxy, I tell you !
Why ? For his pleasure. What'll he get ? He'll get a
mischief, that's what he'll get, for sure and certain. That

Sandri is for ever prowling about the girl ; so Maurin
had best understand there's naught for him to do in that
quarter ; his best way is to leave every blessed gendarme
in the world alone, and let 'em forget his existence. If a
doll were rigged up as a gendarme, *I*'d be in a panic, *I*
should ! Yes, I'd fainer have my enemies to deal with than
my judges. My enemies tell lies, and they know they're telling lies ; and the judge, who knows naught of their per-
juries, sends me to the hulks. Does he imagine, can Maurin
imagine, Sandri's ever going to forgive ? A good Corsican's
a good chap ; but a bad 'un, who thinks he's got a well-
founded grievance, Lord ! he's worse than the worst.
Make yourself scarce, Maurin, and Pastouré after you !
Get up and go, friend Pastouré ; cut and run, Pastouré !
No gendarmes, and no women, that's where peace is to
be found. A woman and a gendarme always go together
—for two reasons : she brings him to the neighbours' by
her quarrelling, and into her husband's—by the horns !

" Yes, horns draw gendarmes, that everybody knows.
Don't marry at all, or else be a widower ; and whatever
you do, beware of a gendarme's girl. If you go interfering
with suchlike, why, it's row after row, trouble after trouble ;
you're in for gendarme for certain sure ; gendarme once
and gendarme twice, gendarme ten times and gendarme a
hundred times !

" We were all quiet and peaceable—and he must go and
provoke war. Then does he suppose his fine friend Caboufigue's going to leave him unmolested ? Does he imagine
young Caboufigue's likely to digest the duel affair ? No,
lads, he can't expect it ! What a business to be sure ! . . .
Halloa ! mark, Panpan ! . . . a water-hen ? No, ducks !
. . . that fellow's got it . . . go fetch, Gaspard, go fetch !
. . . What a business ! that's what I was saying—and
a fine business it was ! A comic duel, a ridiculous duel,
a ludicrous duel, a duel we shan't soon see the like of ; a
duel that set a whole village laughing every man jack of
'em ; a duel they're telling about from village to village
all over the countryside ! Does Maurin think the man's

pride's ever going to forgive the insult ? Beware of Caboufigue, I tell you, Maurin ; you knew him low down, as low as yourself, at the very bottom of the ladder—and that's what vexes him. The higher he rises in the world, the more he's for going back on you. Yes, beware of Caboufigue and young Caboufigue and all the Caboufigues, all the bladders (*boufigues*) puffed out with eating and drinking and the wind of conceit. A pity that duel wasn't a real duel ! A burst bladder, who'd have shed a tear ? If they'd pricked a hole in him with the point of a good sword, it's not blood would have come from a Caboufigue, but just the wind of a broken bladder, the wind I said, the wind of hatred and pride and malice, of vanity and greed. Yes, Caboufigue would have given up the ghost with a little sputter, that's all, the puff of a pricked bladder. . . . As we came out from dinner, when young Caboufigue was driving off in his fine carriage, M. Rinal said : ' When we see them hung, these useless egoists, these traitors to the people, these fellows of yesterday who forswear father and mother to-day, when by good luck—only that never happens—we see them hung or hanged, why, best leave 'em hanging.' And when M. Rinal said that, he said well. I'm not the man would cut the rope. It would only bring ill-luck, the rope that hanged the likes of them !

" Now, M. Noblet, that's a different matter ! A gentleman, but a gentleman who does work in the world ! . . . Hi, Gaspard ! . . . a snipe ! . . . Go fetch, Panpan. . . . Yes, a worker that M. Noblet, with the look of a man about him ; and not a great belly and nothing else, like Caboufigue. What is it he wants, M. Noblet ? He wants folk to work, and for everybody, all over the world, to be less wretched. . . . For a man like that, yes, I'd go barefoot to the end of the earth ! but the others, bah ! I can't abide 'em, I can't stomach 'em, they turn my gorge ! The world's a mighty stupid place, and a mighty rascally ! We must choose out the wise heads, and down with the proud stomachs. Selfishness is all belly. Go, prick the swollen bladder, Maurin. It'll give up its soul with a little puff of wind, I tell you ; for a Caboufigue carries his soul in his belly, as is only the proper thing."

Pastouré was quite right ; Maurin was, indeed, on his way to meet his enemy.

Hardly had Tonia joined him at the *cantine* of Le Don before Sandri entered the house. He had seen Maurin at La Londe-des-Maures in a fish-hawker's light cart on its way to Le Lavandou, and had followed him. Directly Tonia saw the gendarme :

" Get away, Maurin," she told her lover, " get away quick by the back door."

" H'm, after thinking it over now, why should I get away ? " Maurin asked—and he got up to greet the gendarme.

" Good day, Brigadier Sandri."

" I'm not a Brigadier."

" True, you're not. If you were, you'd be married by now, seeing that's the condition Tonia's father laid on you—that you must be named Brigadier for him to give you his daughter. You're not Brigadier yet, so you're not married. Then what right have you to come here complaining ? As Tonia's fiancé ? But you never will be made Brigadier ; so best break it off. Only, seeing you're a good sort after all at bottom, and you know better than most, being a soldier, what honour is (I served myself, you see, and I know what's what), well then, say good-bye nicely to the girl ; don't bear a grudge, and no women's cackling and useless reproaches, mind, against our good and charming Tonia here ; tell her father you've thought better of it, and don't get in my road any more, my man."

Sandri stood gnawing his moustache.

" Tonia," he said presently, " I promised you I would break it off the first time I saw anything in your conduct to displease me ; well, I'll do it now. Only your father must know I have good reasons for it."

" Let me tell him the news myself," said Tonia.

" Then," stammered Sandri, considerably surprised, " then it's all over ? "

" So it strikes me," she said decidedly.

"Very well!" growled the gendarme. "Good-bye,
Tonia. I don't believe you are seriously to blame, and
I beseech you not to become so. . . . That man might
lead you far wrong, Tonia, and be your ruin. I should
be sorry for you. Think—there's still time, I imagine—
think, one day or another he'll get himself into another
bad scrape, and once you're married to the fellow, you'll
come to regret the gendarme, when the other has shown
you the bandit he really is."

" Enough said, Sandri," Maurin interrupted impatiently.
" It's time to part. Off with you about your business ! "

The gendarme looked him hard in the face.

" I know what I know ; I shall catch you yet, Maurin,
my lad."

"If you do, you'll owe me your Brigadier's stripes,
Sandri, and your thanks for getting 'em."

The gendarme had hardly left the room when Maurin
turned to the girl and said simply and straightforwardly :

" Tonia, if your father consents, you shall be my wife."

The words were more or less forced from him. For all
his repugnance to the idea of marriage, he had allowed
himself to be carried away by his sense of justice.

The girl sprang to him, threw her arms about his neck,
and hanging there, her feet swinging clear of the floor, like
a child, she told him :

" Then, if my father refuses, you shall have a mistress
at any rate ready to do everything for you, Maurin, to
defend you to the death, to follow you to the ends of the
earth. You are as brave as you are handsome. Every
girl in Corsica would love you. And if ever they come after
you again, and the *maquis* of the Maures will not hide you
safe enough, we will go to my Corsican fatherland, where
bandits are happy men and honoured by all their fellows."

" For the time being," answered Maurin quietly, " I am
free to do what I please, and I'm going to help my people
to choose a good man to make us good laws."

CHAPTER X

In which we shall see the warlike and quixotic humour, and even the high morality, of the King of the Maures threatening to bring that Potentate once more into collision with the laws of his country.

ALAS! Maurin was not long at peace with the gendarmes. Fresh escapades were bound to occur pretty soon and bring him again under the notice of the officers of justice.

Maurin, in company with Pastouré, was beating the marshes of Fréjus for game. There they came upon a sportsman who, when only a short way off, shot at and missed a snipe. Maurin could plainly see the bird, after the third zigzag, make off and disappear in the distance. The man, a rustic-looking fellow, dressed like a well-to-do bourgeois, of herculean build though not of any great height, with a low-browed, obstinate sort of face, shouted to his dog :

" Go, fetch, sir ! go, fetch ! "

" Sir," said Maurin politely, " the snipe was missed. Your dog cannot retrieve the bird, or any dog on earth."

" Yes, it was a miss," insisted Pastouré.

" Go, fetch ! go, fetch ! " reiterated the fellow to his dog.

" You have a magnificent dog there," remarked Maurin.

" True for you," agreed the man ; " he cost me a pretty penny, and I have not had him long ; in fact, he's bad at obeying still. Search ! go, search ! you scamp."

The dog went patiently to work, but naturally enough failed to find anything.

" Bah ! he's as stupid as he's handsome ! " growled his master.

Then, as the poor beast could not find the bird, which was far enough by this time, he kicked him brutally. . . .

The animal, with a plaintive whimper, took refuge between Maurin's legs.

The fellow ran up to punish him further, breathing savage threats :

" Wait a bit, you scoundrel ! wait a bit, you villain ! You know the taste of my foot already, eh ? Well, you're going to taste it again !

His face red with passion, he put out his hand to seize the wretched creature's collar, but the animal threw itself on its back in terror.

" You shan't beat the dog," said Maurin, coolly and quietly ; " he's not done wrong, to begin with, and he's begging my protection into the bargain."

" And we're two to one," added Pastouré in his short way.

" My dog is my own, I should suppose ! "

" Up to a certain point, yes," returned Maurin ; " but a dog is a dog, and not a slave, I reckon ! "

" Go to the devil," stormed the other ; " I don't know you."

" Well," said Maurin, " would you like to know me ? "— and on the man's once more reaching to grip the dog, Maurin took him by the shoulder and spun him round like a teetotum.

Exasperated at this, the quick-tempered rustic wheeled about and clapped the muzzle of his gun to the breast of this unexpected enemy.

Maurin gripped the barrel in his strong fist, and, pushing it aside, shouted :

" Loose your gun, I say ! "

Maurin's peremptory tone had a remarkable effect. Involuntarily the man obeyed, and gave up his weapon, which Maurin put down on the ground beside his own. Then he unslung his game-bag, and cried :

" Come on now, you brute ! "

Disconcerted for a moment, the would-be sportsman had recovered his wits by this time. He, too, threw off his game-bag and assumed a fighting posture.

Pastouré remarked quietly :

" You'll leave me a small share, eh ? "

" Ha ! it's you are the cowards," the other vociferated ; " you're two to one."

" Oh ! *I* shall only stand guard over the guns," Pastouré assured him.

The two adversaries closed. The bout was short and sharp ; Maurin lifted his opponent clean off the ground, and pitched him on his back on the swampy turf.

The fellow sprang up, and ran savagely at his enemy again.

" You want some more ? " cried Maurin. " Have a care ; I shall hit out this time ! "

But his foe was blinded, maddened with rage, and rushed head down at Maurin. The latter took the man's head, and, clapping it under his left arm, which he pressed hard against his body, held it as in a vice. Then, delivering a series of mighty slaps with his open hand on the stranger's rear :

" Ah ! so you want to thrash your dog, do you ? You are dead set, are you, on thrashing your dog ? Well, just remember this, a man mustn't thrash his dog unjustly ! I'll teach you what justice is, you brute ! D'ye feel it penetrating you behind, eh, fellow ? *Will* you beat your dog again, tell me that ! Now, have you had enough, you dog-beater, you ? "

When he let him go, the man, intoxicated with fury, came at Maurin again, a knife open in his hand. Seeing this, Maurin doubled his fist and hit him in the face, which began to bleed. Finally, he said :

" Now have you got your gruel ? . . . Then, pick up your gun again.

" Draw the charge first, Pastouré, and confiscate his cartridges ; else he'll be murdering us ! "

The victim did as he was bid this time, and made off. But he went straight to the nearest Mairie and lodged a formal complaint against Maurin. Assault and battery, theft of cartridges and theft of dog ! For the sportsman's dog had refused to follow him, and in spite of Maurin's and Pastouré's reiterated orders had stuck obstinately to their heels, asking them with beseeching eyes to keep him with them. It was in such gentle tones his two new friends told him : " Come, off with you, my fine fellow ; go after your master, good dog ! " Whereas his real master mostly spoke to him in a voice that made him long to bolt.

" All the same," muttered Pastouré, " here we are mixed up again in their confounded *procès-verbaux !* "

" So," returned Maurin, " we ought to have let the poor beast be beaten ? "

" No, for sure ! " declared Pastouré ; " but that don't hinder it would have been better if we'd never met either him nor his master."

They were still discussing the event when, far out in the middle of the marshes, they saw another gunner bearing a great resemblance to the first—a wealthy pig-dealer, as it turned out, who had come from Nice to shoot snipe. The man, his gun between his knees, a brand-new game-bag with cord fringes and tassels slung at his side, was seated on a fallen tree-trunk, and at minute intervals was blowing a silver whistle hung round his neck, producing a long, shrill, high-pitched note. His air seemed to say he was engaged in performing an important and urgent duty, one he was never likely to see the end of, and which absorbed his whole attention.

The thing struck the two poachers as so extraordinary that they called a halt to examine further. The man did not appear to see them, but went on whistling with unabated persistency. Manifestly he was losing his wind, and looked quite exhausted.

" Halloa, friend ! " hailed Maurin, in his free-spoken way, " whatever are you doing there ? "

" You can see for yourself, I'm whistling "—and he blew another blast.

" I can see that much," said Maurin, " but *why* are you whistling ? The row you're making is enough to scare the very fish under-water in the sea."

Undisturbed, the man whistled again; then he announced:

" I'm whistling my dog. I've been whistling like that ever since this morning."

" Well, you're both of you fine and patient, for it'll be noon directly. . . . So he bolted from you early this morning, your dog did ? "

" Yes," replied the man (still whistling at regular intervals) ; " he's quite a new dog " (whistle) ; " he cost me a pretty penny at Nice yesterday " (whistle) ; " they said he was a first-rate dog " (whistle); " a dog much sought after. . . . We took train here to go after the snipe together. At Fréjus railway station, eight o'clock this morning, my dog bolted " (whistle), " and I've been whistling him ever since . . ." (whistle). " But my dog's nowhere about "—and, mopping his brow, he heaved a sigh, and with a beautiful and touching air of resignation, observed :

" Luckily, there's no game ! if there had been, running wild as he does, the beast would have scared it all away ! "

"*Moussu*," said Maurin, pulling off his hat with exaggerated politeness : " *Aï vi fouàsso couyouns dins ma pùto dé vido, maï coumo vous, jamaï !* " that is to say, " I've seen manyfools in my unhappy life, but such a fool as you, never!"

The man looked up in amazed bewilderment at Maurin, who added, with a smile :

" We can only suppose your dog, like me, had seen enough of you ! Good day, everybody ! "

The man lost his temper, and a quarrel and scrimmage ensued. The result was that the fellow, still whistling his dog as he went along, carried a complaint to the gendarmerie at Fréjus, where he also took the opportunity of giving his dog's description.

It was easy enough to identify Maurin from the descriptions of the two aggrieved parties, and the conclusion drawn was that the King of the Maures, wishing to keep the exclusive enjoyment of the shooting over the marshes of Fréjus, was by way of forcing a disreputable quarrel on every respectable sportsman who appeared there.

That evening, on leaving Maurin, Pastouré indulged in the following self-colloquy :

" Yes, they could say some fine things, if they could talk, dogs could ! Dogs love you for love. ' Food comes second to love with them. Offer a dog a leg of mutton, and *I*'ll offer him a caress. He'll go after me, for all your joint of meat. . . . To beat a dog is a sin and a shame ; to beat a man who's beat a dog, is a blessing and a good deed. Only it's men have made the laws, and so the laws aren't on the dog's side. Therefore, let the man have it by all means, when he beats the dog, for in beating the dog, he's been hurting something better than a man. The dog don't talk, he yelps, and, even if he wanted to, he'd never betray his own secret."

" Another day like this, and Sandri will be having a fine laugh," was what Maurin said to himself.

Unfortunately the day was not done yet. The same evening, as Maurin was taking a magnificent heron to the Russian Prince's villa, at Saint-Raphaël, he caught sight of his daughter ahead of him. . . .

He was hurrying forward in the gathering dusk to join her, when a well-dressed man approached the girl, who was on her way back to the Prince's villa, where she had been in service for some time past as linen-maid.

Thérèse gave a little scream, and quickened her pace. The man followed, with the gait and look of the sort who pursue women in spite of their wish to be left alone. Eventually she escaped, and vanished swiftly under the gateway of the drive leading to the villa.

Maurin faced the man, who exclaimed in a frightened voice :

" What do you want with me ? "

" Sir," said Maurin, " when an honest man plays the part of cock, which is to go after the hens—it's only natural after all—he ought, if he's an honest man, to apply to wenches who ask no better."

The individual addressed tried to slip by, but Maurin laid a firm hand on his collar and told him gravely :

" Learn your lesson, young man ! I tell you to apply
to girls who may be taken with your ugly face. I've
never done otherwise myself. We must be a bit honest and
manly, eh, my fine gentleman ! When bad girls run
after us, and want to make us marry 'em, swearing they're
good and virtuous, then all's right and fair against such,
for they're trying to catch us under false pretences, and
ruin the peace of our lives. But here it's you want to play
a woman false ! D'ye understand, my fine lad ? . . . You
look a hot customer. But in these cases, I've seen hotter
than you cooled down pretty quick ! "

With these memorable words Maurin let go his prisoner,
who stammered out, with a very pale face :

" Come, now, what do you want with me ? Who are
you ? "

" What do I want ? Just to tell you this, and there's
an end . . . *I'm the little girl's father.* So remember, and
beware ! "

The unknown took to his heels.

Maurin had meant to make a well-hidden allusion to the
Grondard business ; but the speech was repeated and
discussed and canvassed, and from one to another, gendarme to gendarme, and brigade to brigade, came to
Sandri's ears, who instantly exclaimed : " Why, that's a
confession ! " Once more the peasant Don Quixote was
in trouble. A warrant of arrest was issued. The old
persecution began again. But they took care not to
inform the Préfet . . . and Cabissol was kept in the dark.

" He's talked overmuch again," said Pastouré in soliloquy to himself. . . . " Why, I tell you, even Caboufigue's
behaviour at the badger drawing may be turned against
you ! Before you give him a chance, look well about you
if you're in the open, and under your bed, if you've turned
in, for underneath there might be . . . who knows ? there
might be . . . one of your best friends ! And what are
our friends themselves very often ? Why folks—alack-
a-day !—who turn our confidences into weapons against
us ! "

CHAPTER XI

Pastouré's metaphysics.

MAURIN's mother was dying in his old wooden hut, in the middle of the plain of Cogolin, not far from the seashore, under the great parasol pines.

Maurin, with Pastouré to help him, was nursing her.

"Pastouré," he said, "go to M. Rinal's, and fetch my boy Bernard; then you must go to the Prince's for my daughter Thérèse. . . . I want them to see their grandmother die."

As for Césariot, he did not consider he had any right to summon him, seeing the old woman was ignorant of the lad's very existence.

Pastouré duly departed, and returned with Bernard; this done, he went and fetched Thérèse.

"Mother," said Maurin, "here are your grandchildren. They have come to kiss you."

"I give them my blessing," murmured the old woman in her weak voice; and sank back and died.

"Pastouré," said Maurin, "we will bury her in the cemetery of Cogolin. Run to neighbour Labigue's, and ask him to lend us his cart and horse and the new harness. We will put the coffin in the cart. Be quick."

Pastouré went on his errand. In his absence the Cogolin doctor did what was necessary, went to the Mairie, gave notice of the death, and found two friends whose presence Maurin wished at the funeral, and, next day, the burial took place.

The coffin was laid in the cart; this had been carefully cleaned, but still showed some brown stains of good manure,

while a few grains of oats could be detected here and there
sticking between the planks.

To do honour to the dead, Labigue had lent all his cattle ;
in front of the shaft horse was a mule, and in front of the
mule a little donkey.   All three wore their newest harness ;
the straps were well greased, and the copper nails glittered
in the sun, forming rounds and a variety of pretty patterns.
The two friends to whom the doctor had conveyed
Maurin's invitation were there, dressed in their best
clothes ; they fell in on foot behind the cart, which
Maurin drove.   Before them walked Bernard and Thérèse.
Pastouré had sent for his son Firmin, a handsome lad
of twenty-four, who walked by Thérèse's side, and found
her much to his taste.   For love is awake and active
even in the presence of death.   Pastouré himself marched
alongside the shafts, holding in the dazzling white light
of the midday sun the stable lantern with a candle burning inside in honour of the dead, though the dull yellow
flame was almost invisible in the flashing sunlight.

So they moved on along the broad highway, and the
conductor of the diligence, who was returning from Cogolin
to Saint-Tropez, saluted the little procession, as he passed
it, with his whip.   The passengers took off their hats, and
the women they met on the road crossed themselves
piously.

No one spoke ; only, from time to time, thinking himself
alone, no doubt, in the deep silence, Pastouré would begin
gesticulating, tossing his lantern up and down and muttering to himself :

" Afoot or in a cart, lying in a wooden box, stiff and
stark, or walking alongside and stirring one's stumps ;
where are we all bound for after all ?   Why, to the same
place . . . the hole in the ground.   Where do we come
from ? the earth.   Where do we go to ? the earth again.
So say the *boumians* (gypsies), and they say well.   The
poor man ends there ; and the king ends there.   Why
make so many troubles on the way ?   Yours is a sore life,
mate ; then why make it worse ?   You had time to make

the best of things, and you've spoilt 'em instead. What's
before, and what's after ? The earth before, and the earth
behind. The priests say we start living afresh. I reckon
it's done with once for all. Though, truly, 'twould be no
sillier to come again than it was to have come at all. If
there was justice anywhere we should see it, but we don't.
My lantern just now's hardly any use to me, because the
sun's shining. Yet at night it would do me good service.
But what would it show me the sun hasn't ? Children
we come into the world, and children we go out. The
old dame is dead. She had no more concern in the things
of this world, poor old creature, and yet she didn't want
to die. And why didn't she want to die ? To find out
the secret of life—and no one ever finds it out ! And if
to-morrow, and the day after, and always, we had to live
on and on, would I be ready to accept the boon ? No, not
I, upon my word ! It would be too much of the same
thing over and over again. . . . Always going after woodcock, and always hitting on *procès-verbaux* ! There's too
much suffering about. The people suffers. The people
dies. Kings suffer. Kings die. The Pope suffers. The
Pope dies. What do I throw light on with my lantern ?
Nothing. I never see but one God, and that's the sun,
but I could see it without my lantern. My lantern shows
me nothing the sun hasn't shown me already, and the sun
even shows me my lantern ! . . . Well, here's the village
at last, and here's the priest coming to meet you, grandmother ! You're not far now from the only rest poor
mortals get. . . ."

She was further from it than Pastouré thought. A
crowd of people was approaching from the village to
meet Maurin ; but among them were gendarmes, who had
received their orders what to do.

The people, who loved him, and had come to sympathise
in his grief, forced Maurin to come to a halt, and all with
him to do the same.

Thereupon, one of the gendarmes, after saluting the
dead, said to Maurin, without coming too close :

G

" Maurin, I am compelled to arrest you. It is for the matter of the Hyères marshes."

The crowd muttered angrily.

Maurin looked up with a fierce frown :

" To-day ? " he said ; " no, the thing's impossible to-day. To-morrow as much as you like."

The gendarme made as though to step forward, but Maurin stopped him :

" Go away, for the present ! I tell you this, if you push me too far, I shan't be able to hold myself in."

He looked so terrible that the gendarme turned pale, and dared not come a step nearer ; he even drew back a little.

" Let me bury my mother," Maurin went on in a gentler tone.

The bystanders, who were very numerous, began to hoot the gendarmes. . . . " The thing can't be. He's over-officious. He's never had such orders. They don't arrest a man in front of his dead mother's body ! "

Fortunately, the Mayor appeared at this juncture. He said a word or two to the gendarmes, and they withdrew.

So Maurin was allowed to bury his mother in peace. Directly the Curé's prayers were finished, Maurin disappeared with the connivance of all present. Then Pastouré, putting out his lantern, took cart and cattle back to their master. Next day he did the like office for Thérèse and Bernard, conducting one to the Prince's, the other to M. Rinal's.

Once more Maurin was driven to the woods, and the hue and cry grew louder every day against him.

Pastouré, as he made his way back from Bormes, was muttering to himself, as usual :

" What's to be said now ? Nothing ; just shut your beak, old bird. Copy the hare in his form ; he says nothing. He never speaks but once, and that's when he's done for. Then he squeals like a rat, because he knows he's nothing left to lose, even if he told everything, all he's seen and all he knows. So here we are, hunted instead of hunters, once again ! All the same, he's as good—in times like these—as good as good bread or good folk ! Did you see, Pastouré, did you see how they were all ready, the Cogolin men, to defend Maurin tooth and nail ? And did you see how the gendarme doffed his hat ? He did so in honour of the dead. And for the same reason the folk turned good and brave. And that's why I reckon death's a famous thing, because death does this miracle, it makes the people grow good and brave, and even a gendarme polite. He's right, M. Rinal is, when he tells Maurin we should love death, and that death's work is a famous good work. So bide your time in patience, friend ! You'll find the good earth waiting for you, never fear ! "

CHAPTER XII

Wherein Maurin expounds to Tonia his theory of marriage, and the different obligations it involves on husband and wife respectively.

WHEN next they met, Tonia informed Maurin :

" I have spoken to my father ; I told him again I want you, and he did not exactly say no, though he didn't say yes, either. But three days afterwards he had changed his mind. Now he does say no—and he has explained his reasons."

" And what *are* his reasons ? "

" It's because you've got into ugly work again with various people."

" Do you know why ? . . . In the first case for a dog a man was thrashing, though the animal didn't deserve it. Was I to leave a dog to be beaten so unjustly ? "

" Oh, if you mean to champion all the dogs that are whipped unjustly, we shall never get married, my poor Maurin ! Besides, my father says the dog's owner was within his rights."

" Unjust rights," retorted Maurin, " are no rights."

" Anyway," she sighed, " it comes to this ; for the present this dog is an obstacle between us—the dog and the rest of it ! Cannot you think a little more of me when you find yourself blundering into horrid quarrels ? "

" I'm always unlucky ! " groaned Maurin. " The man thrashing his dog, the man whistling his dog, and the one annoying my daughter, all three of 'em well deserved the lessons I taught them ; but everything goes against me."

" Ah ! " she went on, " if those were the only three things against you ! "

" And what else is there ? "

" You and your quarrels about dogs, you set my father against me, but there's another side of your behaviour makes *me* very angry."

" *You* angry ? "

" Yes, me."

" Explain ! "

" You breakfasted with a number of gentlemen the other day at Bormes ? . . ."

" Yes."

" And there was a lady there ? "

" And a very pretty one too ! " laughed Maurin.

" And you looked at her a deal ? "

" A cat may look at a queen."

" I'm not joking, Maurin. François Marlusse and Novarre breakfasted here, at the *cantine*, the other day. Talking together, they related all that was said and done among you that day at Bormes, and they said over and over again you seemed sweet on the lady, and that she gave you many smiling looks."

" Ladies of that sort aren't for the likes of me," said Maurin evasively.

" Is that your only excuse ? now, did you or did you not promise to marry me ? "

" Yes, that's settled, when your father consents ; but," added Maurin, with a fatuous conceit, part real, part assumed in self-mockery, " I don't suppose I can hinder the women from liking me, any more than I can the hens from running after the cock."

" Maurin, don't joke ! . . . *will* you be true to me ? "

" As much as may be I will ! "

" I deserve a better answer."

" Oh ! curse it," cried Maurin ; " you badger overmuch, I tell you. A sporting dog can promise he won't go after the birds, but promising and keeping a promise are two different things, and it would be best not to put one right under my nose, I reckon."

" Where does she live, this fine lady ? "

" At Paris."

" That's a long way ! "

" I know that ; didn't I tramp there on foot ? "

" And you wouldn't repeat the journey for her ? "

" Oh, Lord ! no, not I ! I can't picture myself in her palace yonder . . . but if she chooses to come to see me in my woods, why then, of course, I don't know . . . What would you have me say ? "

Tonia clenched her fist, and struck him like a petulant child. His only reply was to kiss her fondly.

" No, do what you will," he said, " you'll never make me tell a lie. I've always seen the best cocks with a crowd of hens round 'em."

" You know I should kill you ? "

" That's all settled, of course," he laughed.

" Or, come, if you deceive me, I'll pay you back in the same coin."

" No, that can't be," he said gravely.

" And why not ? "

" Tonia," he said, " the woman who goes with another man than her husband commits a more heinous sin than the man who goes with another woman than his wife."

" And why so ? " she protested. " It's the men who arrange things so."

" It's the law of nature," said Maurin.

He seemed buried in thought a moment, then he resumed :

" I have thought about it at times, for myself, and here's how I take it to be, Tonia. It's well I should tell you, for if you're to be my wife, we shall have threshed out this point beforehand. It's a thing of importance, of the first importance. So listen carefully. I've thought sometimes the man is a vineyard full of grapes. If folks pluck one, they don't hurt the others ; neither your ground, nor your vine—nothing is a penny the worse. All you've lost is a grape ; moreover, if you know nothing about it, you don't care at all, and really there's no great harm done."

" Well, it's the same for the woman."

" Oh, no, it isn't ! "

" How do you make that out ? "

" The woman is not a vine, but a wine-cellar that must be always locked against thieves ; for the thing to be feared here isn't that they'll carry off the wine, but, contrariwise, that they'll bring a bad quality of stuff into my cellar, or stuff that, if mixed with mine, will destroy its flavour and freshness.

" A husband, by my idea, can only compromise one single grape, if he *is* unfaithful ; while the wife, if she's not chaste, compromises the whole vintage, and all the chatterers on earth can't alter that one whit. One day can make a man a father several times over ; it needs three-quarters of a year to make a mother."

" And suppose it's as much, by *my* idea," she answered, " for me if they steal a grape as for you if they spoil your wine ? "

" Oh, ho ! " he laughed, " yes, I can understand your feelings, not a doubt of it ; all I say is, the harm done is not the same. We must be reasonable."

" Shall you see this pretty lady again ? "

" May be ! " said Maurin ; " but there, she hardly gives a thought to me. She lives in silks and laces, and I, summer and winter, in the same old canvas jacket."

" That proves you're strong," she said with a sigh—" as strong as you're handsome ! And I know they'd all like to have you, all the women, poor and rich ! "

CHAPTER XIII

Which proves conclusively how, in the eyes of Justice, one and the same act may earn its author a medal or involve him in a misdemeanour, according to circumstances.

MAURIN had just parted from Tonia after the foregoing conversation.

"Good-day, Saulnier; your vixen is as thin as ever, eh?"

"Yes, Maurin; she's always lean, she is."

Saulnier laid down his hammer.

"I've something to tell you," he said; "I saw François the mattress-maker go by on the road yesterday."

"Oh, ho!" said Maurin; "did you?"

"Yes, and he gave, as you two had agreed between you, it appears, he gave me news of a certain lad you're interested in."

"Well?"

"Well, it's high time you put a finger in that pie. Césariot's no longer with his master Arnaud."

"And where is he then?"

"He's not at Saint-Tropez at all."

"But where *is* he?"

"Ah! there you are!" grinned Saulnier.

"What d'ye mean by that? Speak out."

"*Coquin de sort*, Maurin, how sharp you are with a man! If I don't explain more clearly, and if I'm slow about it, maybe there's reasons for it. If I don't speak, maybe it's because I don't know anything more—or, maybe, I don't wish to say more."

"I'm not in a very patient mood to-day," growled Maurin.

" Look at my partridges," said Saulnier.

" I don't care a curse for your partridges just now ! "

" Look at my weasel."

" I don't care a hang for your weasel ! "

" Then look at my fox."

" Confound your fox ! . . . For God's sake, man, tell me where Césariot is."

" My partridges, my weasel, and my fox say no ; they forbid me to talk to you any more, Maurin, for ten minutes or so. My birds have come to know you by now, and they didn't run to hiding when you came up to speak to me, nor my weasel neither, while my vixen wagged her tail when she saw you and her friend Hercules. But now they are all uneasy, birds, weasel, and fox. That means somebody's coming this way along the road, and I shouldn't be surprised if it's the gendarmes. So if you'd liefer they didn't see you, best follow the lead of my partridges and the rest, and hide, Maurin ; quick, man, hide ! "—and the old fellow smiled in the pride of his heart, delighted at the knowingness of his pets.

Maurin darted off the road and plunged into the shelter of the thick undergrowth. A few minutes more, and two mounted gendarmes appeared at the turning of the highway. It was Sandri and a new Brigadier, who were patrolling the country.

On reaching Saulnier they pulled up their horses ; but the road-mender went on steadily breaking stones, as if he had never noticed their presence.

His partridges had taken refuge, and his weasel with them, under his fox's belly, though here and there their pretty little heads could be seen peeping out like chicks from under their mother's wing.

" Ho, there, *cantonnier !* "

Saulnier looked up at the gendarme's challenge.

" What, are those partridges there, eh ? "

" What would you have me say ? " asked Saulnier slyly ; " partridges you call 'em, and partridges they are, I reckon."

"It's not that!" snapped the other irritably, looking down at the road-mender from the saddle.

"What, not that, eh?" grinned Saulnier, who wanted to see some fun. "Well then, say they're snipe."

"I want to know how you came in possession of those birds? What right had you? To take a brood of partridges is a misdemeanour, taking game out of season."

He turned to Sandri.

"You ought to stop these abuses, when you come across them."

Then, turning to Saulnier again:

"A *cantonnier* is a public functionary, and he ought to give a good example. . . . Tell me, now, does your dog pay tax? He don't look like it; he looks more like a vagabond cur. He has no collar."

"My dog don't pay tax," said Saulnier, "because he's a fox. They ought rather to pay me a reward for my fox, because a fox tamed is as good as a fox killed, as he don't harm anybody any more, and only costs me his feed."

"Properly speaking," said the Brigadier pompously, "this fox, by reason of the service he performs, is really and truly a dog."

"Whether you speak properly or not, I don't know," said Saulnier, "but speaking justly is another pair of shoes, and you'd be fine and clever if you could prove my fox is a dog."

"As for the partridges," added the Brigadier, "we must see about returning them to the wild state." ·

"But they'll never agree to that," said Saulnier. "They're too fond of me."

"Then they must be confiscated, and sent to the hospitals for the consumption of the patients . . . or the State hospital staff."

"Fine talk! all very fine talk!" muttered the artful Saulnier—and raising his head, he showed the gendarmes his vast smile, lurking in the wrinkles of his cheeks, the crowsfeet of his temples, about his nose, around his eyes,

at the corners of his mouth—a veritable sun in splendour
of humour and irony.

"I'll tell you all about it, Brigadier. They're friends
of mine, you see, the birds. It looks as if I'd taken 'em,
but I haven't; they're not mine."

"Whose are they then?" demanded the Brigadier,
looking more and more stern.

"They are their own," answered Saulnier, coolly.
"They know me as their father, that's all; they come
when I call them; they eat out of my hand. . . . We got
acquainted one day, because why, they came round my hut
to steal my chickens' corn. I called: ' Hi! little chaps, hi!
and they came back next day, and every day since, and
they won't leave me . . . out of pure friendship; but
they're free, freer than you or I, because we've our duties
to keep us in check. Nobody kills them, for they're always
round me. That's the whole story. So you see I didn't
catch 'em, I didn't trap 'em anywhere, I didn't rob anybody
of 'em. And I don't think anybody can take 'em from me,
neither. Just try, M. le Brigadier. One of two things
will happen; either they'll stick close under my fox, who'll
defend them—and it won't be to eat 'em herself—or off
they'll fly from under your very nose, if I may say so, M. le
Brigadier. Just try . . . try to catch them, for fun."

"I've known the fellow and his pets for long enough,"
said Sandri. "We've always winked at his little doings—
a bit of complaisance we thought ourselves justified in.
And, indeed, his explanation does seem quite natural and
plausible."

"Then you maintain your birds are still free in a sort,
and always have been, while at the same time making
friends with you; so that you didn't rob the State of them?
And you say they would fly away, if we attempted to
touch them. Come, answer, *my good man*, answer!"

Saulnier, who only half liked such a familiar form of
address, only muttered:

"We've never kept our pigs together, have we?"

"What does the man say?"

"I say this ; if you can catch ever a one of my partridges with your hand, you can have it cooked, *my good
man,* for your dinner, or have it stuffed, if you like it better.
I'll gladly give it you."

"Come, I'll see the thing out," said the Brigadier.

He dismounted, gave his bridle to Sandri to hold, and
advanced on the fox. Directly the animal saw him approaching, she sprang up ; every hair on her back bristled,
her sharp, pointed teeth were exposed, and her red eyes
glared at the rash intruder. Between her fore paws
cowered the partridges, gathered round Madam Weasel.

"Egad ! " said the Brigadier, with a touch of more
respect in his tone, " but you've a famous good protector
there."

"For defending partridges," declared Saulnier, " she's
a perfect gendarme."

Then he called his fox to heel.

"My advice to you is to have naught to do with it,"
and he seized the animal by the scruff of her neck and held
her tight.

"I've got her fast. Now, catch a partridge ; just see
if you can."

The Brigadier advanced. The fox growled. The weasel
vanished among the stones. The partridges flew away.

"There, you see for yourself they are free," cried Saulnier triumphantly.

"You might easily have them shot, when they fly off
like that, eh ? "

"Oh ! but," laughed Saulnier roguishly, " they don't
fly off—unless they see the gendarmes coming. . . . So
now, to save yourself making any mistake about my birds,
let me tell you I've taken advice on the matter. Well,
the men of the law at Toulon, the Notary, and the Mayor
of Cogolin, all told me there's no law passed yet to forbid
the friendship of a poor road-mender and a covey of
partridges. I don't kill 'em, I feed and shelter them, and,
if you'll think a moment, you'll see it's just the opposite of
poaching. . . . And if you want to know more . . . I've

always got handy in my game-bag a bit of a proof as how
I'm not in the wrong. It's a medal from the Society!
You see, M. le Maire had me *decorated* just because of my
pets. . . . I was keeping this as a *bonne bouche* for you! "

Saulnier marched over gravely to his game-bag, which
lay on the ground near, and pulled out a little round box,
enveloped in paper. He unwrapped it, opened it carefully,
and taking out a bronze medal, said triumphantly :

" Read that—if you can read ! "

He handed them the medal, which bore the following
inscription :

SOCIETY FOR THE PROTECTION OF ANIMALS.

PRESENTED TO

PIERRE SAULNIER,

Cantonnier,

WHO TAMED

A COVEY OF PARTRIDGES

A WEASEL

AND

A FOX

AND MADE THEM HIS FRIENDS

AND FAMILIARS.

" And you know," said Saulnier roguishly to the amazed
gendarmes, " if anyone hurt any one of my pets, I could
make a complaint, humble as I stand before you, gentlemen,
to our Society, and the culprit would get something very
different from a medal, I warrant you ! "

He put the medal back in its box, saying :

" I might hang it over my stomach, if I chose, but then
it would be jogging up and down all the while ; yes, for
breaking stones, it would only bother me to wear
decorations ! "

The gendarmes went on their way at a round trot, and

Maurin reappeared, to whom Saulnier related his little adventure.

"I had a bit of fun with 'em, to be sure ! And now you understand, I hope, why I waited to tell you what I had to say ? "

Saulnier had dropped his yokel way of speaking, and now talked good, straightforward Provençal.

He went on :

"Instead of a couple of mounted gendarmes arriving, it might very well have been someone coming and hiding yonder to overhear what we said ; and what else I've got to say to you is for your ear only. . . . You know the tobacco smugglers down at Roqueburne ? "

"I know their headquarters, but I never go there. You know I prefer to be on good terms with Government as far as may be. When I get into trouble, it's always against my will. The smugglers think they're not stealing because they rob the State, but once let the State lay hands on them, and they'll find it will treat them as thieves."

"That's the reason why I didn't mention them just now till I had consulted my fox's tail and my partridges' looks," said Saulnier. "Well, you can guess what's coming, eh ? . . . your Césariot has let the smugglers get hold of him. They wanted another hand. He's with 'em now in the cave ; you know where."

"Oh, ho ! I don't mean him to stay there, anyway," cried Maurin angrily. "I shall go and force him to leave them."

"That's what I should advise . . . but to get there, to get to the cave, how will you manage ? You know how things are ? . . . Well, I must explain matters, as François explained 'em to me."

"Go on."

"You must go to the Plain of Fréjus ; there, right in the middle—you know the spot—stands an old gypsies' van, that'll never go on wheels again. Inside lives an old bird-limer, who makes out nowadays to be a harm-

less basket-weaver, and a maker of marsh-reed walking-
sticks."

" Lagarrigue ? "

" Exactly . . . go and see him, and tell him what you
want."

" He knows me."

" Good ! that will prevent his mistrusting you."

" Good-bye, Saulnier, and thank you. . . *Té*, here's a
plover you might like to sell to the driver of the
diligence, and put the coin in your pocket."

"Thank you, Maurin, you're a good chap "—and the
road-mender fell to at his work again, with his pets beside
him to keep him company.

Whenever Pastouré thought of Saulnier's menagerie,
as happened occasionally, his reflections would run :

" If a fox protects partridges in spite of the wish he has
to eat 'em, why can't men protect each other, I wonder ?
You actually want me to admire a Bismarck or a Napoleon,
when I have Saulnier's fox under my very eyes ? 'Pon
my word, that animal gives a lesson to many folks in this
world, I can tell you that."

CHAPTER XIV

Lake-dwellers of the Twentieth Century and their connection with the cultivation of tobacco ; also of the strange complicity sometimes existing between the enemies of law and order and the representatives of the same.

THE Plain of Fréjus which borders the estuary of the Argens river, is a vast marshy tract, washed by the sea which beats languidly on the far-stretching curve of a sandy beach. This tangled expanse of reeds and rushes blocking the banks of the Argens, this labyrinth of swamps and watercourses, invites the stay of migratory birds. On these wide levels Maurin was now busy on behalf of his Russian Prince to secure a variety of specimens—flamingoes, cormorants, teal, ibis, crane, heron, kingfisher, the black and white water-widgeon, past master in the art of diving. This bird skims literally between two elements, at one and the same time swimming with its webbed feet, and flying with its broad, flapping wings, moving faster in this fashion than if it confined itself to the air only.

A few scattered farms, surrounded by their fields, rise here and there amid the levels ; and many of the farmers grow little patches of tobacco.

From all points in the plain can be seen to the northward the grey line of the Maures, along the foot of which lie a succession of sleepy, picturesque villages—Claviers, Bargemon, Seillans, Calar.

To the north-east the red-brown broken summits of Mount Vinaigre hide the Col de Tende, which gives a view of the snows crowning the height of Notre-Dames-des-Anges in the Maures.

North-westwards the buttresses of the Maures end abruptly in precipitous cliffs, at the foot of which nestles the village of Roquebrune.

These lofty, vertical rock faces are seamed with deep chasms, forming regular caverns, only accessible to the martins, owls, and buzzards.

It was in the most spacious of these caves that the tobacco smugglers had contrived very convenient quarters for themselves, admirably sheltered from all prying eyes.

The Government exercises an active and rigorous surveillance over the cultivation of tobacco. The grower is bound to supply an exact inventory of his plants, which are examined several times a year by a sharp-eyed Inspector. It is a well-known fact that the amateur gardener who wishes to grow a few tobacco plants is not legally allowed to possess more than a half-dozen, though as many as seven *may* be tolerated.

Lagarrigue had made himself leader of a troop of tobacco smugglers, or illicit tobacco buyers. He was an old poacher and snarer, now almost beyond work, although he still caught an occasional hare or rabbit in his noose among the hills of Saint-Aigulf, on the slopes of the Maures. But he was getting on in years, and his growing infirmities often kept him at home. This home was a strange place— an old gypsies' van, as Saulnier had said. The dilapidated vehicle stood there, like a stranded wreck, close down by the water's edge, its four battered walls all out of the square. The wheels, which had been stationary for years, rested on four great flat stones, while eight boulders, two to each, wedged them firmly in place. From the roof projected a crooked, black iron stove-pipe, belching clouds of heavy smoke, the product of all sorts of strange fuel—drift-wood and rubbish of all descriptions, rags and sea-wrack and sponges.

The door opened to the south on a wooden platform, supported by eight uprights, and forming quite a verandah.

In the heavy winter weather, when the high tides and swollen waters of the river united and flooded all that

H

portion of the plain, the gypsy cart was a veritable lake-dwelling. In fact, in his last years of unemployment, Lagarrigue had been a lake-dweller. This was at Toulon, where we may still see, in the mercantile harbour, district of La Rode, quite a little floating hamlet. This is composed of seven or eight disused boats, three or four of these being lighters, forty-five or fifty feet from stem to stern, bought up cheap by poor fishermen, who have constructed deck-houses of wood, and even masonry, to serve as habitations.

These often contain rooms furnished just like any others ashore, and, altogether, there are few things to be seen more quaint and curious than the life led by these lake-villagers of the Twentieth Century.

In some odd corner of a boat a miniature garden, a couple of yards square, a few pot-herbs, a rose-bush, some chrysanthemums.

The boat-dogs, which never go ashore, bark furiously at every passing vessel ; the cats live a regular Robinson Crusoe life, without a thought of the rats and mice on land. All round these lacustrine dwellings are tall posts, sticking up above the water, from which are hung by ropes endless wooden boxes and wicker baskets dipping in the sea water, and containing live oysters and prawns, and great con-glomerations of mussels. Of nights, the boldest of these fisher folk venture out to the ships in the roadstead, and even into the naval harbour itself, in search of the forbidden treasure—the Government mussels !

One summer night Lagarrigue, swimming stripped naked and dead silent round a ferry-boat in the arsenal, had got a blow from a custom-house officer's cutlass that had laid open his shoulder. It was a terrible wound, but in spite of the atrocious pain caused by the irritation of the salt water, he had dived instantly, to come up again ever so far away, under shelter of an angle of the harbour wall. Bleeding in torrents, invisible in the darkness, without a groan or a sigh, he had made his way with superhuman endurance out of the arsenal and back to his boat, which he had left in charge of his son, a mere lad.

As the result of this injury—not the first hurt he had got under much the same circumstances, Lagarrigue had left Toulon in search of some means of livelihood within his compass. Then it was he devised his method of illicit dealing with the tobacco growers.

Accordingly, he had settled down within easy reach of the Fréjus farm-lands, installing his new home there in more or less close imitation of the one he had been used to at Toulon. The spot was well chosen. The floods, a bane to others, were his friends and allies ; it was only at certain times and seasons, and with due precautions, that his citadel could be approached, while its defender, who knew every minute elevation of the ground, could leave his shanty when he pleased, and reach *terra firma* at any time he chose. Moreover, at well-chosen and retired spots, he kept two or three small flat-bottomed punts, too old and worn-out for ordinary use, but in which he could always get across the Argens whenever needful. They served another purpose too ; by their means he could explore the marshes for secure hiding-places to conceal for a while any compromising article in, a suspicious tool, a parcel of tobacco leaves, sometimes even the booty from a bit of burglary.

He was a cunning fellow, and far from wishing to give the impression that he was shy of seeing visitors, he actually stuck up a *rama* above his door. A *rama* is a huge green ball of twigs and foliage, sometimes found growing on the pines in the Maures. It is really a disease of the tree, a species of wen, a woody swelling, bristling with half-grown boughs and rudimentary leaves.

Hung up above a door it advertises drink and even food to be had within at a reasonable rate. Lagarrigue was a licensed victualler !

But nobody ever climbed Lagarrigue's ladder. His *rama* was only a convenient blind, enabling him occasionally to invite a keeper or a custom-house officer inside with a—" Come in and drink a drop of *aïguarden*. Didn't you notice my *rama?* " By this means, when dangerous customers, representatives that is to say of law and order, were about, Lagarrigue hoped to escape the risk of any undue inquisitiveness, and results justified his sagacity.

"Ho there! Lagarrigue," hailed Maurin from the foot of the ladder, and Lagarrigue's voice answered : "*Òou ! òou !* " from inside.

"Call in your dog."

"Here, Rognon! Now, who are you ? "

"I am Maurin."

"Maurin of the Maures ? "

"*O !* " (yes !)

Lagarrigue appeared on the platform.

"What d'ye want, *calignaire* (my gay lad) ? So you saw my *rama*, eh ? "

"I knew it was there."

"And you haven't been in up to your knees ? "

"Oh! I know the marshes tolerably well."

"Come up, and you shall have a glass."

"I've a lot to say to you."

"Well, come up then."

Inside, the furniture was scanty enough. The bed—a long, narrow, coffin-like box, full of straw, with a heap of rags lying on top by way of bed-clothes; some nets, a fish-spear for sea-urchins, wretched bits of tackle of sorts, all worn and rusty, fragments of wreckage picked up on the beach, trifles tossed overboard from passing ships, casks, planks, barrels ; dried star-fish, crab and lobster claws, a turtle's shell, a cormorant's beak, sea-birds' skeletons bleached in the sun. It was a sea scavenger's hovel. On the wall, however, was suspended a double-barrelled central-percussion fowling-piece, glittering nobly amid the general squalor. The square window-frame was filled with clear glass, kept scrupulously clean, for it is sometimes all-important to have an unobstructed view of what may be going on without. More than once through this opening Lagarrigue had killed plovers and wild-duck, and made his provision for the day.

" You're in a good place here for the marsh-shooting," observed Maurin.

" Yes, and for the fishing, too, and everything else," said Lagarrigue.

Yet the man was clothed in the sorriest fashion; he really might have been the rags and tatters that littered his bed come to life and walking about.

From underneath the straw that filled the bed Lagarrigue extracted a bottle half full of liquor, and from a narrow shelf above his stove of sheet iron, he took down two big glasses.

" Oh! come," protested Maurin, " you'd make me screwed; I only drink when I'm thirsty."

The man helped himself liberally.

" Now, what brings you here ? "

" I have a favour to ask."

" So have I ; tit for tat, I say ! Well, what is it ? "

" My boy's with you," said Maurin straight out, " my boy Césariot."

Lagarrigue glanced at Maurin :

" Yes ; and then ? "

" I want to see the lad."

" I know, Maurin, you've a sense of honour, and you won't betray me."

" If I wanted to do that, I shouldn't come here to see you."

" So you know whereabouts our 'factory' is, eh ? Nobody else has any suspicions."

" Oh ! yes they have."

" But who ? "

" Oh, several."

" Who told you about it ? "

" What's that to you ? "

" And where *is* it ? "

" In the highest cavern of Roquebrune."

" The deuce ! then we shall have to move."

" Why ? those who know your secret won't tell. You can bide your time. Now, when can I see Césariot ? "

" To-night, it you like ; but I claim a favour in return."

" Well, what is it ? "

Then Lagarrigue proceeded to explain.

It seemed a band of Bohemians, who were not all from Bohemia, had made a settlement in a wood in the Maures, between La Verrerie and the forest of Brégançon. This wood belonged to M. de Siblas, of Port-Cros. The gypsies, like pioneer squatters, had felled a number of pines, and in the clearing had run up not mere huts, but regular wooden houses ; they had settled down as if in a savage country or a conquered land for an indefinite length of time. Evidently they did not mean to go soon, the locality suiting them admirably. There were some forty of them, and their houses formed quite a village, within easy reach of the copper-mines of Les Bormettes, where they engaged in various suspicious forms of trade with the miners. But the authorities were on the alert, and anxious to dislodge them. The new-comers were very angry—and quite right too, declared Lagarrigue, for what harm had they done ?

Was the loss of a few trees a sufficient reason for rousing their ire ? It's not to steal fir-cones, but to make a stew folks hunt the squirrel. Thirty years' occupation would be needed to make the site theirs ; they might surely be tolerated for four or five, or even twenty years. If they were worried, no doubt they would go from fear of the gendarmes, but they would have their revenge first. They would fire the woods here and there, and a thousand, or maybe, five thousand acres, would soon be ablaze. Then he, Lagarrigue, could do nothing, it would be too late in the day. But there was still time to prevent such a calamity. How ? By securing M. Siblas' indulgence. Now Lagarrigue had heard say that Maurin had acted as guide to the Préfet when out after wild-boar. It was only a trifle he asked of Maurin—to wit, just to say a word to the Préfet, to induce him to advise M. de Siblas to do the right thing.

In this way Lagarrigue reckoned upon treating, as potentate to potentate, with the constituted authorities.

" Speak to him, to the Préfet," he concluded with a

coarse laugh, " you who are a king under a republic, the
King of the Maures as they call you."

" Well, I will," said Maurin ; " but what the devil concern
have you with these *Boumians* (Bohemians) ? "

" Oh ! it's a matter of business," laughed Lagarrigue.
" There's times when I want men I can trust to carry my
tobacco, and sell it. . . .' "

" I understand," said Maurin ; " but you've chosen a
wretched trade, let me tell you."

" A man must make a living."

" And how d'you get the tobacco ?   You don't steal it,
I hope ? "

" Why, what d'ye take me for ?   No, I buy it."

" From these land-owners, these big farmers, these
bourgeois who pay tax ? "

" It's just because they pay tax that they're anxious to
get the money back.   It's to grow richer bourgeois that
they think well of me," and with a sly look, the man, who
had served in Government ships in his day, and knew the
world, showed Maurin a greasy newspaper in which a
lump of mouldy Dutch cheese was wrapped.

" Look at that.   The biggest men do the same.   The
smugglers of high finance traffic in money.   As Panama's
now in France, why shouldn't Havana be in the Maures,
eh, mate ? "

" These big men have ended badly, don't forget that."

" I'm quite aware of that.   Caboufigue is shaking in
his shoes at this moment."

" You might end the same."

" And why," demanded Lagarrigue, with a loud, forced
laugh, " why shouldn't I end like a bourgeois ? "

" But anyway, tell me how you've managed with the
farmers ? "

" Well, this is how.   I didn't call a meeting of 'em, you
may be sure !   I went to see 'em, one by one, on the sly.
But I went a bit better dressed, mind you, than I am to-
day, 'cause why, to-day I want to look in poorer fettle.
And I'd tell 'em : ' Before the leaf ripens, and before the

Inspector makes his rounds, I'll come to your place just
to pluck a green leaf here and there, seldom more than one,
from a certain number of your plants. I undertake to
fake the look of the stalk where it's cut so as to appear
as if the leaf had fallen through some disease, or blight.
I have my own ways of managing the thing, ways the
gypsies taught me. My secret's my own, and I won't
sell it you; you can test my skill if you like. I carry off
a few leaves with me, while I give some of the tobacco
plants the look of being diseased. Presently the Inspector will be along. If he says nothing, we shall operate
on a larger scale next year. We must have patience.'
The trick was done, sir. In this way every year I have
a fine crop of tobacco that clean escapes tax, and for that
reason pays the grower better, while I make a living out
of the job. Then the stuff is dried and tied in bundles
and cut and rasped in my cave at Roquebrune, the rent of
which costs me nothing. . . . Where are you going to
dine ? "

"Oh ! I lined my game-bag nicely, with you in view," said
Maurin. "Let's wait here for dark."

CHAPTER XV

A man of the marshes.

DINNER finished, Maurin and Lagarrigue took their seats on a couple of rather rickety stools, and the former began :

" Now, Lagarrigue, listen to me. I must know nothing of the trade you follow. All I shall convey to the Préfet is the advisability of not irritating these *Boumians* (gypsies) and so avoiding a calamity they would be certain to provoke. That much I can safely say, but I won't say a word more."

" That's quite enough for our purpose, and you will only be speaking the simple truth."

" But, this settled, I strongly advise you to change your trade, my poor fellow, soon as you can."

" And will you appoint me Préfet ? What think you, Maurin, I am to make of my grey hairs and old bones ? "

" If you're infirm, aren't there such things as alms-houses, eh ? "

Lagarrigue sprang up, and in a voice of ineffable pride :

" D'ye take me for a mendicant ? *Coquin de bon sort !* I'd not take that from any man but you, Maurin. Why, I'd rather rot in the cane-brakes of the marshes like a wounded duck, *pechère !* and let the sun and salt water eat away my flesh to the bones—as they have that dead heron you see over yonder."

" I didn't mean to hurt you," replied Maurin, " but where I have suggested, with the good leave of the Mayors and Préfets, you might die in peace and quietness."

" Bah ! peace and quietness ! they make me sick ! " cried Lagarrigue. " I'm too old now, after being restless all my life, to like peace and quietness. The only peace I shall ever take to is the last of all ; yes, I shall enjoy that.

In God's own almshouse, which is the good earth—yes,
I shall sleep sound there—or, maybe, far away, far away
yonder . . ."—and gazing through the little window at
the dark sea moaning under lowering clouds, he finished
his phrase:

" At the bottom, like a man who has been a sailor in
his time."

" I've said what I felt bound to say, Lagarrigue. Each
man must manage his life as he pleases. Anyway, I reckon
now's the time to tell you the reason brought me here ;
I've come to recover my boy. *He's* not old yet, at any rate.
Once let 'em catch him with your lot, and his whole life
will be spoilt. When he joins for his military service he'll
join under a cloud as a man who's been convicted ; he'll
be a good-for-nothing, and be sent to one of the African
regiments. . . . So I'm going after him. . . ."

" Ah ! but, by God ! " swore Lagarrigue, " the fact is
I want him for my own purposes just now."

" Find an older man, one who knows what he's after,
and can count up the pros and cons, the advantages and
risks. You've had a youngster yourself, Lagarrigue ?
Where is he ? You must know what I feel. . . ."

Again Lagarrigue sprang up, his face paling suddenly.

" My lad is a petty officer," he said proudly; " he's in the
Navy, and his captain speaks well of him. He writes me
letters to my brother's to make a man cry. . . . If ever
they discover my present trade, which I've kept hid from
him, of course, they'll never sentence me, because why, I
shall be dead first—a small loss for me and a good riddance
for him ! . . . but his father's name shall never be in
there "—and he pointed to the torn newspaper lying on
the table.

He resumed his seat, drank a mouthful, and said seriously :

" I'll give you back your boy this very night. I'll do
my best for you ; you must trust me. So wait here, and
I'll go and fetch him. Our 'factory' yonder may prove
an ugly mousetrap ; any day we may be taken.

" And I've men there whose minds are made up to fight ;
for, as you may guess, there's old scores to settle against
'em, once they're caught. The two you arrested a while
back were my men, and I lost 'em through you, for I'd
got hold of 'em only the day before. They were only waiting an opportunity to join me. So, you'll understand, it
wouldn't do, if by any ill chance the cave were raided to-
night, for you to be found there with your lad. Now
listen. You shall take your youngster away straight off.
But, mind you, things may be reversed some day ; a time
may come in your poacher's life when my ' factory ' will
be a useful hiding-place for you, were it only for spending
one night there. . . . Well, in my cave, the same as here,
being in my house, you'll be in your own, Maurin, because
you've a good heart. . . . There's rich folks who are
scamps ; but at the same time there's many poor wouldn't
be scamps, if only they were rich. The main thing is to
live out one's life, and that you can only do by keeping
alive ! And to live till you come to a natural death, you
must eat, and keep a fire going and have some sort of a
roof over your head. . . . *Té !* look you, the rain comes
down in torrents all of a sudden, and the mountain wind
blows. A good time for me, a winter storm ; it's my best
protection. God keep our young 'uns, mate, better than
He's kept us ! I reckon the Republic's a good thing.
Without the State schools, my boy would be like me,
instead of treading the path of honour. Well, I know
you're a good one to defend the Republic. So . . . get
'em to choose us good 'uns ! "

" Where are you elector ? "

" At Hyères, where my brother is. My true domicile is
where my brother lives, a poor struggling chap like myself.
That's where I'm registered, as the law requires."

" Vote for Vérignon," Maurin told Lagarrigue, " and
make your brother do the same."

" If I were a blind man," said Lagarrigue, " I could be
sure of walking straight, if I had your arm to lean on,
Maurin ! "

CHAPTER XVI

Césariot's regeneration.

HAVING thus rescued Césariot from Lagarrigue's clutches, Maurin took his boy to see M. Rinal.

" Give him some idea of what life means, M. Rinal. Tell him whatever you think fitting, just whatever you deem right without any reserve, just whatever will be for his good."

Then he explained Césariot's present attitude of mind, and M. Rinal talked to him, saying amongst other things :

" There are many orphans who have neither father nor mother, my lad. *You*, at any rate, have a father, and a good and gallant father too, who was under no compulsion to go and save you from the evil and dangerous place you were in. Rely on this good father and give him your love. Follow his advice and mine. If it had been in his power to keep you by his side when you were small, he would have given you other ideas ; but it was impossible, through no fault of his. Like everybody else, you look for a little happiness in life. Believe me, my boy, there is more to be found in industry than in idleness, in the esteem of your fellow-men than in their contempt ; there is more satisfaction in being a poor fisherman on the beach than a smuggler in his cave. It is better to die at sea in a *mistral* than in a sick-ward of a gaol. Both may be poor, hard lives, but, at any rate, the preferable one is where you live in the sunlight, which shines not a whit brighter and warmer and gayer for M. Caboufigue, the millionaire, than for the humblest of crabbers."

Then, turning to Maurin :

" Does he know Bernard ? "

" He has never even heard of him. Tell him about him, if you think well, M. Rinal."

" Go and bring Bernard here, Maurin." But just as he was leaving the room :

" No, stay ; here he is, just coming for lesson," and the boy appeared.

" Bernard," began M. Rinal abruptly, " I am going to put you through an examination. . . . What is a smuggler, do you know ? "

" Yes, M. Rinal "—and then in a rather sing-song voice, as if repeating his lesson, he continued :

" It is a man who obtains commodities subject to customs dues, and introduces them fraudulently. Thus a smuggler is one who robs the State, pilfers the common savings of the people. It is as if a son were to suppose himself no thief, if he appropriated in the home his father's and his brother's goods. What in some slight degree excuses his guilt is the courage he displays in meeting heavy risks ; but what, on the other hand, aggravates it is that from day to day he confronts the necessity of doing murder. There nearly always comes a time when he must take life to defend his personal liberty ; then he makes widows and orphans."

" And can you tell me the reason, Bernard, why a child is bound to obey his father ? "

" I must obey my father, because naturally he wishes what is good for me, and because, having experience, he knows better than I do what is for my good."

" If you were suddenly told you had a big brother, what would you say ? "

" Oh ! " cried Bernard, " I should be very glad."

" You would love him ? "

" Yes."

" Even if he were a bad fellow ? "

" Even if he were bad, yes ! "

" And if he wanted to turn smuggler ? "

" I should take care and stop him ! . . . for his own sake ! " declared the child in a determined voice.

" Well, you have a brother ; there he stands. He means
to be a fisherman at Le Lavandou, and serve under Maître
Antiboul. He will come and see you here now and then.
He will look after you. As he is your elder brother, you
must obey him. He will take your father's place ; he only
wishes your good. . . . And you, Césariot, tell me, do you
want your little brother here to be a smuggler or a fisherman ? "

For some minutes the youth had been bowing his low-
browed head in deeper and deeper contrition ; his chin
was buried in his bosom ; an indefinable feeling of discom-
fort, shame, remorse was torturing him. He would fain
have rebelled, struck someone, uttered some insulting
word ; but all his evil instincts seemed somehow tied and
bound within him, painfully circumvented, impotent to
act. He knew himself dominated by some influence that
was new to him, and stronger and more powerful than
anything in his own nature. Whatever it was, it terrified
and awed him ; he longed to escape it and fly . . . but
his feet were nailed to the ground. He was struggling
against the kindness, the sympathy of his fellows, as if at
grips with material obstacles, mysterious obstacles that
had suddenly risen up to confront his evil propensities,
impassable barriers that astonished him and hurt his pride
and were intolerable.

They were in direct opposition to his whole nature.
What were these forces he had never encountered before ?
By what right did they assail him, and bind him down
and force him to do their pleasure ? He stamped his foot,
and turned away sullenly.

" Go and kiss your big brother, Bernard."

The child went up to Césariot, who burst into sobs.

Suddenly he experienced a strange sense of relief ; he
ceased to fight against all the unknown powers working
within him ; his heart was bursting, and with the tears
that gushed from his eyes flowed forth all envy and hatred
and malice. . . . And love took their place.

" He is saved," said the old doctor ; " but let him weep,

let him weep his fill, let him weep his eyes out. Kiss him tenderly, little lad."

Bernard pressed Césariot as hard as ever he could in his arms.

" Kiss him," repeated M. Rinal, " kiss your big brother, who will always be an honest man ; he has chosen, he is choosing at this instant, for always, to be an honest man."

" Enough ! enough ! " sobbed Césariot, " enough ! "— and they could hear him stammering between the convulsive gasps of his boyish grief :

" I've never, never cried like this before . . . it's the first time, the first time ; don't say any more, sir. . . . I'll do whatever you wish. And I will obey my brother . . . and I'll protect him ! "—and stooping, he took the little lad in his two arms and pressed him to his bosom.

" I will *protect* him ! " It was the word of regeneration ! Yes, the being who protects another wins at one and the same time a consciousness of power, a pride in himself, and a proper feeling of human dignity.

Maurin, hardly knowing where he was, left the room abruptly to go and gaze out to sea from the terrace, and note if the Isle of Le Levant still occupied the same place in the blue expanse.

Next day Césariot was heard declaring to his master Antiboul :

" A fisherman's life, master, is the finest of all callings ! I begin to see that now."

Some while afterwards M. Rinal asked the lad :

" Well, what was it you wanted ? What were you looking for ? Try and explain. What was it you were seeking, my boy ? "

" What I have found, M. Rinal."

CHAPTER XVII

Shows how it only needs two or three good fuglemen so to manipulate manhood suffrage as to make it really record the vote of the select few, and thus escape the well-founded objections of the pessimist.

WAS there to be one single Republican candidate, or several ? This was the point to be settled by a Congress composed of delegates from all the Communes. If the latter was decided on, whichever of the candidates should have obtained the greatest number of votes at the first ballot would be left to fight it out alone with the opposition nominee. All the rest were to withdraw in accordance with a formal undertaking to that effect demanded by the Congress.

At the appointed time, eight o'clock in the evening, the delegates arrived at the little town of N——

The Congress hall was a vast coach-house belonging to an inn, which had been cleared of carts and carriages. A platform was erected at the further end, between two windows, for the officials.

Two enormous lamps were suspended over this platform, and gave a strong, crude light.

The huge door was kept shut and barred, only the small postern in it being left for ingress. On the threshold stood a young man entrusted with the duty of checking the cards' of admission, which were strictly non-transferable.

The delegates soon began to arrive in batches, talking loudly and consulting their watches every moment. The majority were grey-beards, some quite old men with snow-white locks.

All were full of a sense of their own importance, which

they further exaggerated with a view to pushing the
chances of their special candidate. The fact is, despite all
good intentions, the best candidate is still the one of
whom a man can say, if he is elected : " You know so and
so ? the Deputy ? he's an old friend of mine ! We are
quite on familiar terms with one another. . . ."

The audience was now entering the hall. At the door
one delegate, an " agricultural labourer "—the good old
title of peasant is out of fashion nowadays—a simple
fellow of a bygone period, was saying to a Mayor, a
working mason of the same age as himself :

" It's funny, we were cabin-boys together, you and I.
We've always called each other by our Christian names . . .
well, I daren't do it any more."

And the other, with an ineffable air of condescension,
which he believed to be modest deprecation :

" Why not, my dear man ? Because I'm Mayor ? I'm
not that sort, I'm not ; honours don't turn my head. . . .
You can talk to me just the same as you used to ; *vai, I
give you my permission !* "

All arrived to the moment, and there was soon quite
a gathering. Cigalous had just entered with Cabissol ;
and soon the candidates put in an appearance, escorted by
their partisans.

Vérignon, Labarterie, Poisse were at their post, as well
as two or three others of no importance, whose names
would be ruled out directly the sitting began.

A sincere motive of patriotic curiosity had brought
François Marlusse there among the rest. He had no card,
but hoped to get in under the wing of Mayor Cigalous.

" Where's Cigalous ? " he demanded.

" Inside."

" Go and fetch him. . . ."

" I'm bound to keep the door."

" Then let me go in by myself."

" Your card ? "

" I have no card."

" You can't go in ! "

I

Several delegates who did not know Marlusse had gathered in the doorway, which he was blocking, and all began to shout at him.

"You can't go in without a card! Stand aside and let us pass. You can't go in!"

But Marlusse faced his public, signed to them peremptorily to wait, and fumbled for something in the inside pocket of his jacket, muttering:

"Surely I must have it on me to-day! I never come out without it. . . . Ah! here it is"—and he displayed before the eyes of all a bit of rope as thick as a man's finger, and about the same length.

"With that," he said, "I may enter anywhere, *citoilliens!*"

A murmur arose: "What does he say, the fellow? Why, it's a hangman's rope, that is. . . . Let us pass, my good sir! You can't go in," and "No, you can't go in," declared the doorkeeper with decisive emphasis.

But Marlusse, in the voice of a tribune haranguing the populace:

"*Citoilliens!*" he cried.

"*Cassis-cognac!*" answered a mocking voice—but it was the only one.

"Silence!" thundered Marlusse.

A deep silence followed, so true is it that a man of mark can always impress the common herd, and that when the masses make a mistake, it is the lack of men of mark is the reason why.

"You see this rope?" continued Marlusse. "It is the rope with which my poor father was tied and bound, fastened, constrained, garrotted, imprisoned, chained, and haled to Lambessa, time of the *coup d'état* of '51! That is a passport everywhere. My name is François Marlusse, son, grandson, and maybe even great-grandson of victims of tyranny! . . . *Vive la République!*"

"Go in, *citoyen*, go in! . . . Long live Marlusse! Long live the *citoyen* Marlusse! . . . He is a son of the victims of '51!"

" Do you know him ? "

" I ? not I . . . but he's a good man and a true ! . . .
You can see it by his very looks ! . . . Long live Marlusse ! "

And in marched that worthy, as proud as Punch.

At the same moment, inside the assembly hall, one of
the delegates was whispering in Poisse's ear :

" I'm going to do all ever I can to get you nominated
candidate, M. Poisse. Only if you're elected Deputy, I've
a little favour to ask beforehand."

" And what's that ? . . . If it can be done, why, I
grant it you beforehand."

" Just a little place for myself, M. Poisse."

Poisse knitted his brows, as if he were already a Member
of the Chamber, and in a position to . . . refuse.

" Well, and what place do you wish ? have you made
up your mind, eh ? "

" Oh ! for sure I have, *pardine !* . . . I should like a
place as *victim,* if you please ! "

By this time Marlusse had joined Cigalous.

" Why, how did you manage to get in without me,
Marlusse ? "

" Oh ! " replied the latter, " just on the chance I'd
picked up a card of admission, a bit of rope's end that was
lying about, and which will come in useful again."

" I don't understand."

Then Marlusse explained how he had succeeded in penetrating to the " bosom of the assembly."

" Unhappy man ! " exclaimed the Mayor, aghast ; " if
your joke is discovered, we are every one of us compromised ! "

" Don't be alarmed," returned Marlusse, as serious as
a judge ; " I'll prove that what I said is the truth."

" None of your *galégeades* here ! You can't be son and
great-grandson too of victims, come ! "

" Oh ! " declared Marlusse emphatically, " I *had* to get
in ; when it's to serve the Republic, a bit of *galégeade*
becomes the first and most sacred of duties. . . . *Té !*

té! look, there's Pastouré! Are *you* going to speak, my gallant Parlo-Soulet ? "

" And why not, if needful ! " said Pastouré, in his double-bass voice. " In emergencies men come to the front."

" And Maurin ? "

" I'm waiting for him."

Just then a burst of shouting made itself heard outside :

" *Eici, Mòourin!*—Here's Maurin ! Long live Maurin, Maurin of the Maures ! "—and Maurin presented himself at the entrance.

" Delegate from what communes ? " he was questioned.

" From all ! " replied Maurin—and in he marched.

" *Vé!* good evening, M. Labarterie, good evening, M. Vérignon. . . . Ah ! so there you are, M. Poisse ? . . . *Noum dé pas Dioû !* but here's Caboufigue ! "

He stepped up to Caboufigue, who was just making his entrance, accompanied by several clients, delegates from communes to which he had presented some of his cast-metal statues and Wallace fountains, which he called the *monuments* of his Republicanism and his generosity.

Maurin asked him, jokingly :

" You're not coming as a candidate, I presume, M. Caboufigue ? "

But Caboufigue put on an air of importance, and muttered :

" I shall see . . . I don't know . . . public opinion must decide."

" But you undertook not to offer yourself for election. . . . And you know very well what *quid pro quo* you had ! "

Cabissol now came forward :

" I have your written engagement in my pocket," he said.

" Oh ! " said Caboufigue, with a look of royal assumption and settling his hat on the back of his head like a crown, " I've thought it over ; my promise was an immoral one. The law does not recognise promises of that nature, so mine cannot properly be held binding."

" Take care," said Maurin. " If you break your word,
I'll ruin you ; I tell all I know."

Parlo-Soulet stepped forward :

" Maurin, leave him to me. I'll take measures."

" Ah ! then we shall have a laugh ! " grinned Maurin
—and he turned his back on the solemn-faced Caboufigue.

" Open the sitting ! open the sitting ! "

" Let us choose a President by acclamation, *citoyens.*"

" Yes, Cigalous ! . . . Marlusse ! . . . Maurin . . .
Maurin ! . . . M. Rinal ! "

" Choose Maurin," said Cigalous.

" Yes, choose Maurin," echoed M. Rinal.

" Maurin ! choose Maurin," repeated Marlusse, whose
sudden popularity was growing greater and greater, and
was already making him enemies.

The delegates were pointing him out to each other.

" Is that the man ? Yes ! son of a victim, who gains
admission everywhere with a bit of the rope his father was
hanged with in '51."

" Nonsense ! " protested someone. " *I* know him ; it's
Marlusse . . . a mountebank ! . . . Yes, and a dull-
witted fool ! . . . Why, when he speaks, he forgets half
the words."

" That's true," cried another, " I know him too. He
went to the Paris Exposition in 1889 ; he tells a story how
he lost his way there, and wanted to buy a plan of the
Exhibition. . . . Well, would you believe it, the word
plan, he forgets it every time he needs to say it ? "

" Ah ! so that's the man ? We know who he is now.
His story's famous."

" Don't let him speak."

" Never fear."

But at that moment a mighty shout drowned every other
sound :

" Maurin ! Maurin ! Maurin for the Presidency ! "—but
Maurin held back.

" Accept the honour," M. Rinal prompted him. " It's a

good thing for all of us, and for yourself too. I will see
you through ; believe me, it's best to accept."

"I know what you mean, M. Rinal, and I am grateful"
—and Maurin mounted the platform.

"Secretaries ! Assessors ! " cried a voice.

"Cigalous ! . . . M. Rinal ! . . . Marlusse ! . . ."

The Secretaries took their places beside the President,
amid a deafening hurly-burly.

Maurin rang his bell, and silence was restored.

"The sitting is opened," declared Maurin.

M. Rinal was close behind him prompting him with
words, or merely suggesting ideas. Maurin announced :

"M. Cigalous will explain the conditions under which
this Congress is called together."

After duly and explicitly stating these, M. Cigalous
wound up :

"All present must engage beforehand to hold themselves
bound by such resolutions as the Congress shall adopt.
Does everybody promise ? If so, hold up your hands."

It was another oath of the Tennis-Court of Versailles.

Every hand went up except Caboufigue's. But Maurin
had a sportsman's eye, and noted the omission instantly.

"Caboufigue," shouted Maurin, " hand up, or you know
what you'll get ! "

Nobody understood the allusion, but Caboufigue's crest-
fallen look was quite enough to raise a laugh.

"Does anyone wish to speak on the first article of the
agenda ? " queried Maurin.

"What is the first article ? "

"It has just been explained to you ; you are to choose
between selecting a single candidate, or nominating more
than one. . . . If you vote for the former . . . "

A voice thundered :

"Stop ! the President is bound to be impartial ! "

"No, no ! Yes, yes ! . . . Speak out, Maurin ; you
speak first ! . . . Not till the others have been heard ! . . .
The great thing is to come to an understanding. . . .
Caboufigue ! . . . Marlusse . . . A bad beginning this !

. . . *Vive la Liberté!* . . . Labarterie ! . . . Vérignon !
. . . Poisse, Poisse ! . . . Put it to the vote. . . . No, no,
not yet ! "

"Before voting," prompted M. Rinal, "let's hear the
reasons for and against,"—and Maurin's voice rang out
above the din :

"Allow me to explain things to you."

"Be impartial, then."

"To explain isn't the same thing as to advise."

"We demand more than one candidate, more than one,
more than one ! "

"One candidate, and one only ! " Marlusse roared
back in his voice of thunder. "I ask leave to speak."

"François Marlusse to address the house."

It was plain the supporters of a multiplicity of candidates were in the majority, each commune favouring a
different individual—the one that appeared most specially
devoted to its own particular local interests. So when
Marlusse stepped to the tribune, he met with a chilling
reception.

"Who's that ? . . . Shut up, let the man speak. . . .
No, the principle is agreed on. . . . Who told you that ?
. . . . The thing's obvious. . . . Freedom of speech,
freedom of speech ! Let him have his say. . . . Down with
Marlusse ! "

"Citoyen Marlusse, of what commune are you delegate ?"

"Of all ! ¸ . . like Maurin."

"Oh, ho ! the confidence of the man ! "

"And first of all, and before all, and above all, I am
delegate of my own conscience."

"Bravo ! bravo ! "

"He's not delegate of any commune ! he shan't be
heard ! Turn him out, turn him out ! "

François Marlusse took up the attitude of a man who
has no fear of popular clamour. He waited calmly,
his hands in his pockets, with the mocking smile of the
born *galégeaire* he was on every feature of his face.

"When you please ! " he said simply.

M. Rinal got up. His white hair, the simple, unassuming
elegance of his dress and bearing, a something impressive
and superior that seemed to emanate from his whole
person, secured silence.

" The Republicans of Bormes all know me," he began.
" I am an old stalwart of the Republic. In 1851, being
then an officer in the Navy, a surgeon, I voted *no*. It
stopped my career."

He had touched his audience on the quick, and shouts of
approval arose. The memory of 1851, in the Var, is still
an open wound. He went on :

" My grandfather sat in the Constituent Assembly. I
beseech you not to behave like ill-brought-up children.
Listen to your President. Listen to each of your speakers.
Let each have his say in turn ; else to-morrow your
enemies will say your Congress was nothing but a ridiculous,
foolish farce. Give up your petty individual interests
in favour of the general good of the noble cause of your
Republic and your Country."

While M. Rinal was thus speaking from his place,
Marlusse, standing at the tribune, kept up a series of impressive gestures, by way of silently seconding the quiet
eloquence of the old Jacobin. As for Pastouré, he was
sitting in a corner, moving his lips rapidly, repeating over
to himself every word uttered by the orator.

M. Rinal continued :

" The French Republic, the Country of France, are for
the service of humanity, humanity at large—to promote
the progress of us poor human beings, who, having a few
years to live in this world, are striving to render the globe
as a whole more and more habitable for their children,
by lessening—a little every day, within the limits of the
possible—pain and misery, by increasing every day as
much as possible material well-being, by making justice
prevail a little more abundantly.

" Each generation passes away, but humanity remains.
It is reproduced in your children. It is for them you are
working, as they will work in turn for theirs. This is

what you must understand. A legitimate selfishness should inspire men to render their children a little juster than themselves, a little better, a little happier . . . though only a little ! For neither moral perfection nor complete happiness are possible to mankind. Choose, therefore, for Deputies, men of the future, that is to say, of justice and love, and cast away every other thought—or you will indeed be unworthy of the noble name of citizens."

He stopped and resumed his seat, but his hearers still hung upon his lips. Then the applause broke out like a clap of thunder. For a brief while the most commonplace men amongst them had risen above themselves. A divine afflatus had breathed on them and awakened their senses. Then they came back to earth again, and a din of many tongues filled the air.

" *Voui*, but he speaks well, that man ! "

" Suppose we nominated *him*, eh ? "

The thought occurred simultaneously to a number of minds. But it broke the charm ; an opposition instantly sprang into being.

" What is he driving at exactly ? Who sends him here ? *Té*, he wears ruffles ! . . . He said a lot ; let him prove it ! "

The candidates were anxious and uneasy—all except Vérignon ; their friends were disturbed.

M. Rinal got to his feet again :

" I hear say I am to come forward for nomination. No, my friends ; it's not true. I am too old for that ; I have neither the strength left nor the spirit necessary. Besides, I hold with those who deem the political morals of these days disgraceful. A candidate is a man who exposes himself to the basest calumnies of his opponents and even the insults of his own partisans. I admire your candidate's courage, but I do not possess it.

" One last word : as a rule, you will know a candidate by this—he will promise you happiness. *I* have promised you nothing of the sort."

A general feeling of satisfaction diffused itself. The audience was so pleased that the gravity of the reproaches contained in M. Rival's speech passed unnoticed. Again the applause was loud and long.

"We must remember one thing—Citoyen Marlusse still holds the floor," said the President.

It was true ; Marlusse was still entrenched in the tribune, stolid and motionless as his own statue.

"Such as you see me," he began solemnly, "I am for a single candidate, because at the first blow, with a single candidate in the field, you will topple over your opponent and gain time. I will go further. Your adversary's only chance lies in having a number to oppose. It could only be thanks to this false move on your part that M. de Siblas would have the ghost of a chance."

It was felt the speaker had hit the mark. But this did not suit the book of the various candidates and their backers. Even those who were certain to be black-balled craved the honour of having been selected, and approved by the Congress, and their names advertised on the walls. They tried to shout Marlusse down, yelling :

"Siblas has no chance ! . . . Siblas ! down with Siblas ! *Anas sibla óou cúou dóou lou !* . . . No chance at all ! "

"Anybody who thinks Siblas has any chance is a *reac* (reactionary) ; that's my way of thinking," vociferated a friend of Caboufigue's.

"Bravo ! " screamed that worthy.

"Marlusse is out ! Enough said, enough ! . . . Vote now ! . . . Oh, ho ! Marlusse . . . Marlusse at the *Exposition !* "

"What's that ? " cried Marlusse, looking stern. "Who said *Exposition ?* "—and he assumed the port of a tamer of crowds.

"I did ! " ventured a hired partisan of Caboufigue's.

"And you say, *citoillien,* . . . you say . . . about the *Exposition ? . . .*"

"I say, sir, you're known far and wide as a laughing-stock, for a certain story of the *Exposition,* a poll-parrot story, a story you're always repeating and repeating.

You're famous for the silly yarn. . . . We don't know
your face here, but everybody has heard there's an idiot
at Bormes always struggling to find his words—and never
finding 'em ! "

" It's true, quite true ! "

" And a fellow who has this infirmity comes here to teach
other people ! . . . We've had enough ! "

" Yes, enough, more than enough ! . . . Down with the
répépiàré (repeater) ! He's learnt his stuff by rote ! . . .
And *then* they have to prompt him ! . . . Enough ! "

A man of modern ideas shouted :

" Come, shut your phonograph ! "

The noise and confusion were indescribable. People
were telling each other—" Oh ! it's that fellow ? I know
his blessed story, I do. He's a chap with a weakness of
memory. He *can't* say the words, ' a *plan ! a plan* of the
Exposition ! "

A voice overbore the tumult :

" Tell us about the *plan*, Marlusse ! "

Then Marlusse turned on his tormentors.

" It's just that, the *plan*, I want to talk about, *citoyens !*
Ah ! so you know my story, do you ? And there are
actually fools among you who imagine, when I tell it, that
I've really forgot the word, really lost my bearings ? They
positively suppose, the idiots, that I'm a born fool, and
not merely playing the fool, as I do sometimes, out of
galégeade ! But this is no time for joking ! I've changed
my *plan*. So do you change your *plan*, to follow my *plan*.
Yes, I have my own *plan*, I have, friends ! just as you have,
each of you, your *plan*, and I won't go back on either my
plan or your *plan*, never fear ! You are here to draw up a
plan, a *plan* of electoral tactics, a *plan* for the choice of
candidates. Well, I tell you there's only one *plan*, one
good *plan*—one candidate, and one only. Checkmate the
plan of the other side, which is the multiplication of candidates. Adopt *my plan*, one candidate only, and make it
your *plan* ; choose either Vérignon or Maurin, one a clever
bourgeois, the other an ignorant peasant, but both honest

men, both men beloved in the countryside, and both well able, triumphantly, to carry out your *plans !! "*

Marlusse had won the day. The general enthusiasm broke out in thunders of applause. It was a perfect ovation. A unanimous shout was raised :

" Bravo, Marlusse ! Long live Marlusse !—Suppose we nominated *him !* "

The wit of the Southerner had found expression in its most jovial aspect. The cause of one candidate, and one only, carried all before it.

" Well done ! " cried Maurin to the successful orator.

" Vote ! vote ! " roared the meeting.

One or two more speakers took turns in the tribune ; but their only object was to gain time to allow the excitement roused by Marlusse's comic harangue to subside. It was settled, everybody could see that, the wind had shifted ; every voice was raised in favour of the one candidate scheme. The other side saw their cause was hopeless, and declared themselves in favour of one single candidate—Maurin, to wit, feeling convinced that Vérignon was only too sure of a majority. " Maurin ! . . . Vérignon ! . . . Maurin ! " resounded from all quarters ; but eventually Maurin's backers drowned all other voices.

Maurin got to his feet.

" *Voui !* " he laughed, " but this is a bit too much. Just mind what you're after, friends ! . . . You start with one thing, and go slap to the very opposite ! If you want a single candidate, why, choose one to suit everybody, and make sure of returning him. The people's like that— more's the pity ! A wind blows, and round it veers, not because it knows what's right and sensible, but just like a weathercock. Now, supposing I were to say yes, and you chose me Deputy, that would out-Herod Herod. . . . No, no ! . . . Seriously now, just picture me in the Palais Bourbon ! . . . Down here, yes, it would be fine fun ; Maurin it would be here, and Maurin there ; yes, we've a Deputy who's one of ourselves, a matey, a countryman, a poacher ! . . . But when I got to Paris, all by myself, how d'ye think I could work for you, and talk for you, and speak for the Republic's good, and the whole country's ? And when it came to voting, what could I do for the best but just consult my neighbour, who'd tell me, ' That's your ticket, sir ; just vote as I do ! ' . . . Ah ! to be sure, but you manage your affairs finely ! And when you come *sú d'un couyoun coumo iou* (across an ass like me), but who's ready to stand, how much better are you for that ? When you want a driver to take your cart to market, you choose a man (it's only common sense) who understands horses. It seems there's too many already in the Chamber that don't know what speaking means, and amongst five hundred members there's never but a few count for anything. And why is this ? Why, because the electors send Maurins there. It's a bit of luck if they're only honest. No, nominate Vérignon, say I."

" Well, then, bravo Maurin, and let Vérignon be our man ! " . . . cried the meeting with one voice.

M. Rinal sprang up and wrung Maurin's hand.

" Vérignon for a speech ! " and Vérignon mounted the tribune accordingly :

" I have seen clearly enough that at heart the majority favour a number of candidates rather than one only. Well, then, let us adopt that principle. I undertake to retire unless I secure the greatest number of votes in the first scrutiny."

" Bravo ! well said ! "

A tipsy voice made itself heard :

" Say, what's your *platform ?* "

" *Cassis-cognac !* " shouted the assembly, which had recognised a ne'er-do-well in the interrupter.

" I wish to know the Citoyen Vérignon's *platform.* I have a right to question him as to his *platform.*"

" Turn him out ! . . . Ask him for his card ! . . . He's lost his ticket ! . . . Out with him ! "

Six of the strongest men there picked up the fellow and carried him out, held at arm's length above their heads. As he was borne to the door, he kept on shouting

at the top of his voice, continually repeating his word
"platform," which had captivated him with its imposing
sound:

"I tell you he has no *platform!* You're stifling liberty
of conscience and the privilege of free speech. It is my
right and my duty to find out his *platform!*"

But he was soon chucked out, and M. Vérignon was
able to resume the thread of his speech:

"Here is my programme: better regulation of preliminary detention before trial, which is a scandal in this
country; limitation of the powers of *juges d'instruction,*
who have the honour and liberty of every citizen in their
hands; reform of educational methods; proportional
representation; international arbitration.

"We call it liberty, the possession of the plain political
right to choose as we please the men who make our laws;
it is obvious we are very easily satisfied if our laws still
remain what they were under the Imperial Monarchy,
and if, in particular, they afford less guarantee of individual freedom than do the laws of sundry neighbouring
monarchies. Yet such is the fact. A properly worded
accusation, duly executed, is sufficient in France to subject
the personal liberty of any individual, almost without
control, to the good will and pleasure of a *juge d'instruction.*
The tardy procedure of the Courts can turn preliminary
confinement into a veritable torture, and a warrant of
arrest is often every whit as bad as a *lettre de cachet* in the
old days. After thirty years of existence, the Republic
has never so much as thought of reforming these abuses!"

"If they were reformed, I for one shouldn't be sorry,"
interjected Maurin.

"Another evil calls for the attention of the legislator.
While the primary school leaves the child free, while his
family at home, still unenlightened as to the benefits of
education, not only affords the teacher no assistance, but
even destroys his authority with his pupils by siding
almost daily with the child against the master—all this
time the system at the boarding schools, the Lycées, still

continues (in spite of the ameliorations that have been introduced) to make of the young bourgeois a man ready to prostrate himself before authority, before any and every authority, a man bound, therefore, to turn into a mere bureaucrat himself, without initiative, and what comes of the exercise of initiative, a broad sense of humanity !

" This state of things sets the two classes, the working class and the trading class, against one another, when education ought rather to bring them together. It is radically inconsistent with national progress and human progress.

" While the primary school is powerless to teach the children of the proletariat the discipline of duty, the Lycée trains the bourgeois' son to the notion that he will have to obey or to exercise a bureaucrat's authority, without ever enlightening him as to the true needs of the people, which may be summed up in two words—' more justice,'—and again—' more justice ' ! Republican France is still doomed to suffer from a deep-seated, chronic malady—Cæsarism, to wit, while the very essence of a Republic is to recognise no authority but that of the laws.

" To turn to the question of national arbitration, this is indeed the cause of causes, the ideal of ideals. Surely the fate of peoples deserves to be as carefully weighed as that of individuals, and *casus belli*, therefore, ought to be as scrupulously regulated as duels. Granted that universal peace for all time may be a Utopian ideal ; but that war between two civilised nations should ever be possible without previous resort to arbitration is intolerable ! "

The Congress adopted the speaker by acclamation as a candidate.

Several others occupied the tribune in succession, and appealed to their audience with more or less success.

Finally, M. Labarterie spoke :

" No one can be more advanced than I am," he declared, " for as the first article of my programme I inscribe the right of women to the franchise."

A howl of indignation shook the walls, and a voice yelled at Labarterie :

" *Faï-lou téta !* (Go and give the baby suck !) "

" We'll talk about it again when the women begin to do their military service ! "

" Nay, *citoyen*, the woman too has her field of battle."

A Homeric laugh shook the assembly.

" Yes," Labarterie went on pompously, " the woman's battlefield is child-bearing."

" Are you in earnest or pretending ? " the question was shouted from every part of the room.

" Make way for women, I say ! " insisted M. Labarterie emphatically, " make way for them in your meetings ! "

" Then I'll decamp for one ! . . . We've enough already ! "

" We can't agree together, as it is ; if we mix up women in our politics, why, *pechère !* we shall never come to any agreement at all ! "

An individual mounted on a cask in a far corner of the room suddenly drew all eyes in his direction :

" The honourable speaker who has just set down said child-bearing is women's battlefield ? Good ! But men have other work to do besides prodding with the bayonet. They drive the plough, men do. Where is the woman's plough ? Show me the woman's plough, come ! "

" And their *platforms ?* "

" Enough said ! enough ! None of your Labarteries for us ! . . . Out with Poisse's name ! . . . Vote, vote ! . . . Labarterie won't do here ! "

" Citoyen Poisee, citizen Poisse ! "

" Citoyens," declared the last named, " you know my life, and my opinions are yours, all yours without exception, and all M. Vérignon's. I swear to represent them loyally."

" Citoyen Poisse is nominated a candidate of the Congress."

Then a certain Cabantous stepped forward :

" I offer myself as a candidate."

But Maurin sprang to his feet :

"Cabantous is a Bonapartist," he said. "What does he want here?"

"I *was* a Bonapartist," declared Cabantous, "but I am no longer one now. *Vive la République!*"

"I put it to the vote—is Cabantous to be nominated?" —but the proposal was negatived unanimously.

"There are no more candidates to offer themselves?"

"Yes, I am one," shouted Caboufigue, with unabashed effrontery.

"You are aware, *Mossieu* Caboufigue, of the danger you expose yourself to? . . . Well, the word is with you."

"Citoyens," began Caboufigue, "I am a child of the South. Starting from nothing . . ."

"To reach no great things," interjected Maurin.

But Caboufigue went on quite undisturbed:

"Many communes know that I am ready to enrich them with statues and drinking-fountains . . . as I have done before; and now I am going to read my profession of faith. . . ."

A calm voice, a voice of sleeping thunder, rose amid the silence:

"I ask leave to speak for a personal explanation. . . ."

All heads turned about; a giant had risen in the middle of the hall, *cupressus inter calamos*—a cypress among the rushes. It was Pastouré.

"Citoyen Pastouré to speak," cried Maurin, his face beaming.

"*Té!* Parlo-Soulet's going to speak! You going to speak, Parlo-Soulet? Well, that is a good one! What'll he say? *Vaï-li, vaï!* go ahead, forward, to the tribune with you!" But Pastouré spoke from where he stood, and with marked steadiness, hammering out the words in his clearest tones:

"No tribune needed for what I have to say. What I have to say, I don't well know how to say it, but I mean to say it, and say it I will. Citoyens, there's things I want to say to myself, when I'm alone by myself, and then I know how to say 'em right enough; yet I don't know how to say

K

'em, just when I most ought to say 'em. . . . All the same,
I'll get it said somehow—what I have to say ! . . . 'cause
why, I know what I want to say, and it's my bounden duty
to say it."

He took a deep breath, and, emphasising each separate
syllable :

" *Mossieu Ca-bou-fi-gue !* "

The tense silence deepened. Caboufigue looked pale and
anxious. Then Pastouré declaimed, with the fire of a
Danton :

" I have only one thing to say to you, *Mossieu* . . . and
that is, that you have nothing to say ! . . ."

And his voice dropping to a growling bass, as he resumed his seat :

" That's all I had to say," he concluded.

Marlusse himself was eclipsed. Marlusse had only
touched the local mood after all, but in Pastouré it was the
deep, confused, ignorant, just, indignant soul of the people,
at once strong and impotent, yet firmly convinced, that
had uttered its appeal. In vain did Caboufigue brandish
his paper and try to speak. In vain did his posse of friends
strive to help him. He was howled down and pushed off
the platform, and from one to another shouldered to the
door and out into the street.

" Citoyens ! " announced Maurin, " the sitting is closed."

CHAPTER XVIII

Brekekekex, koax, koax! How two bull-frogs stuck straws over
their shoulders, and slanged one another like a brace of coal-
heavers.

HARDLY had he uttered the words when two gendarmes
appeared at the door and pushed their way in.

What did they want there? Sandri being one of the pair,
it may readily be supposed it was no mere curiosity had
brought the officers of the law to the spot. Maurin was
their objective! He realised the fact, and smiled. He
was separated from the gendarmes by the whole mass of
the audience, which showed no signs of opening a passage
through their serried ranks. . . .

"Citoyens," said Maurin in a loud, determined voice,
"it is undoubtedly for my sake these two gentlemen
have taken the trouble to come. . . . Well, I have friends,
dear friends in the room; they have foreseen the event, and
they know what to do. Therefore, whatever happens now,
I beg you all to keep the most absolute silence, that we
may hear the little conversation my friends are going to
hold when the lights are put out."

Next moment the two lamps were extinguished, and
everything was plunged in utter blackness. Maurin's
voice went on in the dark:

"Now's the time I must beg you to listen with the
utmost attention."

Then a quaint thing happened. A voice coming from
the bottom of the hall cried:

"*Chois?*" (pronounce *tchois*, like the *tch* in a sneeze).

Chois is the diminutive of François, and, in Provence, is

131

a familiar and comic form of greeting. The mere sound
calls up to the Provençal mind a ludicrous type of figure,
like Gnafrond for Lyons folks, or Polichinello for the
Neapolitans.

"*Tchois ?*"

The monosyllable was uttered in such a way that it gave
exactly the impression of the first call of a frog all alone
in a half-dried pool, and getting sick of his own company,
when the moon is hiding behind a cloud.

A second voice replied from the other end of the room :

"*Òou ?*" (Well ?)

There could be no mistaking ; it was a dialogue between
bull-frogs.

"*Qué vouàs ?*" (What d'you want ?) struck in a third
voice, just as froggy as the others, for each of the actors
in this comedy managed to give precisely the right tone
and pitch to every word to represent the calls and counter-
calls of a lot of frogs croaking to each other in a marsh.

"*Ìou ?*" (Is it I ?) answered a shrill voice.

"*O*" (yes), went another on a descending scale.

The last of all answered with a deep, hollow croak that
was inimitable :

"*Ren !*" (nothing).

It was such a close imitation, so accurately and naturally
done, you seemed to hear all the frogs in the Almanarre
of Hyères or the Plain of Fréjus giving voice as you stood
at an open window.

It was the very perfection of the actor's art combined
with the musician's.

Then was stirred the artistic impulse within these
Southern souls, and all forgot in a moment differences
and dissensions and political animosities in a burst of
admiration for this happy blending of reality and illusion ;
the whole assemblage burst into one mighty peal of truly
Olympian laughter. The lamps were relighted ; but
Maurin was no longer to be seen ! Then everybody began
to make slowly for the door, discussing not politics or the

rival candidates, Vérignon or Poisse, but the talent displayed by these unknown geniuses in mimicking so marvellously the bull-frogs' dialogue.

And Marlusse, in one corner of the hall, lingered behind to say to M. Labarterie, under the nose of the gendarmes where they stood hemmed in by the crush :

" For my part, I seemed positively to see the moonbeams playing on the marsh water, among the bushes . . . and on a tussock of green moss the great fat frogs, and their big eyes with the gold-rimmed spectacles ! "

Then he added with a far-away look in his eyes, as if lost in an inward vision :

" *Ah ! coquin de bon sort !* if I'd only had a bit of something red at the end of a string, I could have caught a half-dozen of 'em at the least ! "

" These folks are just idiots ! " muttered M. Labarterie in Caboufigue's ear.

But Caboufigue was Southern-born, and protested :

" *Idiots !* not a bit of it ; they're poking fun at you . . . and me, too ; that's all. You take my word for it ! "

Meantime, the large audience was dispersing slowly. The door was blocked every moment, though no one seemed to mind the delay. It really seemed as if a concerted plan governed the strangely inconsequent movements of sundry groups ; they would rush hurriedly to the little door, only to block the exit hopelessly next moment, if it happened to be unencumbered for a second. It was very evident they wanted to hinder the departure of the two officers, who found themselves everlastingly driven back, as if accidentally, under the pressure of a rolling tide of human beings, towards the upper end of the hall.

Outside, each of the chief personages of the gathering was duly greeted on his appearance by a semicircle of the inhabitants collected before the door.

" That's Poisse, that is ! . . . That's M. Rinal, who made a *splendiferous* speech, my boy ! . . . That fat fellow's Caboufigue, the millionaire ! "

Last of all appeared Marlusse, and stood a long time

motionless, and smiling complacently within the frame of
the small doorway open in the great closed gate. He
looked like a picture.

A murmur of approval spread among the onlookers.
All had heard by this time of his successful harangue,
and what power he wielded over the mass of electors.
But approval was not the only note ; some dull spirits still
clung to the legend that Marlusse was a sort of idiot,
a dotard who could never for the life of him, remember the
word *plan*. . . . Then his name Marlusse (cod) made him
an obvious butt for the gibes of the small fry, who struck
up a mocking refrain of " Marlusso ! oh, Marlusso."
Presently, egged on doubtless by one of his political
opponents, they began with one accord to fling a shower
of carrots and turnips, snatched from the greengrocer's
next door, about his devoted head. . . .

None of these projectiles reached their mark, and
Marlusse only smiled and bowed ironically to the hostile
crowd. Then, turning to the friends who stood nearest,
he said calmly, with the accent of a man whose fondly
cherished ambition has been satisfied, and who welcomes
the first gleam of a glory he has long hoped to win :

" *Eh bé ! té*, but I'm delighted ! I see I'm really growing
to be a personage ! "

With the words, he plunged his two hands in the pockets
of his bulging waistcoat, across which hung a gold watch-
chain of abnormal massiveness, and marched off with a
stately step to join a group of politicians engaged in an
animated altercation . . . The quarrel must evidently have
interested him, for he hastened to take an active part in it.

Meantime, the two gendarmes were still imprisoned by
the crowd. In vain they tried to extricate themselves,
they could not succeed, and became the object of a hundred
pleasantries :

" We are on our own premises, gendarmes ! . . . You
two came in without cards, eh ? Well, you had no
right inside. . . . Those who hold no entrance tickets
must go out last . . . that's the rule ! "

The press kept opening, only to close up again the next instant and bar their way, while they hesitated to use force, really not knowing how far their intrusion was justified in such a case.

Outside, the scattered groups gathered together again, and offered a further obstacle to the officers' escape.

Those who were not in the plot lingered near out of curiosity, while a loud buzz of conversation arose, amid which only isolated remarks were audible, having no connection with anything that had gone before:

"It seems his wife is *sadly fatigued;* she won't live out the night."

In Provence a person who is dying is said to be *sadly fatigued.*

"Come here! my bonnie little *Mustapha!*"

Mustapha is a pet name among these Moors of the Provençal sea-board when apostrophising their little ones!

"Tuck up your *taïole* (a long wide girdle), or you'll lose your shape, you will!"

"Oh, yes! I know him quite well. . . . When I say know him, I've never seen him! . . . And, besides, he's dead!"

"When I heard him shout 'Help! help!' I hid myself quick, *noum dé Dioû!*"

"The boar was mortally wounded—and old Pons, he told me the blood spurted out as red and straight as a *penny penholder!*"

"Believe me or not, but in this town there's a dozen bigoted reactionaries have founded a Socialist paper, because it brings 'em in fifteen per cent, . . . So you see, they're not always so shy of Socialism!"

"*Figùro-ti qu'aquèou couyoun dé Parisien* (Just think, that ass of a Parisian) . . . he dungs about the roots of the parasol pines in his park! . . . it's like giving sweetmeats to pigs, it is! . . . What a fool!"

This word (*couyoun*) rose high above all others, and seemed to dominate every conversation by the frequency and vigour with which it was uttered. It is, indeed, the very corner-stone of Provençal speech, as much as *Goddam* formed the burden of English conversation in Shakespeare's day.

Suddenly, two young men, both strong-armed, big-handed fellows—a carpenter and a blacksmith—were seen engaged in a fierce altercation. The loud, angry voices soon silenced everybody else within earshot:

"Hold your tongue, I tell you! I tell you, hold your tongue, you good-for-nothing!"

"Good-for-nothing! You call me a good-for-nothing? Just say it again, and you'll see!"

"Oh, ho! yes, good-for-nothing! Who'll stop me saying it again? *Good-for-nothing*—that's what you are."

"And you, you're no great shakes!"

"No great shakes! say it again, say it again, and *you'll* see. . . . I dare you to say it again."

"You dare me to say it again?"

"Yes, I do, I dare you to say it again. If you do, I'll give you one."

"I shall say it again, if I choose!"

"No, you won't! Now, say it again, if you're a man, and see what'll happen!"

With blazing eyes and clenched fists they stood glaring into one another's faces, as if determined to eat each other up.

"And what d'ye want me to say again, eh?"

"I don't know, not I! I've clean forgot! . . . but you shan't say it again."

The crowd came flocking about them, and the whole breadth of the street was now filled with a curious multitude.

"Separate 'em! They'll do each other an injury!"

"No, leave 'em alone!"

"Say it again, you scamp, you ruffian, you scoundrel!"

"Say what, idiot?"

"That I'm no great shakes."

"No great shakes, no great shakes! Oh! I'll go on saying it over and over again!"

" But you daren't say *I*'m no great shakes ! I dare you to say *I*'m that ! . . . Come, say it, if you're any good ! "

" Oh ! I'll say it right enough ! "

" Well, say it then ; I'm waiting ! "

" Oh, yes, I'll say it ! "

" Say it then, come ! *zou !* hurry up !

" I'll say it, *if* I choose. . . . I'm not here to take orders of you, I suppose ! "

" You're a common beggar ! "

" Beggar ! you called me a beggar ? "

" Yes, I did, you thief ! "

" Thief ! you called me a thief ? "

" Yes, yes, I did, you idle blackguard ! "

The crowd shouted impatiently :

" Get to work with you ! have it out ! "

" Don't ye see they'll never buckle to ! "

" And what's your quarrel all about, eh ? "

" What's our quarrel about ? Now, *is* that your concern ? Just mind your own business, all of you ! "

" We shall have to call the gendarmes."

" The gendarmes are still inside."

" Ah ! then they'll never catch Maurin, the gendarmes won't."

The two antagonists were still measuring one another with furious looks.

" I'll take off my jacket in a moment."

" Well, take it off ! "

Once more the bystanders raised a questioning cry :

" But, come, what's the quarrel all about, after all ? "

To which one of the two combatants replied, shouting like a madman :

" I don't know, I don't ! I've clean forgot ! he called me a good-for-nothing, he said I was no great shakes— all for no reason ! . . . It's politics is at the bottom of it, there ! "

Then the other yelled :

" You called me a beggar, you began it ! "

" That's not true."

" You're telling a lie."

" I don't know what stops me pulling out your guts, you
blackguard ! In a minute I'll knock you down flat on
your back, I will, and trample on your ugly face, and then
you'll see ! "

" You'll knock me down and trample on me, *you* will ? "

" Yes, I will, *I* will."

" Well, do it, then ; I should like to see you at it ! "

" Don't say another word, not another word, as you
value your life ! "

Then turning to the onlookers, and pointing to his
enemy :

" A sparrow ! why, if I were to take him up like that . . ."
and he made as though he was holding in the air a tiny
pinch of snuff . . . or lifting a butterfly by its wings ;
" if I took him like that and blew, *pechère !* there'd be
nothing left of him ! "

" *Eh, bé !* take me like that then ! Just you try ! "

And again they fell to glaring at one another ferociously.

" Here are the gendarmes. . . . I say, gendarmes ! "

The officers were released at last, and now stalked up
to the scene of action, crying :

" Come, come, now, make it up ! What's all this
about ? "

" Is that any business of yours ? it's about politics. . . .
We're at liberty to argue, I suppose, if we choose. . . . It's
a free country ! "

Suddenly one of the mock combatants fell back, took
three steps to the rear, looked about, stooped, and picked
up a straw from the road, broke it in two, stuck it over
his left shoulder, and shouted defiantly :

" *Té !* let's settle it ! Just take away my straw now,
if you dare ! . . . If you do, I'll buy you a white blackbird ! "

His adversary was equal to the occasion ; in an instant
he too stepped back three paces, looked about on the
ground, stooped down, picked up a straw, broke it in two,
clapped it over his left shoulder, and yelled :

" Take away my straw, you take *my* straw away ! . . .
if you do, I'll—I'll give you a green blackbird—a hen bird
too ! "

Marlusse, who was highly amused, turned to Labarterie :
" Look at 'em ! They're worth looking at. I'll tell
you directly why they're squabbling like that."

The two rivals, now separated by some yards, continued
to look each other up and down menacingly, vociferating
both together :

" Beggar ! idle blackguard ! good-for-nothing scoundrel !
There, I've said the word ! you see, I've said it ! "

Then the biggest of the two, his eyes starting out of his
head :

" Oh, you scamp ! you rascal ! Oh ! you God-forsaken
good-for-nothing! *couquin dé padisqui! oh! marrias de sort!
Vé* . . . once I come at you, I'll cripple you, I'll pound
you to a jelly. . . . I'll eat you up alive ! "

Then, turning to the two gendarmes :

" *Vé !* " he cried, " I can't answer for myself any more !
. . . Don't you see I can't ? . . . Hold me, quick ! Hold
me tight, or I shall finish him ! "

The gendarmes seized hold of the madman, and there
ensued between them and their prisoner an interminably
long argument.

All this while his opponent was screaming at him at the
top of his voice :

" Are you going to take my straw ? or are you not, you
coward ? "

Thus apostrophised, the coward shook himself free of
the gendarmes, and ran back at his insulter, carefully
holding the straw in position on his left shoulder with his
right hand all the time. Then, planting himself in front
of his enemy, he withdrew his hand, and folding his arms,
said suddenly with a fine composure and in a soothing tone
of gentle commiseration :

" Poor fellow. . . . You have a wife and family,
pechère ! So I spare you ! "

He shrugged his shoulders, the straw tumbled on the

ground, and turning his back on the battlefield, he walked away with much dignity.

The other ran after him :

" Oh, Chois ! " he cried, " I'm not angry with you. What's to pay, lad ? "

" Oh, Mariu ! " retorted his friend, " I pay you one, and you pay me one, eh ? and so we're quits, lad, as we were at first ! "

And off they marched, arm in arm, as fast friends as ever. The whole comedy, acted in perfect mimicry of the street rows that are often to be witnessed among porters and longshore loafers at Marseilles and such-like seaports, had been arranged beforehand.

Marlusse turned to M. Labarterie, and observed :

" You're still in the dark, eh ? You took 'em for two fools, now, didn't you ? *Eh bé !* man, they're the two frogs of just now. They only pretended to quarrel to keep the gendarmes busy a bit and give Maurin time to get into hiding somewhere. I know the fellows ; they're bosom friends, and stick together like wax. . . . And you could see for yourself, couldn't you ? they can do bull-frogs like a pair of angels ! . . ."

CHAPTER XIX

Marlusse has the choice of weapons.

THAT night Maurin received shelter and refuge in a friend's house, and Pastouré bore him company.

Next day, Marlusse was to be seen seated in a four-wheeled wagon which he had borrowed, driving solemnly up and down the village street ; in his hand he held a new whip, a long, heavy instrument, which he wielded with astonishing dexterity. Click ! clack ! click ! clack ! he went, beating out regimental tunes in perfect time. . . .

The *Casquette du Père Bugeaud* and *Il y a de la goutte à boire là-haut* were easily recognisable, both quite plain and distinct from the *Retraite*.

He kept his horse at a walk, and even then had to hold him in with a strong hand, the everlasting cracking of the whip making the animal restive. The poor beast showed no enthusiasm for military music ! The villagers—the children in particular—came crowding round ; suddenly Marlusse stopped dead in the middle of the *Chant du Départ*, and using the extreme tip of his lash with incomparable dexterity, whipped off the cap of an urchin who was pressing inconveniently close to stare. Then, swinging nimbly round on the seat, next instant he launched his long lash in another direction, with such admirable precision that the end, catching round the tail of a stray cat, hoisted the terrified brute suddenly in the air, caterwauling piteously.

The report of his prowess spread rapidly from street to street, and soon the whole population was grouped round the performer, and giving vent to shouts of admiration.

141

So great was the noise that Maurin despatched Pastouré
just to see if " a revolution was afoot."

Directly he caught sight of Pastouré, Marlusse stood up
in his cart :

" Pastouré ! " he called out. " Come here ! "—and
Pastouré stepped up.

" You're the man I want—you and Maurin," he went on
to say with a look of mystery. " Go and tell him to come !
I'll take you with me in my ' carriage,' and you'll see
what you shall see ! "

" And where are you going to take us ? "

" You shall see all in good time ; but be quick ; it's
a matter of life and death—*neither more nor less !* "

" Come now," said Pastouré, " I know you ; you're
going to play us another *galégeade*, you are ! "

" Pastouré," said Marlusse, as serious as a judge, " look
at me, my face is a bit white, isn't it—if not green ? I tell
you to come quick, if you want to save my life and my
honour. It's no laughing matter ! Just think, I'm
challenged to fight a duel, and I'm on my way there now.
I required two seconds.   And I thought of Maurin and you.
And I felt sure, by kicking up such a rumpus in the streets
with my whip, I'd bring you out of your hiding-hole at
last. I know I can count on Maurin. So bring him along
and be quick ! I'll tell you the rest of the story on the
way. *Zou !* we must be there to the minute. And you've
nothing to see to ; I'm provided with weapons."

Marlusse was in earnest, and Pastouré saw it. Off he went
to fetch Maurin, while the charioteer, shaking his horse into
a trot, left the crowd gaping with surprise and astonishment.
He meant to pick up his two seconds in the high road just
outside the village.

" Quick, get in my cart, Maurin ; in with you, Pastouré—
and away we go ! "

As they drove along, he told his companions the
incidents which had compelled him to fight.

" After leaving the Congress yesterday evening, a
delegate, one of Caboufigue's men, began talking of Vérig-

non (and of you, too, Maurin) in a way I didn't relish.
Then says I straight out : ' A man must be a born idiot
not to see what a fine fellow Vérignon is, and how honest
and true a man Maurin is ! '   The delegate, a M. Desacier,
a Northerner, a half-pay Cavalry Captain, gives me a wry
look, and says he :

" ' D'you say that meaning me ? '

" ' If the cap fits . . .' says I.

" ' I don't know,' he observes, mighty quiet, ' I really
don't know if I ought to demean myself by making you
eat your words ! '

" Well, you must know, Maurin, I'm not a man to eat
the very smallest of any words ever came out of my
mouth.

" ' Sir,' says I, quiet-like too, and as polite as could be :
' if there was a set of dominoes made up of fools, you'd
be double-six, you would ! '

" ' Sir,' he answered back, ' you're a rude fellow. . . .'

" I felt myself getting warm ; something seemed to be
boiling inside me.   I retort :

" ' *Tout áro, ou, vous fàou véirè trento-sié candellos*—and
I translate it for him, like Mascurel : ' thirty-six candles,
sir, that's what I'll make you see, pretty quick ! '

" Well, he looks me up and down again—I suppose he
thought me pretty, and as you can see for yourself, I'd
put my best clothes on to come to the Congress. . . . He
looks at my gold watch-chain, which I wear over my
stomach, well in front, along with the medal of the Republic.
. . . And taking me for a gentleman of his own sort, he
draws me a bit o' one side and tells me :

" ' Here's my card, sir !   My second will call on you
to-morrow.'

" ' Sir,' says I, ' as for a card, I've nothing on me but
a bit of rope's end, the rope my father was tied up
with in '51. . . . And for address—I haven't any in this
town ! '

" You see, I didn't want to tell him I was going to sleep
the night on the hay in my friend Tintidret's horse's

manger—the same horse he's lent me this morning, along
with his cart, to go to the duel in !

" ' You have no address to give, you coward ? but you
shan't get off like that ! '

" At that, I felt something like a whiff of mustard
mount in my nose, and I says to him straight out, says I :

" '*Mossieu*,' says I, ' enough said. You want to fight ?
I'm ready. To-morrow morning at half-past eight by the
clock, I shall be found with my weapons and my seconds
in the meadows of *Martin-l'aï*—anybody will tell you the
place, a couple of miles outside the village. Bring your
arms and your seconds with you, like me, and be punctual—
punctuality is the politeness . . . of the people ! And
sleep well, to be fresh in the morning.'

" ' That's agreed,' he answers in his Frenchified accent ;
' I shall have my swords ! '

" I thought I would go and tell you the whole thing
right away ; but I didn't know where you were hid. So
I said to myself : ' Maybe they've gone off to the mountains, along with the gendarmes. However, I've found
you this morning, and I'm main glad ; for I didn't half
like going alone, going to this duel, you know.'

" Why, couldn't you have taken two other seconds,
instead ? "

" Oh, no ! because I wanted two knowing chaps, two
of your sort, and that's not a thing to be found in the first
donkey's hoof-mark you come to."

" Ah ! " laughed Maurin, " so you've thought of some
trick to get you out of the scrape, eh ? Let me into the
secret."

" It's like this," explained Marlusse. " You know for
fifteen years I horsed the diligences down in Algiers ? My
route was from Algiers to Constantine, and I often used
to drive one of my coaches myself. . . .

" Good ; go on ! "

" Listen, then . . . Now, here's an officer and a gentleman, a fellow whose trade it's been all his life to carry
a great sword dangling at his heels. But it's different with

me'; I'm half ashamed to say so, but so it is—in all my
born days I've never so much as handled the scabbard of
one; I never served, you know, because I've one leg
shorter, or one leg longer, if you like it better, than
t'other. Very good! but this fine military gentleman never
asks if I know his weapon, though he wants me to use it!
And if I use it ill, he's for killing me! That only means
he wants to kill me at his own convenience, without a bit
of trouble for him—and he thinks it shows his courage to
attack me though I can't defend myself! Well, he may
call himself a brave man when he behaves like this, but
I consider he's giving the greatest proof possible of his
cowardice! So there you are, the notion struck me:
to hold my own against his sword, the weapon he's used to,
I had only to take the one *I*'ve practised the management
of—and so I've made up my mind to fight with my whip!
. . . Well, there's nobody but you, Maurin, to explain the
thing properly to him, and Pastouré to make him see,
without ever saying a word, that *he's* ready to back me
up too."

" I take you! " cried Maurin with a big laugh. . . . " Oh,
Marlusse, Marlusse! but you *are* a clever fellow, and a
rare amusing chap! "

Marlusse glanced at Pastouré, who said nothing, but
gravely extended his right arm and closed his fist with the
thumb stuck up stiffly in the air.

Marlusse was radiant. Click! clack! his whip beat to
quarters, and in a few minutes the cart swung out of the
high road into a narrow lane that led to the meadows
of *Martin-l'ai.*

The meadows, a magnificent expanse of rich land re-
claimed from the river, as fine as any in all Provence,
were bordered by a broad avenue of tall elms.

" We are here first," remarked Marlusse. " So much
the better. Let's tie up the horse to this tree here."

After doing this, Marlusse still had plenty of time to give
his friends any final explanations he thought necessary.

Before long his adversary arrived, also driving, and

L

accompanied by two seconds, who had brought a pair of swords.

The evening before Captain Desacier had at once set to work to find a couple of retired *sous-officiers*, whom he had eventually run to earth in the village café ; and who had agreed to act for him.

All the gentlemen exchanged bows, Marlusse and the Captain coming to a halt at some little distance from their seconds, who entered upon the preliminaries.

" Gentlemen," began Maurin to the Captain's representatives, " my name is Maurin, and this is my friend, M. Pastouré, a sportsman like myself. Whom have I the honour of addressing ? "

The other two mentioned their names : Rompinaz and Cassadan, retired *sous-officiers* of Dragoons, one being now a harness-maker, the other a grocer and dealer in china.

" Gentlemen," resumed Maurin, " I have served myself in the Navy, and I am a fencing-master into the bargain."

The two old *sous-officiers* repeated their bows, this time *à la militaire*, while Maurin and Pastouré raised their hands to their hats. The Captain did the same, and Marlusse followed suit.

" Gentlemen," proceeded Maurin, still addressing the Captain's seconds, ' I am directed to make a statement, which I beg you to hear with the utmost attention. My client has never touched a sword in his life. I am aware that by the customs of duelling, if one of the two principals knows how to use his weapon and the other does not, the former is not expected to take into account his opponent's unskilfulness. But, besides being men of honour, *we* are men of progress, and you are, I trust, the same. And this is why we have assumed you would not wish to take the responsibility of pitting against one another a well-armed man and one who, as a matter of fact, may be described as unarmed, seeing he would hold his sword about as cleverly as an old woman clutching a candle in church."

" You mean to say ? " exclaimed the Captain, interrupting, in spite of himself.

" You have no right to speak," protested Maurin in his *presidential* voice. " But, anyway, what honour could you reap from so easy a victory, won over an enemy whose defeat is assured from the very beginning ? . . . In one word, to cut it short," he continued, turning afresh to the seconds, " our two friends here, one a trained fencer and the other not, can never fight on equal terms, though their weapons may be of equal length to the fraction of an inch, and of equal weight to the fraction of an ounce."

" What are you driving at ? " growled the Captain ; " you haven't brought me out here for nothing, I should hope ? "

" You have no right to say a word ! " declared Pastouré, as solemn as a Bishop, and looking imposing enough for anything with his immense stature.

" In fact," concluded Maurin, " we ask for fair play ; let each of the gentlemen fight with the weapon he understands best."

" Which means . . . ? "

" Which means that the Captain, who has been for years a soldier, can fight with his sword . . ."

" And the other with a pistol, I suppose ? " suggested the officer, with manifest ill-humour.

" The other, who has been for years a diligence driver, will fight with his whip. . . ."

" It's all a piece of insolence ! a gross impertinence ! " blustered the Captain, furiously angry.

" Excuse me, it is only justice," corrected Maurin—" and the more so (if you still think it just and fair for one of you two to use a weapon he does not understand), inasmuch as we will, of course, allow you—you, Captain, if you choose— to fight with a whip too."

The Captain was stamping about with rage.

" And," Maurin proceeded calmly, " thinking you might likely come in your carriage with a fancy whip, we have brought a couple of fighting whips with us,"

"*I* sold 'em to M. Marlusse," declared the harness-maker, "five-and-forty sous apiece ; forty each, if you take a pair."

"Bang went four good francs ! " sighed Marlusse.

"So you see they're whips no honourable man need be ashamed to use," added Maurin imperturbably. "Come, gentlemen, to work ! "

"I will not put up with it, gentlemen, I will not ! " growled the Captain. "I'm not come here for fun."

"And I tell you we're not in fun neither," Maurin assured him. "Get it into your noddle once for all that in M. Marlusse's hands the whip is a deadly weapon ! "

"Come, come ! " sneered the Captain, shrugging his shoulders.

"Sir," replied Maurin, his characteristic ingenuity suggesting the master word of the situation, "I know what I'm talking about, whether it's fighting gear or fighting courage. Now, the sword is a weapon ; and skill to use it is another. If you wield a sword, a weapon you understand and we don't, you will have two weapons and we only one ! Now, is that fair, I ask you as man to man ? Answer me, *as a Frenchman should !* "

At bottom the Captain was a good fellow and a sensible, if hardly a genius.

"True for you," he muttered ; "it does *not* seem quite fair, does it ? "—and he broke into a laugh.

"Ah ! " went Pastouré in a tone of relief.

"If it'll amuse you to fight me," declared Maurin, "I'm quite ready, with sword or sabre or musket—or big guns, if you like ! But I think it will be pleasanter for us all to see how M. Marlusse makes play with the whip ! Then I'll ask you if it wouldn't need some pluck for two honest Frenchmen to fight with that terrible weapon, the same as the wagoners do ! "

Finally, the Captain came to see his best way was to treat it all as a laughing matter.

"Well, let's see the performance," he said, making up his mind.

"Light up!" Marlusse gave the order to Pastouré in a ringing voice.

Then the latter, in accordance with instructions previously given him by Marlusse, went to the cart and, opening the box under the seat, pulled out three packets of candles.

Next, he extracted from the same receptacle a number of little candlesticks of yellow crockery-ware, which, with Marlusse's help, he arranged here and there, to right and left, some on the cart, others on the ground, more or less at random, but all within a confined space.

The Captain was getting interested by now, and watched the proceedings more in astonishment than in anger.

"*I* sold Marlusse those candlesticks," observed the grocer ; "one sou apiece. Ten sous the dozen."

"Bang went thirty sous, oh dear !" sighed Marlusse.

Then, facing the enemy :

"Now," he said, "watch carefully ! I'm going to begin."

He settled his hat on the back of his head, and whip in hand, assumed the posture of a duellist on guard.

"Look you," he harangued, "with my whip in my hand, I'm afraid of nobody. Show me a *tavan* (gad-fly) on my horse's back, I can kill it you without the nag feeling the faintest touch of the tiniest tip of my whip-lash. There, see that grasshopper on that blade o' grass, d'ye see ? Now, clack ! I've hit it. Where's it gone ? Ah, ha ! search and ye shall find. . . . Why, before you can advance a step— I'm supposing you standing on guard with your sabre facing me, it's only a supposition—click ! I twist my whip-lash round it and I twirl it up in the air out of your hands, like a smelt at the end of a fisherman's line ; and have a care, I say, as it comes down again, butt first, it don't split your head open ! Next shot, I blind your right eye, clack ! and third shot, your left, click ! Fourth shot, I entangle both your legs, I haul in, and plop ! you tumble on the tip of your nose. Then you're a lost man, *pechère !* in two or there more click ! clack ! click ! clack ! I leave you as good as dead. . . . Why, sir, with my own weapon in my fist, I shouldn't care for a lion—if he was a one-eyed lion, 'cause then I could knock him blind with one blow, clack ! . . . Well, now I'll finish up by giving you a proof of my deadly dexterity, as you haven't managed to find the grasshopper . . . you didn't look properly, you know . . . we'll find it presently. . . .

"Now—first candle ; click ! . . . there, didn't I put it out without shifting it, without upsetting the candlestick, without touching anything but the flame ! Second candle . . . hold it in your hand, Pastouré ; no, no, not at arm's length, man ; put it just before your nose ; never fear, you can trust to me ! . . . Now, clack ! . . . out ! neater than ever an extinguisher could have done it. . . . And now, just count up in your mind the candles left, beginning with the last out . . . there . . . that's right . . . now, I'm going to douse all the even numbers for you— two, click ! four, clack ! six, click ! eight, clack ! . . ."

Marlusse dashed swiftly to and fro, darting nimbly hither and thither, according to the distance separating him from the particular candle aimed at.

" . . . sixteen, click ! twenty-four, clack ! . . . Well, gentlemen, you see for yourselves . . . thirty-two, click ! . . . I might have got a place in a circus . . . thirty-four, clack ! . . . only my poor mother didn't fancy the life. . . . Now, a moment's rest. . . . Now, thirty-six, click ! clack ! and out ! . . . Well, what d'ye think of it, Captain ? Didn't I promise to make you see six-and-thirty candles . . . and you've seen 'em ! . . . shall I finish the rest ? "

"Ample ! ample ! " cried the Captain gaily ; " and now, let's to breakfast . . . it's my treat ! . . . Well, it's prodigious ! "

"I thought somehow it would end as it has, sir," said Marlusse genially ; " I read the papers, and they describe plenty duels, and they all of 'em end with a *bouille-abaisse*. So, I put in the cart-box all we want for a good breakfast— and good wine to wash it down. . . . Pack up the candles, Pastouré ; the good gentleman who sold 'em me didn't let me have 'em at the price of tallows, I can tell you."

" Prodigious ! " repeated the Captain. " I'd never have thought it possible ! "

Everybody was laughing, and soon the whole party sat down to breakfast on the turf under the great elms ; the horses were unhitched, and browsed their fill of the rich grass.

At dessert, the Captain, who was a trifle " elevated," kept making the same remark over and over again :

" Prodigious ! prodigious ! it's prodigious ! "

Marlusse, who seemed to be really drunk, suddenly began to weep hot tears.

" Come, come, my dear boy," the Captain addressed him affectionately, " you've no reason to be so sad ? . . . prodigious ! prodigious, I say ! "

" *Sian touti d'amis !* " (Let's all be friends !), said Pastouré, with exemplary seriousness.

But Marlusse threw himself into the Captain's arms, and dropping his head on his shoulder :

" No, sir, I never, never get drunk, because in these parts it's not the thing ; but your accent told me you were a Burgundian, and you wouldn't despise me if you saw me fuddled like one of your own compatriots. . . . Ah ! what a pity, sir : what a pity ! . . ."

" A pity ! what's a pity ? " stuttered the Captain, drunker than he'd meant to be. . . . " Prodigious ! prodigious ! . . . Come, tell me your trouble, and I'll comfort you. . . . Prodigious, I say ! "

" Ah ! M. le Capitaine," said Marlusse, " I'm crying because before ten years is out, there'll be nobody left in France knows how to use a whip. It's fast becoming a lost art ! the *totos mobiles* (automobiles) have killed it ! "— and he sobbed bitterly.

" Sir," said the Captain, " I owe you a breakfast. It's prodigious, prodigious ! . . ."

" It's only the mountains don't come together again, after once knocking glasses," said Marlusse sapiently—he didn't care a medlar about mixing his metaphors !

When at last the two parties had separated :

"All the same," remarked Maurin to Marlusse, who had suddenly grown sober, "you were precious drunk just now."

"Alas, alas!" sighed Marlusse, with the calmness of despair, "it's my fate, *povre mi!* always to be taken for what I'm not. Every time I pretend to be something, egad! they think I'm that really. *Et tu*, Maurin! Oh, Mòourin! oh, Mòourin, you too! . . . Why, couldn't you see I was stuffing him? *Galegeàvi!* (I was mystifying)."

At the word, the silent Pastouré extended his arm, and doubling his fist, held up the thumb in the air—very stiff and vertical.

CHAPTER XX

A brief but important interview between M. de Siblas and
our friend Maurin.

NEXT day Maurin thought it best to pay a visit to M. de
Siblas. So he set off . . . without his gun.

" Ah ! so there you are, M. Maurin ? "

" Yes, M. le Comte ; I thought it was my duty to come
and tell you how things are going."

" Political things ? "

" Yes, M. le Comte."

" Well, what news is there ? "

" The papers will tell you all about it better than I can ;
but I may tell you the Congress has adopted the plan of
running several candidates. Vérignon was accepted as
one by acclamation."

They talked a bit, and M. de Siblas finally said :

" You see, M. Maurin, we're not so far from an understanding after all. It's not the Vérignons and the Maurins
bother me, but the Caboufigues."

" Oh ! they're flattened out, those fellows ! " declared
Maurin—and he told M. de Siblas, who laughed till he cried,
first the story of his duel with walking-sticks with young
Caboufigue, and then Pastouré's famous speech against
the father of the same Roman Baron.

" M. Caboufigue has been here to see me, but he never
said a word of all this," remarked M. de Siblas slyly.

" I don't suppose he will talk about it much," replied
Maurin.

Then, just as he was leaving the room, he turned back
suddenly :

" Well, well ! . . . so you still want badly to have a

king, eh ? . . . What a pity ! . . . Without that, I should like you fine ! " he told the Count, who was delighted with his friendly frankness.

" Egad ! " exclaimed M. de Siblas, " I could still get on very well without a king, if all my countrymen were fit for it."

" Fit for what ? "

" Fit for going without—in other words, fit for freedom. A people fit for freedom, M. Maurin, that means an honest and intelligent people. Now it's far from easy to find a large supply of honesty and intelligence ; it would be readier to find a good king. In a word, it's harder to discover twenty million honest and intelligent men than one man of these qualities."

" Good," said Maurin, who was thinking ; " all we want is good laws."

" Who is to make them," retorted M. de Siblas, " if you don't know how to choose your legislators ? Alas ! what's wanting is good conduct and honesty and strength of character."

" We have children," said Maurin with a sadder gravity.

The Count sighed ; then, after a pause :

" You may rely on my not withdrawing my candidature " —and he held out his hand to Maurin.

" By the by, M. le Comte," said Maurin, " since I saw you last, things have occurred that concern you. I've been backwards and forwards, coming and going, with my eyes and ears open. I've something to tell you I was very near forgetting. . . . I should have had to come again to say it. On your land, in your Brégançon woods, you've got . . ."

" A lot of gypsies—and they annoy me very much," M. de Siblas completed the sentence. " They have been ordered off, and they refuse to go. They treat my woods as a conquered country or a virgin forest in America. I shall end by calling in the gendarmes and evicting them."

" Don't do it for the present, M. de Siblas ! " advised Maurin. " If you take these measures, they'll revenge themselves. . . ."

" But how ? "

" They'll set fire to your woods, you may make sure of that. . . . And your woods," laughed Maurin, "are very important to me, M. le Comte, more than they are to you, because you don't shoot in 'em, and I do ! . . . Oh ! only woodcock and rabbits . . . yes, and partridges, but not pheasants ; besides, there ain't any ! "

The Count burst out laughing.

" Wait a while longer," Maurin continued. " These gypsies have a reason for squatting there I mustn't tell you, but which may cease to act at any moment ; I'll do my best to that end. Better for you to use patience in the matter ; I'll say a word to some poor chaps I know who are urging them now to stay where they are, and between us, we'll get 'em out of the place. But it's a question of time."

" Very well," agreed the Count, " I'll trust to you. When all's said and done, they don't hurt me much, and if they won't fell more than an acre or so . . ."

On parting, he observed :

" But you are not so cheerful, I think, Maurin, are you, as usual ? "

" One gets tired of things, sir. The gendarmes amused me finely at first ; now they annoy me. I suppose I must be getting old. Then sometimes I go and listen to the lessons my son's getting from a good man, a man of a thousand, and that sets me thinking. . . . For instance, some days ago I made up my mind I could never come here any more to kill your pheasants, M. le Comte. It would strike me as stealing—nothing less ; I should feel myself no better than a smuggler. All this because my little lad repeated a lesson to me he had learned about smuggling."

" We shall be fine friends yet, Maurin. You are an honest fellow, Maurin, and a heart of gold. Come and see me again when the shooting opens. We'll take our guns and make the round of my island together."

" Delighted, M. le Comte. . . . Till we meet again, sir ! "

CHAPTER XXI

Maurin and his prospective father-in-law Orsini hold a conversation, in which the former hears of something greatly to his disadvantage, and is thereby confirmed in his belief that "Justice is blind."

A VAGUE, half-defined wish to settle down to a more peaceful life had been growing on Maurin for some time. At last one day he donned his best clothes and set off to find Orsini; but the Forester was out.

"For God's sake, Maurin," cried Tonia the instant she saw him, "go away! . . . I can't tell what's wrong with my father some days past; he never speaks, and only grinds his teeth when he looks at me."

"I'm not going away," declared Maurin; "I mean to ask him for you as my wife this very day!"

Orsini walked in.

"What, you here!" he exclaimed angrily, as he caught sight of Maurin. "'Pon my word! you're a bold man! . . . Now listen; you've come in as a guest, and you shall leave unharmed. But I give you fair warning, from an hour after you're gone, I shall hunt you down without mercy, wherever I may come across you."

"Oh, dear!" said Maurin, "I'm sorry you take it so; I didn't quite expect this! And I wanted to talk to you to-day on a matter of importance. Clap the muzzle on your anger and listen. Maybe it concerns all our happiness, your own, and Tonia's, and mine."

"And what, pray, has Tonia to do with you?"

"I have taken a new resolution, Orsini. The things they are after me for deserve, I consider, rather reward than punishment; and I mean to convince the law of this. I shall give myself up to the police; they can judge me

by the facts, and I shall be acquitted—there's no doubt of
that. Then, Orsini, I shall come back to you and say,
' Now give me Tonia ; I love her, and she doesn't altogether
dislike me, I think. . . .' "

Orsini made an impatient movement, which Maurin
stopped with a wave of the hand :

" But I don't feel in the humour to give myself up to
justice till I have your promise. You understand ? "

" You're a bit late, man ! " cried Orsini. " It's not a
mere inquiry now you've got to face, it's not a mere order
to come up for examination that's out against you now ;
it's a warrant to clap you in gaol ! You're not suspected,
my fine fellow, you're condemned ! "

"Condemned!" exclaimed Maurin, turning pale. "Great
God ! what to ? "

" Three days' imprisonment and fifty francs fine," replied Orsini. " You have a pigeon-hole now of your own
in the police records. You've been convicted by default of
assault and battery ; as to the dog-stealing, that wasn't
proved."

Maurin was thunderstruck ; surprise and consternation
held him dumb. Tonia was in the like case.

" Sorry ! " cried Orsini ; " no, I'm not sorry ! Why
should I be ? It's a disaster has naught to do with me or
mine. Sorry ? no, but angry, furious, yes, to see a man of
such a sort come into my keeper's lodge, into an honest
man's house, and have the effrontery to ask me for my
daughter ! . . . Out with you, you scoundrel ! "

" I always thought," said Maurin quietly, " Corsicans
were more hospitable to guests, and less hard as a rule on
bigger bandits than I am, even if I *had* done the things
they charge me with."

Orsini seemed to feel the reproach.

" And how d'you know I've nothing else to bring against
you myself ? "

" Why, what ? "

" Can't you guess ? Didn't you speak at the Congress
t'other day against Cabantous, a faithful supporter of the

Bonapartist cause—the cause every Corsican has at
heart ? "

" Oh, ho ! " said Maurin, " so that's where the shoe
pinches, eh ? "

" Yes, that's it."

" In that case, my good father-in-law," said Maurin,
with a scornful, mocking laugh, " you're concerning yourself with what's no business of yours surely."

" A man like you could only make discord in my house,"
stormed Orsini. " We could never hit it off. I should vote
one colour, and you another. I want a son-in-law of my
own ways of thinking, and not a sort of rebel, a fellow
who's against all rules, a Republican and an Anarchist !
Out you go, you dog-stealer ! "

Tonia took a step towards her father ; but he pushed her
away.

Maurin shrugged his shoulders.

" It's quite true," he said, " I gave a good lesson to a
gunner who was thrashing his dog ; it's a fact, too, his dog
followed me and has refused to leave me since. The man's
name and his address at Cannes are on the collar ; I always
meant to return his animal to him one day or another.
Well, I won't now. The beast has chosen its master. I give
it full liberty to go back of its accord to Cannes, by road
or train as it likes best, and what more can I do ? About
the conviction, I'm vexed, but after all I don't care a hang !
It's just so much waste paper. I shall never do one single
day in prison, not I. It's an unjust punishment, and I
won't recognise it. True justice is on my side. Saulnier,
he holds a medal from a Society for Protecting Dumb
Animals, because he loves foxes and weasels and makes
them love him. It shall never be said a citizen of France
is to go to gaol for having defended a dog against cruelty !
Good-bye, Orsini.

" Neither you nor your friends the gendarmes will ever
catch me. And if Sandri resumes his plans of marrying
your daughter, it'll not be for laying hands on Maurin
he'll be made Brigadier ; you may tell him that from me,

and it's God's truth. . . . Good-bye, Tonia. Your father *is* your father, and you're bound to respect him.

" I'm not the man to entice you out of his house ; but I reckon you don't agree with him, and you're not the girl to scorn Maurin nowadays when he's unhappy—a deal more unhappy than he was yesterday."

Tonia made a step to go to Maurin, but he drew away. Orsini put out his arm to seize his carbine.

" Come here, Tonia. . . . And you, out with you, thief ! "

Maurin, standing just within the door, turned round to say a last word to Tonia, who was all quivering with distress :

" You see how he is, Tonia ; it's no fault of mine. Maurin would have gladly married you this moment, you are so brave and so pretty. But Maurin has no luck. Forget me, Tonia, and forgive me the pain I've given you "—and he marched out.

Stick in hand and Hercules at his heels, he started off along the high road.

CHAPTER XXII

An ugly encounter on the high road and its unpleasant sequel;
Maurin displays his bravery and good common sense, and reaps
his reward in vexation and annoyance; he pays an unexpected
tribute to the great Pasteur.

HE had been walking over two hours, when Hercules,
who had been gambolling ahead, suddenly ran back, to
take refuge between his master's legs, where he lay on
the ground trembling all over, and positively refused to get
up.

" Halloa! " exclaimed Maurin, " what's up now, I
wonder? "

He listened, but could hear nothing. He waited awhile,
and presently vague noises became audible in front.
He walked on, and there in the middle of the road was a
huge bull-dog, biting savagely at a fir-cone that had
dropped from a tree by the roadside. The animal was
tearing the wood to pieces with his teeth; his tail was
down, squeezed spasmodically against his belly. As
Maurin drew nearer he could see the slaver dripping from
the beast's jaws, and hear a hoarse roar that bore no resemblance to the sounds a dog usually makes.

" Good Lord! " he cried, " a mad dog! "

Hercules had got on his legs at last, no doubt ashamed
to desert his master in the moment of danger. Maurin,
who had looked round and seen him, waved his arm as
much as to say, " Lie down, sir! Lie down! "

Proud to have shown such spirit, but not at all sorry to
see any further display of courage was not required of him,
the dog cowered down again in the dust.

As Maurin advanced upon the infuriated creature, it

lifted its head to look at him, and forgetting the fir-cone it was gnawing, turned its rage against the man.

Maurin grasped his ash-stick by the thin end ; the other ended in a formidable knob studded with rugged knots. Slowly, cautiously, he marched upon the foe.

" A bad job ! " he muttered. " I'd a deal rather have my gun ! "

The dog left the fir-cone for good—it was all torn and broken by this time—and came straight at the man. The lips were drawn back and displayed the powerful teeth in the frothing jaws. The eye, dull yet bloodshot, was terrible to look at, glaring upwards, though the head was held low.

Maurin, one arm guarding his body, held his stick almost horizontally in his right hand, which almost touched his left elbow.

When the brute was within half a dozen yards of him, he suddenly whipped off his hat with his left hand and pitched it right into the face of his terrible adversary. The dog seized it savagely. Then Maurin crouched and sprang forward ; his stick mowed the air, and came down with a will, breaking the dog's two front paws. . . . The animal gave a howl of pain. But next moment Maurin had clubbed his weapon and beat out the creature's brains.

" Ough ! that's done ! " went Maurin. But the fight over, his nerves gave way ; he ran hurriedly back, gripped Hercules by the collar, and feeling his legs giving way under him, sat down on a stone post by the roadside.

" My poor old Hercules ! " he half sobbed, " you've had a fine escape ! "

The dog got up, put his two paws on his master's shoulders, and licked his face. The latter took a box out of his game-bag, and out of it produced a slice of jerked meat, which he gave to his four-footed friend.

" That'll do you good ! " he said. " If you were as terrified as I was, *pechère !* lad, but you'd want something."

He pulled out his flask of *aiguarden* and took a pull.

M

Above him, on the hill-side, a shepherd was on the move, calling together his flock of mountain goats.

"Oh, dear! oh, dear! Maurin," he shouted; "a mad dog's been along the road there! He's bitten two of my goats, if not more, and my good dog into the bargain!"

"Poor chap!" said Maurin; "you'll have to kill 'em, both your dog and your two goats."

At that moment men appeared on the road, marching cautiously along, armed with guns. In front strode a *garde champêtre ;* you could see his badge glittering on his breast.

With infinite precaution, very slowly and gradually, this body of seven or eight men advanced upon the dog's dead carcase. All held their guns at the ready, finger on trigger.

"You're a day after the fair," Maurin hailed them, "the beast's dead."

On the hill-side above, the shepherd was still lamenting his losses.

The little band stepped more briskly forward, and the boldest spirits ventured to touch the lifeless body of the mad dog with a twig they had broken off a bush.

"Yes, he's dead right enough!" said one and another.

Then, the *garde* leading, all marched up to where Maurin was sitting.

"Halloa! is that you, Maurin?"

"Who else should it be?"

"Well, you've done a fine stroke of business!" growled the *garde* in a voice of reproach. "M. le Maire won't be over and above pleased!"

"What d'ye mean?" cried Maurin in amazement. "Whether it's I killed him or you, what's the odds, so long as the beast's put beyond doing any more hurt? If there's any reward you can get, I'll give it up to you with all the pleasure in life, along with that pretty bit of game yonder."

"It's not that," explained the man. "We had different orders, you see; we were not to kill the dog."

"And what *were* you to do with him?"

"Oh!" said the official, "you don't understand! We had been driving him for an hour—and no easy job, neither!"

"Driving him? but where to, man? So now you're shepherding mad dogs—is that your trade? A fine profession, 'pon my soul! Where were you driving him, may I ask? My brain's giving way, surely."

"Into the next commune."

"What! into the next commune? Do they collect mad dogs there, like my Russian Prince collects rare birds?"

"Don't you know the custom?"

"Custom! what custom d'ye mean?" gasped Maurin, more and more bewildered.

The others had recovered their calm, and were now standing round Maurin, shouldering their guns.

The *garde champêtre* answered :

"When they kill a mad dog, it's the custom for the commune to pay the expenses of the post-mortem. The commune has to pay these charges and also for the vet's time coming and going. So, to avoid all this useless expenditure, they chivy the beast across the line into the next commune. I got my orders to-day, and these gentlemen came with me, because several guns are better than one if the creature turns at bay."

Maurin was dumbfounded, and could not believe his ears. Still seated on his post, he replied :

"Nonsense! I don't believe you, it's a *galégeade* of yours! But it's no joking matter, this isn't! 'Pon my word, I don't think it is. Either you're poking fun at me, or your Mayor must be a more dangerous and savage brute a hundred times over than that mad dog there ; it was by itself, all alone, to work its mischief, while to do his, your master seems to have in his employ all the mad dogs of the countryside! But you're only pulling my leg, eh, my lad?"

"What!" one of the men asked with perfect seriousness, "didn't you know that, Maurin? . . . It's really the

custom, as they've been telling you. I've always seen
the thing done that way, all my life ! "

" You mean it ? "

" Mean it ? Yes ! And, what's more, we're going now
to drag the carcase into the next commune ; the boundary's close to where we are," was the *garde's* only answer.
" They can do as they like with it there. The eagles can
eat it, if it's to their taste, and the ratepayers won't have
to pay for sauce ! "

" A pretty business, 'pon my soul ! " protested Maurin,
" to poison the very eagles with your rottenness ! For
that carrion, it's only by men's interference it can be
prevented from infecting the polecats and martens and
foxes. I killed him in your commune ; I say so now to the
garde champêtre, and I'll make the same declaration
directly at the Mairie, and you shall pay for what's happened. I tell you, you shall, including the shepherd's
goats and his dog ! You'll see. . . . Come here, shepherd ! "

But the man, who overheard what they were saying in
the road below, shouted :

" Thank you, thank you, Maurin ! but in such a case,
if I do make a claim for the loss of my two goats and my
dog, I can't bring 'em to life again ! And I shall only have
a thousand worries to put up with from the lawyers. I'll
bear what I have to bear, and not add to my troubles.
Go your own road, is my advice, and leave policemen and
judges to go theirs ! "—and he vanished over the hill,
groaning and growling.

" He knows," said Maurin, " it means another forty
sous for me out of pocket."

" No ! what he knows," corrected the *garde*, " is that
I'm under orders, under orders, d'ye hear ? "

" Orders like that," cried Maurin angrily, " a sensible
man doesn't obey ! If I were you, I'd pitch my cap,
the badge of slavery, in the Mayor's face, or any other
idiot's or rascal's who'd issue such orders ! . . . And if
that mad dog, which you could have killed a hundred times

over, had bitten some woman or young girl, or a child coming home from school, anyone, old or young, or even me,
Maurin, would the poor mad beast be to blame? No! you,
you reasonable folks, you would be the murderers! And
to think France has a great and learned man, whose name
the youngsters are taught at school, a man who has spent
his life in studying how to cure men who have been bitten
by mad animals! I'm hardly sure even of his surname.
He's been called the ' Great Shepherd ' or the ' Great
Pasteur,' to let the world know he chose to lead men in
spite of themselves—for they're stupider than so many
sheep—to lead them into the right road. Yes, it's for you
he worked, that brave, innocent-hearted savant, *pechère !*
for idiots like you, fellows who can't understand the simplest
thing! God bless him, but he's gone on a fool's errand!
Oh! generation of slaves and dullards, as noxious as your
masters, and more maleficent than madness itself! . . .
Aren't the folks in the next commune Frenchmen, too,
like yourselves? What else are you doing but playing
traitor towards them? yes, traitor, I say! Nay, if they
were Prussians even, would you drive a mad dog into their
midst with its deadly slaver? Savages and fools, that's
what you are! Go and tell your precious Mayor that, and
I'll tell him the same myself when you're done! "

" Well, well, Maurin, don't get angry," said one of the
party soothingly; " we hadn't thought about it so much
as all that, you know . . . and we were risking our skins,
anyway? "

" Yes, and what for? to save forty sous! and wasting
a hundred times as much time over it as if you'd done your
duty; you could have shot the beast in one second.
That's just why I call you brute beasts. . . . Rabies!
rabies! " Maurin repeated the word in tones of burning
indignation, " they bandy rabies and death backwards and
fowards, from one commune to another! To save forty
sous among a population of two thousand! And the
fellow there calls himself a *garde!* What is it, pray, you
guard, when, to save the commune a few dirty pence, you

endanger the lives of the very people you're paid to guard !
. . . but if it were forty sous' worth of absinthe, you
wouldn't be so stingy, tipplers that you are ! "

The *garde champêtre* began to lose his temper under this
tirade.

"Look here, Maurin," he said, "you're going too far ;
my patience is nearly done ! Once I'm really roused,
you'd best have a care ! I might chance to remember,
mate, there's orders out against you, too."

"Now," said Maurin, "when these good people, who
followed you without ever thinking, have been shown how
shamefully they've been acting under your gallant orders,
there's not a man of 'em all will help you to arrest me,
at the very moment when, at the risk of my life and limbs,
and my dog's too, I've delivered their district of such a
terrible scourge—but not so terrible, no, not one hundredth
part as terrible as you who, instead of killing it, were
driving it before you as one takes a turkey-cock to
market ! "

"Oh ! that's it, is it ? " roared the officer. "Well, to
begin with, we're going to look after *your* dog, which
I mean to take away with me, and I'll have him shot,
were it only because he went near the other."

"Shoot yourself, jackass ! If you touch one hair of
my dog's coat, I'll smash you. My dog contributes to the
revenue ; he pays tax. And he's a better citizen than
you ! "

So saying, Maurin loosed Hercules, who showed his
teeth.

The *garde* stepped suddenly up to Maurin to seize him
by the collar, but stopping half-way :

"You insult me," he said, "in the performance of my
official functions."

"Official functions ! say rather functions of a chattering
fool and a blatant ass ! You guardian of mad dogs, when
your superiors issue orders against sick animals, and you
go to arrest dogs there's nothing the matter with, dogs
you know perfectly well, and leave the dangerous ones at

large, because you're afraid of 'em. All you care about
is to save yourselves trouble ! "

The functionary again advanced a step, and again put
out his arm. Maurin seized his opportunity and brought
down his fist heavily on the man's extended arm ; then,
snatching the gun the representative of the law held in his
left hand, he whipped it out of his clutch, and hurling it
into a bush by the roadside twenty yards away :

" To heel, Hercules ! " he cried to his dog.

The latter had just torn a great rent in the regimental
trousers.

" Pick up your pop-gun and your dead dog, and begone
with you ! " he ordered the *garde*. " I've said my say. . . .
Ah ! poor France ! "—and, with Hercules trotting behind,
Maurin walked quietly away.

The gunners, sensible men enough, were a good deal
embarrassed. All liked Maurin, and one of them shouted
after him :

" Keep a cool head, Maurin. You're quite right in
what you say ; but all the same, you're a bit hot-tempered,
old man ! "

" I shall make my report dealing with the facts," said
the *garde*; " you are my witnesses."

" But all the same, Maurin's in the right. We hadn't
thought properly. The law is the law, M. le Garde. Let's
make a litter out of branches, and carry the foul brute
back to the village.

" The commune must just pay what it must."

" But I shall make my *procès-verbal !* " insisted the
garde savagely. " Authority cannot be flouted. A Mayor
is a magistrate, and we officers have taken an oath. Yes,
I shall send in my report. He spoke to me *too* insolently,
and my gun's damaged."

Maurin, as he disappeared down the road, looked back
and shrugged his shoulders.

CHAPTER XXIII

In which, for no other reason but the satisfaction of paying a visit to a good and honest fellow, the author introduces the reader to Victorin Pastouré, Parlo-Soulet's brother.

VICTORIN PASTOURÉ, brother of Parlo-Soulet, lived in the heart of the Maures, four leagues from Roquebrune. His house was a lonely habitation, standing isolated among fields, the creation of his own hands. It lay in the deep forest, in the district of the Cabanes Vieilles. He had fired the woods and cleared the ground himself in earlier days.

The house was a poor place, but the land was not without value. Victorin was a perfect type of the working peasant, fanatically devoted to the soil, and miserly to the last degree.

The two brothers, moreover, owned another *bastide* and another piece of land in the Estérel, not far from the legendary farm of Les Adrets. Their tenant was a good farmer, who came punctually every year to the Cabanes Vieilles to pay the rent. The Pastourés were men of means.

It was a passion for solitude and hard work that induced Victorin to live at the Cabanes as he did, all alone, digging, ploughing, sowing his wheat and oats, pruning his vines, shooting too, sometimes. But, while Parlo-Soulet ranged the length of the Maures from end to end by Maurin's side, Victorin only made a heron's flight round and about his own house, describing a circle that never altered, and coming home quite contented from his outing, whether he had killed or no, secured game big or little.

He poked into every hole and corner of his property,

and knew the particular tastes of every sort of wild creature
for such and such a tuft of broom or heath, such and such
a wet ravine or sun-scorched hill-side.

He knew a certain oak, in a low-lying bottom, at the foot
of which he had killed, every season for the last thirty
years, one, two, three, or even more woodcock. Victorin
was as much tied and bound to his land as one of his
cork-oaks. True, his feet had the power of motion, they
were not roots, but his heart and mind were fixed firmly
to the soil, To wrench them loose would have meant
tears and blood.

" How can you bear to lose sight of the roof of our little
home ? " he would sometimes ask his brother.

Penurious, or saving to the verge of penuriousness,
Victorin, who was Parlo-Soulet's elder, never employed
any help, never. He *did himself by himself.* He could
sew and mend and wash ; he always lit his own fire and
cooked his meals. He ground his flour from his own corn,
kneaded it himself, and baked it into loaves, every Satur-
day, in a primitive oven he had built with his own hands.

He was now over sixty. He had six fingers on each hand,
and was all the better for it. The deformity had secured
him his exemption from military service. Never going
" to town," he had never recorded a vote. When this was
thrown up against him :

" I have six fingers," he would reply, " I'm exempt ! "

Since the day he had appeared before the military
tribunal, he had never set foot in Roquebrune. His
brother, of whom he had assumed the care about that date,
after the death of their parents, when Parlo-Soulet was
barely five, worshipped him. Victorin had been father
and mother to him. Even at that distant epoch, the little
lad would go alone to the village to buy this or that, a roll
of cloth, a pair of ready-made trousers. François, the
mattress-maker, too, would call from time to time at the
Cabanes to deliver articles which Victorin had com-
missioned him to bring from the town. Poachers, again,
would cross Victorin's land, and in return for his tolerance

of their presence would also run his errands and keep him
supplied with smuggled powder, in big, round grains,
like black peas, as well as shot (eights) for miscellaneous
game, and buck-shot for wild-boar.

Victorin never joined in the chase openly; but when a
hunt was held in his neighbourhood, he would keep a
look out at home; and in this fashion, or else by taking
ambuscade at night, he had brought down wild pig more
than once.

He had had a mother; so he knew women existed.
The fact had been further impressed on him when, at the
age of twenty-five, his younger brother had vexed him
by getting married and leaving him, to go and live at
Roquebrune. But his sister-in-law was dead, and Victorin
had recovered his brother, whose room always stood ready
for him at the Cabanes Vieilles. " A runagate ! " Victorin
would say; " but such a good chap ! "

Parlo-Soulet's son had not found this lonely life to his
taste, and when quite a lad had removed to Roquebrune,
where he was working on the estate of a wealthy landowner,
learning not only the management of a vineyard, but
ornamental gardening as well.

If Parlo-Soulet invariably began to talk directly he was
by himself, there were two good reasons for the habit.
The first—that lonely livers almost always love to talk out
loud in this way, whether speaking actually to themselves,
or endowing the material objects around them with ani-
mation, asking them questions and making them answer—
for man was never meant by nature to live alone.

The other reason that had led Parlo-Soulet to adopt this
amusing trick of his was his instinct for mimicry. Some
habit which seems ludicrous at first, we often adopt
eventually when another's example urges us. " You see,
it's not so extravagant after all; others do it, though
you're afraid."

As a child Parlo-Soulet had seen his brother waving
his hand and saying to his gun :

" You'll go off this time, eh, slow-coach? You *do*

play me tricks. . . . Mind I don't lose my temper, *Jôousé!*"

Victorin called his gun *Joseph*, his pipe *Marietto*, his stew-pot *Vidasso* (fat living), his bottle *L'Amiguo* (his doxy), his bed *Consolation*, his plough *Tiro-dré* (drive straight), his spade *Pico-fouart* (smite hard), and so on, and so on with everything.

He would address his pipe :

" Marietto, you're getting blacker than a *pète* (goat's dung). Yes, you wear the breeches, Marietto ! (*une pipe culottée*, a coloured pipe). Never a wench but you'll ever wear 'em in my house ! "

He would say to his pot :

" Oh, Vidasso, so you're still full, eh ? It's to keep you supplied the world drudges ! Yet the more I fill you, the more I empty you ! " It was like the bottomless jar of the Danaïdes.

He would tell his bottle :

" L'Amiguo, you've got a fine hat ; off with it, and let me drink your heart's blood ! "

To his bed :

" Consolation, *préni-mi* (take me). Every night you take us for fun, but the day will come when you take us for good and all ! Then the folks cry, but you comfort 'em ; and, presently, it's their turn too."

To his plough :

" Oh, Tire-droit," he would say, "when you don't drive straight, it'll be no fault of yours, but because your old master's all twisted, arms and legs, and all of a tremble ! "

To his spade :

" You, Pico-fouart, smite hard, for the ground's stiff. Dig me holes will give me life-bread, and at the end you shall make me the pit that'll take my dead body."

These and such-like speeches had been Parlo-Soulet's education.

One day the mattress-maker François came to tell him Victorin was feeling ill, and asked him to come to the

Cabanes Vieilles. Parlo-Soulet begged the mattress-
maker to inform Maurin and also pass on the bad news
to his own son at Roquebrune. If Victorin sent for him
it was serious ; it meant the end for certain, thought
Parlo-Soulet, and Parlo-Soulet was right. A fever and
a chill, a touch of *peremonia* (pneumonia), and Victorin
was dying.

Directly his brother arrived, the sick man insisted on
dressing. His brother protested, but without the smallest
effect. The obstinate old man got up, put on his oldest
jacket and fell back utterly exhausted on *Consolation*.

Presently he said :

" It's the fashion hereabouts to dress the dead, so I
wanted to help you ; you'd have found it overmuch trouble
all alone."

Parlo-Soulet burst into tears, at which Victorin made
a jocular remark :

" The silly asses of these days would put on black-tailed
coat and *kalitre* (tall hat), as that's the wear for weddings.
. . . One's oldest jacket is good enough, surely, for
making manure underground ; and the Almighty, if there
is one, will welcome me just the same at His dance,
in the emerald hall of Paradise."

He heaved a great sigh and ejaculated :

" Parlo-Soulet ? "

" Yes, Victorin."

" All the things I've done in my life, I'd like to do 'em
each just once again, *pechère !*—but I can't. So, d'ye
see, I want to watch *you* do 'em. So, lay the table and
eat your dinner. The onions are here, the ham there.
I shall smell the steam of the last soup. , . . Pity ye
haven't the stuff handy to let me taste the savour of a
good, rich *bouille-abaisse !* "

While the soup was preparing :

" Take Joseph, and make him give voice. It's just the
time of day the partridges come and steal my oats from
the threshing-floor. Go and stop 'em. Take my dog
Cæsar along with your Pan-pan."

So Parlo-Soulet went out and found birds pecking at the
oats on the threshing-floor, just as his brother had said.
He killed an old hen-partridge, which Victorin's dog
carried to his dying master's bedside.

"Good dog! a good dog, old Cæsar ! " he said, patting
the animal with his thin, weak hand.

"Now, give me a drop of soup. . . . Good-bye,
Vidasso ! "

He just tasted the soup, and said :

" Hand me Marietto, lad. Light her for me."

He took a couple of pulls, and then :

" Ah ! when Marietto won't serve you any more, it
shows you're good for nothing."

He threw the pipe down and broke it, and muttered to
himself :

" You'll never smoke again, Victorin ! "

Hour succeeded hour ; the old man dropped asleep,
and woke shivering in a deathly sweat. He felt the end
was come. Then he said :

" I'm glad to have seen you again, little lad (the little lad
was an old man). I'm going back to our forbears, to
find out which of 'em parched wheat and which grew vines.
What we've eat or drunk, takes its turn and eats and drinks
us. Good-bye, lad, I'm dying . . . I've polished up the
new harness and repainted the cart, by way of precaution,
when I saw I was so ill, to do you credit at the burial.
You'll take Pico-fouart and dig my hole yourself—yourself,
you understand. I'm set on that. My money is for you,
Pastouré." Victorin looked upon himself as dead already,
and gave Parlo-Soulet the family name, the hereditary
appellation. " My money is for you and your boy. Soon as
I'm gone, you must take Pico-fouart and dig under the big
fig-tree, all round the foot in a wide circle just six yards
from the trunk, like a crown. . . . A golden crown under
the potato roots ! But dig deep, dig deep, you know,
all round. Money don't rot like us. There you'll find
my fortune, which is yours—what I got from my father
and mother and what I've made myself ! "

He sighed heavily, and, after a short silence :

" Put my pillow straight, will you ? I'm mortally sleepy," and he yawned painfully several times over.

In the death agony it often happens that, before the last convulsions come on, the dying person makes some habitual gesture, speaks some well-remembered word. . . . When he was dying Victorin put his left hand on top of his right, and laid his cheek on his left. He always slept so, as dogs sleep with their head on their crossed paws ; and as all his life long he had seen his thoughts turn into persons, he now saw death, as it were, standing before him, and accosted the Prince of Terrors :

" *O vé !* so there you are ! " he muttered. " Death, is it ? Well, I was expecting you ! But, *coquin de sort,* you're not a pretty sight, not a pretty sight ! . . . *Zou !* do your work quick ! "

He was a strong man, and the death struggle lasted an hour longer. As he died, he had only one word to say :

" Parlo-Soulet ? "

" Yes ! "

" *Parlo-mi !* . . ." (speak to me)—and he breathed his last.

CHAPTER XXIV

Parlo-Soulet's reading of the "rights of man," and his gross ignorance of some of the most elementary rules and regulations of civil society,—albeit he had figured at many electoral meetings and voted the social ticket under the auspices of his King, or shall we say his friend, Maurin.

WHEN he saw his brother was dead, Parlo-Soulet lit a half-dozen tapers and sat down by the bedside.

A sportsman passed the door, whom he hailed, offered the man a drink, and begged him to warn his son and Maurin, if possible, to hold themselves ready to join him next day, about noon, at Roquebrune, as they had clearly not received his first message.

When night fell, he lay down on a heap of old sacking spread on the floor, with the two dogs, Pan-pan and Cæsar, snoring beside him.

Next morning, before the sun was up, he put the horse called Loubùou (the ox) in the cart, all fresh painted a bright blue, harnessed the little donkey tandem, took his seat on the shaft, pipe in mouth, and with a *hi! hup! Loubùou!* the creaking contrivance got under way. . . .

Over the cart Parlo-Soulet had thrown his brother's great woollen cloak, which was quite new, and so over the rugged mountain roads the heavy vehicle, bumping and creaking, made its way, lifting over protruding boulders, like a boat at sea, to fall back again with a crash into the intervening hollows. When the shock was too violent, Parlo-Soulet would turn round and carefully rearrange the folds of the new cloak, being afraid, no doubt, of losing it.

Down the hills he walked behind the cart and held on to the rope of the brake, leaning his weight back to keep the block tight on, and shouting to his donkey :

175

" *Hue, l'aï ! hi ! gia ! hue ! gia, l'aï !* "

The surrounding woods murmured like a great sea beneath the bright stars. Then, presently, in front, in the eastern sky, Parlo-Soulet saw long horizontal streaks of gold and crimson form across the heavens, fretted by the countless black limbs of the pines that looked like regiments of giants struck motionless. Then the east grew rosy, then white, till finally the sun flashed out in blinding splendour, and, little by little, the world grew warm. Then a host of flies and wasps began to follow the cart, and Parlo-Soulet cut himself a branch of heath to drive them away whenever they settled on Victorin's new cloak.

When, after making a circuit, he reached the level road which led to Roquebrune, he reseated himself on the shaft and rekindled his pipe. But he still kept his long twig of heath in his hand, now tickling up his horse's quarters with it, now waving it over the great cloak, which the swarm of brown flies obstinately refused to quit.

For the moment, though absolutely alone, Parlo-Soulet did not unclose his lips.

Arrived at Roquebrune, he drove straight to the joiner's, and pulled up in front of the shop.

" *Oou !* is that you, Pastouré ? What can I do for you ? "

" I've come to order the box."

" What box ? "

" Why, the dead box, to be sure ! "

" And who's dead ? "

" My brother Victorin."

" Have you measured him ? "

" No, I've brought him with me."

" Eh ? What have you brought ? "

" Why, my brother, I tell you ! "

Parlo-Soulet raised the great cloak. Underneath, his brother lay sleeping, the head raised on a bag of oats. He only said :

" Get to your job and be quick ! Dead men crave to be underground."

The joiner objected :

"But they don't lug about dead people like that!" Had he called in the doctor? Had he given notice to the Mayor? Parlo-Soulet shook his head.

"I know it's not allowed to bury folk on their land, and that's the reason I've brought my brother here with me. But what's that you say about a doctor? Since when have dead men wanted a doctor? I'm in no mood for joking? Dead folks need nobody, and a doctor least of any! As to the Mayor, my brother never set eyes on him, and the Mayor doesn't care a hang for him. My brother's my concern and no one else's. You make the box for me to bury him; I'll pay you now, on the nail."

"*Oou!*" wondered the joiner. "You talk stern and quick. I never saw you like this before!"

"It's a special occasion, man," replied Pastouré. "A chap doesn't lose his only brother every day of his life."

In vain the carpenter tried to make him understand about the formalities he had to fulfil. Parlo-Soulet was dead obstinate, and only said ten times, twenty times over:

"My brother belongs to me. Isn't he my brother? It's nobody else's business. He lived alone, and died alone. His death only concerns nature! And I shall bury him all by myself; I promised him I would. Show me the place, and I'll dig the hole, as he ordered, with Pico-fouart, that I've got in the cart there beside him under the big cloak. *Zou!* you do your job, and I'll do mine!"

Hearing what was afoot, people came crowding round:

"It's your brother who's dead?"

"Yes."

"He's there? really and truly?"

"Yes, he's there."

The carpenter sent to tell the Mayor, who came hurrying up in person. Giving up all idea of getting Pastouré to listen to reason, he made up his mind to carry out the necessary formalities in his official capacity there and then. The doctor arrived next, and wrote out a death certificate in the carpenter's house.

N

Pastouré, still sitting on the shaft smoking his pipe, shrugged his shoulders and told him :

" As to a doctor, you're the first he's seen. He never saw one at all—and he's dead nevertheless ! "

He smoked in silence, surrounded by a ring of staring villagers, who treated him with as much consideration as was compatible with a lively curiosity. He sat there very calm and quiet, mechanically timing the puffs of smoke that issued from his lips and danced away in the sunshine to the blows of the Joiner's hammer nailing the coffin together.

Now and then he would pick up his green bough again, and drive off the buzzing flies :

" The silly brutes ! " he would exclaim out loud. " Well, it's natural enough ; there's more of 'em in the village than in the woods."

When the coffin was finished it was hoisted into the cart side by side with the dead man ; then the body was laid in it, and the lid nailed down. Pastouré helped, to ensure the Job being done quicker and more thoroughly.

Then, resuming his place on the shaft, he shook up his team and drove off, followed by an ever-growing crowd, whose minds were divided between curiosity and sympathy, Parlo-Soulet being a familiar figure to everybody present.

" There's a fine lot of you, good folks, and no blame to you," he observed ; " but forgive my saying so, the ones I wanted to see were my boy Firmin, and my good Maurin, too. I didn't forget to tell 'em. Will one of the lads there go see if they're coming, and say we're at the cemetery, my brother and I ? "

When this was reached, they found the sexton, who had had word from the Mayor, already engaged in digging a grave.

" There's the hole for your brother to go in, Pastouré."

" *My* hole I shall dig myself, and no one else ! My brother gave me those orders. *Zou* ! stand back, good people all ! "

He had taken care to bring a shovel too, and he fell
to excavating the hole in presence of the whole population,
which had assembled by this time to see him at work.

Down in the grave Parlo-Soulet said a word or two now
and again, not to the spectators, but to himself, for down
there he was alone.

" Eh ! what fine worms, my lads ! and what tap-roots !
Good, rich soil, and bound to rot us quick !   If all the earth
were like that everywhere, all the world over, yes, we
should have less trouble to break it up and make it bear
crops !   It's all good manure, there's such a many burials !
Pico-fouart, you needn't smite hard here ; it's an easy
job to drive you in, as easy as into so much sand ! . . .
Now, hole, you're deep enough—and such nice soft lying,
and so rich in good shoots and growing roots, 'pon my
word ! we might call *you* ' Consolation,' for I never saw a
better bed, never ! "

Just then Maurin appeared, as Parlo-Soulet climbed out
of the new-made grave.   He had deposited the coffin near
it, and now proceeded to pass the cart-ropes round it,
same as the undertaker's men do.   Accosting Maurin,
without so much as a good-day :

" Let's move it," he said.   " Give me a hand "—and
the two raised the burden between them.

There was a slip, and the coffin slid over hastily towards
the gaping hole, the head sagging downwards.

" God save us ! " screamed a woman in horror.

" What odds ? one way or another, head first or feet
first, he'll always reach where he's going, never fear ! "
said Pastouré.

Then Maurin helped him to fill up the grave, and they
piled a mound above it.   On this Pastouré planted a cross
made of two twigs tied together with a rough hank of hemp,
and the crowd dispersed.

A wag shouted at him :

" *Oou !* Pastouré, I thought you were a free-thinker,
man ? "

He faced about and answered quietly :

" Whatever I've thought, joined to what you have, stupid, wouldn't fill the noddle of a *darnagas* (shrike), *pechère !* So your bits of thoughts and mine, lad, be they free or be they not, I'd advise you not to put 'em in the scales ; that'd only set folks jeering at the pair of us ! "

At the end, when all was over, Firmin, Parlo-Soulet's son, put in an appearance.

His father pressed the lad's hand without a word, and the three men set out together on their return to the Cabanes Vieilles.

They called a halt half-way to bait the cattle, while they sat down themselves by the roadside and finished off the provisions which Maurin's game-bag supplied, as well as what was in the cart-box ; then they set off again.

Heath and rosemary and cytisus, the cork-oaks and pines, sang in the wind, suggesting dreams of life and love. The three men told shooting stories. The three dogs gambolled round them, darting hither and thither, now pretending to mark down a rabbit in a tuft of thyme, now galloping after an imaginary hare.

Presently the men fell silent, and not a word was exchanged for over an hour, each pondering his own thoughts. Then, suddenly, young Pastouré spoke, saying calmly and quietly :

" If it met with your approval—yours, father, and yours, M. Maurin—I should be glad to make your daughter my wife."

" If she'll have you, that's all right, . . ." answered Maurin.

" Oh ! she'll have me, I reckon. I think I gathered what she thought the other day at her grandmother's funeral, though I saw her then for the first and the only time."

The lad had hardly spoken when, in a moment, something jocund and health-giving, something that banished the thought of death, breathed into the hearts of the three men, who went on their way without another word.

CHAPTER XXV

How Maurin and Pastouré, the day their two children were married, set their enemies the gendarmes dancing an impromptu and involuntary jig.

PASTOURÉ's son Firmin had for some time occupied an excellent and promising position. He had rented the shop and goodwill of a gardener and nurseryman at Saint-Raphaël — a small business, but with an ever-growing clientèle. This was evidently calculated to advance his prospects in love-making and marriage. Once his wife, Thérèse could retain till further orders her place in the Russian Prince's household.

For his part Pastouré was bethinking him of unearthing his brother's hoard under the big fig-tree and making a liberal provision for his son.

Such were the projects of the two fathers and of Firmin himself. It only remained to ascertain the girl's sentiments.

Two days later Firmin, duly installed in his little house at the end of his garden by the seashore, was expecting Thérèse, whom Maurin had undertaken to sound on his behalf.

" Would Firmin Pastouré suit you for a husband, Thérèse ? "

She looked up at her father with a bright face.

" For sure," she said. " I've only seen him once, but I like him very well, and he's your best friend's son."

" And an honest lad," said Maurin heartily. " I'm glad to see service hasn't spoilt you. By having places in too grand houses, girls often acquire a love of fine rooms and fine clothes. They think they're going to marry princes, and end by dying old maids, or going to the bad.

. . . Why, 'pon my word ! " he added with a look of
surprise, " you're not even wearing the fal-lals you used to
have at your first mistress's, Mme. Labroque's. Your frock
is quite plain, and there's not so much as a bit of lace to
your apron ! "

" Madame la Princess has very simple tastes," replied
Thérèse, mincing her words a little to appear *comme il faut*.

" And Madame la Bourgeoise was a very fine lady ! "
retorted Maurin. " I'm pleased to see you've changed for
the better. Our peasant lasses you see on the high road
through the villages wear *Princesse* gowns and open-work
shoes, while it's just the opposite with the fine ladies from
Paris ; they walk about the country in short skirts and
thick boots. Fools sport their pride on their backs and
on their feet, people of sense keep it for home consumption.
. . . Yes, I authorise you, go and see your lover, your fine
spark, little girl ; I will meet you there presently. Talk
it out betwixt you, and arrange matters."

He was going to explain where she would find Firmin,
what garden it was he had bought. . . . But she knew all
about that already, the slyboots !

She made her way thither, and knocked at the door of the
little house. Firmin opened it himself. For a moment
the two stood facing each other without a word, framed in
the doorway that opened on the sea. They only stared
in each other's faces with a stolid look of surprise, not un-
mixed with pleasure. He was the first to break the silence.

" And so ? " he said questioningly.

" And so ? " she asked in reply.

" Would you like to see my garden ? "

" Oh yes ! I should indeed, M. Firmin."

He showed her his fine collection of trees and shrubs,
phœnix palms, date-trees, as well as agaves (American
aloes) and mimosas. He counted up his customers, en-
larged on his chances of success, and gave the figure of his
monthly incomings, which he said he could certainly
improve in time. He was going to grow rich, or, anyway,
if he could not do that, one might live very well on what

he could make. He would send mimosa blooms to Paris
in winter, to say nothing of roses. Thérèse could stay a
while longer with the Prince, and then in two or three years'
time leave her place to live as mistress in her own house.

She smiled, and agreed to everything, but noticed he
had never once said the words she wanted to hear : " I
love you, dear ! and I admire you, oh ! so much ! " It had
not occurred to him.

When he had shown her all over his garden and pointed
out every detail, another long silence fell between them ;
then he repeated his original question in the same abrupt
phrase :

" And so ? "

" And so," she said, " why, yes ! . . . seeing I'm come
to it ! "

She laughed, and he broke into an answering peal.

" I came here," she added, " with my father's leave."

" Then you will really have me, Mademoiselle Thérèse ? "

" You look so good-natured ! " she told him, " and your
father is such a friend of mine."

With this Maurin appeared :

" Is all going well, children ? "

" Yes, we know each other's minds, father."

" The Princess is pleased with you, and the Prince
satisfied with his birds. I've just seen him, and he is giving
five hundred francs for the wedding. You must thank
him very kindly. They're waiting for you at your master's
now ; so off with you."

" Good-bye, Firmin."

" Good-bye, Thérèse."

" And is that the way you say good-bye, you ninnies ?
Come, kiss each other, nom de padisqui ! "

Firmin took Thérèse in his arms, and she offered no
opposition to his salute. . . .

" Your turn now," Maurin urged the girl ; " kiss him,
come ! "

She did not do this, but gave him a punch on the shoulder
with her doubled fist, and scampered away.

And so the engagement was hanselled.

" A marriage isn't a thing to be put off and put off," was Maurin's dictum. " What's postponed over long may come to nothing."

And within the fortnight the wedding took place. It was a festivity in which both Maurin's and Pastouré's handiwork was plainly evident.

One night the two of them drove away from the Cabanes Vieilles in the same cart that had borne Victorin's coffin to the cemetery. In it they had arranged two rows of chairs, tied with their backs to the sides of the wagon, while all along either side they had fastened pine-boughs, and branches of heath. Among the greenery they had stuck flowers, with which they had likewise decorated the shafts, the wheels, the horses' harness and even the whip-handle. On the road they gathered more still at the friendly farm-houses where they stopped to pick up the four groomsmen. At Saint-Raphaël they called for the *novi* (bridal pair), first Firmin, and then Thérèse. The latter came proudly out of her master's door dressed in her white wedding-dress, which she had made beautifully with her own hand. Moreover the kind Princess had condescended to cast an eye over the bride's costume before she left the house. . . .

In this fashion, seated in their garden on wheels, the eight chief actors, bride and bridegroom, Maurin and Pastouré, and the bridesmen, proceeded to the Mairie, and thence to the church.

" How imprudent ! " said the Deputy-Mayor, who married them, turning to Maurin. " Luckily the local gendarmes have no suspicion you are here. . . . You must get out of the place as soon as ever you can ! "

M. Rinal and M. Cabissol had expressed a wish to be present, and stood beside the brothers Pons, the two famous shots of the Estérel.

Maurin and Pastouré were wreathed in smiles, well pleased with the day's work.

To the latter someone remarked :

" You've married your boy very soon after your poor
brother's death, haven't you ? "

" My brother's right glad," he replied ; " and so is
Maurin's good mother there under the mould."

M. Rinal seized an opportunity as they were leaving
the Mairie to draw Maurin aside :

" Here's your daughter well married, Maurin," he said.
" I congratulate you, and I tell you it makes me happy.
Your little lad Bernard is working excellently too. Now
I have some small, very small savings, and no relatives.
They will be for him. Césariot is getting on well now. He
is pleased to come and see me, and he begins to understand
things. We will put him too above the most troublesome
of life's worries, and you will die a happy man, because
you deserve happiness."

Maurin gave M. Rinal a look of infinite gratitude. His
dog Hercules had not a gentler, more loving eye.

" M. Rinal," he said, " for men like you one would
fain live and die, one would follow you to the ends of the
earth. I can say no more, for I've never learnt how to
make speeches. . . ."

He thought a moment, then added :

" No, the world is not wicked, it is only stupid. Take
my case ; I can't tell what to say, and there's nothing I
can do for you ! . . . Ah ! if you were a doctor still in
practice, I would drive your carriage gladly. . . ."

M. Rinal pressed him in his arms.

Next day Pastouré and Maurin stripped their cart of its
decorations, and started off soberly on their way back to
the Cabanes Vieilles.

The gendarmes had received private information, and
set off an hour later in pursuit.

On the way Pastouré said to Maurin :

" Now I've space enough at the Cabanes ; there's room
for you. It's one of your houses."

" Houses are not safe places for me," said Maurin.
" Houses are mouse-traps a man sets for himself. All these
stupid *procès-verbaux* will keep the gendarmes on my track

for many a day yet. . . . I've just had a happy thought,
Pastouré. The fine weather's coming now, and I mean
to choose different spots in the Maures and build myself
in the tops of trees a number of *agachons*, or look-out platforms, carefully hidden away amongst the tallest foliage,
like those they make sometimes for shooting wood-pigeons.
There, in summer-time, I shall be able to spend a peaceable
night sometimes."

" Yes, and if they're out after squirrel, they'll pepper
you with shot."

" I'm not afraid. The squirrels will keep their distance
when I'm there."

" Well, I'll bear you company sometimes," said Pastouré, without expressing further surprise. " It'll feel
funny up aloft ! "

" I shall build the first of my hiding-holes somewhere
near your house, to see how things work out, and if we
find it fairly comfortable, I can then make some more in
other places."

" It's a quaint notion, just what I should have expected
you to think of, lad," was Pastouré's summing up.

Just then the cart was going uphill in a hollow way,
between high, echoing banks. The animals stopped to
recover breath, and the creaking of the wheels ceased.
In the sudden silence Maurin thought he heard a suspicious
noise. He turned swiftly, and caught a glimpse at the
bend of the road behind him of a gendarme's cap, which
vanished in all haste.

He signed to Pastouré to say nothing but restart the
horses. The latter was quick to guess what was wrong,
and promptly did as he was told.

Maurin slipped away noiselessly. On leaving Saint-
Raphaël he had put his boots in the cart-box and resumed
his *espadrillas*. Besides, the noise of the wheels drowned
that of the stones rattling and rolling under his feet. He
was already away and in the open when his tormentors,
who, to their undoing, had thought fit to call a halt and
lie low a bit to " mature their plans " instead of acting on

the spur of the moment, made up their minds to go on again.

Arrived at the spot where the cart had halted momentarily, one of them happened to lift his eyes and saw a sight that made him touch his comrade warningly on the arm. He said nothing, but pointed to Maurin climbing the steep hill-side above.

They reckoned up the chances of a successful capture in a man-hunt hereabouts. As the crow flies, Maurin was not above a hundred yards from them. But, unfortunately, they could not fly! The only practicable way of reaching the spot where he stood was to follow a long, roundabout, winding goat-path. A bee-line was out of the question.

The hill rose in a series of terraces, forming a sort of stairway, part natural, part artificial, one step being of the native rock, the next the result of human handiwork.

Without further hesitation the gendarmes sprang up the ascending pathway, which wound deviously in and out of rocks and gullies, and the chase began.

Maurin never lost sight of his pursuers, halting from time to time to crane over the rocks bordering the track like a parapet, and note his enemies' precise position.

A momentary bit of heedlessness made him lose ground. The track divided ; he took the wrong line and found himself in a cul-de-sac. When he got back again to the parting of the ways, he could hear one of the gendarmes, only twenty yards below him, say to the other :

" Let him have it now. I know the ground. I'll catch him by doubling back. We shall collar him on the other slope."

Maurin had been delayed and had almost lost heart. His only chance was to try and recover his advantage by sheer speed of foot, and he dashed on again. Three steps more and he swung round a clump of dwarf-oak, and suddenly found himself in the middle of a settlement of bees.

Some on the stony platform, some close up against the boundary wall of the rock, were thirty hives, each just a-rough section of the bark of a cork-oak stem, with thyme and rosemary in bloom all about. Already the denizens of this workmen's city were buzzing excitedly.

Maurin broke into a voiceless laugh. He threw both arms round one of the hives, lifted it, leant out over the precipitous drop at the foot of which the two gendarmes were holding a final consultation before separating, and dropped his fragile load plump on their heads. He heard a terrific oath. The hive had lighted on Sandri's back and opened out like a water-melon.

Smothered in wax and honey and bees, the gendarmes stood for a moment, struck motionless with amazement. A second, then a third, hive came and broke at their feet. Then the angry host of the offended insects swarmed round the unhappy representatives of public order, and set upon them and enveloped them. With a hundred unavailing oaths, the two victims tried to fly ; but how could they escape ? a whole population was in pursuit, buzzing round their heads and stinging their faces. The different swarms joined forces to punish the two villains whom they naturally concluded to be their enemies, for were they not carrying off their honey smeared all over their coats and coat-sleeves and hats. The fiercest individuals of these stinging hordes soon discovered the dark defiles of trouser-leg and coat-sleeve, and pushed their way in. . . . Meantime, down below, Parlo-Soulet, looking up, beheld the two officers dancing a wild jig together . . . while Maurin, on the hill-top above, was waving his hat gleefully in token of victory.

Then he vanished behind the hill.

At first Pastouré failed to account for the gendarmes' eccentric polka.

"They're dancing ! why, they're dancing ! " he shouted with a great laugh. " It can never be said they didn't dance for my son's wedding ! Oh ! look, look, how they're dancing ! But it don't seem natural somehow . . . What's the music they're tripping it to ? . . . Ah, ha ! I have it ! I understand ! he's smothered 'em in honey !

and the bees are making a fine music in their ears, to make
'em foot it ! . . . Good ! that one's lost his hat now ! . . .
Pick it up, man—if you can ! . . . Well, I never saw gendarmes dance to one another like this before out on the
hill-side ! So never you make fun any more, good folk,
if you see me, times and again, wave my arms about a bit
when I am talking to myself, all by myself, because here's
a sight a thousand times droller ! . . . A bees' quadrille,
with a couple of gendarmes doing *vis-à-vis* ! . . . Look,
now they're slapping their legs, as if they were bursting
with laughing ! . . . Ah ! no, I see how it is ; they're
hitting their legs to kill the bees, that's what they're after.
Now, advance partners ! . . . The best thing they can do
is to wind up with a grand gallop ! "

To complete the poor fellows' discomfiture, two great
regiments of clouds that had been drifting in opposite
directions for the last hour, now met and joined forces.
The united mass swept across the sky and piled itself up
to form a vault of dark, sullen vapour, hanging low above
the earth. Then the thunder-cloud burst, and poured
out a steady, drenching downpour as if from the rose of
some gigantic watering-can. This calmed the bees and
relieved the pain of the stings the men had received,
but at the same time it pretty well drowned the two
gallant minions of the law.

There was no house for miles round ; and they could
only retrace their steps to Roquebrune in this draggled
plight.

Unfortunately for Parlo-Soulet, the rain had not, like
Maurin's bee-hives, a special and particular reason for falling solely on the gendarmes. It drenched him too, with
entire impartiality.

Under these unpleasant circumstances, Pastouré departed from his usual custom and, though quite alone,
never opened his lips. He apostrophised neither the clouds,
nor the wind, nor the rain. Sitting tight on his shaft he
kept a stout heart against ill-fortune, and really seemed
insensible to the fury of the storm. It can only be sup-

posed that the gendarmes' ridiculous dance, Maurin's lucky
escape, and his son's happy marriage combined, had given
him strength to bear in unbroken silence the miseries of this
tempestuous evening.

The rain put out his pipe ; he put it away in his pocket.
The rain flooded the brim of his hat ; he took it off from
time to time, and emptied the water away. Then his hat-
brim turned to pulp, and poured gallons of water down his
neck and along his shivering spine ; he only shook himself
and wound a handkerchief round his throat. His new cloak
got so wringing wet it passed on its moisture to his jacket
underneath ; he took handfuls of straw, stuffed them under
this cloak, while he tied that garment tight over it with
string. His whip-lash was more sodden than a fishing-line,
and refused to act ; he put it down in the bottom of the
cart and began to whistle.

At last, after a two hours' drive beneath a continuous
deluge, he reached his own door. It was still raining, and
Parlo-Soulet was still obstinately silent.

He unharnessed in the rain, rubbed down his cattle,
horse and donkey, with a wisp of straw, then put himself
between the shafts and hauled his cart into shelter under a
shed. It poured all the time.

Finally, everything being properly arranged and shelter
for himself close at hand, Parlo-Soulet decided to let his
temper go and looked up askance at the heavens. Yes, up
there's where Fate sits enthroned. Anyway, it's plainly from
up there the rain comes down. So Parlo-Soulet fixed his
indignant gaze on " up there." He seemed to see with his
own eyes the Obstinacy of God that for hours had been
abusing his patience—his, Pastouré's, patience.

It was too much ; suddenly, leaving the shelter of his
cart-shed, he planted himself squarely under the still
dripping sky, beneath the mouths of the invisible water-
pots that were being emptied up there by the hand of the
unassailable and exasperating unknown power. . . . He
leant back, unbuttoned his jacket with both hands, threw
open his waistcoat and shirt, and offering his naked bosom

to the sky, he shouted his challenge of defiance to the
heavens :

"Ah ! if you want to drench me . . . then, drench me,
there ! *Mi vouas bagna ? eh, hé, té, bàgno-mi !*"

Maurin, who arrived presently by devious ways, found
him in this attitude. They dried themselves together
before a good fire of heath, while they amused each other
by telling sporting tales. Then they went off to bed, wishing all good wishes for their children's happiness.

And what stories did they tell ?

Some of the finest in the world ; but inasmuch as they
themselves repeated the same anecdotes over again a
short while after, we will wait, if you please, for this fresh
opportunity of hearing them.

CHAPTER XXVI

In which the King of the Maures makes Tonia think of the Three Musketeers,—who by the by, were always four.

THIS year, on the fête-day of the Patron Saint of his native town, Saint-Tropez, the 15th June, Maurin was to figure in the traditional processions as a *bravadeur*.

The *bravadeurs* of Saint-Tropez wear the costumes of Musketeers and Dragoons of the days of Louis XIV, some adopting one, some the other.

Such is the prestige of this solemnity, its character as a national institution is so venerable, so sanctified by tradition, that Maurin, Republican as he was, had never even considered the possibility of renouncing the honour and satisfaction of taking part in the customary display. Your true *bravadeur* plays his part without asking whys and wherefores ; he is above logic and above criticism.

Maurin seemed to have tired out the gendarmerie. They had forgotten him—or perhaps only pretended to have.

His most formidable enemy, Sandri, made no sign, and whenever Maurin played off some good prank on the officers of the law, those unfortunates, if no witnesses had chanced to be by, took excellent care to hold their tongues ! The story of the bee-hives had come under this category, and had been hushed up ; but the settled conviction remained that Maurin was untakable.

No doubt it was still the dream of Gendarmes and Gardes Champêtres to arrest the King of the Maures some day ; but for the present they were a trifle ashamed of themselves, and never alluded to the subject.

The general public, on the other hand, amplified and exaggerated the Maurin legend. . . . It wasn't ten times only the beggar had slipped through the gendarmes' fingers, but a hundred times ! . . . He was a wonder-worker ; some admirers came near believing him a wizard.

Well, one fine day in early June, Maurin was sitting quietly at the door of his hut in the plain of Cogolin going over his *bravadeur's* uniform, his musketeer dress in other words, which was an heirloom from his fathers, and threading his needle to sew on one or two loose buttons more securely, when a certain Terrasson, a friend of his and a " free-thinker," passed that way.

Pulling up and facing the other :

" *Oou !* " he began, " aren't you ashamed of yourself, Maurin, a Republican like you, to countenance these silly shows with your presence ;. and in that tom-fool's get-up ? I can see you're furbishing up your costume to appear as a musketeer in the procession. . . ."

Maurin had no liking for counsel or advice he had not sought—a feeling of repugnance closely connected with his native ideas of personal freedom and individual dignity. He pricked up his ears.

" *Oou !* " he cried, " here's a fine fellow very ready with his good advice ! I don't think I ever asked you, did I ? to say more than *good-day* when you go by my house ! By what right, sir, do you dare to talk to me in that strain ? "

" Aren't we both of us," protested Terrasson, " aren't we both of us members of the ' Free Thought Club ' ? "

" It was to think freely as *I* please," retorted Maurin, " and not to take your orders about it that I went there once, went to your Club ! . . . But Lord ! d'ye call that a Club ? Because you've stuck up over the door of your hovel, away there in the pine-woods of the Maures, a bit of a placard with the words ' Free-Thought Club ' in big letters, and because I went there once in a way to see what it was you were thinking over, you chaps inside, you four tom-tit and wren shooters that had got together, d'ye suppose that gives you any right to hinder me living as I choose ? "

" Are you turning *réac* (reactionary), Mòourin ? "

o

" What I say," pursued Maurin calmly, as he threaded
a needle, " what I say is you've spoilt a pretty little cottage ;
it's no bigger than my hand certainly, but still, it would
make a first-rate butt for shooting thrushes ! You've
spoilt it by scrawling up over the door a rigmarole you don't
understand a word of. Call yourself a *free-thinker*, when
you won't let me think as I please ! Why, there's not a soul
away yonder in the pine-woods to read your old placard—
except the thrushes and blackbirds, and they know more
about it than you do ; at any rate, they've sense enough
to make 'emselves scarce when you put your nose outside,
you pinchbeck sportsman, you ! "

" Come, come, Maurin, have you lost your wits, man ? "

" What it is you think about inside I've seen for myself,
for I went there once ! There was four of you there, of
whom four-and-a-half, counting me, could hardly read,
and we thought of nothing else whatever, I was there and
I know, but eating a dish of mushrooms and leveret, and
a leg of mutton and salad. I'll take my affidavit we never
thought of another blessed thing ! So go your ways, man,
and don't make me lose my temper. ' Free-Thought ' !
you'd find it a hard job to say what you mean by that, you
ass ! "

" It means," explained the other, " it means to think
the opposite of the Priests."

" A friend of mine, M. Rinal, who has more savvy in the
little toe of his left foot than you have in all your carcase,
told me this much. Free-thinkers are dullards who think
they're very clever, and try to expound how the world
managed to make itself all by itself, and how the first man
came without ever a mother, and the first egg without a hen
to lay it. And God's thunder strike me, if *I* can guess such
a complicated riddle ! So I just don't try, I should only
addle my brains ! I'd rather give it up, and rig myself out
as a Musketeer, if it gives me pleasure, and bang off my
blunderbuss at the Feast of Saint-Tropez, which is a
festival has come down from our ancestors, who were born
of women like you and me. It takes wiser chaps than you

and me to say if the Sun is or isn't the only God we've got.
I see no harm in taking my fun as my fathers did before
me, whether I'm singing the old songs, the ' Distaff ' and
the like, or making the powder speak. So now get out of
my sunlight, and let me thread my needle, my gallant
Free-thinker ! . . . No, but just look at the silly wiseacre !
He calls me names, calls me a *réac*, the noodle ! . . . All
the same, if they come attacking the Republic, the same as in
'51, my *bravadeur's* blunderbuss would defend it to the
death, let me tell you, while you—they'd clap the barrel of
your gun up your rear, and the new Emperor, blowing by
the breech, would puff you out like another ass of Gonfaron !
. . . Be off, or maybe my boot may find its own way to your
person ! "

" Come, Maurin, beg pardon ! I didn't mean to anger
you."

" Well and good ! " said Maurin, calming down instantly.

" Now, will you have a drink ? " he asked amicably—
and they clinked glasses.

" You're pretty quick to go off ! " observed Terrasson.

" Quick as a blunderbuss ! " laughed Maurin.

" On fête-days they go off of themselves—and don't you
forget it ! "

They shook hands, and Terrasson took his leave, saying :

" Good friends as ever, eh, Maurin ? "

" Yes, as long as you keep your place," answered Maurin,
as he returned indoors to finish his tailoring job in peace
and quietness.

A few minutes later there came a tapping at the door—
three little timid knocks. He threw it open :

" *Té !* why, it's you, Tonia ! "

" Yes, it's myself, dear Maurin. *Pauvre de moi !* I must
be deep in love."

" The deuce ! " he exclaimed. " How came you to
leave your father's house ? You must go back there, my
pretty Tonia. Life with me would be over hard for you.
Best remain as I said—forget me and marry someone
else."

" Maurin," she said earnestly, " I love you. How rash of you to be here in your own house ! "

" Well, I must be somewhere," said Maurin. " I've thought it over, and I reckon the last place where they'll expect to find me just now is at home. How are they to guess I'm no longer in hiding ? "

" *I* guessed it right enough," she said.

" *You* are different, Tonia, because you love me, you say. . . . Come, be a good girl and go back home."

" Why do you send me away ? "

Then, with a sudden access of jealousy :

" You're expecting another sweetheart ! '

" No, indeed I'm not ! But where does your father think you are ? "

" I told him I had things to buy at Cogolin, and he saw me into the diligence. I have one or two errands to do for him too."

" In that case you have a bit of time to spare," observed Maurin. " Well, now, you'd be a good girl, Tonia, if you'd just sew these buttons on for me."

" Why, whatever costume is that ? " she cried in sudden amazement when her eyes fell on the top-boots, sword, and plumed hat ! . . . " We're not in carnival time ! "

" Nor is it a fancy-dress," said Maurin in an offended tone. " It's my uniform as a *bravadeur*. . . . And," he added proudly, " it was my father's before me, and he had it from *his* fathers."

She picked up the needles and thread and began to sew.

Maurin watched her busy fingers and proceeded to explain to the best of his knowledge the ancient costume of the *Bravade*, that festival so dear to the men of Saint-Tropez.

It is a fancy costume with a long and venerable history of over two centuries and a half, which Maurin summed up in the phrase : " Yes, it comes down from our ancestors, long before automobiles were invented, in the days of King Herod." And no description could be truer, for, indeed, the tradition is connected with the name of Torpes

" who was cupbearer to the Emperor Nero ; as much as
to say, he poured out his liquor for him."

" And so," she remarked, spreading out the old costume
she was mending, " you'll be dressed like that ? "

" Yes, Tonia."

" Oh, Lord ! you *will* look droll ! "

" Why ? " he asked, with some annoyance.

" I should just love to see you ! "

" Come to the show with your father, and then you can
see me from a window."

" Oh ! I'll come for sure ! . . . It's a fine sight, is it ? "

" It's the finest fête in all our country of the Maures,"
asseverated Maurin, with deep conviction. " Why, they
burn as much as five hundred kilos of powder ! "

" That must make a fine noise ! "

" It's on purpose to make a noise ; that's the custom."

" But why kick up such a row ? "

" To do honour to the memory of our ancestors," explained Maurin in vigorous tones ; " for why ? they were
attacked, I tell you, hundreds of years ago, by one-and-
twenty galleys from Spain ! and they forced 'em to go
back to their own country. . . . And, you know, that day
I'm on horseback ! "

" You have a horse, Maurin ? "

" They have a stud here, you know. I was a horseman
from my cradle ; I can ride like the breeders themselves.
The folks hereabouts know what I can do, and they're
always glad to lend me a nag for me to show his paces in
the *Bravade*."

" Say, did your ancestors ride after the Spanish galleys
on horseback ? "

The question rather disconcerted Maurin.

" I never thought of that," he stammered. " In a sea-
fight, why, yes, there's no cavalry, of course. But, I suppose, they waited on the beach for the Spaniard fellows to
land. . . . I'll ask M. Rinal about it."

" There, your buttons are fast on again. Put the coat
on ; I want to see."

He obeyed, while the girl laughed merrily.

Yes, he was quite the Musketeer ! top-boots, breeches, slashed doublet, lace ruffles, rapier, and plumed hat, all were complete.

" I once read a book," she said, " full of pictures, and they always had three or four chaps dressed like that. . . ."

" They were soldiers of former days," Maurin told her ; this was the limit of his historical information.

" Only," Tonia pursued, " in the pictures, they all had moustaches and a pointed chin-tuft, and didn't wear a full beard like you ; you must shave, Maurin."

But the King of the Maures drew himself up, his hand on the pommel of his sword.

" My Arab beard," he cried, " no, I will never give that up ! A free man sticks true to his beard, and his beard sticks to him ! "

Thus accoutred, he looked odd, without being ridiculous. The dress suited him too well for that.

" It's getting late ; you must be going, Tonia "—and they bade each other good-bye.

In the long evening shadows it was the quaintest of spectacles, this group of a gay Musketeer of the Grand Monarque kissing farewell to a pretty girl of the Twentieth Century !

CHAPTER XXVII

Supplies authentic and official documents relative to that ancient and admirable, but pre-eminently noisy institution, the *Bravades of Saint-Tropez.*

EVERY year, on the fifteenth day of June, from early in the morning, is to be seen hung on the great door of the *Maison Commune* of Saint-Tropez a glazed frame exhibiting a copy of a municipal resolution of the said town, running to this effect :

" In the name of God, Amen ! The year one thousand, six hundred, thirty-seven, and the fifth day of July, in the Town Hall, in presence of Maître Honoré Marquès, Deputy Judge of the said town, met together the old and new Council, after the customary procedure, by sound of bell, blare of trumpet, and public proclamation, for to deliberate on the urgent businesses of the Community. In attendance the undernamed and in especial : Jacques Antiboul, François Fabrenand Antoine Augier, Consuls ; the Captain François Cocorel ; Maître Jacques Marquesy, Notary ; the Captain Abel Peyre ; Antoine-Martin d'Honoré, Merchant ; Barthélemi Aubert, Shopkeeper ; the Captain Charles Antiboul ; the Captain Jean Croust ; Balthazar Taurel ; André Gattus ; Joseph Cocorel ; the Noble Antoine Antibert ; Jean Augier ; the Captain Sébastien Martin ; the Noble Balthazar Raimondy, Co-Seigneur of Allons ; Honoré-Martin d'Antoine, Merchant ; and Jean Peyronnet, Shopkeeper.

" The Lords Consuls duly laid before the Council how that the Community and the inhabitants of Saint-Tropez have cause to render thanks to Almighty God for the grace and favour He did vouchsafe us, *the fifteenth day of the month of June* last, in the morning, by giving us the strength and puissance to defend ourselves against the

199

attack made upon us by one-and-twenty galleys of Spain, the which did fight us for three hours, or thereabouts. Whereafter, the Council was prayed of its graciousness to resolve and decree that in time to come that same day be kept a feast-day for the town, and a general procession be made thereon as a meet token of gratitude.

"The which Council, by common accord, did resolve that the Worshipful the Prior Antiboul be requested, an it please him, in consideration of the grace and favour Almighty God hath done us, the aforesaid fifteenth day of June last, by safeguarding us from the assault of the Spaniards, of his kindness to arrange, whenas it seemeth to him best, a general procession to the honour of Saint Tropez, our Patron and Protector ; and that in time to come, for all years and on the same fifteenth day of June, anniversary of the aforesaid attack, shall be held a like general procession in token of gratitude.

"*Signed :* MARQUÈS, Judge's Deputy,
ANTIBOUL-SENGLAS, Clerk of the Council."

On June 24, 1558, there was appointed at Saint-Tropez, with the title of Captain of the Town, an Officer to take general command ; he was entrusted, in the terms of the Municipal resolution, with the duty of safeguarding the town by day and night against enemies ; powers were assigned him to enrol such men as were needful for the defence, to put the artillery on a proper footing, *to buy powder* for the bombards, as also for the smaller arms, to enforce his orders on every man to keep his weapons in order, and so forth.

In 1562, his powers were re-enacted, and the Municipal Council confers on him the additional right to " enrol all the men he deems needful for maintaining the watch, to go against the Turks and the enemies of our Lord the King, of the Country and the aforesaid town."

We read in the " Life " of Saint-Tropez, as told by the Abbé Espitalier (Saint-Tropez, 1876) :

" The powers which had been accorded him (the Captain of the Town) by the said township of Saint-Tropez were

confirmed by letters patent of all the French Kings, down
to Louis XIV.

"But under the reign of that powerful Monarch, standing
armies having been created, the inhabitants were no longer
held bound to obligatory and regular military service ;
the defence of the town was *committed to the King's soldiers*
in garrison in the Citadel ; and the Captain of the Town
lost the authority he had hitherto exercised.

"But, *while ceasing to employ their arms for the defence
of their town, the men of Saint-Tropez still kept them in
possession to honour their Patron Saint. The Captain
of the Town*, accompanied by the Major and Ensign,
*continued to put himself at the head of the ' Bravade ' or
Procession*, and the inhabitants, robbed of their erstwhile
military prestige, *were only the more zealous* to resume, on
the fête-day of their Saint, *the costume* and the weapons
they had once boasted."

Alas ! there are occasions when the Captain of the Town
fails to appear at the *Bravade* at all ! . . . Then, in 1759,
the Municipal Council decides that henceforward the Captain of the Town shall every year be presented with a
silver sword, on the express stipulation that he put himself
personally at the head of the procession on the fête-day.

Later on, the silver sword, weighing a hundred pounds,
is replaced by a pike of honour, "not so costly."

The Captain of the Town is appointed by the Municipal
Council every year, on the Monday of Easter Week ; he
receives special powers, the pike, and three hundred francs
to cover expenses. It is only since 1806 that the pike
has superseded the sword.

Here, according to the *Guide de la Bravade*, by MM.
Lally and Condroyer (Saint-Tropez, 1888), is the cere-
monial attending the appointment of the Captain of the
Town :

"On Easter Monday, so soon as the Municipal Council
has chosen the Captain of the Town, a deputation of three
Members of the Council repairs immediately to the residence
of the individual appointed, to inform him of the good news.

The latter, if he accepts office, at once presents himself before the Council, which then nominates him officially.

"The Mayor presents himself with the newly-elected officer on the steps of the Hôtel-de-Ville before the assembled population. The drums roll and beat to quarters. Then the Mayor proclaims the Captain of the Town.

"A volley of musketry, followed by another roll of the drums, accompanies the approving cheers of the people. On the same occasion the Captain of the Town, escorted by the Mayor, Deputy-Mayors, and Municipal Councillors, marches in triumph through the main streets of the town, at the quick step, to the sound of the drum and more volleys of musketry, finally returning to his own house.

"The custom is for the vesper bells to defer ringing till the Captain of the Town has reached home.

"From that day forth, the supreme direction of the festivities, *with all its expenses*, falls upon the Captain of the Town.

"*The Sports and pastimes are at his discretion;* he regulates their order and combinations. . . .

"On May 16, the *joys* (prizes—trophies, scarfs, cups, etc., etc.) are carried round the town, suspended from a horizontal hoop attached to the end of a staff. The drums salute all the Civil and Religious authorities in succession, all the Functionaries of the State, the Officers of the *Bravade* and their Ensign, as well as the Staff of the previous year.

"At three o'clock, the Captain of the Town, with his Staff, and all his escort, repairs to the Place in front of the Mairie, where he is to come to a halt right in front of the Maison Lavagne, forming the angle of the Rue Sainte-Anne.

BESTOWAL OF THE PIKE AND OF THE FLAG.

"When the Mayor, wearing his official scarf and the pike in his hand, appears on the threshold of the Mairie, the Major gives the word ' Drums ! ' and orders them to beat to quarters.

"By *beating to quarters* is signified the march of the Captain of the Town, by *beating to the flag*, that of the Ensign. These ceremonial marches are derived from our ancestors.

"The Captain of the Town and his Major advance and take

position in front of the Mayor. The Major then steps forward alone, and at three paces distance, salutes that dignitary with his sword.

" After returning it to the scabbard, he takes the pike, which the Mayor hands him, retires three paces, and turning to his left, advances towards the Captain, halts three paces in front of him, to receive his salute, and passes him the pike, which he salutes in his turn. After lining up with the Captain of the Town, he moves with him towards the Mayor.

" At a corresponding distance, the Captain of the Town, leaving his Major in the rear, steps forward majestically by himself towards the Mayor and executes in his honour his first traditional salute, which is followed by a general volley of musketry.

" The Major advances in turn, salutes the Mayor with his sword, and returns with the Captain of the Town to resume his original position.

The excellent *Guide de la Bravade*, whence these particulars are taken, gives, with illustrative plates, " the ten several salutes demanded of the Captain of the Town. Number 1 is for the Saint exclusively."

" The dispositions are identical," adds the *Guide*, " for the bestowal of the flag as for that of the pike."

" This ceremony completed, the Mayor gives the word for the march past.

" The newly embodied corps always go by after the *Musketeers*, who form the *bodyguard* of the Captain of the Town.

" The march past takes place before the Mayor and ends at the lower extremity of the Place, where each corps takes up its proper position. The Captain of the Town, his Staff on his left, occupies the centre of the Place, having the Rue Blanche on his right.

" When all are placed, the Major steps out and goes to inform the Clergy that the whole body of *Bravadeurs* is assembled ready to receive the benediction of arms, and this done, returns to his post.

" The Clergy, cross in front, and escorted by the Saint's retinue, marches into the Place by way of the Rue de

l'Horloge. As the procession files in, the Major orders
his men to port and present arms.

" He stands beside the celebrant priest throughout the
ceremony.

" The prayers ended, he orders a general volley.

" For some years past ships of war have put into the
harbour of Saint-Tropez to salute the Saint as his procession
goes by."

These extracts give an excellent idea of the ceremonial
attending the festival of the *Bravade*. But no description,
verbal or written, can do justice to the extraordinary,
the unparalleled spectacle presented by the town of Saint-
Tropez at the time of its annual fête. The imagination
is powerless to picture certain aspects, if one has not seen
them ; the memory fails to represent them adequately,
even when one has.

Nothing is more touching than the veneration and love
the town feels for its time-honoured legend.

Unfortunately for Maurin and for Saint-Tropez, the
dignity of the ceremonial was to be marred this year by a
ludicrous incident.

It was the 15th June, 19—. The Captain of the
Town, Souventy, a friend of Maurin's, had already twice
occupied the exalted position, the duties of which he
fulfilled to everyone's satisfaction. He was to carry out
the return of the pike and flag the same evening, with the
usual ceremonies accompanying its bestowal. Maurin
was proud to address a word now and again from his saddle
to his friend Souventy ; for the office of Captain of the
Town confers a real and not insignificant distinction on its
holder, as we have read above, and as another circumstance
will show, viz., the fact that on Corpus Christi Day, the
Captain of the Town takes precedence of the Mayor.
He it is holds the first cord of the canopy, a privilege
to which the Mayor in person cannot aspire. Souventy
wore an admiral's laced coat and a hat with a white
feather. The Captain of the Town, five-and-twenty years
ago, used sometimes to wear the complete suit of armour

of the Montmorencys, which the town of Draguignan possesses, and which it lent to its sister town of Saint-Tropez. But as the result of many appearances at the festivities, it was getting spoiled and disfigured with scratches and dents. . . . Draguignan has had the joints of the leg and arm-pieces re-riveted, and now keeps its treasure jealously locked up in the local museum.

It was a strange sight to see Souventy in the uniform of a modern Admiral, and surrounded by his bodyguard of Musketeers, some on foot, some mounted, to the number of a hundred or so.

Souventy was a past master in the art of wielding the pike with elegance and dexterity. Every movement of that weapon demands a long and laborious apprenticeship. But Souventy was a faithful servant of tradition, and a true captain of men, one of those who can command obedience because they have first learnt how to obey. It was a pleasure to see him salute those to whom it was his duty to pay homage.

Now he would raise his pike above his dead—a twirl in the air—then steady on the shoulder ! Now he would present it with the left hand, the right on the seam of the trousers ; then reverse point to the ground, " present, then steady on the fingers of the left."

Beside the mounted Musketeers danced the *chivaous-frux* (or hobby-horses) under the guidance of the lads of Lougeon. These, as everybody knows, are horses made of cardboard, the flowing housings of which hide the legs of the rider who manages them and puts them through their paces, making them gallop and caracole, leap and rear.

The Musketeers bore themselves proudly, and really looked well when they pranced along, Maurin in front, on their Provençal thoroughbreds with their beribboned trappings.

All these Musketeers, as well as the newly enrolled *Corps de Bravades*, are armed not with muskets, but with blunderbusses, tremendous-looking weapons, the muzzle of which opens out like the mouth of a hunting-horn, and

which the town of Saint-Etienne manufactures specially
" for consumption in the town of Saint-Tropez."

From time to time, at a sign from the pike, the Saint's
retinue drop their blunderbusses on their fore-arms,
the enormous mouths pointing obliquely to the ground.
Another signal, and twenty blunderbusses, loaded to the
muzzle, simultaneously vomit fire and flame.

Hardly has the thunder died away ere another *corps de
bravade* follows suit. . . . Already the first have reloaded
. . . and it is a never-ending crash ! crash ! of fire-arms,
so well kept up, so well timed all together, that each dis-
charge seems the single explosion of one gigantic field-
piece, one Titanic cannon.

The *bravadeurs* follow the prearranged route, halting
every ten minutes for fresh, and ever fresh salvoes. The
smoke envelops the whole town. The smell of saltpetre,
mixed with the fumes of incense, intoxicates the entire
population. Everybody is at the windows or in the streets.

The town trembles, the walls, the very ground shakes.
If a well-known citizen appears, or a stranger, to be honoured or terrified, at a given signal he is surrounded by a
body of *bravadeurs*. They form a complete circle round
him, of which he is the centre, with a radius of barely four
paces. Blunderbusses are lowered, and only wait for
another signal. Then follows the tremendous uproar of
thirty pieces going off all together—bang ! The earth
seems to open ! Thirty gaping mouths strike the ground
with their sulphurous breath, and the pebbles fly, peppering
the face of the unfortunate in whose honour the salute is
fired ! Neglecting to stuff their ears with huge plugs of
wadding, *bravadeurs* have been known to have been
deafened for life. . . . Vesuvius in eruption is not so fierce
and furious. Never a year passes but a woman's skirts
catch fire on this 15th June at Saint-Tropez, and require
the firemen's help.

Anyone who should try to escape these compliments
of the *bravadeurs* would be regarded, very rightly, as a
discourteous boor ; and besides, it would be quite im-

possible to get away. The Musketeers encircle the citizen
they propose to honour; he is a prisoner within a ring of
iron and flame . . . and bang! bang! the lightning and
thunder salute him to the grave danger of life and limb.

Sometimes a *bravadeur* darts out of the ranks, pushes
his way into the passage of a friend's house, and there . . .
bang! . . . his weapon roars and spits fire! . . . The
panes of staircase windows crash down in fragments—
unless the householders have taken the precaution of
opening doors and windows beforehand.

Hour after hour these bangs and crashes, these rolling
discharges and booming explosions, these roarings and
thunderings and bombardings, all this unprecedented,
incredible, inconceivable uproar goes on, setting nerves
quivering, blood galloping, and hearts palpitating. From
minute to minute the whole town grows more frenzied,
more intoxicated with the acrid scent of gunpowder, the
rhythmic repetition of volleys, the vision and the memory
of ancestors and their crusades and their battles against the
Spaniard and the Turk, and their fights with the Saracen,
of whose blood, nevertheless, every native of the Var has
an inherited drop or two running in his veins.

And away yonder, the Mountains of the Maures, Maurin's
fatherland, tiptoeing on their bases all they can, gaze down
at Saint-Tropez over the Gulf of Grimaud. La Garde-
Freïnet is all alert, and every eagle's eyrie, where the
victorious Saracens rested for so long, recognises in the
mighty voice of the *bravades*, that dominates the roar of
waves and wind, the very voice incarnate of their past,
the challenge of their history, something like an appeal
of race and blood, recalling far-off centuries of blood and
slaughter, of doughty deeds and desperate onslaughts,
of victory and triumph, of joy and terror, of glory and
disaster—all vanished into the limbo of futility!

CHAPTER XXVIII

Of the incredible yet veracious circumstances of the quarrel between the two rival brass bands of Bourtoulaïgue, which ended in a battle royal, and how Maurin and Pastouré, finding themselves involved in the deplorable scrimmage, got honourably out of their difficulties, after the latter had borrowed a clarinet from a bandsman and lent it to a horse.

THE worthy Parlo-Soulet all along foresaw the likelihood of trouble arising out of Maurin's presence at the fêtes of Saint-Tropez—and this in spite of the supposed inviolability of the *bravadeurs*.

François the mattress-maker warned him : " There are ugly rumours afloat ; they're talking of concentrating all the brigades of the district of the Maures upon Saint-Tropez to take some decisive step against the poacher ; detachments are for ever to be seen moving on the roads and exchanging information." In a word, François was decidedly of the opinion that Maurin would have done better this year not to attend his favourite fête.

But Maurin had too keen an appreciation of what is due to national traditions, too fond a feeling of instinctive respect for the past, father of the present, to give up his part of the *bravadeur*.

Tonia had heard nothing of any disquieting reports. She was eager to see the famous festival, and Orsini, not knowing that Maurin would be at Saint-Tropez, accompanied his daughter thither. He was as curious as she was to witness the celebrated *bravade*, and both secured places in a first-floor window, on the Quay, at the house of one of Orsini's friends.

The procession was filing past. . . .

Parlo-Soulet, as a mounted Dragoon, kept circling round the troop of *bravadeurs*, in the guise of a scout, a real scout—ready to warn Maurin at any moment : " Look out, the enemy's coming ! "

He had mentioned his fears to the Captain of the Town, who reassured him :

" The gendarmes will never dare to stir up such a scandal. If they touched a *bravadeur* under arms, the town would rise to a man, and something serious would follow. No, they will never dare, believe me, except some incident should authorise their interference; but there will be no untoward incident. . . ."

The procession advanced slowly, from time to time saluting the Saint, borne along on his litter, then greeting with a volley the notables on their balconies, or such as they met in the streets and instantly surrounded and subjected to the terrible ordeal above described.

It was a quaint figure of the Saint which his devotees carried ! Saint Tropez, a body without a head, lies full length in a boat, as if in a coffin, while his head rests beside him. A dog sits and guards his corpse, and a cock, perched on the gunwale, looks on. . . .

Every time the Saint's retinue honoured the sacred image with a well-sustained volley, the drums rolled and the brass blared simultaneously.

Two bands, this year, had been given permission to take turns in playing their finest pieces. They brought up the tail of the procession, and were only to strike up, of course, when the Captain of the Town gave the word.

Both these sets of musicians belonged to one and the same commune, Bourtoulaïgue, near Saint-Tropez, with a population of some six hundred males all told.

Two brass bands for something like twelve hundred people is surely excessive. A few years before this Bourtoulaïgue had possessed only one, boasting the name of the *Gloire de l'Harmonie*. But the leader of the *Gloire de l'Harmonie*, holding Republican views with certain qualifications, and having thought fit to offer himself as a

P

candidate at the Municipal elections, the stalwarts whose
Republican opinions were *un*qualified, had turned the
tables by establishing a rival Musical Society of their own.
And thus the *Victoire de la Symphonie* came into existence—
harmony out of discord.

Not a soul at Bourtoulaïgue, or in all France, could see
the smallest use in having a second band, but anger and
animosity make men blind, and often drive them to do
ill-considered things. This accounts for the fact that
Bourtoulaïgue now possessed two several bands for the
delectation of twelve hundred people, say a hundred and
twenty performers, say, approximately, one bandsman for
every six male inhabitants.

The two associations, as might be expected, were per-
petually quarrelling. While the *Gloire de l'Harmonie*
took its vermouth at one café, the *Victoire de la Symphonie*
consumed its absinthe at another. The result was that
the two landlords, who were brothers, had a deadly quarrel,
and henceforth they had but one object in life, at least
they said so, to eat one another's liver.

Whenever the *Symphonie* asked the Mayor's permission
to play in the public square of Bourtoulaïgue at a given
hour, the *Harmonie* was instantly taken with a morbid
and imperious craving to perform precisely at the same
hour and the same place. The population, already divided
by the thousand and one petty bits of gossip that form the
staple of village talk, was henceforward cruelly torn in
two by the bitter rivalry of the two factions.

We must go back in the history of France to the Hundred
Years' War and the struggles of Armagnacs and Bur-
gundians, to find so fierce a hate as now animated one
against the other the two brass bands of Bourtoulaïgue,
in the Department of the Var.

One of the two Bourtoulaïgue bakers having died, his
shop remained closed for some time. He had been
attached to the *Symphonie*, and that Society immediately
asked itself the question : should they establish a special
bakery, all their own, or should they import their daily

bread every day, on mule-back or by boat, from Saint-Tropez ?

The latter scheme carried the day at the general meeting. Honorary members and active members all voted with one voice that the baker who kneaded the *Harmonie's* bread must be put on the index, boycotted. It was resolved that the trombone, who was a fisherman by trade, should go every day to Saint-Tropez in his boat to fetch the *Symphonie's* supplies of bread.

" And when am I to go fishing ? " asked the man.

" You needn't go any more," he was told ; " we appoint you our Superintendent of Provisions. The *Symphonie* will pay you for your work ; we shall merely have to increase the contributions of our honorary members."

This meant, in times of tempest, exposing themselves to the risk of famine ; but nothing is more provocative of heroism than pique and music, combined together and each exacerbating the other.

This became manifest before long. A terrible *mistral* blew, and for six days kept the boats of Bourtoulaïgue wind-bound in the little harbour. The members of the *Symphonie* were like to perish to a man for lack of a crust of bread to gnaw. The first day not one visited the rival bakery to buy a single loaf. A fine, a noble example of stoicism—had it only been in a better cause !

Not a bandsman faltered. On the second day the *Symphonie*, transformed into a Choral Society, paraded the streets of Bourtoulaïgue, singing :

Mourir pour la Symphonie
Est le but le plus beau, le plus digne d'envie ! [1]

Happily the women proved less obstinate than the men. To feed their children, they consented to buy bread in their native village at the *Harmonie* bakery.

The baker at first refused to sell them any ; but M. Cabissol, hearing of what was happening at Bourtoulaïgue,

[1] To die for the *Symphonie* is the noblest fate and the most enviable !

had hurried to the spot to study the phenomenon; he telegraphed to the Préfet, who telegraphed to the Mayor, and the *Harmonie* was forced to feed the *Symphonie!*

This disgraceful pusillanimity on the part of wives and mothers exposed the members of the *Symphonie* to the scorn and insolence of the *Harmoniens*. The latter sneered audibly at the sight of one of their rivals in the street. It was a plot, that was evident. The instant they set eyes on a *Symphonien*, they made a show of chewing something, then rubbing their stomachs with an assumption of gastronomic enjoyment—an unpardonable allusion to the torments of hunger their enemies had had to undergo.

The bravest member of the *Symphonie*, a bachelor, had fasted two whole days. He upbraided the others with their weakness. They lost their tempers. He gave in his resignation . . . and immediately offered himself and was accepted as a member of the *Harmonie*.

The Minister of the Interior was informed, and the commune kept under observation. This state of things could not go on. For the 14th July (Republican fête), the Préfet required the two rival organisations to join forces and play together the piece of music always performed on that morning in the Mayor's honour. The two bands protested, and only yielded under threat of being *dis*banded. But the authorities had forgotten to mention what piece of music was to be played under the Mayor's windows, with the result that they attacked simultaneously, the one contingent the *Marseillaise*, and the other the *Bourtoulaïguoise*, a war-song composed by the leader of the *Symphonie*.

" We must combine the two bands into one," opined the *Receveur Buraliste*, " and call them the *Triomphe de la Cacophonie* " (Triumph of Discord).

The Mayor felt like going mad. No marriages were contracted any more except between partisans of the same factions. Now the Mayor was a doctor, and maintained that judicious crossing is the only hope of degenerate races.

Things were in this condition when the fête-day of

Saint-Tropez arrived. But the Captain of the Town had one brother-in-law in the *Harmonie* at Bourtoulaïgue, and another brother-in-law in the *Symphonie.*

Consequently he sent a message to both the two bands, to say that he counted on their common devotion and veneration for Saint Tropez, once martyred ; that they must both forget their differences provisionally, at any rate outside the borders of Bourtoulaïgue ; and that they might both of them take part in the procession, if they promised to behave sensibly and play one after the other—" for you know," he added, " the sun shines for everybody."

The two associations agreed. . . . But, alas ! the smell of powder is suggestive. Compelled for hours to carry their silent instruments about with them tucked under their arms while the guns spoke, the two bands grew more and more impatient. Every bandsman burned with the desire to be heard and admired and applauded. They made wry faces at one another, standing there so peaceably amidst the exciting hurly-burly of war ! They stamped and swore, ashamed of their inactivity, while the thunder of battle was roaring round them ! At each crash of artillery the musicians all gazed sadly at the bell-mouths of their cornets and bugles, and bitterly regretted their trombones were not *tromblons* (blunderbusses).

The story is familiar which tells how the great Saint Tropez was beheaded at Pisa, and his headless trunk laid in a ship along with a dog and a cock—and so launched from the shore, and how Providence brought the vessel ashore at the place to which the Saint has given his name.

The group of carved wood, carried on men's shoulders, and representing the Saint, the dog and the cock in the boat, rose high above the countless heads of the crowd. This awe-inspiring image alone kept the rival bands in restraint. One of the big drums was heard to mutter : ' Ah ! if only the Saint wasn't there ! "

But the Saint *was* there, and called for proper respect.

In due course the procession reached the Quay where the statue of the Bailli de Suffren stands, and right before the

window where Tonia was seated beside her father, looking
with all her eyes at the imposing ceremony.

In the Square below everyone fell into his proper place,
each *corps de bravade* taking up the assigned station.　For
the two bands, these were lined up, one to the right, the
other to the left, of the Great Admiral's statue, face to the
sea, back to the houses.

Maurin, the gallant Musketeer, was just raising his
sword to the salute in honour of his fair lady at the window,
making his horse prance and curvet the while, when suddenly Parlo-Soulet, Dragoon and scout, rode up and
whispered a word in his ear:

"Have a care, Maurin!　I scent a trick of Sandri's.
The Saint-Tropez men won't dare to budge; but the
gendarmes I see coming in yonder are not from Saint-
Tropez.　They won't be afraid of scandalising the towns-
folk.　Keep your eye open!"

"Where are they?"

"There, at the end of the street the tail of the procession is just coming to.　There'll be others, perhaps,
guarding the other roads, and so you'll be caught like a rat
in a trap, my poor lad!"

"Not I," said Maurin, with a wide wave of the hand;
"the sea is free; I shall jump into a boat, if needs must,
or even plunge in and swim my horse"—and then—bang!
bang! calm and composed on his plunging horse, once,
twice, he fired off a brace of blunderbusses.

The frightened horses of the Musketeers reared and
wheeled at each report.

As a rule the mounted men do not carry blunderbusses;
to make up for it, most of the footmen—in top-boots, and,
nowadays, wearing a costume pretty closely modelled on
that of Napoleon's veterans, with the figure of the great
Saint Tropez painted on their caps—have at least two of
these weapons apiece.　Directly they have discharged one
their attendant hands them another, and proceeds at once
to reload the first.

To carry a blunderbuss on horseback was a whim of

Maurin's, a bit of audacity, a piece of bravado in the *bravade*. Maurin had three attendant squires and three blunderbusses . . . and bang ! bang ! bang !

To return to the two rival bands, each of these deemed itself represented by its leader, indeed, in a way, incarnated in his personality. Alas ! it was only too likely the two leaders would end by getting into a dispute ! And what a place for a quarrel—there, on the open Quay, in a strange but friendly town, in presence of the Bailli de Suffren and the great Saint Tropez !

Amidst the deafening thunders of the volleys they exchanged the most biting invectives, though no one could make out what they said. Like two Homeric heroes, they bandied "winged words" to and fro, their voices sounding shrill and harsh between two salvoes. Excited by the smell of powder, they presently strode forward to the fray, their leader's baton brandished menacingly in each other's faces !

In a moment, urged by irresistible impulse, driven by overmastering fate, the two bands met in a wild, confused mêlée, each man selecting in the rival ranks his own pet aversion. Insults hurtled in the air. In vain the Captain of the Town signed to his Musketeers to make a diversion by moving between the two opposing forces. Too late ! the two ophicleides were already at grips. It was the signal for a general engagement.

The two armies flew at each other, whirling their instruments furiously above their heads like battle-axes—fragile, yet formidable weapons.

At every window along the Quay women stretched despairing hands to heaven, supplicating divine succour—in vain ! . . .

Then, from the extremity of the Place, up rode the gendarmes at the trot !

" Run, Maurin, run ! " cried Pastouré the Dragoon.

" Not yet ! " replied Maurin the bold Musketeer ; and discharged a defiant blunderbuss . . . bang !

The explosion roused the other *bravadeurs*, who had been

struck motionless and dumb for a moment by surprise
and curiosity. Then thirty guns went off in one tremendous bang !

"We call upon the Clergy to withdraw," a gendarme
said, addressing the Curé. "Things are looking ugly."

Hastily, to avoid the sight of a battle that promised to
be bloody, worthy of the cruel days of Nero, the Priests
tucked up their *soutanes* and took to their heels, while
the Saint's bearers, imposing in their purple gowns, put
down their burden and gallantly formed square round
their Patron.

Maurin and Pastouré were still separated from the gendarmes by the two brass bands, that is to say, by a tangled,
inextricable, struggling mass of two hundred and forty
warriors !

"Stop fighting, bandsmen ! you are violating every duty,
breaking all your promises ! " cried a loud commanding
voice, that strove ineffectually to dominate the hurly-
burly. It was the Captain of the Town, waving aloft
with his arm that glittered in its rich embroideries his
pike of office, once so implicitly obeyed. . . .

There was a momentary hesitation among the combatants. The tumult seemed to slacken. The Captain of
the Town went on :

"*I* am the only one to give orders here,—the only one,
I say, and don't forget it ! . . . I beg, I beseech you,
gendarmes, not to interfere, or I cannot answer for the
consequences. My authority must suffice ; I represent
a tradition there is no disputing ; for centuries it has not
been violated ! Come, enough ! let *Harmoniens* and
Symphoniens separate at my command, and profit by the
occasion to combine henceforth in one single, one undivided
musical society. True, that would be a miracle, but it
would not be the first we should owe to the great Saint
Tropez."

As he spoke, the Captain waved his pike involuntarily.
The *bravadeurs* thought he was ordering a volley . . . and
bang ! went fifty guns as one !

"That's it, a salute, *bravadeurs !* " he shouted, cleverly turning the accident to profit and hoping to disarm by his eloquence the fury of the two hesitáting bands, and change the wavering purpose of the gendarmes ; " that's it ! a salute in honour of the twin bands of Bourtoulaïgue ! Surround them ! ring them in ! and now another salute ! "— and again he waved his pike.

Instantly the two companies of musicians were penned in by the combined forces of all the *Corps de Bravades* . . . and bang ! . . . the whole town might have been flying skywards, blown to atoms by an exploding powder magazine ! . . .

The effect was disastrous ! sundry pebbles, driven before the all-compelling breath of the firearms, struck the faces of the músicians, who were still facing one another and exchanging insults amid the uproar. The unexpected impact let loose again the fury that was half assuaged. The powder seemed in literal fact to fire their passions. . . . And the pistons, the bugles, the trombones, the saxophones, began a veritable devil's dance ! Oboes, ophicleides, hunting-horns rose and fell, rose and fell like so many tomahawks. . . . The hurly-burly was beyond description. Clubs at first, next moment bucklers, the brass instruments beat and pounded against each other ; some slipped from the grasp of the combatants, who stooped hurriedly and groped about to recover them, and were instantly sent sprawling in the mud, where they wallowed half suffocated. Neither mounted Musketeers nor gendarmes durst push into the press for fear of injuring the exasperated musicians or the lads of Longeon, who, riding their *chivaous-frux* (hobby-horses) and entangled in their flowing housings and paste-board framework, tried in vain to escape ; while not a few toppled over with a yell, their four hoofs tossing wildly in the air !

Seated at her window, Tonia displayed the light-hearted gaiety of her quick, excitable temperament. " Good Lord ! how funny they all are ! " she burst out, clapping her hands, and laughing loudly to see so fine a battle.

At this moment Pastouré caught sight of the gendarme Alessandri, who, sitting very straight in his saddle on a very tall horse, was manœuvring to get Maurin between two groups of police.

"*Gueiro, Móourin!* Look out, Maurin! Mark!"

"Let me be!" Maurin called back. "I've got my eye on him all right."

Sandri was just upon him ; but at the very instant one of the musicians in the mêlée swung his hunting-horn high in the air, evidently meaning to bring it down crash ! on the skull of an enemy, Maurin snatched the instrument from the man's hand, clapped it to his lips, and, still calmly bestriding his fiery charger, blew a discordant blast, so sudden and so terrific, that Sandri's mount, now close to his own, shied, stumbled, lost its footing all four legs at once, and rolled over . . . sending the handsome gendarme sprawling a dozen yards away.

In a jiffy Sandri was up again, had dragged his horse to its feet and sprung again into the saddle, for he had caught sight of Tonia up there at the window laughing like a mad-woman !

Pulling his beast together, he drove in his spurs savagely. The animal, frightened and furious, cocked up his stump of a tail proudly in the air.

But Pastouré, Pastouré the Dragoon, was watching. He caught a clarinet in the air as the instrument went whirling past, sent flying by a blow from one of the big-drum sticks, and quick as lightning leapt from his horse and shoved the aforesaid reed instrument well in under Sandri's horse's tail, laughing lightly as he did the trick :

"Who knows ? perhaps he'll fly away !"

And he did fly—at least that's what they say. He sprang into the air, as if he had had wings.

Resenting at once the bitter outrage to his pride and the deep hurt to his posterior, dropping his tail erstwhile borne so haughtily, chafing at the feel of this artificial tail he could not even guess the nature of, thinking confusedly, amid the roar of battle, that he had been wounded, wounded

to the death by some savage lance-thrust, the noble animal
bolted helter-skelter. Then, seeing the wide, cool sea
spreading before his fevered eyes, he bounded into the
waves, carrying his rider with him, who exhausted himself
in ludicrous but entirely ineffectual struggles to hold him.
Poor, unhappy beast! the pain he hoped to escape
followed him with dire persistency! Straight before him,
without ever a thought of the despair and shame of his
master, he swam on and on in an undeviating line, as if
magnetised by the opposite shore! . . . On he swam,
cleaving the blue waters of the Gulf.

Pastouré gazed after him pityingly :
" Poor devil ! " he said. " *Pechère !* he'll go on like
that till he gets to Sainte-Maxime ! . . . He thinks all
the while he's going to drop it on the road (*it* meant his
clarinet). He wants to leave it behind ; that's what
makes him tear along at that rate . . . but I don't think
he'll get rid of the thing. It sticks too tight for that ! "

" A horse, a horse, my kingdom for a horse ! " was
Richard III's despairing cry when he found himself dismounted on Bosworth Field. But Pastouré was a happier
monarch ; he had nothing more to do but swing himself
heavily back into the saddle.

" Victory ! " shouted Maurin, waving his plumed hat
in salute to the fair Tonia, who sat there laughing on the
balcony.

" Well, now we've won the day," observed Pastouré
to his chief, " we'd better be going. . . ."

Maurin handed him one of the blunderbusses, and the
pair, threading their way through the tortuous streets and
making a clever short cut, struck into the high road that
winds round the Gulf of Saint-Tropez and leads to Cogolin.

Meantime, if we are to credit the legend, Sandri's horse,
still swimming and still carrying its rider, was nearing the
beach of Sainte-Maxime, a delightful little place that faces
from across the Gulf the proud town of Saint-Tropez.

The men at the signal-station of Sardinaux, which
lies above Sainte-Maxime, fixed their telescopes on the

strange object they could see down yonder moving across the tranquil surface of the bay.

"What can it be?" asked one—to which the other, after a long look, declared:

"It's very funny! it might be Napoleon returning from the Isle of Elba."

"What! again!" cried the first, incredulous, but evidently puzzled.

But, as he was "a reading man," he pondered a moment, and then:

"No, no; that's impossible," he added. "History does not repeat itself."

CHAPTER XXIX

Where we shall see how that gallant and illustrious musketeer, Maurin of the Maures, saw in Spain the hereditary foe of his Moorish ancestors and his forbears of Saint-Tropez.

To wear, with musket and sword complete, a costume that is an heirloom from your ancestors, and that on a day of dignified festivity; to be subsidised by the State, to take part in a national review of arms;—then, notwithstanding a grotesque triumph achieved over a solitary gendarme, to beat the retreat and take to flight—the situation as a whole was not precisely glorious for a Musketeer of Maurin's intrepid character.

It is beyond a doubt that, to the man who wears it, any special costume, no matter what, is bound to suggest thoughts in agreement with the associations it calls up.

Maurin was chagrined, in a vague, half-conscious way. . . . In the worn folds of his patched doublet resided a whole past of glorious traditions that seemed to cry shame on him and tell him he was but masquerading as a Musketeer, for all his protests to the contrary when Tonia had made such fun of him the night before, as she sewed the buttons on the time-honoured relic.

After all, Tonia had seen the hero take to his heels! True, she had likewise witnessed Sandri's ludicrous disaster and his involuntary bath. Still . . . Maurin was not happy!

He told himself, indeed, that flight was the only reasonable thing he could have done; that any other course would have been only a piece of silly fanfaronade. . . . No matter! he had run away, a hunting-horn in one hand, a blunderbuss in the other; yes, he had run away! He, Maurin, had run away! He could not altogether explain these impressions of regret and disillusionment, but he felt them strongly; he was a mere burlesque Musketeer, unworthy of his native town, unworthy of the glorious past recalled year after year by the placard posted outside the *Maison Commune*.

Soon the very presence of his faithful henchman Parlo-Soulet, galloping behind him, was only a reproach the more, spurring his self-contempt to greater activity. What! between them they had two horses, two muskets, and a horn! They were inflamed by the spectacle of battle, intoxicated with the fumes of a thousand kilos of powder—and they were in full flight!

In his irritation Maurin kept pricking his spurs into his horse's flanks, and Pastouré, whose weight was almost too much for his mount, was left far behind. Presently, observing this, Maurin pulled up under the Berthaud Pine, once witness of his victory over Césariot. Pastouré came up panting.

"Oh! Parlo-Soulet," Maurin broke out, "what if we rode back to Saint-Tropez? what if we had a bit of a rise out of the gendarmes? Now's the time. Why, we're bolting like a brace of stinkards. Running away, always running away. I'm sick of it! There comes a moment when the wild-boar turn at bay and lash out at the dogs. I won't spend my life in being chivied. Suppose *we* give the other chaps a taste of chivying this time?

"Sandri, I make certain, by this time must either have reached Sainte-Maxime or else sunk like a lump of lead to the bottom! Another of the 'Charleys' fell with his horse in the *Place*, I saw the spill, and he couldn't get up again in time to come after us. . . . He'll have a sore set of ribs. . . . So come, let's play off some fine trick on his mates. . . . There were only four or five of 'em altogether."

"Yes, but how?" questioned Pastouré, cautious and hesitating.

"Oh! I don't know," returned Maurin; "but with two horses, you know, and two blunderbusses, *and* a horn! and with only three fellows against us! Why, surely we can find some road to a bit of sport—though I'm bound to say I don't just see how."

Parlo-Soulet shook his head.

"It's the smell of powder has turned your head. Just think, Maurin; isn't it enough to have the gendarmes coming after you, without our going to seek 'em out of our own *sicar* (of our own initiation). So forward, say I!"—and Pastouré gave spur to his horse.

"You say 'forward'; but you're turning your back on the enemy!" sneered Maurin—and heaved a great sigh.

All the same, he knew that Parlo-Soulet was in the right, and much against the grain he put his horse into a gallop and caught him up,

"I say 'forward,'" Pastouré then proceeded to explain, "because we shall certainly find gendarmes, if you must have 'em, at La Foux. There's never a fête without those gentry. Gendarmes and *gardes*, there'll be plenty at La Foux, on the race-course, where they have just lately erected a great amphitheatre of planks, and to-day Spanish bulls and Spanish bull-fighters are flocking to it."

Maurin pricked up his ears.

"What!" he cried. "Spanish? You're sure they're Spanish?"

"Spanish they're called, anyway, on the bills I've read."

"Spaniards!" Maurin exclaimed in a voice of consternation. Then, with a burst of unfeigned indignation:

"So here we have Spaniards at the gates of Saint-Tropez! at La Foux! at Cogolin! on the very day of our *Bravade*, which expressly recalls the memory how, hundreds of years ago, we put to flight, after three hours' fighting, one-and-twenty Spanish galleys! And now here's Spanish barbers come to clip our beards, the very day of the *Bravade!* Spaniards to hold their fête cheek by jowl with ours! They're to shed the blood of poor, harmless beasts under

our very eyes, while our muskets only fire blank charges
and make an empty boast ! . . . I reckon the Spaniards
think light enough of us ! "

He gripped his blunderbuss hard in his hand, which
shook with anger. Then he spurred on his horse. His
excited brain was stirred with a new enthusiasm. No, he
was not flying now ; he was advancing to confront a new,
an unknown peril. Now he scorned domestic broils, he
turned his back on civil war, to face the foreign foe !

" I don't think," said Pastouré seriously, " we have
anything to fear just now from these Spaniards."

" And who told you so ? " retorted the Musketeer
fiercely. " You know very well, Parlo-Soulet, that several
times I've convoyed stallions from the Gulf here to the
Camargue, to a great landowner's stud-farm yonder. He
wanted to try crossing our Grimaud breed with that of
the Camargue horses, which, like our own, were originally of Saracen or Moorish blood. . . . So I know the
Spaniards ! "

" I never knew," said Pastouré diffidently, " I never
knew the Camargue was in Spain."

" The Camargue is in France, yes ! " returned the other ;
" but for some years now you must know the inhabitants
have wanted to turn Spaniards."

" Well ! I didn't know that ! But how ? And why
do they want to be Spaniards ? " objected Pastouré.

" This is how it is," explained Maurin, pulling his
horse into a walk, a manœuvre immediately copied by
his faithful comrade. . . . " This is how it is : in the
Camargue, which is an island in the Rhône and in the
sea . . ."

" Is it in the sea, d'you say, or in the Rhône, this
island ? " questioned Pastouré, bent on accuracy.

" In both, seeing it's in the Rhône where that river flows
into the sea."

" And what's it like ? "

" Oh ! there's sand and swamps, cane-brakes and furze-
brakes, and reeds and rushes ; look you, it's very like the

marshes of the Salins d'Hyères, and not unlike the shore
about here, at the head of the Gulf."

"I can see it, your Camargue," said Pastouré.   "And
what's in it, this island ? "

"Breeders of horses and wild bulls."

"Any sport ? "

"Every sort of game—barring wild-boar. . . . But to
come back to Spain," Maurin continued; "every year the
folk of the Camargue brand their young bulls with a red-
hot iron, so as to know them again and tell whom they
belong to. It's made the occasion of a public holiday, and
they amuse themselves with the bulls. The bull-tenders
show off their strength and skill by making the creatures
chase them ; sometimes, when the bull is just upon them,
they escape by leaping clean over with a pole, other times
by planting a foot on the bull's head at the very instant he
lowers his horns to toss them, and making a spring. . . ."

"They show a fine pluck of their own ! " commented
Pastouré.

"Pooh ! " went Maurin, "I've tried the game down
there and I could manage the trick as well as any of 'em.
You must be nimble and keep your head, that's all. The
bull is slow at turning, and an active man can dodge him
pretty easily."

"It's a job I should be no good at," remarked Parlo-
Soulet parenthetically, "a big fat fellow like me. Why,
l'you know I weigh two hundred and fifty livres ? . . . I
should smash any pole ; indeed, the nag I'm riding this
present moment must be regretting his old master, the
gendarme ! "

"To come back to the Spaniards," resumed Maurin ;
'they make sport with bulls in Spain too, but it's in
quite a different way—and not a pretty one, one I don't
over and above like ! "

"I know," said Pastouré, "they kill the bulls in public,
before everybody."

"Exactly ! And what's more, they torment the poor
beasts ; they stick in darts all over their body, like pins

Q

in a pincushion. I've seen the thing at Arles, where the Spaniards came to earn a heap of money, thinking their barbarous amusements would please the people of our Camargue. Indeed, it can only be supposed these Rhône folk did enjoy them, seeing they've begun to claim the right themselves to exhibit those horrid spectacles the Spaniards call *corridas*, or bull-fights to the death. But, after all, in Provence, d'you understand, Pastouré ? a bull-fight was a sort of game in which the men ran risks in plenty, but there was no danger and no cruelty for dumb beasts to fear. The bull was never tortured."

" I've heard tell torture was abolished," observed the well-read Pastouré, " by the Great Revolution."

" Exactly so. Well, the Spaniards are introducing into our native Provence the torturing of animals. Disgusting ! And now, by what you tell me, here they are at the very gates of Saint-Tropez, these Spaniards ! Ah ! if only I could stop 'em, these performances ! "

" Pending which consummation, *I* should be very glad to see 'em, 'cause why, I don't know what it's all like."

" Well, let's get on there then ! "—and they shook up their horses into a hand gallop.

The *arènes*, or amphitheatre, at La Foux was actually on the road Maurin had to follow on his way back to his hut, where he intended to resume his everyday habiliments.

The horses travelled well, and the two friends were not long in reaching the race-course at Cogolin and coming in view of the amphitheatre or bull-ring, a wooden erection all covered with parti-coloured posters, half red, half yellow.

Red and yellow, these were the Spanish colours, the rivulet of gold between banks of blood.

These placards were everywhere—even plastered on the trunks of all the umbrella pines in the neighbourhood.

" There you see ! " exclaimed Maurin, " it's the Spanish flag ! they've planted it everywhere on the soil of Saint-Tropez. . . . Well, we shall see ! "

The headlines of the posters ran thus :

Courses nationales du Midi

dites

GRANDES COURSES ESPAGNOLES

OU

COURSES DE MORT

Primera espada :

GONZALÈS TORTILLADOS EL FUEGO BARDILLAS

Le Célèbre Matador de Seville

ESPAGNE.[1]

---

[1] National Sports of the South, otherwise Grand Spanish Bull fight, or *Corridas de Muerte :* First swordsman : Gonzalès Tortillados el Fuego Bardillas, the famous Matador of Seville, Spain.

CHAPTER XXX

THE race-course at Cogolin, at the head of the Gulf of
Grimaud, is situated on a vast sandy expanse, dotted here
and there with magnificent umbrella pines. Standing there,
if the eye does not travel to the hills (which stand too near,
however, to bear out the comparison properly), a man
might fancy himself in the Camargue itself. Pines, sand,
tamarisk-scrub, lentisk-thicket, all are identical.

It is on this ground that every year are held the horse-
races, which draw a crowd of spectators from Toulon,
Hyères, Draguignan, Saint-Raphaël, Cannes, Marseilles,
and a score of other places.

This year it had occurred to certain *impresarios* to take
advantage of the fame of the Cogolin race-course to promote a bull-fight in that locality, the close proximity of
which to Saint-Tropez was yet another advantage. They
calculated that the day after the *Bravade* they would attract
practically all the visitors from a distance, while even on
that day they might make sure of all such as are satisfied
with a brief attendance at that exceedingly noisy festival—
and they were not far out.

A vast and many-coloured crowd swarmed on the
ground, beneath the tall, spreading umbrella pines, when
Maurin arrived on the scene with his companion.

Nor was it the promoters only were interested in the
experiment, but also the sellers of assorted beverages, who
follow the bulls about from place to place, as they do an

army corps at manœuvres, pushing their merchandise before them on hand-barrows.

Moreover, besides promoters and in addition to these humble, itinerant "licensed victuallers," the enterprise appealed to a host of elegantly dressed young bloods —high-collared, immaculately gloved, eyeglass in eye and stick in hand.

Under the very French-sounding name of *afficionados* (amateurs of the bull-ring), these young men had found it necessary to give the title of *National Sports of Provence* to the *corridas de muerte*, which are essentially Spanish, and never, no never, were Provençal.

The standing reproach, and a terrible one it is, that may legitimately be raised against the *corrida de muerte* is that it rouses, under the misnomer of enthusiasm for the ring, the vilest of all human passions, that of cruelty glutting itself without any personal danger whatever.

The whole pleasure of the spectator at a bull-fight consists in watching, himself in perfect security, the risks run by one or more performers, and the sufferings of a wretched animal, the target of a score of wounds before death puts an end to its agony.

An odious pleasure surely—to feel oneself safe and sheltered from the pain one has procured by a payment of fifteen or thirty sous, five francs or twenty-five. For a civilised people, it is impossible to imagine a less civilised pastime.

This was precisely what two distinguished individuals, M. le Sénateur Bésagne, to wit, and M. l'Instituteur Letourel, were saying at that very moment under a big sun-umbrella and under a still bigger umbrella pine.

When Maurin and Pastouré rode up under the giant pines of La Foux, the day's sport had not yet begun. The crowd, especially those from a distance, stared at the pair, Musketeer and Dragoon, at first in amazement, then inquisitively, but the most part supposed they formed part of the *personnel* of the bull-fight. "It's the *picadors*," passed from mouth to mouth.

"Look," said Pastouré, "here's the gentleman, the teacher, who 'learned' my boy. Good day, M. Letourel," —and bending from the saddle, he wrung M. Letourel's hand, where he stood listening to M. Bésagne the Senator.

"Two *bravadeurs* from Saint-Tropez, are they not?" observed the latter.

Maurin lifted his plumed felt in salutation.

"We were speaking," said M. Letourel, addressing Pastouré and Maurin, "of the bull-fights, the *Corridas de Muerte*, we are going to witness; and," he added, turning back to M. Besagne, "I shall take the freedom of asking you, M. le Sénateur, how it comes that the Chambers don't vote a law once for all against these disgusting exhibitions, or else, if there is such a law already—and they say there is—why it is not rigidly enforced?"

"The promoters of these amusements," answered the Senator, "have devised a name for them that paralyses governmental interference; they have called them (see the posters) *National Sports*. This word 'National' has the virtue of shielding whatever it is applied to from attack more or less. If we laid hands on games so denominated, we should have against us, so it is feared at any rate, the whole French Nation, or, if not that, the whole Provençal Nation."

"My nation! no, never!" protested Maurin.

"I take the further liberty of pointing out," said M. Letourel, "that the motive you mention would seem only to emphasise the feebleness of the Government without excusing it. There should be other considerations. . . . It is a great grief to me, who have devoted my life to the endeavour to teach children the lessons of gentleness, justice, kindness to animals, to see these savage performances encouraged everywhere. Think of it! Does it not recall the most barbarous epochs? Is Republican France anything but a decadent France, M. le Sénateur? And who is responsible? tell me that."

"Bravo!" cried Maurin, the mounted Musketeer.

"Who is responsible? Well, I will tell you!" replied

the Senator, roused at last. "I will tell you, since you
'press me; I don't wish to let a good man like you charge
me with indifference to the hideous evil you deplore. . . .
Universal suffrage is to blame!"

"Oh! come, come!" protested Maurin indignantly;
he thought the Republic was in danger.

But the Senator went on unheeding, while Maurin and
Pastouré sat silent and imposing on their horses, listening.

"Universal suffrage," declared M. Bésagne, "is like the
tongue, as Æsop describes it, the best thing and the worst
in the world. . . . Now mind what I say: the curse of
our country is drunkenness; there are towns where the
liquor shops are so numerous that there is one to every
seven inhabitants, including women and old men!"

"It's more than there are musicians at Bourtoulaïgue!"
put in Maurin.

"It is dreadful!" exclaimed the schoolmaster.

"Now the liquor-sellers in France are one and all
electors to be reckoned with, for they exercise an influence
that cannot be gainsaid over their customers. Do you
follow me?"

"Only too well, M. le Sénateur."

"Who the deuce could ever have guessed such a thing!"
ejaculated Maurin ingenuously.

"Therefore the Deputy, if he cares anything for his
reputation and chances at the next election, deals judiciously with the dealers in alcohol, in other words, he is
careful not to hurt their trade, and that means, to give
them a free hand to poison the people with their adulterated
stuff. To keep his seat in the Chamber, a man must allow
the people to be poisoned at the hands of the trade. Is that
plain?"

"*Noum dé pas Dioû!*" cried Maurin; "I understand
the thing! All these alcoholic drinks are poison! . . .
And to think that, while they concoct 'em out of different
sort of grains, and even wood, and all kinds of abomina-
tions, a good native wine can't find purchasers! And so,
M. le Sénateur, you say our Representatives protect the

cheats ? If M. de Siblas had told me that, I should have refused to believe him, and maybe lost my temper—because he is an enemy of the Republic, as he has every right to be ; but you, you're one of its staunchest defenders. So if you say so, it's a serious thing. But, come to think of it . . . liquor-sellers and bull-fights are two different things, eh ?."

" No, only one ! "

" How so ? " exclaimed Pastouré, hitching his blunder-buss from his left arm to his right.

" It is easy to see ; the people that attend bull-fights are first-rate customers for the vendors of liquid refreshment of every sort. An excited crowd drinks, and drinks again, and calls for more. The spectacle is one that promotes thirst."

" Ha ! ha ! now the hare's in sight ! " muttered Maurin with a thoughtful air ; " and a big 'un too ! "

" Excitement makes dry throats," went on the Senator, " and drink the fellows must. In the bull-fighting towns, the liquor-sellers have everything to gain by dubbing the *corridas de muerte* ' National Games,' to make them seem more reputable ; and many a Deputy, thinking more of his seat than of the real good of the people, whose interests, nevertheless, he has undertaken to defend, is content not to go against the dealer in absinthe and bogus Turin vermouth, who, when all is said and done, is the veritable King of the Country ! . . . To sum up : it was to turn France into a shambles and make the dealer in alcohol the actual King of France that our fathers made the Revolution of '89. . . ."

" Good Lord ! " swore Maurin, passing *his* blunderbuss from his right arm on to his left.

" And that is why, M. L'Instituteur, your sermons on kindness and generosity to animals will bear no fruit. . . What can I do ? I am old and disillusioned."

" Say all this in the House."

" I am a Senator. The initiative is with the other Chamber."

" Get the newspapers to say it."

" Most of them would refuse. . . . The Trade is a formidable organisation. It holds in its hands the life and death of the great Dailies. . . . In a word, it holds in leash the two mightiest powers of modern Society—universal suffrage and the press. That is why and how the dealer in drink is the new king of this world. . . . But the performances are beginning. . . . Let us see what will come next."

Maurin dismounted, looking vexed and angry, and Pastouré followed suit.

" M. le Sénateur," said Maurin, " we of the people, we cannot explain things, but we often make use in our country of a phrase that means a good deal. We say : ' *Aï, pauvre France !* ' and I see it is indeed ' Poor France !' nowadays. . . ."

" Pooh ! " returned the Senator more cheerfully, " the life of a great nation is a mighty power too, and sooner or later a cure can be found for everything ! "

" After all," muttered Maurin, " it's no worse than my affair of the mad dog. . . . but it's much of a muchness."

The Senator did not catch the remark. He was just entering the great enclosure with his friend the Schoolmaster.

Then Maurin turned to Pastouré :

" I'm full of dreadful thoughts, friend Pastouré. If all that M. Bésagne has told us is true, the day will come when we shall have to undertake, we Republicans, a revolution against the Republic, to reconstitute you a new France ! And the notion frightens me ! Yet, no matter, if my people required it, I'd put myself at their head, *noum dé pas Dioû !* I would. I've been to Paris once before, on my own account, on foot. I'm a plain man, as you may see for yourselves, who might come back another time with a Nation behind me ! "

" I know it, I know it," said Pastouré. " And I'm the man to go there with you—as is only my duty."

" Meanwhile, let's go with the crowd," laughed Maurin.

" I've a mind to show 'em, these Spaniards, what stuff I'm made of ! "

They tied their horses to the stem of an umbrella pine, and made for the entrance of the bull-ring.

Pastouré the Dragoon stuck close to the heels of the gallant Musketeer, who drew many an engaging glance from the girls; for, indeed, he bore a bold and fascinating mien with his blunderbuss over his right arm, his left hand to his sword, which stuck out horizontally behind, and his plume waving in the wind, albeit a trifle dishevelled by this time. . . .

CHAPTER XXXI

JUST as Maurin entered the building, followed by Pastouré, Tonia also arrived with her father in the light cart they had borrowed from their neighbour, the landlord of the *cantine* of Le Don.

Orsini tied his horse to the stem of a pine not far from Pastouré's and Maurin's animals, which he knew by the fluttering ribbons decorating their harness, and made his way into the amphitheatre with his daughter.

Pastouré pointed them out to Maurin :

" Look at your Tonia yonder, with Orsini. One would think they were after *you*."

" It's the bull-fight they are after," said Maurin ; " then, you know the Corsican girls are half Spanish ; they carry the knife in their garters."

Tonia smiled at Maurin across the wide space dividing them. He could not help a glow of satisfaction to feel she loved him so ardently ; yet it made him only the more unhappy to have to run away from the gendarmes under his inamorata's very eyes.

The building was entirely of wood and had been hastily run up, but it was of great size. It was an amphitheatre, open to the sky, forming a vast ellipse ; the external walls rose to an altitude of fifteen to twenty feet, while the partition which separated the spectators from the ring was five feet or so high.

All round inside this interior barrier ran a projecting step, from which the toreadors could take off when they wanted to vault over to escape an infuriated bull.

There were eight or ten rows of seats rising one above the other. A special box hung with tricolour bunting was

235

occupied by several Mayors of neighbouring localities, grouped round M. Bésagne, the Senator. The two front rows, known as *reserved places*, were filled by tradesmen, well-to-do landowners, provincial dandies from various towns and villages, sightseers from Marseilles, Cannes and Nice ; amongst the rest two or three wealthy proprietors of houses of doubtful reputation in those towns were to be seen, who had driven out in flash gigs, behind spirited trotting horses. In the same place sat five or six country gentlemen of the district, habitués of the Cogolin race-course. In fact, the most incongruous elements of society were represented in the vast audience.

The performance began. . . . Two mounted men (picadors) wearing leg-pieces of thin iron plates and armed with lances, galloped round the ring.

The first bull was let loose. . . . This was described in the bill as the dreaded *Emperor*—a famous and formidable Spanish bull, the same which had gored to death the illustrious El Tato, the sole inheritor of whose renown was Gonzalès Tortillados !

Emperor showed no great alacrity to leave the *toril* and enter the ring, but out he came at last, and Maurin knew the beast at once, a wretched little bull of the Camargue, worn out with thirty recent baitings, and as many forced marches along the roads of Provence on his painful way from circus to circus !

" If they're all Spaniards of that sort," he remarked, " the *afficionados* will be justified in demanding their money back."

Presently, accoutred in the correct costume of a Spanish toreador—padded calves in silk stockings, a short jacket glittering with spangles, and all complete—an individual with a head of hair as black and shiny as pitch stepped forward. He was armed with two banderillas, which he planted in the bull's heaving flanks, capering and waving his arms about like a ballet-dancer.

Emperor shuddered. Two trickles of blood appeared where the two darts had pierced the hide. The animal shook himself and twitched his muscles, but could not get rid of them ; then, carefully avoiding the picadors, he trotted two or three times round the ring. . . . His wounds were bleeding where the banderillas tossed up and down as he went and tore the flesh ; it soon became plain *Emperor* was only looking for the best way out, and thinking of nothing more bloodthirsty than the good hay in his manger, unless it were the wide horizon of the Camargue, bounded by the encircling sea.

A howl of derision from the crowd greeted this display of cowardice. *Emperor* was not going the way to fill the promoters' pockets. These worthies had stationed confederates here and there among the spectators to voice the wishes of the public :

" Now then, fireworks ! fireworks ! " yelled one of these bogus *afficionados*.

Then a second toreador, in just the same get-up as the first, planted in *Emperor's* neck two fresh banderillas of a new sort. These carried crackers, with a slow match attached. Soon the powder caught, and the bull, smothered in sparks of fire, shook himself again, the two crackers finally fizzing out with a ridiculous sputter. . . .

The bull, dashing hither and thither, got too near a picador, who pricked the animal in the forehead with the point of his lance. The blood spurted out, and trickled into the unhappy beast's eyes..

A storm of hisses broke out. The hunted creature was roused at last, collected its energies, and dashed at a picador, whose lance missed its mark this time . . . the beast's two horns gored the horse's belly, and it fell, rolling over its rider. . . .

" Bravo, toro ! " shouted the young *afficionados*, sucking their gold-headed canes.

Then the *primera espada* (first swordsman) made his entrance and marched straight up to the bull, shaking his scarlet cloak.

Emperor, forgetting the fallen horse, plunged at the cloak. . . .

The horse tried to regain its feet. The picador, hampered by his clumsy leg-pieces, worked himself free at last, and, moving with difficulty, reached without assistance the door of exit, which opened to admit him, and immediately shut to again behind him.

At last the horse had managed to stand. Then the poor animal could be seen, in the centre of the arena, staggering a few feeble steps, the bowels pouring out and getting entangled in his hoofs. Giving a final stagger, he fell over sideways, stretched out his legs, raised his head for a moment by a last effort, dropped again, and died. . . .

The women, happy with horror, pressed close against the young men's sides. . . .

The *primera espada*, pursued by the bull, made a feint of flying—then suddenly wheeled round, and faced the brute.

Emperor stopped dead in surprise. The crowd clapped frantically.

The paid amateurs among the audience shouted : " Gonzalès ! long live Gonzalès ! long live Tortillados ! Bravo, the great El Fuego ! Bravo ! bravo ! bravo ! Tortillados ! "

Tortillados turned this way and that obsequiously, and bowed low to every quarter of the compass in succession.

Presently the man turned his smiling face towards the Musketeer and the Dragoon. Then :

" *Noum dé pas Dioû !* " ejaculated Maurin, . . . " but I know the chap, this Tortillados of theirs ! It's Mouredu, from Six-Fours, who was my mate, when he was in the service and fencing-master at Arles ! . . . He was a Keeper in the Camargue at the time they demolished the village of Six-Fours, on top of its hill, to put a battery in its place ! If he's the pick of the company, *pechère !* the public's finely done ! Why, they're no more Spaniards than I am, the lot of 'em ! "

The *primera espada*, winding the scarlet cloak about his left arm, advanced and aiming his point at the fatal spot between the shoulders, he struck out—and missed !

The paid *afficionados* kept a discreet silence, but an independent member of the audience hissed.

The bull, wounded for the fifth time, seemed debating whether to charge his enemy . . . but ended by turning tail. The hissing grew fast and furious.

A picador dashed up to the bull, waving his lance. . . . The animal seemed to prefer the sword, and wheeled back to face the *primera espada* again.

The graceful Tortillados, whose fat posterior was squeezed into very tight breeches, swaggered about with infinite elegance. Once more he took his stand before the bull, which rushed head down at the cloak. Then Gonzalès El Fuego Tortillados swung round on his heels. . . . *Emperor* tore past, just grazing the red rag. . . .

The same manœuvre was repeated several times.

Once, pressed by the bull, Tortillados Mouredu leapt lightly over the dead horse, which lay there a hideous mass of bleeding carrion, and the crowd applauded enthusiastically.

Then Mouredu Gonzalès Tortillados El Fuego Bardillas set about finishing his bull. . . . Again he lunged, and this time struck home ! . . . *Emperor* rolled over.

Thunders of applause, storms of cheers, broke out instantly, and the *primera espada* bowed to the ground.

But the bull was only wounded after all. The poor beast was exhausted, and had stumbled and fallen from sheer weariness. . . . He was up again in a moment. He galloped for the gate in the barrier, which at that moment was thrown open to admit the mules into the arena whose duty it is to drag out the dead animals, and dashed away out of the building altogether. He fled past the officials and the privileged amateurs permitted to stand with them near the *toril*. . . . Then, between two planks, he caught a glimpse of daylight coming from outside, charged wildly, to the panic terror of all near, battered down the wooden wall with his head and horns, and suddenly found himself in a wide plain like his own free saltings of the Camargue. . . . Yells and howls filled the vast building as the crowd lashed out distractedly by every exit.

CHAPTER XXXII

A form of sport not recognised in Provence, in which Maurin and
Pastouré, albeit poachers by profession, decline to have art or
part.

"A BULL got loose !   A bull got loose ! "

The great amphitheatre was left almost empty.   Everybody was eager to see how the fugitive would behave
outside.

The bull, free at last, excited by the sense of rapid
motion, urged on by exasperation and the keen desire
of liberty, charged at random at the scattered groups that
ran nimbly for shelter behind the great trunks of the pines.
In a flash, seven, eight, a dozen men and more—who were
they ? where did they spring from ?—appeared around
with guns and revolvers, and started in pursuit of the
animal. . . .

Then followed a wild chase over the sands.   At last,
hunted down by some mounted men, the beast turned
back and made for the circus.

Maurin and Pastouré, like everybody else, stood watching
the pitiful chase. . . .

" Take your horse, *bravadeur !* and go after the creature ! "
someone called to him.

" Why should I ? " answered Maurin, with a shrug.
" I only wish it could escape for good and all ! "

The wretched beast was close to the great building again
now, and recognised the scene of its martyrdom ; panting
and exhausted, with bloodshot eyes and red dripping
nostrils, blood on its flanks and blood all over, it halted,
dazed and beaten.

At that moment a shot was heard.   A valiant fool had
fired his revolver at the quarry.   The light ball, too small
to do serious harm, grazed the animal's back.   The flesh

quivered as if stung by a troublesome gadfly, and a fresh trickle of blood showed on the black, shiny coat. And that was all.

A second shot rang out—this time a musket-shot. A full charge of shot, intended for the ducks of the Bay, riddled the quivering muzzle, which began to drip blood from a score of wounds. The bull shuddered, but still stood there without a sound—piteous victim of human brutality!

Maurin and Pastouré looked on at all this with a dull air of helpless disgust, as if they shared the poor beast's contemptuous amazement.

"All the same," muttered Maurin, "they're a set of savages! But what can we do? There's the box full of Mayors and Sous-Préfets, whose business it is to have the law respected; I can't take all their duties on my own shoulders! . . . And, besides, what use could we be, as things stand? . . ."

Poor *Emperor's* butchers had neither ball nor buckshot; one after the other, eight or ten guns, loaded with small shot, made a target of the martyred animal. Now one eye was struck, and hung half out of his head. His tongue drooped from the foaming mouth . . . a charge of shot riddled it with thirty holes. . . . The animal drew it in, only to let it hang out again, torrents of blood coming with it.

Once more the bull, worsted by its human foes, fell to its knees, then pitched over on its side and lay panting on the ground.

Then, slim and elegant, in his jacket of purple and gold, a sham Spaniard ran up, squatted on the back of the once dreaded monster, and with the orthodox dagger-thrust, gave the *coup de grâce*. A last shudder shook the ponderous carcase that had once been an active, living creature, and the bull expired.

The public, discussing the incidents of the hideous chase in divers moods, poured back into the circus.

The authorities had consulted their dignity and had not left the official box. Nor had Tonia, either, left her seat.

R

CHAPTER XXXIII

Maurin of the Maures does eventually bear a hand—or rather a foot
—in the National Games, after a fashion of his own, and to the
huge delight of four thousand spectators.

A SECOND bull made its appearance in the arena.

Like everybody else, Maurin and Parlo-Soulet had resumed their places, where their grave faces had at once a
comic and a disquieting effect, as they sat in their *bravadeur*
costumes with their blunderbusses laid across their knees.

The ring was clear, and clean swept; the dead horse's
blood had disappeared under the sand carefully raked
over the spot.

The second bull that was let loose seemed in better
fettle, and likely to show more spirit.

"He's only another chap from the Camargue, all the
same," sneered Maurin, "this Spanish bull of theirs!"

The picadors' horses were afraid of the new bull and
turned tail, baulking their riders and rearing, as they
were forced several times round the ring. . . .

When Mouredu Tortillados appeared, a volley of hearty
hisses greeted him. He was resolved, however, to wash
out in blood the memory of his previous check; he made
his best bow to the audience, and without a moment's
delay drew on the bull with his red cloak. .

The bull charged, and the toreador slipped on one side.
The bull charged again, and this time Mouredu Tortillados
faced him, striking an attitude of defiance.

Three paces from him, the bull halted, head down.

The public quivered with pleasurable excitement, thinking man and beast in instant peril of death.

Taken separately, each single individual composing the
vast assemblage held bloodshed and cruelty in abhorrence;

242

yet the assemblage as a whole was overjoyed to feel itself waxing cruel and bloodthirsty.

Safely sheltered behind the barrier, the spectators one and all waited impatiently to see the death or disablement of the toreador or the bull. But neither one nor the other had the least wish to die, or even to be hurt, and both kept their original position.

There they stood like two statues—forming a striking picture. . . .

This lasted over a minute. Then a shrill whistle was heard, in unequivocal token of disapproval, but neither of the two opponents stirred.

"Egad! but he's getting on my nerves, that Spanish chap!" Maurin suddenly broke out in a loud voice.

"Who is that idiot?" one of the young bucks who still sat composedly sucking the knobs of their canes asked his neighbour, pointing to Maurin.

The latter gave him a wry look, and pretending to think he was speaking of the toreador :

"That idiot, sir," he said politely, "is a Spaniard of your kidney, no more a Spaniard than you are ; and what's more, a *bravadeur* from Saint-Tropez, with or without leave, is going to show the fellow how our ancestors treated the genuine Spaniards, years and years ago."

So saying, Maurin left his seat, sprang down from tier to tier, set one foot on top of the barrier that separated the spectators from the arena . . . and without ever letting go of his blunderbuss, the bold Musketeer leapt lightly into the ring.

The bull never shifted when he saw this new enemy approach . . . nor even moved his head. There he stood, immovable, horns lowered, but beginning to paw the earth savagely with his hoof.

The toreador, whose back was towards Maurin, had seen and heard nothing of his arrival ; his attention was absorbed in watching his opponent, for the most pacific of bulls may turn dangerous at any moment.

The crowd held its breath, Maurin's interference serving

rather to increase than to divert the eager expectancy of the spectators, who sat motionless and silent.

A Musketeer in the arena,—to begin with, the circumstance surprised nobody; some recognised the *bravadeur*, the rest only thought it was a new performer come on the stage, dressed as a Spaniard of former days. . . . But all realised one thing—the plot was thickening!

Events moved rapidly. Maurin marched composedly, his blunderbuss over his left arm, towards Mouredu Tortillados, who, standing like a post in the posture of a fencer on guard, exposed his hinder parts to the best advantage.

Arrived close to the toreador's unguarded rear, the Musketeer lifted his right boot and . . .

And Mouredu Tortillados jumped as if he had been shot, the well-delivered kick having fallen exactly where it should—on that finely rounded surface.

Amazement held the crowd silent for a moment; then came a prodigious burst of merriment, a colossal, a brobdingnagian laugh, from two thousand throats at once, answering the far-off explosions that were still shaking Saint-Tropez away yonder at the other end of the Bay.

At first Mouredu Tortillados did not even realise he had been kicked; he had jumped, but he had not altered his position, or looked round, observing with great prudence and scrupulous exactitude the first duty of a *primera espada*, which is to look a bull between the horns, his very life possibly depending on a false step. . . . It was true, true enough, that death was there, mixed up in this ridiculous burlesque!

Mouredu felt it was no time for fooling! and far from wheeling about, he stood rooted to the ground, still as a statue, his eye fixed on his opponent, the only one of his two enemies he saw or could see.

A second vigorous kick was applied to the satin of his breeches . . . Mouredu Tortillados jumped a second time, and with heroic self-restraint stuck to his post without moving a hair's-breadth, his eye on the foe, his sword at the ready.

At the third blast of the trumpets the walls of Jericho
fell. . . . At the third kick behind received by the toreador
Gonzalès Tortillados el Fuego Bardillas, his breeches split,
and let a corner of his shirt escape to flutter like a banner
in the breeze ! At the sight the bull suddenly turned tail
and bolted.

The crowd shook with uncontrollable laughter.

What is known as a "game" bull, a really game one,
is a rarity ; most of the poor creatures alternate between
impetuous valour and rank cowardice. This particular
one appeared to think : "Well, well, let the two fight it
out betwixt them ! . . . Perhaps the new-comer is a friend
and ally."

Thus rid of the foe in front, Mouredu Tortillados, still
sword in hand, turned at last to confront the mysterious
enemy assailing him in the rear.

"You pasteboard Spaniard," Maurin then accosted
him, " the men of Saint-Tropez put to flight, three centuries
ago, one-and-twenty Spanish galleys . . . and *I*'ve just
knocked the bottom out of one ! . . . "

The white flag which Maurin's kick had set flying in the
wind was now visible to that section of the public which had
not hitherto seen it. The spectators pointed it out to one
another, and the merriment of the multitude rolled out
in loud, never-ending peals of laughter, rising and falling
like the chorus of the cigalas in the forests of the Maures
in the dog-days.

The toreador was not aware of the full force of the blow
his dignity had received, but even he could not help seeing
he was the butt of general derision.

But next moment the sea-breeze penetrated to his skin
by the orifice Maurin's boot had opened, and Tortillados
realised the gravity of the situation. Maurin's insulting
words and Maurin's threatening sword together enlight-
ened him as to the serious risk menacing at once his
personal honour and the success of his commercial enterprise. . . .

He turned scarlet, and sprang with uplifted sword at his

enemy. . . Maurin broke a step and unsheathed without letting go his blunderbuss, which he carried in his left hand. . . . The swords crossed. . . . The bull, from twenty paces off, watched the glitter of the steel as the weapons clashed. The tumult of laughter and applause grew positively deafening. The two men, both fencing-masters in their day, took stock of each other, feeling their way, as it were, along the blades.

Then a great cry, a great whole-hearted cry arose, of glad approval, but an anxious cry withal; the people understood at last what the *bravadeur's* interruption meant, what this homespun Don Quixote had in his mind.

"Bravo, Móourin! hurrah for Saint-Tropez! down with the Spaniards! cheers for the *bravadeurs!* Provence for ever! death to the foreigner! bravo, toro! bravo, Móourin!"

Standing correctly to his guard, the Musketeer, noble champion of the local and genuinely national traditions, borrowing the words he had heard from the Senator, M. Bésagne, in a voice of thunder his own blunderbuss could not have drowned:

"Citoyens!" he shouted, "France is not a shambles! The Spaniard is not King of France! nor the liquor-seller neither! *Vivo Sant Troupé!*"

"Yes, Saint-Tropez for ever!" echoed the crowd with enthusiasm.

Then the Musketeer began, parrying tierce, parrying carte, trying every parry, lunging and feinting! His blade never quitted his adversary's. No matter where Mouredu's sword went it could not escape Maurin's, which followed it and clung to it, for all the world as if it had been a magnet, in spite of the owner's skill. . . . Suddenly Maurin hit out.

The *primera espada*, Gonzalès Tortillados Mouredu, sprang a pace to the rear—and the crowd danced with delight.

"Death to the Spaniard! Provence for ever! *Ten-ti! Móourin! vivo Sant Troupé!*"

At once terrified and delighted like the crowd, Tonia was clapping her hands frantically.

"Well, he is a wonder, anyway, that Maurin!" muttered Orsini.

The bull was still staring at the duellists with a stupid look of surprise. By this time Maurin was pressing Mouredu hard, forcing him bit by bit to fall back, each time a pace; at last, when the man was pinned close against the enclosing barrier, he whipped his enemy's gilt sword out of his grasp with a sudden pass . . . and ran and clapped his foot on it. . . .

Suddenly the bull darted between the two men. When it was quite close, the Musketeer lowered his noble blunderbuss and pointed it at the animal's feet . . . and bang! a roar of thunder bellowed round the amphitheatre, pealed over the plain and roused the echoes of the Gulf and the surrounding hills. . . . The bull was half stunned, and once more wheeled suddenly about; whereupon Maurin, treating the bull as he had done the bull-baiter, calmly planted his boot under the animal's tail.

At the unheard-of spectacle a very frenzy of delight, a glee that went beyond words, seized the crowd and set them dancing with joy. The women threw their fans at Maurin, their handkerchiefs, every favour they could think of, pelting Mouredu with oranges and halfpence in mockery. The latter was thunderstruck; propping himself with bent knees and back set against the planks of the barrier, in the attitude of a man sitting on nothing, contrite and pitiful, hiding as well as he might his rearward shame, the full enormity of which he now understood, he gazed with lack-lustre eyes at those startling manifestations of disfavour, the reasons of which he, even now, only imperfectly comprehended.

The Musketeer stooped and picked up the toreador's sword, which he handed back to him with a noble gesture; then, returning his own weapon to its sheath, he ran to the middle of the arena to secure the *espada's* red cloak, and stepping quietly up to the still half-stupefied bull,

he clapped it over the animal's head, winding it about the
horns and muffling the eyes in the folds of the waving
scarlet rag. . . . To end up, assuming his gravest look, he
seized the beast by the tail and, hauling with all his might,
forced it to walk backwards as far as the gate of the *toril*,
which opened to let them pass out. . . . Mouredu Tortillados el Fuego Bardillas, the Spanish bull-fighter, the
Provençal of Madrid, Director-in-Chief of the National
Sports, had clean disappeared.

Instantly, as though some instinct told them what was
the proper logical ending of a scene at once so painful and
so ridiculous, the crowd, intoxicated with merriment and
rage, mockery, indignation and a reckless spirit of horse-
play, set to work to tear down the rows of wooden seats
and the barriers, and pitch the remains into the ring.
A drinking-booth was outside, quite handy. . . . A
madman ran and looted the jars of spirits, which were
emptied over the pile of débris in the middle of the building.
. . . The enormous bonfire was set alight, and a wild
farandole was formed round the blaze.

A fantastic ring of laughing and cursing dancers began
its frenzied gyrations about a pillar of ruddy flame and
eddying smoke. The women had fled in panic, and the
notabilities and "respectabilities" had followed suit, while
Senator Bésagne muttered to his friend Letourel :

"It always ends up like this; yes, their *corridas de
muerte* are a bad school, a bad school. . . . But where
can the *gardes champêtres* be ? "

Just then the *Gardes Champêtres* were busy enjoying
themselves in the surrounding drinking-kens.

Maurin, looking grave, turned to Pastouré, who had
rejoined him :

"There's bad work beginning," he said ; "let's go
fetch the gendarmes ! "

As they pushed their way through the confusion to the
tree where they had tied up their horses, they passed
a number of travelling liquor-booths. A drunkard was
staggering in front of one of them, holding out for the tenth

time to the barman the price of a glass, and hiccuping :
"Give me whatever you please, if it's only got a bite in it!"
Then, just as the vendor was tilting his bottle, Maurin,
seized with a passion of disgust, swung round his blunderbuss and smashed it to atoms with the butt.

"*Té!*" he cried, "take that for the King of France!"

"You'll hear news of me, Maurin! I know you, and *I*'ve
witnesses who saw you do it."

"Oh, dear! another *procès-verbal*, eh, Pastouré?"
groaned Maurin philosophically—and the two mounted
and rode away.

A hundred yards further, before an open-air counter
set up under a great pine, they came upon a couple of
gendarmes seated at a table and busy with their liquor.

"Gentlemen," Maurin addressed them politely from
the saddle, "gentlemen, look yonder; the bull-ring is
smoking."

"Ah! smoking, is it?" replied one of the men. . . .
"Well, and we're drinking"—and the pair went on with
the business in hand, which was to get drunk.

"Please yourselves," laughed Maurin good-humouredly.
"As a rule you chaps do your duty—too well, sometimes!
Well, I've warned you, and so I've done mine. Good
night to you!"—and spurring up his horse, he said to
Pastouré, who still followed him like his shadow :

"As a rule it's the gendarmes are after me ; now, for
once, I'm after fetching the gendarmes, and you see with
what success! . . . All the same, I've never seen the like
of this sort of Sports before! But now we *have* seen 'em,
we know there are such. What say you, Pastouré?"

"I say this," answered the giant; "I don't know where
we're going at this pace, and perhaps it would be best to."

"To my hut!" returned Maurin. "I can't stay all
my life, you know, rigged out as a Musketeer! . . .
Liberty, French liberty, forbids a heap of things, but above
all, to dress as a soldier of olden days. As Musketeer,
friend Pastouré, the State subsidises me only two days in
the year, and then it's only to pay me for the powder I use."

They were still pushing on steadily at a round trot, when :
" Halt ! " cried Pastouré suddenly. " If you want
more gendarmes . . . there you have 'em. I can see one
hid behind your hut there ; he thinks he's well out of sight,
but I spy the corner of his cocked hat. He's waiting
for you, never fear, and no one else."

" Then," said Maurin, " it seems to me beyond a doubt
that the great Saint Tropez means me to remain a
Musketeer. Just let me reload my blunderbuss, one never
knows what may happen—and then away for Bormes !
Won't M. Rinal laugh to see us arrive in this kit ! "

After they had been travelling in the new direction
for a considerable while, without any fresh remarks on
either side :

" All the same," observed Parlo-Soulet, à propos of
nothing, " it needs a good pluck to pull a bull by the tail
as you did ! "

" Pooh ! " said Maurin, " in the amphitheatre at Arles,
all the little boys do the like ; why, many a time the tail
actually breaks and comes away in their hands ! "

The horses fell into a walk, and soon after the two
riders greeted with a double salvo from their blunderbusses
a light cart that overtook and passed them on the road.
It was the one conveying Orsini and his daughter Tonia
home to the Forester's lodge.

Maurin and Pastouré shouted with one voice :
" Saint Tropez for ever, and death to the Spaniards ! "—
and urging their horses into a wild gallop, they dashed
ahead of the cart again, and soon left it far behind.

" He's a fine, reckless devil, that Maurin, anyhow ! "
Orsini growled in reluctant admiration.

Tonia felt proud and happy ; but, " All the same,"
she laughed, " they needn't have smothered us in dust ! "

CHAPTER XXXIV

Showing how the African lion enters into the plans adopted by the
great Algerian wine-growers to secure abundant vintages,—to the
detriment of their Provençal rivals.

OLD Saulnier's vixen pricked her ears, the weasel scuttled
into the darkest corner of the game-bag, and a perfect
panic spread among the brood of partridges. It took a
good deal to excite the easy-going road-mender, but he
could not help noticing how they all stiffened their necks
suddenly, stood still a moment, peering about anxiously,
then rose with a rush and dispersed in every direction,
some disappearing over the slope of the hill, others making
for the bed of the torrent. . . .

The vixen got up hurriedly, seemed to sniff the air,
and then, scenting an invisible enemy, darted into the
undergrowth and disappeared.

For her part the weasel lay still as death, cowering in
the recesses of the leather bag, in between Saulnier's loaf
and his bottle of wine.

" My partridges," Saulnier muttered to himself, " don't
fly away except for gendarmes ! . . . But now, they must
have marshalled all the brigades at once, surely ! They're
going to march a regiment by ! It can only be meant for
you, Maurin, poor lad ! "

He removed his goggles, and looked his hardest down
the road. . . .

" The deuce ! what's this I see coming ? strolling players,
is it ? . . . or robbers in disguise ? "

He slipt half behind a leafy oak near by. . . . The gallop
of hoofs—two horses—approached, and stopped quite
close.

" *Oou !* is that you, Saulnier ? "

" Lord, Lord ! but it's Maurin ! *and* Pastouré . . . in *bravadeurs'* rig, I wager ? "

" Yes, of course."

Musketeer and Dragoon came forward and began a conversation without dismounting.

" So you've never seen *bravadeurs* before, eh ? "

" I only see what goes past along my road," said the road-mender resignedly ; " the roads I make are not for me. I only go from kilometre 40 to kilometre 80."

He wiped his brow, and went on :

" I make the roads, I don't use them. . . . Ah ! but you scared my pets finely ! Scarecrows like you, they've never set eyes on before ! All the same, I see all sorts of things go by along here, I do ! And the funniest I ever saw was the other day, that menagerie with all those lions roaring fit to terrify you, while alongside marched the two camels, great beasts as tall as those you see in the *crèches* in church at Christmas-time, following the negro king. The lions, shut up in carts that were really cages with iron bars, were hauled along by elephants. Just think, they stopped right here—because just yonder, where the road was up, Martegàou had found nothing better to do than leave his waggon, loaded up with pigs of metal, and sunk in the mud to the axle-trees. . . . Martegàou's team of four couldn't shift it an inch. . . . So then they out horses, and hitched the waggon behind one of those great beasts with a short tail and a long nose at the end of their arm, or a long arm at the end of their nose—take it which way you like, and *pechère !* he just leant forward a bit, like that, and out he pulled the heavy waggon like a tooth ! . . . That time, too, my partridges made off instantly, only to smell 'em coming in the distance ; my vixen took three hours to get over her terror ; and my weasel nearly squeezed herself for protection into my stomach ! "

Dragoon and Musketeer were listening with serious faces.

" Yes, it's amusing at times," went on Saulnier, " to

watch what goes by on my roads. I'm here in the first
seats . . . but elephants don't pass every week . . .
luckily! They're a size too big . . . they'd destroy my
work a bit too quick ! "

But now the Musketeer thought good to put in a word :

" *I*'ve seen elephants, too," he said, " and more than a
few, when I was a sailor in the Navy. I've seen 'em in
India. As for camels, why, I've ridden 'em, down in
Africa, no less. . . . That's where I hunted wild-boar in a
very queer sort of mountains ! "

" And what made 'em queer, these African hills of
yours ? "

" The fact is," said the Musketeer, " the dwarf palms
and *kermès* oaks, and all the growing vegetation there is
there, were so thick, so thick and close, that all day long
I used to travel without ever setting foot to ground. . . . I
used to walk in the air—that's the best way to describe it ! "

" I once saw," said Saulnier, " a long time ago at
Toulon, a tumbler fellow who could walk like that on the
necks of bottles, without ever knocking one over. . . . .
And " he added, with evident curiosity, " you must have
hunted the lion, no doubt, down in Africa ? "

" Hunted lion ! " exclaimed the Musketeer with a sly
look ; " hunted lion, indeed ! I should rather think so !
You don't expect to go to Africa and not have a taste of
lion-hunting, surely ? Marlusse is the only chap to go to see
the Paris Exposition, and then come back without having
seen it."

" So," said the road-mender, resting the head of his
hammer on his pile of stones and leaning on the handle,
" so you've killed lion in your time, eh ? "—and he gazed
with enhanced respect at the man who had hunted such
terrible beasts.

" And you, Parlo-Soulet," he asked the Musketeer's
companion, " have you ever hunted lion ? "

" I'd a deal rather," laughed Parlo-Soulet, shrugging
his shoulders, " hunt fleas all my life than go after such-like
big game, which is more like to kill good Christians than

Christians are to kill it. But . . . look, there's your vixen come back . . . and your weasel poking the tip of her nose out of your bag . . . and your partridges collecting again. . . ."

" Come, now, tell me one of your lion-hunting stories," Saulnier begged, " if you're not in too great a hurry. It'll give your cattle a breather. . . . A poor road-mender, as I've often told you, hasn't a chance of news every day."

" Then wait a moment," said Maurin; " we'll get down, and our nags, like us, will rest all the better for it."

The two riders sat down by Saulnier's side, holding their horses' bridles in their hands. The Musketeer felt no disinclination to seeing Tonia and the light cart appear again presently; no doubt it had stopped a bit somewhere on the road.

" Well," he began, " when I had made up my mind to go lion-hunting, like our fellow-countryman Gérard, the lion-killer, who came from Pignans, near Gonfaron, I started for Africa and set to work."

" Did you have a dog ? "

" No, I had a goat."

" I see. To act as bait ? "

" Exactly so; I heard all about our gallant Gérard, whose name is known the world over. I knew how you must set about this kind of sport. I went into a district the Arabs pointed out. The spot I chose was near a spring, at the foot of a wild-looking mountain, from the foot of which a plain stretched away to the horizon covered with vines. A lion lived in the caves thereabouts, and every evening, at sunset, he was in the habit of coming down to drink at the spring that glittered there before my eyes. I tethered my goat securely at the foot of a tree . . . and waited, listening; for the fellow used to roar every evening at the same hour."

" I know what that is," said Saulnier; " though the menagerie ones were in good, strong cages, they terrified me, all the same ! . . . Now, get on quick with your story. . . . Well, you heard him roar ? "

"No, not yet!" said the Musketeer. "He wasn't to roar—they said that was his way—till sunset, and I had come a bit beforehand, so as not to scare him."

"Good!" said Saulnier. "So you made sure it was the lion would be afraid? You were perched in a tree, I suppose?"

"Never such a thing, never!" cried Maurin indignantly; "get up a tree, yes, that's all right for killing rabbits at Sainte-Maxime; but a lion, a lion's easy enough to see when he breaks covert; a tuft of scrub won't hide *him*."

"Ah! so a lion just breaks covert out of a bush, like a rabbit, eh?" asked Saulnier suspiciously.

"Out of a bush of dwarf-oak, for instance, yes—and just like a rabbit, as you say. . . . You're strolling round . . . you chuck a pebble into a thicket . . . crack! out springs a lion! But don't be alarmed, for many a time, if it's broad daylight, he just walks majestically off—if he has dined, or if he hasn't young ones. . . . And more often still you can throw your stone into the bushes, and nothing will come out!"

"Come, now, come, you do keep a fellow waiting to hear the end. . . . So, you were not in a tree, but sitting as you are now?"

"Just so; I was sitting on a rock, my gun between my legs, with my goat tethered in front of me and the spring beyond."

"I am all shaking with impatience!" ejaculated Saulnier.

Maurin went on:

"Then, suddenly, he appeared. . . ."

"*Noum dé pas disqui!*" cried Saulnier; "he came with a spring, did he? without having roared to warn you?"

"It wasn't a lion that came," observed the Musketeer.

"Why, what other wild beast was it, then?" questioned the road-man.

"A forest keeper! . . . He was most polite, the worthy man. 'Sir,' says he, 'I beg your pardon, you must excuse me, but lion-shooting is not allowed on this property. Kindly remove your goat, and take her somewhere else

for her supper,' and he pointed to a notice-board nailed
up on a tree, which I had not observed before :

LION–SHOOTING
STRICTLY PROHIBITED
ON THESE LANDS,
WHICH ARE
PRIVATE PROPERTY.

" ' Very good,' I told the keeper ; ' I'll go and take
station t'other side the water." But the man pointed out,
still very politely, that to get off the private grounds
where I was, I should have to walk all day and a couple of
nights. It was the one and only spot in the whole province
where, after careful search, you could find a lion !

" ' But, *sacrebleu !* ' I said to him, ' how comes it lion-
shooting is prohibited on this property then ? '

" ' Because,' he told me, ' we've only a few left, and we
want badly to keep 'em, for why, the wild-boar eat our
grapes, and if we hadn't the few lions still remaining to eat
the wild pigs, there'd soon be no vintage here at all ! ' "

" Ah ! and so that's why," exclaimed Saulnier, " there's
so much wine in Algeria, and we can't sell ours here !
But for the African lions, we should be selling our wines of
the Var ! Well, that whips creation ! "

" However," remarked the Musketeer, " our nags are
getting restless, and we must be off again. . . . "

" Ah ! *parbleu !* " laughed Saulnier, " if it weren't for
your coming by now and again along my road, I should
have a blessed dull time for my forty-five francs a month !
It's chaps like you, with their *galégeades*, are the life of
the country ! . . . But where are you bound for, the two
of you, in your clothes of other days ? "

" Oh ! " grinned the Musketeers, " that's just what we
don't know. . . . We're marching straight before our
noses, trying not to meet the gendarmes," and in a few
words he recapitulated the incidents of the day for Saulnier's benefit.

" Here's dark upon us, and the best thing you can do,"

advised the road-man, " is to spend the night in my hut.
Then, to-morrow, our friend Pastouré, who has nothing to
fear for his part from the gendarmerie, can go to his house
to change his clothes, and afterwards to yours to get you
yours. I've never regretted so much before I've only one
pair of breeches to my name ! "

" We were thinking, perhaps, of going on to Bormes
to-night," said Maurin.

" Dressed in that rig ! " cried Saulnier. " Why, the
folks would set up such roars of laughter when they saw
you, you'd have the police telegraphing in all directions,
and every gendarme in the Var and the Bouches-du-Rhône
and the Basses-Alpes on your track in about no time ! "

Saulnier swung his hammer over his shoulder, and the
Dragoon, the Musketeer, and the road-mender set off at an
easy pace, followed by the two horses, the weasel, the vixen,
and the partridges, clucking and chattering.

" But our horses ? where are you going to put *them* up ? "
Maurin asked.

" In the scrub up yonder," said Saulnier, " out of sight
of prying eyes ; I keep a little ass now of my own, so
there'll be hay enough."

Just then they had all three to draw to the side of the
road ; Orsini's light cart, which had stopped a bit at La
Molle, overtook them, and passed them at a round trot.
But before it disappeared, Tonia turned round and threw
a kiss to the King of the Maures, who was amply consoled
for the time he had wasted in chatter with the master
of the weasel, the partridges and the fox.

" But," said Maurin, as they plodded on towards the
road-man's hut, " shan't we put you out very badly, coming
two of us, like this, to your sentry-box of a place, where
you've not overmuch elbow-room, when you're all alone ? "

Saulnier's face, the cunning old face, with its network
of wrinkles, beamed merrily :

" My lad," he grinned, " you know the proverb, I
reckon : ' There's always a pleasure in having friends
visit us ; if it's not when they come, it's when they go.' "

s

CHAPTER XXXV

Which reveals the secret of a new and unheard-of type of sport, and shows Parlo-Soulet positively avowing an urgent desire to talk.

" AND how about supper ? " asked Maurin.

" We'll sup on bread," said Saulnier ; " I lay in a stock every week. I've three days' supply left still. We shan't eat all that."

He went to a board, hung from the ceiling by four bits of rope to form a shelf, and took down two enormous Aix loaves, as big as paving-stones—and as hard.

Maurin felt them, and :

" A bit tough, aren't they ? " he suggested.

" Lord ! yes, in this hot, dry weather ! "

" You'll never find a knife strong enough to tackle 'em."

" Oh ! haven't I got my hammer ? " said Saulnier.

He laid the two loaves on the doorstep, which was of ashlar, and grasped his great hammer.

" There ! " laughed the Musketeer, " and I thought you only broke stones with the old thing ! "

" Stones, or crusts, it's always the same thing I'm hitting —my daily bread," said Saulnier sententiously ; " but I'll show you both presently something a deal more curious."

With a few blows of the heavy hammer he broke up the two loaves into several big pieces, adding :

" The crumbs are for my partridges."

The birds had taken refuge under the bed along with the fox and the weasel. Now they ran out to peck at the food.

After a while :

" Now's the time," announced Saulnier, " for my sort of sport ; come along with me."

Maurin laid hold of the old single-barrel that was hooked up along the great roof-beam.

258

Saulnier noticed what he was after, and said :

"Please leave the gun behind, Maurin; you'd only frighten the game ! "

"Amazing ! " grunted Parlo-Soulet.

"I'm out of it now," said Maurin ; "it beats my comprehension."

"Put the gun back, and follow me, both of you."

He gave a peculiar whistle, and vixen and weasel came out from under the bed. The latter Saulnier stuffed inside his loose shirt, "in his stomach," as he called it. Then the three men, the fox at their heels, set out along the hillside.

Pastouré and Maurin could make nothing of it, and said nothing.

"You can talk," Saulnier told them. "The more row you kick up, the better for my sport."

"Well, I've seen sport of most kinds in my day," said Maurin, " but never this sort, never ! "

"You hadn't the opportunity, you see," observed Saulnier.

"And that's why," remarked Pastouré, " the old mother would never die, because she was sure she had something fresh left to learn."

They passed by a threshing-floor, where a neighbour to whom it belonged had left several heaps of straw ; and not far off, under a little lean-to of branches, Saulnier had made shelter for his donkey and his supply of hay. There was well near, beside which Maurin's and Pastouré's horses were tied to two pines.

"They're well off there, in the fine fresh air." said Saulnier.

He led his friends among the rosemaries making a hedge to right and left, and through the heaths and cytisi, over the pine-lands and across the rabbit warrens.

Suddenly the fox left his master's heels and slipped into the undergrowth. Saulnier went on his way undisturbed, escorted by his two friends. Then the animal reappeared, disappeared again, darted across their path.

" Things are going well ! " chuckled the road-mender.
" Come on."

Coming up to a rabbit-burrow, he stooped and pointed
to a gaping hole among the big stones ; he picked up one
of these, and, strange to say, it fitted the hole exactly,
so as to plug it as if made on purpose.

In the same way he visited three or four other burrows,
each time stopping a hole with a stone that was " just the
size."   🖾

Finally, coming to a last hole, he gave a curious cry on
a falsetto note—and the weasel darted out of his bosom.
He picked up the little creature and placed it in front of
the hole, down which it scuttled without any pressing, and
which he then blocked as he had the others. He whistled
his fox, which came running up, and showed it two little
eggs.

" Magpies' eggs ! " he said. " I destroy nests and earn
the reward ; the eggs I keep, and find 'em useful for
teaching my fox all sorts of tricks ; she'll sit up and beg,
at the word of command, to get 'em. Look ! "

He held up the little eggs in his hand. The vixen got
up on her hind legs, her long pointed nose sniffing at the
dainty. Saulnier gave her an egg, which she munched up,
and told her :

" You shall have the other, lassie, when we're back at
the house."

" And the weasel ? " demanded Pastouré, his curiosity
unloosing his tongue.

" I see this much," said Maurin ; " she acts as a ferret ;
but how will you get hold of your rabbit, if there is one
down the hole ? "

" You wait a bit, mate ! " said the road-mender with
a low chuckle, like a man very well pleased with himself.
Two things contributed to this self-satisfaction : his companions' wonder and the pretty trick he was playing " the
Government " on the sly.

It was a warm night, and the dusk was falling softly.
The deep rustle of the hot pine-lands, as a barely perceptible

breeze blew over them, seemed the very breath of the
coming summer.

Once more back in his hut, Saulnier carefully fastened
the door behind him, and gave his fox her second magpie's
egg.

" No one anywhere about ! if there were, lassie would
have told me. Now, look here ! "

He pushed aside an earthenware jar that stood in a
corner of the hut. This done, he pointed to a little trap-
door in the ground in the angle of the wall ; he lifted it
and showed a square hole underneath. . . . At the bottom
cowered two young rabbits, half dead already, over which
the weasel was squatted sucking their blood.

" There ! " said Saulnier triumphantly.

Then he dropped a miniature gate running in vertical
grooves which closed the underground passage by which
the rabbits had reached the hole.

" *Osco manosco !* " went Pastouré, arm out, fist closed,
and thumb in air.

The young rabbits were soon skinned and opened, and
duly deposited on a gridiron above a quick fire of rosemary
and heath. The vixen feasted on the offal and heads.

" You see, I can trust Maurin and Pastouré," Saulnier
said to his pet ; " they're men of discretion, they are."

" Have you any wine ? " asked Pastouré.

" Unluckily for the growers," said Saulnier, " I can
always afford myself wine, and the best stuff too—seeing
I get it free, gratis, for nothing."

The door was thrown open again, and outside, by the
light of an oil lamp that flickered feebly in the light breeze,
beneath the stars that were beginning to wink, they ate
and drank to heart's content.

" What I like about you, Maurin," declared Saulnier
when they had reached the dessert of cheese and pounded
figs, " is that all the tales they tell of you show you're
a free man. And when you see a foolish thing done, you
never let it pass."

" I can't help it," replied Maurin ; " I don't do it on

purpose, for I hate these *procès-verbaux*, and if a man tries
to do things as he'd like to see 'em done, one's dead certain
to displease the gendarmes and the *gardes*, and sometimes
the Préfets into the bargain. Ah! if I chose to tell you
all!"

"For instance?" questioned Saulnier.

"The fact is . . . it's not always amusing . . . there's
sad stories too."

"Tell us, all the same."

"You've heard of my affair about the mad dog?"

"Who hasn't?"

"Well, this one's no worse, but it's even sadder. One
day, not so long ago, I came across—I won't tell you
where—a village sexton engaged in drowning a drowned
man."

"Drowning a drowned man?"

"Yes; the fellow was perched on a rock beside a sailor
who had been drowned; he had tied a big stone round his
neck, and was preparing to throw him into the sea below,
where it was two or three fathom deep."

"And what for, good Lord?"

"He was carrying out his Mayor's orders, to save the
commune, in whose borders the poor body had been cast
up, the expenses of the doctor, and the coffin, and goodness knows what. I couldn't stop him. . . . He did his
job."

"I don't wonder now," said Saulnier, "if we often read:
'Such and such a vessel was lost; the bodies were never
recovered!'"

"The Mayor of that commune was a friend of mine.
I spoke to him about it. 'Ah! my good fellow, what
would you have?' he said; 'we're forced to do it, and
it happens only too often. Our *budget* don't allow us to
indulge in extravagances.'

"That's what the Mayor told me. But, all the same,
it makes me angry, when I see the same men who drown
the drowned like that spouting fine phrases in the ceme-
teries over the graves, and prating, without ever a smile,

about the respect we owe to death. The world is too full
of lies, that's what riles me."

" And when you said so to that Mayor (I know you too
well to doubt you did say it), what answer did he give you?"

" He said : ' Oh ! sailors, it's their fate to find a watery
grave.' "

" Well, it's more or less true. . . . And about your son,
the *pescadou* (fisherman), how's he doing now ? "

" Very well," said Maurin ; " he has turned over a new
leaf ; he knows by now his back'll be the better for it."

" Ay ! to have children," said Saulnier meditatively,
" is a heavy responsibility. . . . Too often they repay
you for the pains you've been at to be good to 'em by
turning out ill. . . . My poor father used often to say :
' Better have a pig than a son. . . . You can always kill
and salt him ! ' "

They lit up their pipes.

" You've a fine pipe there, Maurin ! '

" It's a present I made myself to have an excuse for
paying a visit to the pretty pipe-makers at the Cogolin
factory. They *are* fine girls, they are ! The sawdust of
the briar-root, flying all about, makes 'em all as rosy as
their new pipes, and they have a way of protecting their
hair from the dust with a kerchief they tie round their
faces, that frames them like a picture !—it's so pretty and
becoming, I'm in love with the whole lot of 'em."

Maurin had an artist's eye, and he understood the es-
sential charm of the pipe-girls of Cogolin. They *are* all
amazingly pretty, that's a fact, and it's a pleasure to see
them at work !

They stand holding against the steel disks of the circular
saws the little squares of hard briar-wood. The impalpable
rosy dust dances in the air and falls in a steady shower on
the pretty work-girls, so that one and all, their hair shielded
by a coloured kerchief, which they arrange like the head-
dress of an Egyptian sphinx, are one uniform rosy pink
from head to foot. . . . They might be so many terra-
cotta statuettes, of a fine, ardent tint.

Maurin omitted to mention that he had loved one of them, till an American one fine day carried her off for money down, and heedless of artistic possibilities, dressed her as a Paris *cocotte !*

"Maurin," said Pastouré, puffing out a gigantic cloud of smoke, "women will be your ruin, I've always told you so."

"*I* make my pipes," observed Saulnier, "of reed ; for the bowl, I cut a length of full-grown reed, just above the knot, and a little half-grown one for the stem."

"*I* carved out mine," said Pastouré, "with my knife from a rough bit of root, and the stem's of reed, like yours."

"To the bonny pipe-makers' good health ! " laughed Maurin, roused to a burst of enthusiasm by his recollections.

"And Tonia ? " put in Saulnier slyly.

"You shall go and tell her to-morrow her Musketeer's here," said Maurin, "in his *bravadeur's* breeches and top-boots ! "

They smoked in silence awhile under the stars.

"To come back to your ways of killing game," Maurin said presently. "I can see now how your weasel and your fox help you . . . but what about partridges, eh ? "

"When first I had my weasel and my fox, it was just for the pleasure of having 'em, I swear that was all," explained Saulnier. "They're good friends and dear pets. It was only *after* making friends with 'em, without a thought of asking any return, that it struck me there should be a bit of give and take between true comrades in the way of a helping hand. It was the same with my partridges ; but the help they are to me at present " (here Saulnier dropped his voice) "is to give me the look of a chap who feeds useless pets for the fun of the thing. You understand, they remove the impression folks might have that my fox and my weasel get game for me. Besides, it's not game I ever go after. Rabbits are vermin."

"H'm ! then what's your gun for ? "

"Pooh ! . . . a hare or two a year,—though I count more on the ones that catch themselves—I'm not responsible—in the snares I set for the pole-cats !

"Oh ! ho ! " he grinned, " when that happens, it's no fault of mine, now, is it ? And then a man must have a taste of the good things of life when he can."

" All mouths are sisters," observed Pastouré sapiently.

" Well, come, Maurin, give us a song, and then we'll get to the straw."

Maurin sang a little Provençal song :

> "On marie une jardinière
> À Saint-Michel ;
> On lui donne pour dot cinquante
> Chapelets d'oignons
> Et des radis !
> Et, avec quelques melons
> Et beaucoup de pastèques,
> On lui donne cinquante piments ! " *

" And now for the straw, that's the ticket for us ! "

It was decided that Maurin, for fear his strange costume might betray him, should remain in hiding at Saulnier's till Pastouré had been to La Foux to fetch him his everyday togs. For to-night, he could sleep in the road-mender's hut, either on a good litter of straw on the ground or on the bed, as he preferred.

" Nay, keep your own bed, Saulnier," he said, to decide the matter ; " you're hard at work all day, and you're not as young as I am neither."

" Very well, then you shall have a shake-down of straw on the floor, you and Pastouré."

" Not I," said Pastouré ; " I saw my bed all ready made for me in the straw on the threshing-floor, beside the nags. Besides, I've got to water them and keep an eye on 'em a bit."

---

* The gardener's daughter, she's wedded at Saint-Michel. For dower they give her fifty string of onions, and radishes galore ! And pumpkins plenty and water-melons they give her—and fifty head of pimento !

"I'd go with you, Pastouré," said Saulnier, "but, you see, what with my pets and what with my guest, I can't very well leave my hut."

"It's all right as it is," Pastouré summed the matter up. "So good night all!"—and while Maurin and Saulnier turned in between the narrow walls, Parlo-Soulet made himself at home in the open air, after watering the horses.

Presently, when he was ensconced in the straw littered about the threshing-floor, and lying comfortably on his back gazing up at the stars, Pastouré began a soliloquy as usual:

"*Noum dé pas Dioû!*" he broke out; "it's high time! I was just dying, I must confess, to say a word or two! All day long, in all that crowd and noise, never a chance to speak a thing! . . . Well, friend Pastouré, and are you snug there? Pretty fair, thank you, and you?—Yes, you can see I'm all right. Capital, that's good hearing!—Return the compliment, old chap.—Eh, but what a heap of things all happened in one day! The shooting's just deafened me.—Anyway you can hear me; I know that much, because you answer."

Pastouré chuckled; he was charmed with his own wit.

"Oh, ho! I could hear you right enough, even if you never spoke, my lad!"

Then he was struck with a brief spasm of wonder at the immensity and marvel of the universe:

"It's a strange world anyway!" he muttered—and after a pause and a glance at the starry expanse above him:

"They're winking!" he laughed. "Yes, it's a funny world!"

Then, shutting his eyes:

"Now that Saulnier," he went on, "with his fox and his weasel, he *did* amaze me above a bit! The clever scamp! his fox is a first-class beater and his weasel as good as a ferret! Who'd ever have thought it?—Should you, Pastouré?—No, never!"

His thoughts began to wander.

"I only hope our dogs are well looked after! Yes, I wanted to leave 'em in charge of a friend at Saint-Tropez during the *bravades ;* but there, Maurin liked better putting them at Saint-Raphaël, at my son's . . . and he was right! . . . All the same, that vixen, you know, she hunts in close time, she does! . . . But she's as mum, she is, as mum as a mouse. . . . And just to think, he asked me to sleep indoors! Nay, nay, there's nothing better this time of year than sleeping out. Then, indoors there, along with them, why, my lad, you couldn't have spoke a word ; and I'm bound to confess, I've said so before, I'm bound to confess I longed for a bit o' talk with myself, like a pregnant woman craves for a thing—for I never say a word before folks, remember! But inside, not to keep 'em awake and not to set 'em laughing at me, I shouldn't have breathed one word, that's certain sure, and I *should* have been in a stew! "

Then, with eyes shut, he could see Sandri once more in the thick of the battle royal of the two rival bands. He broke into another guffaw :

"Now you'll see if ever—and it's like enough to happen —if ever the newspapers, where they put everything, come to tell the story about me and the clarinet, they'll add a whole lot of details, because, mind you, when a thing's as long as your little finger, the papers always stretch it out as long as your arm. They always exaggerate everything! I can hear from where I am now what they'll say ! . . . They'll say I shoved the blessed clarinet under the nag's tail till it disappeared altogether, and there it stuck, and with the instrument projecting behind like a ship's rudder, the brute steered himself all the way from Saint-Tropez to Sainte-Maxime over the sea !, . . Oh! ho! what a joke! yes, and I'll swear myself, if need be, the thing was so—just for the fun of seeing the folks taken in and chaffing the gendarmes over it. . . . And yet, what did I actually do ? I just barely touched up Sandri's horse behind with the very tip of the clarinet—and I took good care to stand well o' one side at that, for fear of his heels !

" But I knew that would be quite enough to set him flying like an ass of Gonfaron ; for it's a remarkable thing, I've noticed—if you want to set a beast flying, it's always behind you must set to work ! . . . Yes, they'll have some fine stories to tell about the clarinet adventure, once they begin embroidering, as they did over the affair of the great Saint Tropez. Yes, they'll print some noble stuff ; but there, all journalists are liars ! "

Pastouré was chuckling to himself, but suddenly his face grew serious :

" 'Pon my word ! " he muttered, " I believe the *bravade*, with the Spanish bull-fight to follow, and Saulnier's *aïguarden* (brandy) to help, have got to my head a bit. . . . Here I am lying abed and telling myself stories like so many waking nightmares ! Yes, and these fairy tales will be repeated—everything is—and in a hundred years it'll all be put down as sober history, how a gendarme's horse swam across the Gulf of Saint-Tropez with a clarinet under his tail ! . . . After all, I'm bound to allow, the thing's no more amazing than the story of the great Saint Tropez himself, and how he came sailing over from Rome in a long-boat, with a dog to steer, a cock for admiral, and his own head on the thwart beside him. . . .

" After that, why, anything's possible. One miracle's as good as another. Allah is great ! Put one brick to t'other, and it makes two bricks. Thirty-one, thirty-two ; when all goes well, all's well ; when all goes ill, why, what's the odds ? Life lasts as long as it may, and when there's naught left, there's still some over, and the last to bed must shut the door ! So good night all ! "

He tried to get to sleep, but could not.

" Now I ask you, suppose I was with 'em at this moment in the hut—it's about the size of a double pig-stye !—whatever should I be doing if I couldn't talk, and I couldn't sleep, and I couldn't think of a blessed thing but the great doings I've seen to-day ! . . . Oh ! yes, I know what folks will be saying : 'There's Pastouré, and there's Maurin, they've just had death in their families—Pastouré's brother's dead, and Maurin's mother—and there they've been processioning about at the fête ! ' But mind you, to begin with, there's different sorts of fêtes, a procession is not a dance ; besides, what harm can it do 'em, when they're dead, for a man to go to a *bravade* and to see a bull killed, so long as he don't forget 'em ? Mourning's best worn in the heart. Perhaps they'd like to see me going shooting all dressed in black, and a *kalitre* (tall hat) jammed on my head ! Why, it would be ridiculous ! . . . Ah ! yes, and we married our youngsters, Maurin and I, too soon, before we were out of mourning ; yes, I know they've made a lot of talk about that, I've been told so. But I come from Auriol, I do, and the world can just say what it chooses. The rain falls on the just and on the unjust—and I snap my fingers at 'em !

" The pot's over fond of calling the kettle black, neighbour, when likely one's just as smutty as t'other. And my brother in his grave, where I put him myself, I did, my brother knows my heart's sore for him. But there, why worry ourselves about dead folks ? They've only gone where we're all bound to follow . . . and the longer we can put it off, the better—at least, that's how the thing's put generally."

He was surprised at his own sentiments, and declared : " There's no denying it, I'm a bit screwed ! "

However, this time he felt his eyes growing drowsy, and sighed with satisfaction. He had another brief vision, brief but complete, of all the sights of the busy day, and muttered :

" Anyhow, when he hears how the King of the Maures bested the Spaniards, it's the King of Spain won't be over pleased ! . . . For he will hear . . . I tell you everything gets known. Folk always talk overmuch."

The thoughts within him seemed to rock him as if aboard a ship at sea. Darkness descended on his senses, and he fell fast asleep.

CHAPTER XXXVI

How the fair Corsican and her gallant musketeer enjoyed a pleasant
chat together; and how Parlo-Soulet returned from doing scout
duty and reported progress at great length, though for once he
had another audience besides himself,—and a deeply interested
one !

At peep of day, when Saulnier went to his day's work,
Pastouré set out on his way to the Cabanes Vieilles to
change clothes. On his way back he was to go round by
Cogolin to secure Maurin's, and bring them back with him
at once. Saulnier was all graciousness, and even went so
far as to work that day within hail of the *cantine* of Le
Don. Thus he could let Tonia know how Maurin was at
his hut all alone, and with nothing to do, being compelled
by his conspicuous costume to keep well in hiding.

She joined him as soon as possible, following his example
in the way of concealing her movements all she could.
She had provided for his comfort by collecting a supply
of good things to eat and drink.

She liked her gallant lover better than any gendarme,
and he, too, liked better than any other this girl who
went about armed and ready for self-defence. They were
as happy as could be together, and he had really given
up all other intrigues for her sake, though she hardly
believed it could be true. He had told her so before, and
he said so again, but a jealous woman will take no man's
word.

"When I think," she said, gazing round her angrily
at the four walls of Saulnier's hut, "when I think you
met that Secourgeon woman here, and others, too, most
likely, I don't know how ever I brought myself to say I'd

270

see you here. I long to take every stick there is in the
place and pitch it out of doors, because other girls have
been here before, running after you ! "

" Don't do anything of the sort ! " cried the Musketeer,
who was sitting in his shirt-sleeves, very much at his ease,
with nothing else of the Musketeer about him except the
breeches.

His sword was hung on a nail above his doublet, which
was crowned by his hat, while his great top-boots lay in a
corner beside his blunderbuss, which was leant upright
against the wall. His hunting-horn figured on the top
of a rickety chest of drawers. . . .

" Remember, barring my Musketeer things, which
haven't done you any wrong, and which are heirlooms
from my ancestors, everything here belongs to Saulnier.
. . . We mustn't spoil his property, *pechère !* He's such
a good chap . . . poacher as he is ! "

" Yes, I long to get out of a house where you've wel-
comed other girls," she stormed, angry at the thought
of his past infidelities. . . . "It all disgusts and horrifies
me ! "

" Well, such is jealousy ! " laughed the Musketeer,
sitting down, and pulling the pretty girl down on his knee.
" Come, there's no sense in it. Why should you be wroth
with the furniture and the walls ? Have my skin off my
bones, that would be a more reasonable proceeding, for
it's my skin's in fault ; and, after it, what's underneath,
my heart and my soul. Yes, jealousy would destroy
everything. Then, if it's a sign of love, after all, as they
say it is, you'd be sorry next minute to have deprived
yourself of what you love. That seems to me mighty
silly, Tonia, as silly as I am myself."

She sat there sulking, angry and sore, exasperated by
the pictures the room suggested to her imagination.

Suddenly tearing herself away from him, she ran to the
other corner of the hut :

" You shouldn't joke about such things, Maurin ! " the
girl cried furiously. " Your skin you talk about, your

living skin that has wronged me, I could drag it from your
flesh very well—I love you so, I *hate* you so—as easy as
they skin a rabbit ! "

" Lord ! " he grinned, " but it wouldn't be such a light
job ! . . . Come, come, don't be jealous of past times,
anyway . . . 'Pon my word, little girl, I'm so fond of you,
I've not given a thought to the others for days now."

" Truly ? " she asked him, suddenly softened.

" Really and truly. . . . Why, yesterday I had no
eyes for anyone but you."

" Oh ! Maurin, you hardly looked at me ! "

" Because there were so many things to look at," said
Maurin ; " to begin with, those confounded musicians,
then the gendarmes on the look out for me, and afterwards,
toreros and bulls and all the rest of it. But you may
bet your life, Tonia, out of all those pretty girls swarming
there in their finery, I'd have picked up one at any rate in
the old days, while yesterday, I never so much as thought
of such a thing, 'pon my soul I didn't ! Even the bonny
pipe-makers from Cogolin—and they were all there at the
games—never made me forget you, no, not for an instant.
I thought of you, my girl, directly I had a moment to spare ;
when I read the Spaniards such a lesson as I did, I was
really drunk with the smell of powder and the longing to be
up and doing, but it was more still because I knew you were
there, and could see it all, and because I wanted to please
you ! . . . Doesn't it always please the pretty girls to
see their lovers, sword in hand, fighting a gallant fight
like men ? "

Tonia broke into a smile ; she was fascinated, mastered.

" It's true," she said, " you were splendid, Maurin !
You looked like a king—king of them all. Even my father
said : ' Ah ! but he's a good sort, after all ! ' And their
grand Senator and the Mayors clapped hands . . . in spite
of themselves, for it seems you were in the wrong."

" A man's for ever in the wrong in this country," grumbled the Musketeer. " In France, everything's forbidden.
If I chose to break stones in place of Saulnier, he'd be in

the wrong, I wager, and I too. If I wanted to work o'
Sundays, I should be doing wrong, just as much as in the
old days, when the priests ruled us. Under the Republic,
you must be Emperor to have any rights."

"Emperor," she laughed, "or King! King of the
Maures ! "

They kissed gaily. Then she added :

"To talk of you again, the Senator—I went close past
him—was saying as we came out : ' He's a rough customer,
that Maurin ! Let me tell you this, we've just been looking
on at a real duel, a fight in earnest ! . . . The toreador
would have run him through, if he could ! ' "

" H'm ! I thought as much ! " said the Musketeer.

" And yet, only think, it was all so funny, so funny,
one clean forgot you were both of you risking your lives."

"That's where the merit comes in," declared the Musketeer. "We each of us had three sharp points to evade,
for we must count on the two weapons the bull carries on
his head, same as my old gossip Secourgeon ! "

She pulled his beard in a spasm of quite unfeigned
irritation at this last allusion. But he rather liked her
violence than otherwise, the bold *bravadeur*.

" Yes, he must have looked precious funny, the toreador,"
he laughed, " when my boot burst his breeches, and he
daren't for the life of him turn round, he was so busy
watching the dreaded horns. If he'd thought of guarding
his rear just then, he'd have been done for, that's certain."

And the two, the Musketeer and his pretty companion,
in Saulnier's hut, laughed gaily, and mingled their fresh,
young merriment with ardent kisses.

She told her lover :

" *I* wasn't laughing all the time, I can tell you ! . . . I
was trembling all over to think of your danger. . . . But,
all the same," she concluded, " here you are, in a fine pickle
again ! They'll certainly charge you with having incited
the mob to set fire to the building ! "

" Oh, they charge me with all sorts of things," laughed
Maurin ; " a little more or a little less just now, what odds

T

does it make ? Everything must have an end ; we shall
see what comes of it and what'll be the end of it, we shall
know in time. But one thing's as sure as death, they
won't catch me yet awhile."

"And where are you going now ?"

"My Russian Prince, now he has finished with his birds,
means to collect all the stinking vermin of the hills ;
he wants pole-cats, weasels, martens, and the rest, down
to the very shrew-mice and tortoises of the Maures ! I
shall take Lagarrigue into partnership—he's a famous
snarer, and all August and till the opening of the shooting
season, we shall be trapping, the two of us, all this sort of
small deer. When the season does come, I've promised
a lot of fine gentlemen, and our Deputy among the rest,
to go with them. . . ."

In this kind of talk the pair spent two very pleasant
hours, till the time came when Tonia had to part from her
lover. She left him a supply of good things to eat, and
promised to come back again next day.

She was there accordingly, as evening was drawing in,
when Pastouré reappeared.

"Well ?" demanded Maurin, "and my togs ? You
come empty-handed ? . . ."

"I had to ! I was forced to leave 'em in the woods. . . .
It's the gendarmes are to blame."

"But, *sacrebleu !*" swore Maurin, "I can't spend the
rest of my days dressed out as a Musketeer ! . . . If only
Saulnier had two pairs of breeches, he'd lend me one ;
but he hasn't, *pechère !* and he must keep what he has to
look decent on the public road. I can't go on like this,
with great boots as old as King Herod and a plumed hat
that would scare away the very tortoises in the Maures !
I look like one of those scarecrows they stick up in the
middle of a field of peas to frighten away the sparrows.
Do find a costume a man can wear without being stared at,"
he groaned. "I'm getting as sick of being a Musketeer
as I am of Spaniards ! I'm downright tired of being kept
prisoner here all along of the great Saint Tropez !"

" You'll soon be packing," Pastouré assured him. . . .
" Your clothes are not far off."

" But where are they ? "

" I'm going to tell you."

" Let's go and get 'em, then," cried Maurin, donning his
doublet, and pulling on his top-boots. "I'll leave the
costume of my ancestors down yonder, and you can bring
it to me at home afterwards."

" Oh, yes ! let's go ! let's go ! it's easy saying that ! "
growled Pastouré, shaking his head. . . . "First hear what
I've got to tell you. After leaving you I took the diligence
and went home to the Vieilles Cabanes; I put my Dragoon's
uniform away in the chest, and then back to Cogolin. . . ."

" To my place ? "

" Yes—and in I go, and get together your everyday
clothes. Then out I march, and come face to face with a
certain gendarme you wot of ! "

" *Noum dé pas Dioû !* they're at it again ! " sighed
Maurin. " Have the gendarmes never anything to think
of but me? And what did the fellow say this time ? "

" There were two of 'em, as there always are, and they
said : ' We know Maurin has fled in the dress of a *bravadeur*.
Evidently you have come here to fetch his everyday
clothes. We demand to know where Maurin is hiding
at this moment.' "

" You wouldn't betray me, I know that, *pardi !* So, what
did you say ? "

" Wait a bit, lad !—' Oh ! I'd be very glad to tell you,
gendarme,' says I, ' if I knew.' ' Come now, you've got
his clothes in your hand, you must know where he is to be
found ! ' ' That's where you're mistaken, sirs, as I'll show
you. Friend Maurin is too clever, look you, a deal too
clever, not to foresee you might come across me like enough,
and question me as to his whereabouts. So, to save me
the trouble of inventing lies, or maybe, giving him away
without meaning too, he took the precaution of not telling
me where he makes his hiding-place.' ' And where was he
when he refused to tell you ? ' ' He was on horseback,'

' Yes, but where ? ' ' On the road from Saint-Tropez to Cogolin.' ' And where were you bound for just now ? ' ' H'm, h'm ! yes, you see, he asked me to, so I was going to a particular spot in the woods which he described, to leave this parcel there, so that he can come and get it when he finds it convenient ; but I can't say when that'll be.' ' And what is the spot ? ' I wanted to have a bit of a laugh, so I told 'em : ' Oh ' says I, 'it's called the *Darnagas* (Shrikes') Spring.' ' H'm ! I don't know the place ; it's not in the map.' ' You'll know it when you get there. It's not a place just generally known by that name, seeing as how it's Maurin and I christened it so.' ' Lead the way, and we'll follow.' So away we went, and I took 'em to the Ringdoves' Oak, you know, near the Spring, in the Wood of Les Arnauds.

" When we came by the Spring, I put down the parcel, and there they stick at this moment, posted a few yards off, like gunners in a butt ! They're fools enough to suppose you'll come to fetch your clothes, and so tumble slap into their trap."

" But how is it they didn't guess you'd come and warn me ? "

" They thought they'd make sure enough of that when they put me in the diligence going back to Cogolin. . . . They ordered me in, and in I went, and they saw me take my seat . . . but a mile further on I got out again, took one of our short cuts, and here I am ! It is surprising, all the same, come to consider it, they never thought of coming to look for you in Saulnier's hut."

" It's a place a bit too likely to remind Sandri of a certain transaction where I made him look a precious fool once."

" So it's like this, is it ? " put in Tonia, who had been listening with all her ears, but had not said a word ; " it's like this—there's those two poor dear gendarmes posted out in the woods, staring their eyes out all the while at a parcel of old clothes ! "—and she broke into a peal of laughter at the idea.

Pastouré rounded off the scene :

" Yes, staring hard at Maurin's breeches, his jacket and hat and shoes, all nicely tied up in a tidy parcel with two long ears ! . . . They're waiting for you, lad, they're on the look out, ready to clap hands on your collar the instant you show up. My word ! but they may keep your breeches as long as they choose, provided you're not inside 'em ! "

" But that's just where I want to be ! " groaned Maurin. " I've had enough, I tell you, of this trade of Musketeer ! I mean to go there ! I'm going now ! and I'll have back my property from under their very noses, I will ! "

Tonia, till she was obliged to go, and Parlo-Soulet half through the night, and Saulnier, who presently came in from work, to back him, all begged and besought Maurin to give up this mad scheme, but in vain ; he only grew more obstinate. . . .

" You'll get yourself caught ! "

" Not I ! "

" But you will ! "

" Anyway," said Pastouré at last, " to-morrow's coming ; we shall see plainer by daylight."

CHAPTER XXXVII

How they hunt the musketeer in the Crown Forests of the Maures, in Provence.

SANDRI and his comrade crouched furtively in the undergrowth within a few yards of each other, and not far from the Spring; they were on the look out for game! Beside the grassy pool lay the parcel of clothes in full view. The contents were wrapped in a large piece of coarse cloth, tied at the four corners; on the top the tails of the knots made two great ears that waved in the light breeze, and were reflected in the clear water.

The two gendarmes, expecting to see Maurin appear at any moment, strained all their eyes. Soon night fell, and they searched the darkness with the same eager scrutiny. They had taken the precaution of putting each a loaf of bread in his game-bag, and a few slices of Bologna sausage. They dined frugally. They had wine, each his flask, and they sipped it, in strict moderation. . . . Maurin could not be long now; he really could not go on for ever living *en mousquetaire!* he must arrive almost directly now! It was too fine an opportunity of capturing him to be neglected. . . . And so they waited and waited, more and more impatiently. They refrained from speaking, for fear of scaring the quarry, and could not shift their position for the same reason. When their flasks were empty, they durst not go to the fountain. Martyrs to duty, they could only gaze at the water, dying to approach and quench their thirst, but not venturing.

They durst not sneeze or blow their noses, they could not spit or smoke or make any noise whatever. They were

sorry their bread was so crusty ; it made such a crunching
under their teeth. They enjoyed all the emotions of lion-
hunters on the watch for their prey. . . . One by one the
stars peeped out in the sky ; they could see them twinkling
above their heads through the fir-boughs. They seemed
to move . . . and the gendarmes could not. . . . At times
a rustle shook their nerves . . . a fir-cone, in this hot
night of early summer, falling and knocking against the
branches on its way to the ground, or a pole-cat on the
prowl creeping through the bushes, or the squirrels
gnawing at the kernel of a fir-cone.

Once they thought they saw something move beside
the Spring. . . . Was it he ? was it Maurin ? No, only
a marten that had been startled by the mysterious parcel,
and sprang at a bound into the brushwood. . . .

This time, it *is* he ! . . . no, it's a wild-boar, a ' solitary.'
The fellow is grubbing about near, looking for food, and
snapping the dead branches under his feet. . . .

The wood cracks under his tread as if the bushes were
catching fire and crackling. Tantalising beast ! Fain
would the gendarmes have turned poachers, had not stern
duty held their wills in check.

All they can do is to wait, wait, wait. . . .

The first gleams of dawn broke, then the sun appeared
over the skyline of the hill and threw a narrow band of
gold, here on the caps of the two sleepy-eyed gendarmes,
and there on the long ears of the parcel that lay still
wrapped in its piece of cloth. . . . Now the gendarmes
lift their heads a little to see if it is still in the same place.
. . . Yes, there it is, nobody has touched it. So Maurin
has not been there during their fit of drowsiness.

Then the pair, pushing aside the sheltering bushes slightly,
looked at each other with startled, feverish, wondering
eyes. It is six o'clock in the morning. . . . Suddenly . . .
what is it ? . . . the noise of a stone rolling down a pebbly
path. . . .

A stone does not move of itself. . . . A foot must have
stirred it.

The two gold-laced caps, gilded by the sun, once more rise furtively above the bushes. . . . The two gendarmes cast their eager glance towards the spot the sound came from . . . no, they are not mistaken ! Yonder, still a considerable way off, between that great oak and that fallen pine. . . . It is he ! there can be no mistake ! no error ! . . . It *is* a Musketeer !

Again they cowered down in hiding ; they crouched, made themselves small, became invisible. They were ready for the crisis, ready to spring upon their man, like tigers in the jungle !

Their hearts beat high at the thought of the triumph within their grasp ; for they knew the Musketeer, hampered with his sword, like themselves, and his big boots, would not escape them so easily as if he had been shod in his *espadrillas*. . . . His great plumed felt would be another obstacle, too.

So thinking, they crouched lower still, like a hare in her form, and kept a careful look out ; but there was now nothing to be seen !

Had the quarry scented them ? . . . They lifted their heads again a bit to see better. . . . *Nom de nom !* the Musketeer was slipping away. . . . Already he was only a tiny figure in the distance, no bigger than a child's doll. He must have caught sight of the top of the military caps . . . and he was making off at an easy pace, stopping and looking back now and then with an air of anxiety, to make sure he was not pursued.

No doubt about it, he had seen them ! he was going to escape them after all ! . . .

At a bound they were on their feet, without a word between them of their fears ! . . . They dashed off on his track. . . .

Then the Musketeer put on the pace, and they saw he had made up his mind to give them a long, stern chase. . . . He knew all the cunning short-cuts ; they would have their work before them to come up with him ! . . . The fellow was familiar with all the paths, and they were not, *parbleu !*

He led them by impossible ways, now scrambling up a cliff to dive down next instant into the depths of a ravine. Then, when the two heavily booted gendarmes thought to nab him at the bottom of one of these steep clefts, lo ! the Musketeer, in his mad costume that seemed to mock them with its absurdity, would suddenly appear above their heads, high aloft, perched on a pointed rock, under the open sky, like a Corsican mouflon or a Swiss chamois, insolently flouting them, waving his arms in derision, taking off his plumed hat sometimes to wipe his brow with a handkerchief that was a red rag of defiance. . . . And when he restored his felt to its place, his streaming plume would shake in the wind in bravado—yes, *bravado* was the word, there was no other to express his attitude.

. . . The chase threatened to be eternal. It had lasted two hours already.

Presently, on the extreme edge of a rock rising against the sky, the gendarmes saw him sit down gravely. The effrontery of the thing made them long to send a bullet at him ! But there he rested calmly . . . and there, clear cut against the sky, a weird figure . . . he was taking off his top-boots !

" *Nom d'un chien !* " swore Sandri, " he's going to put on his *espadrillas !* "

" Ah ! the villain ! " growled the other gendarme, " and already we've had five leagues of mountain travelling after him ! and now his light foot-gear will give him wings ! "

Yes, up there above their heads, the Musketeer was quietly and methodically changing his shoes ! Maurin was donning his famous moccasins, thanks to which, swift and sure-footed, he could challenge the wild-boar and the birds in speed.

" Once he has his *espadrillas* on, we are done for ! " groaned Sandri.

The gendarmes looked on in impotent consternation. They saw the Musketeer's legs lifted one after the other in the air, and the redoubtable *espadrillas* bound carefully on his feet. Then they beheld the fellow tie the two great boots neatly together. Next he got up, unbuckled his belt, and fastening the boots over the end of the scabbard which the sword kept stiff, he threw it with a fine swing over his shoulder.

At that moment, perched high aloft in the full blaze of the morning light, he looked, presumably by some optical delusion, as if he had grown bulkier and his doublet was too narrow to close over his capacious chest. The two gendarmes both simultaneously noted the curious effect. Then, preparing to resume his flight, Maurin pointed with a sweeping gesture, as if in defiance, to the wide distance he had still to traverse.

It was too much ; Sandri reached the limit of his patience, and putting his two hands together to form a speaking-trumpet, he shouted at the pitch of his voice :

" Halt, in the name of the law ! or we will send you an ounce of lead in your carcase ! D'ye hear, Maurin ? "

Thereupon the Musketeer, turning haughtily upon the gendarmes from his lofty position, shaded his eyes with his hand—as if to see them better down there below his feet, at the bottom of the depression, and, doffing his hat, the plume seeming to sweep the blue space of the sky, he shouted back :

" Oh ! is it you, gentlemen ? I hardly expected to meet you here ! . . . you must pardon me, I didn't see you before ; but if you're looking for Maurin in these parts, you're on the wrong tack, my fine fellows ! . . . *I* am Pastouré . . . you know, Pastouré ! Very much at your service ! "

Sandri was blind with rage ; his legs bent under him, and he had to sit down on a boulder.

The figure of the Musketeer vanished at the same moment. Parlo-Soulet was already descending the opposite slope of the hill, and with wide, waving arms, was saying to himself :

" Who'd ever have thought the ill-luck of life would have brought my brother's brother to be wandering about the great woods, first with a sword hung at my rump,

and now with a pair of big boots dangling from a sword ! It
bothered me a bit just now, when it knocked against my
legs, the old thing ! Now I've hung my boots to it, at
any rate it's some sort of good to me. . . . My word ! but
I'm surprised myself to be rigged out this fashion ! It
only proves that no man, till he's dead, can know all that's
going to befall him in his life ; and the things that do
happen him are just what he'd have least expected ! . . .
I'm precious hot . . . and this jacket's plaguy tight !
but there, I can throw it off now. . . . Oh, the deuce !
though we unstitched every seam, it has split again in five
places. . . . Well, no matter, that's a small hurt ! Tonia
can mend it. I *had* to put it on to befool those two who
were out musketeer hunting. I know I look ridiculous
like this. . . . I might carry the sword in my hand and the
boots too, but that would be just as funny, and less convenient. If folk from the towns could see me now as I am,
they wouldn't believe their eyes ! I'm acting like an idiot,
I see that, but then, if we won't play these foolish pranks
sometimes, we must give up having friends. I'm doing it
for Maurin's sake, and I don't regret anything. . . . All
the same, I shan't be sorry to be back at the Cabanes
Vieilles, and after trapesing so many miles in a day, sword
in hand and boots on back, against all my habits, too,
I shall be main glad to find myself at home, and see *Vidasse*
and *Consolation* again. . . . Lucky my poor brother's
dead ! else, *pechère !* if he'd seen me arrive in this zany's
dress, he'd have gone crazy, thinking I'd lost my wits
altogether ! ' *La vido ès ùn carnava !* ' (Life is a carnival !)
. . . *Té !* . . .''

And the stout Musketeer, in the lean Musketeer's doublet,
tramped on his way from pine clump to pine clump, up
hill and down dale, gesticulating and soliloquising, alter-
nately grumbling and congratulating himself.

CHAPTER XXXVIII

M. Rinal, prompted by Maurin, discovers a human heart in a melon.

MAURIN, having recovered his sportsman's kit, returned to his regular course of life.

He did not fail to tell M. Rinal the story of Parlo-Soulet masquerading as a musketeer and mistaken for Maurin of the Maures, and the ludicrous discomfiture of the gendarmes.

M. Rinal continued to take a keen interest in all Maurin's tales of adventure.

"These men of Provence," he remarked, one day, to M. Cabissol, "have a genius for anecdote. Every one of the gallant Maurin's gestures is a story in itself and brings the scene before you like one of those roguish *fabliaux* that delighted our fathers. His movements are as replete with natural wit as his words. Our native *galégeaïres* are French of the French in their satire, but their laughter rings freer and franker than that of your northern humorists; it displays a row of good, sound teeth that bite only honest bread and fine rich grapes!"

"We think alike," said M. Cabissol. "So I am glad to know that Jean d'Auriol is writing a book where we shall find all our Maurin's adventures related.

"It is the sort of book could never be written except by a man of old Provençal stock, one who has spent the most part of his life among his compatriots—I mean among the last relics of the true Provençal population, the folks who live in the scattered villages or the woods far from railways and towns—a Provençal who is thoroughly familiar with their accent and speech, their ways of making fun and talking seriously, of losing their tempers and regaining

284

them, all in a second, and even their characteristic trick
of shoving their straw hat or wideawake on to the back of
the head. . . . The more I think of it, the more convinced
I am Jean d'Auriol can write the book, for the indispensable
ingredient is an ardent sympathy for the race he wishes to
depict ; it is by sympathy, and sympathy only, you can
fathom it and really understand. Viewed from outside,
there are many sides of our local life that risk being looked
upon as merely ridiculous, but which, on adequate examination, prove to be burlesque and satirical. Our Provençal friends are fond of displaying their perversities to
get amusement out of them as artists and as moralists.

" That is the very spirit of Molière, the spirit of a very
' olden time ' France. To write a book of the sort it will
be needful to forget the literary methods one has been
taught, and forgo the niceties of style one has cultivated.
Each French sentence must have a Provençal turn, a
spice of solecism, a sprinkling of neologisms and bar-
barisms. In decanting one language into another, we
must take care the wine does not lose too much bouquet."

M. Cabissol was warming to his subject :

" At last," he cried, " I have found in Jean d'Auriol a
man who understood what I meant, as you do. Argufy as
I may with our Préfet, I cannot make him admire, as we
do, this most remarkable, most diverting, very serious and
very romantic Maurin.

" Romantic—yes, that is the word. When his love of
old tradition persuades him, notwithstanding his political
views, to dress up as a musketeer, and play the part of a
bravadeur, he is indeed wearing the costume that suits him
best. He is a knight of the days of St. Louis and Saladin.
He speaks of women, when he does speak of them, in the
contemptuous tones of a Mussulman—and when he speaks
to them he wears the self-confident air of a Duc de Richelieu.
From the *Fronde*, the most French of all periods of French
history, he has acquired in the highest degree a passionate
predilection for mocking and defying the powers that be—
or the Commissary of Police as representing them. He is

first cousin of Karagueuz and Guignol. . . . With it all, the loyalty of a true Frenchman of olden days, and a heart as clear as rock crystal. . . . We shall make something, I think, of his son Bernard, and I am delighted to do my best in the work. . . ."

One day, when M. Cabissol and M. Rinal were engaged in telling each other a hundred times over the same things about him, Maurin arrived on the scene.

M. Rinal was in the habit of finding occasions for asking Maurin's advice on all sorts of subjects, declaring that his natural common sense and his vernacular way of expressing his ideas often gave him valuable lights.

"You have come in the nick of time," he told him. "What do you think of manual labour? Is it a pleasure or a pain?"

"Ah! M. Rinal, perhaps I have little right to speak of it, for it's long since I abandoned the plough for the chase—which is not work to me, because I love it passionately—but I know people who have a passion for work. I had once; and in the days when I laboured in the fields I used to put the same fire into my ploughing as I do into my sport now; I made it a point of honour to have everything done punctually and in the best way. Without work, for want of enough movement, we should run mad, and be capable of anything—regular savages. So I am far from pleased, let me tell you, when I hear our Deputies tell the workers, by way of flattering them, in a thousand different fashions, that politics will ensure the people's happiness, and that happiness consists in doing nothing! and so on, and so on, and all the rest of it!

"They say that many people who were not obliged have worked all their lives, and have been well pleased to do so, and I think, if they worked with so much satisfaction to themselves, work cannot be a bad thing. But there are other people who would fain spend their lives staring at their navel—and the Republic leaves them to think that is what makes the happiness of the rich! My notion is that, when we teach the little ones to read and cipher, we should

seize the opportunity to give them better ideas on this
question of manual labour, for if things go on as at present,
the children of our workmen will despise the forge and the
bench, just because they have learned to read and cipher.
I think books ought to lead the ploughman to plough
better, and the carpenter to be a better carpenter."

" Bravo ! Maurin," said M. Rinal.   " A rebel against the
necessity of work is working his own destruction ; as well
deny the necessity of breathing. . . . I am trying to teach
your son the things you have just been saying. If I
see he has any marked aptitude for this or that, I shall
urge him that way ; if not, I shall train him to be a culti-
vator, well taught in the scientific improvements of
agriculture, or at any rate well prepared to assimilate
them.   But above all I shall guard him against this idiotic
pride of those children who, having learnt a few rudiments
of science, immediately begin to despise the working father
who begot them, and set to work to read bad novels, or
dream of writing romances themselves,—for I have seen
several such cases. . . . By the Lord ! yes, my dear
Cabissol, if we don't look out, the elementary school is
going to drown us under a deluge of uneducated scribblers !
. . . Why, look you—only the day before yesterday it
was—there comes a knock at my door : ' Come in ! ' and
in there comes a young man with a chubby face, sad and
smiling at one and the same time, nicely shaved and without a trace of beard barring a bluish tint on chin and
upper lip.

" He was tidily dressed like a workman in his Sunday
clothes, and he carried under one arm a big oval basket
with a lid.

" ' What is it, my friend ? '

" ' M. Rinal, I have heard of you ; and you will forgive
me if I've come to ask you for advice.'

" ' I am all attention.'

" ' I have written a book, sir, which I should wish to see
printed ; here it is '—and therewith he handed me a
bundle of manuscript, which I glanced through.   It was

childish, pitiful stuff. Then I fathomed the melancholy smile of the author. He had imagined himself to be writing a book on Sociology! He had a new gospel of humanity, and a new conception of the universe! I handed back his papers as soon as I decently could :

" ' My friend,' I asked him, ' are you married ? '

" ' Yes, sir, I am.'

" ' Have you a trade ? '

" ' Joiner.'

" ' Where ? '

" ' At Caroubière, near Draguignan.'

" ' You came by train? '

" ' Yes, with a return ticket.'

" ' Very well, my friend, go back quick to the station. There's a train for Draguignan in three-quarters of an hour. Take it, go back home, and tell your wife : "The gentleman told me to plane smooth and that I was crazy to write books." '

" ' Why, sir,' he replied, with his wan smile, ' that's just what she has always told me, my wife has—and no later than this morning too.'

" ' Then believe her, and love her true. Off with you, my lad ! '

" But he seemed very much embarrassed when he got to the door. . . . He turned, and came back to me, swung his basket off his arm in an awkward, frightened sort of way, put it down on the table, opened it, and said :

" ' Your pardon, M. Rinal, excuse me, but I've brought you a fine melon to thank you for your advice.' "

" That was the least he could do," observed Maurin.

" There you have the exquisite feeling of our Southern common folk," said M. Rinal. " They love to give, and have a feeling that any piece of trouble taken deserves an acknowledgment. Give me what you can, and I'll give you the same."

" When I was a boy," said Maurin, " I've seen actors of wood, marionettes—they were still to be seen in those days—represent the scene of the manger at Bethlehem,

and when the infant Jesus was in the stable the poorest
used to bring him whatever they had of the best, some
walnuts, some dried figs . . . "

" Some a tune on the pipe and tabor," M. Rinal
continued the sentence. " It is admirable ! it is the
quintessence of exchange by sympathy ! Jesus introduced
into the world a renovation of ideals . . . and in return
the poor man gave Him what he had to give—his heart.

" The poor fellow I am telling you about, he offered his
heart in a melon ! "

Maurin laughed.

" Was the melon a good melon, anyway ? " he asked.

" I cannot say," answered M. Rinal. " I told him : ' Take
back your melon, my friend ; you can eat it in the train,
and I'm going to get them to pack a bit of lunch for you
in your basket.' "

" M. Rinal," said Maurin gravely, " I feel sure you hurt
him very much. I know my people ; you should have
accepted his melon. You may be sure he had chosen it
long and carefully in the market at Draguignan, with his
wife's help, for she hoped, of course, you would dissuade
her husband from working at book-making. You should
have accepted the melon, M. Rinal, because, as you have
just said yourself, all his heart was in it."

M. Rinal thought a moment :

" Plainly I was wrong," he said at last. " And I thank
you for teaching me the lesson, Maurin."

Then, turning to M. Cabissol :

" The delicately modulated expression of human sympathy will alone save the democracies of modern days
from an inevitable and fatal fall into a condition of un-
emotional physical comfort, organised on a purely
mechanical basis, and more degrading, more stupid, more
immoral, and more mischievous than any errors of passion."

" A pretty dream ! " scoffed M. Cabissol, " but as a fact,
democracies scorn politeness as an artificial mask, and the
mistake they will make is not seeing that sentiment is a
positive force. . . ."

U

CHAPTER XXXIX

Wherein it will be seen, thanks to a quaint visit paid M. Cabissol by a heart-broken widow woman, that there are morals *and* morals.

" IT is my turn now," said M. Cabissol, "to tell you a story in connection with what you said about this love of giving, which is so touching a trait of our country-folks."

" Let us hear your anecdote," said M. Rinal. " It may well prove more interesting than mine, which, properly speaking, is only by way of an instance of the ease with which our elementary scholars are carried away by their own self - importance and think themselves very clever just because they have discovered the alphabet—a very fine invention it was, too, in its day. We are all attention, M. Cabissol."

" As you wish," agreed M. Cabissol ; and he began :

" The other morning a worthy woman in deep mourning knocked at my door. She had come from a neighbouring village to consult me.

" ' I am a widow,' she informed me. ' My husband died not a fortnight ago.'

" ' And what can I do for you ? '

" ' I have come to see you, M. Cabissol, to ask you to write me a bit of *a moral !* '

" For the moment I was out of my depth, and you would have been the same.

" ' *A moral?* What do you mean ? '

" ' Put me down on paper a bit of a moral ! '

" ' *Coumpreni pas* ' [I don't understand].

" ' A moral, sir, that everybody can read in the newspaper.'

" ' Explain yourself, my good lady ! '

" And this is the explanation the widow gave me :

" ' Ah ! sir ! Just think, my husband, poor man, all his
life, never drank anything but water ! I used to tell him
sometimes : " Marius," I would say, " a drop of wine
would do you good ; a drop of wine would comfort your
stomach ; wine gives a man strength ! " But I might
just as well have sung *A wet sheet and a flowing sea !** to a
gavot [peasant of the mountains] who had never seen the
sea ! He always said no : " My *Touninetto*, water is good
enough for me ; the good God made the water, but He
did not make the wine. You wouldn't give wine to a new-
born babe, would you, now ? Then why d'you want to
give it me ? " And you may be sure, sir, if he didn't
take wine, it wasn't to take absinthe or any shape or form
of strong liquor—no, nothing of the sort ! He knew very
well all those devil's drinks poison your blood, and make you
savage-tempered and passionate ! He was a sober man,
so be sure he was a good and a kind one. In nineteen
years and a half of married life he never spoke one word
louder than another ; he never so much as lifted his little
finger against me, to threaten me the very smallest little
bit ! No, indeed, but he always said : " I'd rather cut
off my hand than strike you, *pechère !* "

" ' And all day long it was *Touninetto* here, *Touninetto*
there ; my heart melts now, only to think of it ! . . . Well,
just imagine, sir, how wicked and spiteful the world can
be ! The folks about us, the whole countryside indeed, sir,
declare he was a drunkard, and used from morning to night
to beat me like a devil-fish ! ' †

" The poor widow wiped her eyes elaborately, and, after
a silence, during which I felt deeply moved, she concluded :

" ' Then I said to myself : " M. Cabissol, who is so good
and kind, will write me a bit of a *moral* in the paper, so

---

* The song is actually entitled " Le Patron Vincent qui a gagné la
targue " (Old Captain Vincent who won the prize at the water-sports).

† These creatures are beaten to make them tender before being
cooked.

that everybody may know my husband never got tipsy in all his life and never, never beat me ! " '

" More and more touched, I asked for some further particulars ; then I took a fair sheet of white paper and wrote, taking pains to be very legible :

" ' *Here lies Marie-Marius Siblet, a shoemaker by trade, a clever workman at making old as good as new. Public rumour has unjustly charged him with being a drunkard and a wife-beater. Above his grave his inconsolable widow declares these statements to be pure fabrications. She swears this before God, treading base calumny underfoot !* '

" ' There, my dear lady, is the document you asked for.'

" She took the paper, looked at it carefully, gave it back to me and made me read it over to her twice, thanking me after each reading with words that flowed faster and faster, as did her tears.

" ' Ah ! how well that is expressed ! It is just what I wished ! . . . And the newspaper will put it in ? '

" ' No, you shall have it framed instead, like a picture, this paper I give you, and hang it up on a post which you must plant, in the cemetery, on your husband's grave.'

" ' Oh ! M. Cabissol, what an excellent idea ! '—and with the words the poor woman put down timidly on the edge of my table a new five-franc piece.

" ' Take it back,' I told her, ' I only wished to please you. I don't do it for a living, you know.'

" She pocketed the coin, got up with reiterated thanks in a very paroxysm of emotion, dropped her long mourning veil over her face and made for the door.

" Suddenly, at the threshold, she turned, hesitated, then suddenly came back, and in an excess of grateful feeling, her words coming in gasps through her sobs :

" ' You are so good, M. Cabissol,' she said, ' I cannot, I really cannot deceive you. . . . I feel I owe the truth to a man who will not take money . . . it costs me a good deal to tell, but I know I ought. . . . No, no, I ought not to keep my secret, I must tell *you* all ! . . .'

" She broke off, shaken by spasms of grief ; then in the

shrillest of voices, as if to dominate the sound of her sobs, she said, very, very rapidly, almost screaming the words :

" ' He was always tipsy, sir, always tipsy, *pechère !* He used to beat me every night, very badly, and a bit every day ! . . . Thank you, kind sir, thank you ! '

" So she took her departure in a calmer frame of mind, and I was left admiring the pious falsehood of this noble widow, who really deserved to have married a better man.

" Well, Maurin, and what do you think of it ? "

" I think with you, M. Cabissol—the poor woman was noble, sublime."

" And ought I—tell me what you think—ought *I* to have accepted her five francs ? "

" No, no, of course not ! " said Maurin. " When she came to see you she thought at first you sold advice professionally, like a solicitor or a doctor. So she wished —her sense of justice demanded it—to pay you a fee. You made her see that *you* only hoped to do her a neighbourly kindness, out of pure good-heartedness. Then *she* is bound, out of consideration for you, to accept your gift. When she realises this she finds herself unable to pay you now, and yet she *must* offer you something, because she is a good-hearted woman in her way, a true daughter of our people. . . . So, out of the fulness of her heart, M. Cabissol, she gave you the most precious thing she had to give—her confidence and her secret. I think it *superb*, M. Cabissol. Yes, indeed, indeed, I see my people there ! They are good folk at bottom, yes, they are ! Only, among the poor no less than among the rich, those who get themselves the most talked of are not always the most worthy ! . . . "

M. Rinal and M. Cabissol exchanged glances, well pleased with their friend Maurin and his sentiments.

CHAPTER XL

The Ceremony of the Blackbird !

" By the by," said M. Rinal, " do you know, Maurin, what occurred at Bourtoulaïgue on the last 14th July ? They say your two brass bands, which pitched into each other so finely at Saint-Tropez the day of the *Bravade*, have now been reconciled, with the quaintest ceremonial."

" Oh, ho ! " laughed Maurin, " *voui*, yes, that *is* a good story ! Just think, on the eve of July 14, the Mayor sent for the two leaders of the two rival bands, and said to them, just like this :

" ' I have a blackbird at home ! ' "

" A good beginning ! promises well ! " grinned M. Cabissol, delighted.

M. Rinal gave him a nod not to interrupt with needless remarks the flow of the narrator's eloquence.

" ' Yes, I have a tame blackbird,' said the Mayor. ' And this morning, as I was looking at the bird through the bars of his cage, a happy thought struck me. . . .

" ' Liberty is the best of all good things. . . . My blackbird is a prisoner . . . let us give him his freedom— and give it him in a way useful to the community. I will tell you how. My daughter, this very evening, shall measure the bird's neck, and before she goes to bed she shall make him a little cravat of tricolour ribbon, red, white, and blue. And to-morrow, the 14th July, the National Fête, if you are all agreeable, I will summon the two societies, the *Harmonie* and the *Symphonie*, to meet in the great hall of the Maison Commune. We will shut the door and throw open the windows. Thither we will bring my blackbird in his cage, which we will set on the big Council-table.

" ' The united musicians, with their instruments, will all surround the table.

" ' At a signal from me, the door of the cage will be solemnly opened. Instantly the two bands of music will strike up with one accord the *Marseillaise*, and the blackbird will fly away to the sound of the famous air, bearing off on its wings for ever the memory of all our discords ! '

" The two leaders received the proposal with enthusiasm, and replied :

" ' M. le Maire, it is a sublime notion ! "

" Indeed, the plan was highly approved by everybody at Bourtoulaïgue. If the two rival associations had been asked right out to forget and forgive their grievances and differences and mutual grudges, they could not and would not have done it, but the mere idea of so touching a ceremony at once paved the way to a prospect of peace in the land. Everybody could see already in his mind's eye the blackbird, with its tricolour, flying out at the window and carrying away all recollections of former discord on its little black wings. The announcement of the proposed ceremony transported the whole population of Bourtoulaïgue with delight. It would have stirred the enthusiasm of all France if the papers had spoken of it, but the Press is still unrepresented at Bourtoulaïgue.

" On the morning of the 14th the blackbird's cage, standing on the Municipal Council-table, right in the middle of the sea-blue cloth blazoned with the town arms in red, was surrounded by the two brass bands and the Town Council, the Mayor at its head.

" Below, in the *Place*, before the open window, the crowd, which included the whole population of Bourtoulaïgue, was waiting.

" Three little girls, dressed one in blue, the other in white, the third in red, entered the Council Chamber. The first opened the cage, the little spring door of which she tied back securely with a string, the second took the bird very gently in her hand, while the third adjusted round its neck a little tricolour riband.

" Then the blackbird was put back in the cage, the open door of which was right opposite the window, also wide open. An impressive silence followed. . . . Then the Mayor appeared on the balcony and addressed the people :

" ' Citoyens,' he said, ' to-day, a day made glorious by the overthrow of that odious State prison called the Bastille, and to honour the birth of our national liberties, my blackbird is to be set free too ! Already he wears the national colours, which have gone round the world on the wings of the Revolution. The bird is still in his cage, his prison ; he only waits to fly forth by yonder window to hear the first notes of the *Marseillaise*. . . . Say after me : "Bravo, blackbird ! hurrah for peace ! liberty for ever ! " '

" The acclamations of a united people came in at the window ; but presumably they only frightened the black-bird, for he huddled back in his cage.

" Then the two leaders waved their bâtons, and the united bands struck up the *Marseillaise*. The noise was terrific in the confined space of the Council Room, which was quite a small apartment.

" Each bandsman, sir, kept his eye fixed on the black-bird. . . ."

" So you were there, eh ? " put in M. Cabissol.

" H'sh ! " went on M. Rinal, " he thinks he was ; that is enough. Do not interfere with the artist at work on a work of art ! "

Maurin heard nothing—except the crash of the *Marseillaise*; and he could see the blackbird !

" And the blackbird," he went on, " the blackbird looked at the musicians, cocking his head now on one side, now on the other ; but for all that, he was incommoded by his cravat, tiny as it was, for you see he was not used to wearing a necktie ! He looked greatly surprised, and instead of persuading him to fly away, the crash of the

instruments only seemed to make him more loath to move ;
he might have been a stuffed bird !

"The people crowding the square, seeing nothing fly
through the open window, began to wonder.

"'Why, what can be the matter? Isn't he coming
after all? Surely the music ought to frighten him away.
. . . *Oi !* what a joke ! the thing's gone awry altogether ! '

"Well, gentlemen, the blackbird heard the *Marseillaise*
out without budging ; but when the bands had finally
stopped their row . . . burr ! . . . in a moment, without
a word, he flew out of the cage and out of window.

"The crowd never saw him, and began to shout with
impatience fit to bring the houses down. Then they
started singing to a popular air *Blackbird ! blackbird !
blackbird !* over and over again.

"The Mayor reappeared on the balcony, and said :

"Citoyens, he's gone ; he has borne away on his wings
the memory of all our discords. Long live the Republic !
. . . And, above all, citoyens, mind and be very careful
when you go shooting after the 15th August not to kill him.
You'll know him by his little cravat ! He is under the
protection of the three national colours !

"Then the crowd dispersed in high content. It made
for the *Place* by the seashore, and everybody strolled
up and down there, discussing the ceremony over and
over again. It was noticed as significant that each of the
bandsmen of the *Triomphe de l'Harmonie* gave his arm to
a musician of the *Victoire de la Symphonie*.

"Then, suddenly, a word passed from mouth to mouth :
'The blackbird is back again ! Yes, yes, he has come
back ! ' It was true ; there he was, perched on one of the
trees in the Square ; there was no mistaking him, naturally,
because of his necktie.

"Two bandsmen went under the tree and, nose in air,
called in dulcet tones : ' Come, dickie, come ! '

"' *Pechère !* ' said the girls right out, ' he has forgotten
the way to find his living for himself in the woods, and he
has come back to be fed.'

" An old veteran gave it as his opinion that the bands-men ought to adopt the poor bird, as it could make nothing of its freedom.

" In the interval the blackbird had hopped down on to the shoulder of one of the two musicians who had been coaxing him.

" The man was for keeping him ; but the other, who belonged to the opposite faction, had seen him first, and disputed possession ! . . . First came abuse, soon followed by fisticuffs. I blush to tell it ; but all the musicians, who had been made friends the same morning, dashed up to interfere ; each took sides with his own champion, and an appalling scrimmage—as bad as on the day of the *bravade*—ensued, under the eyes of the Mayor, Deputy-Mayors and *Gardes*, who were helpless to stop it.

" At long last the Mayor himself resumed possession of his bird, and announced :

" ' Citoyens ! we will try again on the 14th July of next year.'

" In fact, M. Rinal," concluded Maurin, " I believe myself they'll repeat their ceremony of the blackbird year after year at Bourtoulaïgue, and century after century, because, look you ! men will be always men—and bandsmen bandsmen ! "

CHAPTER XLI

How the shooting season opened under Maurin's auspices; and how
that worthy held an important conversation with a *juge d'instruction*
who was fond of melon, rivalling M. de Montesquieu, the illustrious
author of the *Esprit des Lois*, in the judiciousness of his remarks.

MAURIN paid two or three visits to M. Rinal, who found
much amusement in the accounts he gave of his different
bravades, and who promised to remind M. Cigalous and
M. Cabissol of the shooting-party planned for the opening
day of the season.

This took place as arranged on the morning of 15th
August. The night before the sportsmen had arrived at
Sainte-Maxime. Maurin had chosen Sainte-Maxime for
the greater convenience of these fine gentlefolks, who found
the same luxurious accommodation there as in a Parisian
hotel.

It was agreed that they should all meet at daybreak at
the foot of the signal-station of Sardinaux.

Everybody was punctual. Cabissol, Cigalous, M. and
Mme. Labarterie, all were there; and M. Cabissol had also
invited the *juge d'instruction* from Draguignan (a Parisian
quite lately installed as an official in the chief town of the
Var), the *procureur du roi* of the Royal and Imperial Republic (as M. Rinal delighted to style that dignitary), and
sundry other magistrates. M. Cabissol in his good-nature
hoped to interest these gentlemen in Maurin's favour, but
for fear of their refusing his invitation, he had not mentioned his intention of bringing them in contact with the
famous King of the Maures. . . .

Maurin and Pastouré were waiting, leaning on their

guns, in front of the semaphore, and three dogs were leaping gleefully about their feet.

"A start! a start!" cried Maurin, seeing the arrival of the distinguished guests. "Now look out, partridge, hare, and rabbit; the season is begun."

"You've got some fine dogs there," the *juge d'instruction* said to him.

"Only one of them, the pointer, belongs to me," replied Maurin, not knowing who and what the speaker was. "The other one here is a dog—would you believe it?—they say I stole."

"Oh, ho!"

"And those fools of judges at Draguignan found me guilty!"

"Oh, ho!" repeated the other in a tone of anxious surprise, "tell me the particulars."

Maurin explained:

"A sportsman, a man I didn't know from Adam, was beating his dog unjustly. . . . I try to stop him. He loses his temper. Then, of course, I leather him. Off he goes with two black eyes. His dog goes after me and won't have anything more to say to his old master. What could I do? Well, they sentenced me! . . . There's no justice anywhere! . . ."

"You ought," said the judge, "you ought to have taken the animal back to his master."

"So I did, but the beast always came back to me again. They have some sense, those creatures! they'd rather be petted than beaten! Yes, she came back to me from Cannes, where I had taken her to restore her to her owner. You'll admit I was not *bound* to make the journey, which costs money. Well, the poor brute came running up to me in the Estérel, just in front of the inn of Les Adrets."

"An inn with a reputation!" exclaimed the young *juge d'instruction*, looking askance at Maurin.

"I should think so!" cried Maurin; "it was often visited, though you don't seem to know it, by Gaspard de Besse, a robber who is beloved to this day by all my people

of Provence, for why, he never robbed the rich save to do
good to the poor."

And Maurin took his turn to cast a sly look at the judge's
face.

The latter was young still, and chock full of old prejudices.
The mention of the inn of Les Adrets and Maurin's enthusiastic praise of our beloved Gaspard de Besse* set him
against his interlocutor, and instinctively he began to harbour suspicions of the man's character ; a dangerous fellow
evidently, he thought, and edged away.

Maurin walked up to M. Cabissol :

" Who is that gentleman, M. Cabissol, with the gold eyeglass, who has just been speaking to me ? I can't say I like
him ; he looked at me in a very funny way ! "

" That," said Cabissol, " is Maurice Couder, the *juge
d'instruction* at Draguignan."

" The deuce ! " returned Maurin in his simple way—" a
dangerous man ! "—and he left the other's side.

" Who is that lean, poacher-looking fellow I was talking
to just now, my dear M. Cabissol ? " questioned the *juge
d'instruction.* " I can't say I like his looks."

" That ? that is the celebrated Maurin of the Maures."

" By gad ! " said the judge, " a dangerous man ! "

" He ? why, he is the most honest fellow I know. He
is accused of a heap of trumped-up misdemeanours, every
one of which only proves his goodness and right feeling.
He is the personification of the good, natural common
sense of the people, that man," declared M. Cabissol emphatically.

" Oh ! at bottom, Maître Cabissol, I think *you* are a
revolutionist . . . an anarchist."

" There are some good notions in all the *isms*, my dear
judge ! "

---

* Gaspard de Besse, condemned to be broken on the wheel by the
Parlement of Aix in 1786, marched to his doom in a dove-coloured
silk coat and a rose in his hand, which he waved in salutation to the
noble ladies who crowded their balconies in tears. All Aix wept that
day.

The sun was beginning to beat down hotly. Hats were decorated with white handkerchiefs to keep off the blaze from the back of the neck, and everybody looked warm. Three rabbits and two brace of partridges had been bagged with some difficulty, but it was Pastouré and Maurin who had brought them down.

"Gentlemen," observed the *procureur du roi* of the Royal and Imperial Republic (Cabissol's phrase again!), "I have not been long in Provence, but I see what your Provence is."

"And what is it ? "

"A terribly hot place. I refuse to go a step further, and I should say the very same though you promised me a rain, a deluge of partridges—a thing I certainly don't expect to see here. . . ."

"'Pon my word," said the *judge d'instruction*, "I think I shall have a sunstroke ; my brains seem boiling in my head already."

"You're not so hot as all that, sir, are you ? " laughed Maurin slyly.

"I'm bound to say," put in M. Labarterie, "I came for pleasure, and I fail to see where the pleasure comes in."

In a word, everybody owned themselves too exhausted to go on with such poor sport in such suffocating heat. Only Mme. Labarterie volunteered, if Maurin would be her guide, to see if she couldn't bag a few partridges.

Maurin declared gallantly he would go shooting in a potter's oven to please so pretty a lady ! "So the rest of you," he said, " had better sit down in the shade in this pine wood ; there, just at the foot of that telegraph post, you see there's a circle of boulders for arm-chairs. We'll come and rejoin you when we've killed, Madame and Pastouré and I, something to save the noble company from taking home empty bags like so many duffers. Now they're seated there very pleasantly in the shade . . . we'll be with them again by midday."

"One thing strikes me as disagreeable here," complained the judge—" those telegraph wires ; they sing a song that gets on one's nerves. . . . Listen, they hum, and hum, and never stop. . . . Let's try further away. . . ."

"Pooh!" laughed Maurin, "what's wrong with that? It's as good as having canary birds to sing to you!"

The sally was greeted with a universal shout of laughter.

"Take my advice and stay where you are," added Maurin; "there's nowhere, near about anyway, where the shade is better."

They were on the crest of the hills, which descend in gentle slopes to bathe their rosy feet in the sea. The spot chosen for a halt was really beautiful and charming, and there was a well in the near neighbourhood—no bad thing under such circumstances.

From these summits the whole stretch of the Maures was visible, Saint-Tropez to the south, Saint-Raphaël to the east; in the distance the Estérel, the Alps, and in front the murmuring sea, all quivering with dancing shafts of sunlight. In the offing the Mediterranean Squadron was full in view, steaming past, a veritable floating city, the smoke of which trailed behind, like waving pennants of the huge fighting ships.

Away went the astute and enterprising Mme. Labarterie in the wake of the handsome poacher, in hopes that old Pastouré would presently slip away to talk to himself in some ravine he considered a likely place for game.

No sooner were the three—Maurin, Pastouré, and their fair companion,—a few yards away, than M. Couder addressed the most animated reproaches to M. Cabissol for having brought him in contact with a fellow like Maurin without previous warning! . . .

"There can be no doubt, you see, that one day we shall have him before us and sentence him. You are compromising two magistrates, the *procureur* and myself."

"What childishness!" laughed M. Cabissol; "why, Maurin is the particular friend of the Government. I wanted, by making you acquainted, to do both you and your colleagues a service. If ever you should see him brought to Draguignan between a couple of gendarmes—

and I for one will be greatly surprised to see any such thing
—you will know all about him beforehand, and this knowledge will afford you good reason for acquitting him."

" Meantime," snapped M. Couder, " I cannot understand
how M. Labarterie comes to have trusted his wife to a
brigand of the sort."

" You may be sure," said Labarterie with unconscious
malice, " my wife does not bring either jewellery or money
with her on a shooting-party ! "

M. Cabissol took advantage of the interruption :

" Maurin has never hurt a soul," he cried indignantly.
" In fact, gentlemen, you would be wounding my personal feelings if after this you should speak slightingly of
my friend."

" My own idea is," said the *Imperial procureur of the
King's Republic*, " we should do well to leave the party.
Are you coming, my dear judge ? "

The two magistrates rose from their seats.

" Remember, gentlemen, it is a distinct personal insult
you put upon me if you part from us like this," said
M. Cabissol in a very grave voice.

" I can only do my duty," returned the *procureur* dryly.

" And I will second you, my dear *procureur*," said the
judge. " Anyway, we shall find it cooler in the hotel
garden at Sainte-Maxime."

When he saw they were determined to carry out their
intention, M. Cabissol told them roundly :

" Very well, gentlemen, before three days are out, we
shall read in the local papers the account of our opening day,
over my signature. The part you are now playing will be
described, and your names given. My friend Maurin being
well and truly loved by everybody in the countryside,
despite his little differences with the representatives of
the law, I am sorry to have to assure you your popularity
will be seriously compromised—not to put it more strongly.

" You, M. le Procureur, you have a brother in the
Chamber, and you, M. le Juge, you have one, a Sous-Préfet ;
well, perhaps you won't be long in learning, both of you,

that your brothers' influence is nothing compared to
Maurin's ! You may yet discover it would have been
better, for the honour and success of your fortunes, to leave
Maurin in peace !

" This is the first time in my life I have ever allowed
myself to threaten a public official with the thunders and
lightnings of the press ; but I feel bound to warn you of
my intentions, that I may not take you unawares. . . .
Now, are you going, gentlemen, or will you stay ? "

" Once you give us your guarantee, you know," stammered the magistrates, " seeing you take up the cudgels
. . . so warmly and enthusiastically . . . for your friend
. . . a man of your indubitable respectability . . ."

" Good, gentlemen, good. I am delighted. Let's say
no more about it."

The incident and M. Cabissol's plain speaking were not
unnaturally followed by a considerable period of constraint
among these enthusiastic sportsmen who had abandoned
their sport. . . . But little by little the heat seemed to
melt away the awkwardness, and soon all were amicably
engaged in the absorbing business of fanning themselves
and wiping their streaming brows.

" I am curious to know," M. Labarterie said, suddenly
breaking a prolonged silence, " I am curious to know if my
wife has killed anything."

His curiosity was promptly satisfied. No sooner did
the idlers sight Maurin in the distance returning from the
chase, with Mme. Labarterie at his side beaming with
satisfaction at having shot a brace of partridges, than they
hastened to spread the white cloth over a carpet of soft,
golden pine needles. Pastouré arrived almost simultaneously from following a line of his own.

Then every game-bag disgorged pies and assorted
dainties, bottles of wine and soft white bread. Picnic
napkins were unfolded, and metal cups clinked against
goblets of cork-oak or briar-wood.

When all the company was seated in a circle round the
cloth :

x

" Gentlemen," asked Maurin, " which of you here fired a shot just now, while we were still a hundred yards off ? "

" I did," said the *juge d'instruction ;* " a magpie flew over, and I took a shot . . ."

" And an unlucky shot it was, sir ! I was just aiming that very moment at two rabbits at once, in a melon-garden there is yonder, down in the bottom of the hollow, beside the water-wheel, and for certain sure I should have potted 'em both, when your confounded gun banged off fit to wake the devil, and the rabbits, of course, bolted."

Everybody laughed.

" So," Maurin went on, opening his enormous game-bag which lay on the ground beside him, " so, instead . . . I took a couple of melons "—and he pulled out of his bag two fine melons, beautifully ripe and as juicy as could be, and, clapping them down on the cloth :

" When you've had a good look at them, I'll go and put 'em to cool in the well."

The fruit was duly examined by the company. But the *procureur du roi* of the Imperial Republic threw a look of understanding and reproach combined at his neighbour, M. Cabissol.

" Well, sir," he whispered in his ear, " and what do you say to that, eh ? "

And the *juge d'instruction* summed up without more ado :

" It's thieving, nothing more nor less ! "

" Pooh ! " said M. Cabissol, with a light laugh, " out shooting, you know . . . in Provence . . . when it's so hot . . . a grape or two ! . . . a melon or two ! . . . If the owner sees you, you just shout : ' I'm taking so and so,' and he calls back : ' By all means, help yourself . . . take what you want. . . .' "

" You think so ? " said the magistrate.

" It comes just as natural in our parts as to sing out to people you guess are off to bathe in one of the neighbouring coves : ' Well, so you're going to see if there's still any *water* left in the sea, eh ? ' "

" Just as natural ! " echoed the two magistrates at once, in a tone of incredulity.

" Well, ask Maurin."

The latter was all alive, and had not missed a word of the little conversation.

" 'Pon my faith ! " he broke in, " it's God's truth I took the two melons without a thought of stealing. The earth offered me them, and the sun too. . . . I just thought, you know, how everybody would enjoy them at dessert ; why, a wild-boar might as likely as not have gnawed 'em to the bones this very night, *pechère !* . . . Anyway, I shouldn't have told you how I got 'em, and you'd have eaten 'em up without any scruples. . . . Come, fall to, gentlemen ! . . . I'm ravenous, let me tell you," he wound up.

He got up and carried away the melons to put them in the water to cool.

When he got back, his companions had already begun the attack on the good things spread on the white cloth.

" Egad ! you make me say it—if I'd stayed away three minutes more, you'd not have left me a blessed mouthful ! "

" Look at your plate, man," Labarterie told him ; " my wife has taken good care of you."

" Madame," said Maurin, " I don't know how to thank you properly."

Presently, when the stimulus of a good breakfast, with heady wines to wash it down, had had its effect, and talk and laughter were in full swing :

" Do you know, M. le Juge," remarked Cabissol gaily, " Maurin called you a dangerous man this morning ? "

The judge drew himself up :

" A judge," he said gravely, " is only dangerous to guilty consciences."

" Excuse me," Maurin spoke, as he drained a final draught from his drinking-cup, carved out of a briar-root, a legacy of affection from his sporting friend Casimir, who had himself been left it by Prime, predecessor of Maurin in his kingdom of the Maures—" excuse me, M. le Juge. With all respect to you, it *should* be as you say ; but as a matter of fact it's just the opposite, and in these parts, at any rate, it's more generally the innocent have to fear the judges ! "

" How so ? "

"*Eh, bé !* " said Maurin, " getting mixed up with the judges, the guilty are never a penny the worse . . . but the innocent always suffer. I don't say it to offend you, but you may take it from me it is so."

" He's giving it you straight," observed Pastouré the taciturn, laughing in his beard.

" There's some truth in what M. Maurin thinks," declared Mme. Labarterie.

This time her husband gave her a reproving look.

" What do you know about it ? " he asked her.

" Oh ! " she said, smiling, " suppose an honest woman whom her husband believes to be wronging him ; he demands proof of an imaginary act of folly. The judge sides with him and gives the necessary instructions. Then the Commissary lays a trap. The thing appears proven, and the wife is compromised, although perfectly innocent."

" In that case," said the judge, " it is the husband has misled justice."

" And take just the opposite case," argued Maurin, more and more interested ; " suppose a pretty woman who has forgotten for a moment she's married ; nobody knows a word about it ; there's no judges in the business at all ; everybody's quite happy. Yes, it's the judges always spoil everything. I'm sorry M. Vérignon, our Deputy, isn't here. He'd explain it all for you first rate."

" It is very true," said Labarterie—who was thinking of his own eventual candidature—" it is very true that M. Vérignon on the day of the Congress said some most sensible things ; I can repeat his words almost by heart. He said :

" ' A *juge d'instruction* holds in his hands a terrible power.'

" Yes, M. Vérignon," added M. Cabissol, " maintains

that a *juge d'instruction* can, if he chooses, protract the period of preliminary detention to a scandalous extent—till it becomes the most flagrant injustice. Warrants of arrest may become, to use his expression, veritable *lettres de cachet*, and a judge, while keeping within the text of the code, if he does not strive to satisfy equity before everything, may bring an honest man into dire dishonour, making the law a slave to his own purposes."

" It was I set him off ! " cried Maurin gleefully.

" Come now ! " protested the judge, who thought his best course was to take the situation lightly ; " are we on a shooting party or in the Chamber of Deputies ? "

" We are at table, sitting on the ground," laughed Maurin, who saw his jokes were appreciated by Mme. Labarterie. " And I'm not sorry to be one of the party with judges and grand folks, to let 'em hear a few home truths, now I've got the chance. . . . Such as you see me, I've been condemned for assault and battery, as they call it, and for dog-stealing ! and I never did steal the dog ; a dog's not a melon ! . . . I have a half-dozen *procès-verbaux* out against me. . . . The gendarmes are after me by brigades. . . . And all for what ? for so-called misdemeanours that are none at all really."

" The faults Maurin may have been guilty of," said M. Cabissol, " were all committed in the interests of true justice."

" I have heard of some of them," the judge admitted, " though I have hardly been a fortnight at Draguignan."

" Then, M. le Juge, you must be aware that the most serious of them all ought by rights to have earned the congratulations of the Chamber—my adventure with the mad dog. But then, who cares ? we're all more or less d'Auriols in our parts, and in the long run the public opinion of my subjects judges me as I should always wish to be judged."

" But why not surrender to justice, stand your trial, and make your defence ? "

" Ah ! that's just where the shoe pinches ! " cried

Maurin. "I'm not going to enter into parleys with justice, because . . . well, because I distrust the whole thing! If I go to your Palais de Justice and say what I'm saying to you now in this palace of God's free air, you'll clap me in prison to a certainty."

"Egad! I'm afraid I shall be forced to," the judge admitted.

"While I should wish to get justice done me without being punished by anticipation."

"The law is the law! We have to judge by facts and not by motives."

"And we must have laws," asseverated Maurin emphatically; "but only the other day the papers told how a young mother, *pechère!* having nothing really her own save her poverty, stole three halfpenny loaves from a baker's shop, because her little one was hungry. She is clapped in gaol till her trial. This comes on a month later, and she is sentenced to be imprisoned and pay a fine. Now what do you say to that? *I* say she has been robbed."

He went on, his voice rising with indignation:

"You have robbed her of twenty-five days' work, *mossieu!* Five-and-twenty days, *noum dé pas Diou!* it's a little fortune gone which nobody can give back! Five-and-twenty days you've no right to; you're a pack of thieves, not judges,—you force me to say so!"

Everybody burst out laughing; and the judge and the *procureurs* had sense and humour enough to do like the rest.

"And that's why *I*, Maurin, condemn *you*—but much you care! Still, it's maybe a pity. *You* judge with your law books in hand; if I were you, I should use this, and this . . ." and slapping brow and breast vigorously, he added:

"I don't know if I make myself understood!"

Another peal of laughter greeted this unconventional speech, and if the judge pulled a wry face, at any rate he let no one see it.

Maurin, excited by his oratorical successes, continued hotly:

" After all's said and done, so long as a Government protects the Spanish ruffians who come to kill bull-calves in France as a public spectacle, and allows them to give the people lessons in butchery, nay ! encourages them, simply to bring business to the dealers in liquor, who choose our Deputies, the men who make our laws, I reckon it's no wonder if our judges speak a French jargon only a Spanish bull could be expected to understand, and if the people go from bad to worse ! . . . No offence meant, M. le Juge, if you please ! I speak as I think, like a rough, ignorant fellow ; but at bottom I've no personal grudge against you. . . . All the same . . ."

A barely perceptible smile of raillery ran over his moustachioed lips :

" All the same, being what I am, I'm confoundedly glad to have made your acquaintance ; for I quite see it's a good thing, a capital thing, even a necessary thing, to have a friend at court such as you. Then, if ever I got into serious trouble, you'd only have to be a bit obliging to get me off scot-free, seeing it's the very same nowadays as it was under the old Kings, and nothing's ever to be got except by black favour ! "

After which, without another word, he got up to fetch the two melons he had put to cool in the well near by.

CHAPTER XLII

A sequel to the foregoing, in which, after a statement of reasons
showing why the sportsman who shoots small birds is not necessarily beneath contempt, two Magistrates of the Republic are
seen confronted with a suspicious melon, and Pastouré is heard in
violent altercation with a rabbit.

By the time Maurin reappeared, the conversation, thanks
to M. Cabissol, had taken another turn. They were talking
of the *chasse au poste*, or butt-shooting,* beloved by the
Marseillais, and the immortal *Chasse au Chastre* of Louis
Méry.

Maurin deposited his melons on the table-cloth in front
of him.

" Why, they make one's mouth water," he declared.
" They seem to say to you, ' Come and eat me ! ' "

And he set to work to cut them up into equal slices
of goodly proportions.

" The *chastre*," said M. Cabissol, " is a wizard-bird, a

---

* For an explanation of this form of sport see Dumas' *Chasse au
Chastre* (The Bird of Fate), chapter I : " All the more knowing
sportsmen of Marseilles have shooting-butts. These are little
retreats partly dug in the ground, the earth which is excavated being
heaped up so as to form low walls, over which numerous branches
with withering leaves are strewn as roofing. On either side of these
huts, as one may call them, stand two or three pines, near the
summits of which some long bare spars stretch out like skeletons,
two as a rule being placed horizontally, and a third vertically.
Before daybreak, every Sunday morning, the sporting gentlemen of
Marseilles usually install themselves in their burrows. so arranging
the branches that only their heads protrude ; and even these are
generally disguised by caps of a faded green. which blends wonder-
fully well with the hue of the withering boughs. Thus the Marseillais
sportsman is invisible to every eye, . . . He waits for thrushes,
blackbirds, ortolans, fig-peckers, red-breasts, or other small birds, for
his ambition never rises to quails. . . . The Marseillais sportsman
is generally attended by a boy carrying various cages, in each of

bird that, from tree to tree, enticed Méry's sportsman all
the way from Marseilles to Rome, gun in hand."

" I don't know the tale," said the judge, " but it reminds
me of the chase of the enchanted bird in the *Arabian
Nights.*"

Then, with a keen glance :

" Yes, from one thing to another, pecking and *picking*,
a bird will bring a man sooner or later to the deuce."

" How witty ! " sneered Mme. Labarterie ironically.

" We must learn to master our passions," declared the
judge. " Buddha is wise when he bids us to kill desire
within us."

" It's easy done for rich folks, who can command
whatever they want," retorted Maurin—and he passed
round on three or four plates his two melons, divided into
slices that looked ready to melt deliciously in the mouth.

The guests passed the delicacy to each other with many
polite phrases : " . . . After you . . . no, no, I beg you
. . . no, after you, sir, . . . what an aroma ! . . . most
delicious ! "

The judge passed the fruit to his neighbour without
touching it himself. The *procureur*, as if in absence of
mind, secured a slice as the plate went by—and not the
smallest neither.

The judge's nostrils quivered with the pangs of baulked
appetite.

" To come back to your wizard-birds," said Maurin,
" have you ever heard of the *fig-mocker ?* "

which one of the birds enumerated is imprisoned. These captives
are of both sexes, the males being designed to call the lady birds,
and the females the gentlemen. The cages are hung on the lower
branches of the pines, and the captive birds call the free ones. It is
expected that these unfortunates, deceived by the call, will perch on
the horizontal spars."

As to the *Chasse au Chastre*, the *chastre* is a fabulous bird (*avis
castorum*), which lures sportsmen on and on by all sorts of miracu-
lous devices from place to place and country to country. In Méry's
famous story *La Chasse au Chastre* (and Dumas' even more famous
elaboration of the same tale), the *chastre* entices its would-be slayer all
the way from Marseilles to Rome, involving him in all sorts of
absurd adventures on the way.

"No, no!" cried the company with one voice—a voice softened by ambrosial melon juice.

"This melon," cooed Mme. Labarterie, "is the very best I ever ate in my life; it's as juicy as the finest water-melon."

"And more tasty than a cantaloup," insisted her husband.

Pastouré was lost in a brown study:

"The *fig-mocker*," proceeded Maurin, "is a bird resembling a fig-pecker, but blue-black in colour, like a *mouïssonne* (a sort of fig). The gunner in his butt, when he sees it light on a fig-tree, keeps his eye steadily on it and brings his weapon smartly to the shoulder . . . and then, in an instant, he can't see the bird any more! There's nothing whatever on the fig-tree now—except figs. That's because the *fig-mocker*, the instant he saw the sportsman bring up his gun, hung himself head downward from a twig, holding on by his claws; tucking his head well under his wing, and suspended between two figs, he looks for all the world like a third! Next moment the man comes out of his shelter, gun in hand, his eye still fixed on the twig where he saw the bird light. . . . 'He's not gone, I'll swear! then where is he, the wizard? . . . I can't see a movement!' Once close to the tree, he forgets he has a gun . . . he thinks he was mistaken, for certain . . . he feels sure the bird has flown. . . . He gives it up, dismisses the idea, and seeing on the identical twig he has been staring at all the while the finest fig of all, just where his bird was, he puts out his hand . . . f-r-r-r-t! the bird flies away, dropping a little remembrance in his eye, just to say good-bye!"

"No doubt that is the origin of the expression we use— 'Not to care a fig for anyone,' when we mean to defy a person," remarked M. Cabissol.

"Very likely!" assented Maurin, stuffing his mouth full of melon under the poor judge's very nose. . . . "What's very certain is, we mustn't despise this butt-shooting altogether; it has its merits, for there's other

wizard-birds, too, that make it a difficult form of sport.
We have the *stone-dodger*, that hides behind a stone, and
dodges round all the time, so as to keep it always between
him and the man with the gun ; then there's the *death-
shammer*, that falls on its back and shams dead, so that
the sportsman, instead of firing, goes up quite unsuspecting
to pick the bird up in his hand, and just as he's going to
seize it . . . f-r-r-r-t ! good-day to you, mister simpleton !
. . . Then, in former days, when they used flint-locks,
there was the *missfire-bird*, that used to come and drop his
little compliment from under his tail neatly on to the
touch-hole to wet the priming ! . . . but that's an extinct
species, as is only natural. Anyone any more melon ? "

"Talking of wetting the priming," said M. Cabissol,
" you would never guess what I noticed—I saw it with my
own eyes—in the church at Bourtoulaïgue . . ."

" Yes, what ? "

" A very quaint picture ; it represents Abraham offering
up Isaac. Isaac is tied to a post, and Abraham—armed
with a flint-lock gun ! !—stands ready to kill his son. . . .
But lo! God the Father appears in the clouds. His hand
is raised in command, and a sweet little angel, a tiny
cherub from up there in heaven, wets the priming of the
Patriarch's gun—I leave you to guess how. A naive picture,
work of an age of simple faith ! I have always thought it
charming. . . . Anyone another helping of melon ? "

A renewed chorus of approval greeted the invitation,
and the delicious fruit, whose suspicious origin was entirely
forgotten, once more made the rounds.

M. Couder, the *juge d'instruction*, could bear no more,
and as a plate passed under his nose, he laid hands upon it,
casting a furtive glance first at Maurin, then at M. Cabissol,
to see if they were looking. But both pretended to be
utterly unconscious of his proceedings.

Soon the conversation grew general under the agreeable
influence of good living and good wine. It was a perfect
babel of talk and anecdote, animated questions and inconsequent replies, careless wit, and heedless laughter.

Pastouré presently, wishing to leave the talk for a moment, slipt away into the woods, taking his gun with him. He was not the man, you may be sure, to leave it behind for however short a time, on the opening day of the season. He got up accordingly, and disappeared among the trees, weapon in hand.

Ten minutes later, the general cackle was at its loudest, and the judge, deaf to the reproaches of conscience, was attacking a second slice of melon, when suddenly Pastouré's voice was heard thundering under a clump of pines in the neighbouring woods. Parlo-Soulet seemed beside himself with fury :

" You cur ! " he was roaring at the pitch of his voice, " you hang-dog thief ! you robber, you brigand, you convict ! So you think you're going to escape, do you ? No, no, I've got you ; you won't get away, see if you do ! It's you stole the melons ! it's you likely ate 'em ! If you stole 'em to eat 'em, well, that's bad enough ! But, bandit, murderer that you are, if you've sold 'em, I'll complain to the judges ! They're no joke, and they'll send you to the hulks, they will, you vagabond, you beggar's brat ! "

The abuse went on thus, fast and furious. . . .

" The man will be doing someone an injury. Go and see what's wrong, Maurin," cried the judge. . . . " Come, gentlemen, we must interfere."

" Don't trouble your heads," said Maurin calmly ; " there's no reason why you should. . . . I know what's up. . . . "

Pastouré's voice had been roaring and ranting all the time :

" Tory ! scamp ! royalist ! blackguard ! reactionary ! good-for-nothing ! clerical ! thief ! scum ! I'll skin you alive ! you wait, just wait a bit ! "

The judge sprang up in genuine consternation.

" I will not allow it," he cried ; " within two steps of me. . . . Who is it he's insulting, tell me ! "

" Leave him alone," said Maurin lightly, " just leave him alone ; I know what it is—he's insulting a rabbit ! "

A shot put a full stop to Pastouré's invective; he appeared the moment after, and threw down a rabbit at Mme. Labarterie's feet.

The company stared at each other, more and more puzzled.

" Tell us what has happened, M. Pastouré."

" I ? . . . *sabi pas parlà* (I'm no speaker). You explain to 'em, Maurin."

" It's only this," said the latter; " when you come upon a rabbit crouching and cowering in its form, squeezed up under a tuft of thyme or broom, you're mostly too near to him to fire, even at the head, without blowing the creature all to pieces. So there's only one thing to do— you must insult him."

" The man is poking fun at us," purred the *procureur*.

" You must insult him with all your might and main. . . . Oh! don't be afraid; it's not to hurt his feelings. It's for this reason—so long as he hears a great rumpus, he'll take good care not to show, thinking you don't see him. The louder you shout, in fact, the closer he sits, and the more he won't move. The gunner knows that the instant he stops speaking, his rabbit will bolt . . . and you may guess he'll precious soon be lost in the scrub—though this, of course, depends on the sort of place he's in. That's why you've got to hold him where he is, keeping a careful eye on him all the time, till you have stepped back yourself to a decent firing distance. So you start shouting at him, as loud as ever you can, the biggest insults you can turn your tongue to; I say insults, because, of course, it's always abuse comes most natural to a man to shout. Pretty speeches and endearing epithets would never do, they'd sound too gentle, and you couldn't yell 'em out without making yourself a laughing-stock! So that's the reason why you call your rabbit all those names— royalist or republican, emperor or anarchist, convict or judge, as the case may be, according to the sportsman's political opinions, social position, or simple caprice. Even supposing a man has no opinions at all, he adopts a set for the time being, and insults his bunny for all the world as if it were a question of electing him Deputy. Meantime, you see, the sportsman has secured time to step back gradually ; at last, when he finds himself at the right distance, he ends the business with a charge of shot . . . then you roast your rabbit—unless you like it better stewed."

It took endless trouble to make M. Labarterie believe Maurin's explanation corresponded to the actual reality. He would have it the poacher was playing on his credulity.

Pastouré and Maurin returned to the chase by themselves in the afternoon, and by evening had twelve brace of partridge, eight rabbits, and a couple of hares to divide among the company.

" But," observed Maurin, " they're not tame creatures like Caboufigue's pheasants ! "

The magistrates had to accept their share of game like everybody else.   As he stuffed the judge's game-bag, Maurin took the opportunity to ask him, under his breath :

" Well, M. le Juge, and were the melons good ? "

The poor man started guiltily.

" Come, come, don't worry. . . . I'll put you out of your pain. I gathered them, on my word of honour I did, in a friend's garden, with his leave. All the same, I'm bound to say, if I must tell the truth, that on occasion, hunger or thirst prompting, I would make no bones—as you didn't—about eating two or three slices of stolen melon—not more than three, else I should have stomach-ache. And that's why, if I were a judge, I should very often be inclined to take into consideration *extenuating circumstances !* "

CHAPTER XLIII

Lagarrigue owns to the soft impeachment of using scent, and enumerates his favourite perfumes ; also a little misadventure to two gendarmes which they deemed it more judicious *not* to own to.

FROM time to time Lagarrigue would join Maurin in his quest after the different sorts of vermin which the Russian Prince required for his collection. For this purpose they had taken full advantage of the month preceding the opening of the shooting season. Now that date was come, their energies were concentrated on regular game. However, Maurin wanted to secure a pole-cat, and the pair set off together one day to lay fresh snares and to visit the old.

"*Sacrebleu !*" said Maurin presently, turning to Lagarrigue, as they were tramping along on this expedition, "there's surely some carrion near by ; the stench is awful."

They did not stop, and after a while :

"*Sacrebleu !*" swore Maurin again, "the stench gets worse and worse."

Lagarrigue said nothing. They went on a bit further, and Maurin remarked for the third time :

"What a vile stench ! It's very queer, it seems to be everywhere ! You'd think it was following us ! "

Then Lagarrigue explained, in the most matter-of-fact tone :

"It's *I* smell," he said.

"What ! what d'ye mean ? *qué mi diès ?* "

"It's *I* smell foul."

"*Coquin de sort !* man ! you mean to say it's *you* stink like that ? "

"Yes," explained Lagarrigue. "You see, I get good out of ill! . . . You must smell like that, *I* say, if you're going to catch foul-smelling vermin. Not to frighten 'em, the best plan is to stink the same as they do."

"But how do you set about it, eh ? "

"I keep a lot of pomades of sorts I made once with the fat of all these kinds of stinking beasts ; and according to what I mean to go after next day, I grease myself the night before, after first stripping naked—now with pole-cat, and now with marten. I grease my game-bag the same fashion, and my gun too, till I stink all over. It's done to prevent the vermin being afraid of me. So never you mind if I do smell a bit ; your Russian Prince will owe his collection to my little ruse. The fish-cask smells of herring, *pardi !* and the cod-fisher of brine. For to-day I've chosen weasel ! "

"I'd have thought," growled Maurin, "it was rotten badger, myself."

"Well," admitted Lagarrigue, no whit abashed, "it is, a trifle rancid."

"'Pon my soul," declared Maurin, "rather than be compelled to go out with you every day, I'd rather—though I love sport above everything—I'd rather forswear it for the rest of my days and go and live at Grasse, and never stir from my chair all the days of my life—at the good town of Grasse, where they grow the finest flowers of every sort, and make 'em into scent and bottle 'em. . . . It's not just orange-blossom you remind me of, my lad ! "

"Come, let's drop the subject," begged Lagarrigue, suddenly overwhelmed by a sort of shame.

"Whether I talk about it or no, my poor chap, you'll stink me out, all the same. It's not fair play."

"Did you speak to the Préfet, Maurin, as I asked you to ? " demanded Lagarrigue, by way of changing the conversation.

"For your gypsies ? "

"Yes."

" I explained to him it was best to leave them in peace."

" I guessed as much, for they've not had a word said to them since."

" Good! But you, Lagarrigue, aren't you thinking of leaving that vile hole where you work at making up your contraband tobaccos ? "

" Yes, I have thought over your advice, and for my boy's sake I'm going to drop the trade."

" You'll be doing a good job," said Maurin. " A man's easily involved in a quarrel with the judges, without having done any real harm. So it's best not to rouse 'em and leave 'em in the wrong! God—no, I'm not afraid of God, if there is one, because He knows what I think at the bottom of my heart—but the law, Lord! Lord! man, that's another matter! "

For the next few days Pastouré joined the two other snarers, and the three hunters of vermin made fine fun of the gendarmes.

" If only they knew how you stink! " said Maurin to Lagarrigue, " they'd soon catch us by following their noses up wind, without dogs."

The officers were now out after Pastouré as well, for his crime of giving them a wild-goose chase and dressing up as a Musketeer. For poor Parlo-Soulet had made himself liable to the penalties of an offence technically described as " illegal wearing of uniform," the Musketeer's doublet being one of the official costumes of the *bravadeurs*.

But the three artful snarers were constantly shifting their quarters and moving about in so impenetrable a *maquis*, the devil himself might well have lost his bearings. For the present nothing more was heard of Grondard.

As for Tonia, she several times visited her lover in various *agachons* (hiding-places in the trees), which he had by now finished building in the tops of sundry tall pines separated by great distances from each other. There was one at Collobrières, another at La Garde-Freïnet, and at ever so many other points. On the huge, spreading arms of the pines, the oldest and most intricate he could find, he had

Y

constructed rough platforms of interlaced branches. High
aloft on one of these, keeping watch on the neighbourhood,
Maurin had many a time murmured in his sweetheart's
ear the charming couplet of the King of Aragon's song*
that runs :

> Y'a ren qué lís estélos
>   Qu'an vis
> Lou parèu amourous
>   Din lou nis.
>   Lis an vis
> Si douna la bécàdo
> Coumo d'òoucèu óou nis—
> Si douna la bécàdo
> Coumo d'òoucèu óou nis ! †

The existence of these hiding-places was revealed to the
gendarmes by Maurin's old enemy Grondard ; obstinate
in his hatred as in everything else, he continued to spy
on all the poacher's doings.

"Yes, there's one in M. de Brégançon's spinney," he
told them. "I've seen it with my own eyes."

"Will you take us there ? "

"I don't much care about showing myself. . . . You
can find the way very well by yourselves, the wood's quite
small. However, as it's very thickly grown, I left a
blaze near the place. Not far from the pine where Maurin
has made his *agachon* right in the middle of the wood,
there are two or three cork-oaks—only two or three, and
in the bark of one of them I've cut a gash with my knife
and stuck in it a twig of arbutus. It's in the side facing
the hiding-place you're in search of."

Sandri and a comrade often prowled about the place,
but for all their zeal failed to discover Grondard's *blaze*.
The little wood was not quite so small as the latter had

* Masterpiece of the "félibre" (member of the society of poets
and literary men devoted to the revival and cultivation of the Langue
d'oc, the Southern French of Provence, headed by Mistral) Félix
Gras.
† "There's nothing but the stars to see the amorous pair in the
nest. Look and see if they kiss and coo like a bird in the nest—if
they kiss and coo like a bird in the nest !"

made out. And then, were they really in the one he
had intended ?

One day they made up their minds to discover at any
cost the famous hiding-place. Then they would devise
some means of luring Maurin into the neighbourhood ; they
would chase him, but in such a way as to give him time
to take refuge in his *agachon*. This done, they would lay
siege to it, and be certain of capturing the bird in the nest.

The two gendarmes started light-heartedly on the
expedition. On reaching the scene of action, they parted
company, so as to be able to beat twice as much ground
in the same time. It was agreed that each of them should
take one side of the hill covered by M. de Brégançon's
wood, and search that thoroughly.

For all their care, they could not help paying more
attention to the tops of the trees than to the stems where
Grondard's *blaze*, a twig of arbutus stuck in the bark of a
cork-oak, was to be looked for, and thus wandering with
eyes aloft, they soon lost each other's bearings. . . .

Suddenly Sandri's eye fell on the arbutus twig. He
ran up ; yes, it was the token, not a doubt of it ! He
shouted to his companion, but received no answer.

"Never mind ! he'll be back directly. Let's see
exactly where this vile bird's nest is, to begin with."

Nose in air, he looked long and carefully, but could see
nothing. It is a fatiguing exercise, keeping the chin
always up, and he was soon tired. His neck ached ; so he
thought he would take a rest, and sat down on the ground,
which was carpeted with dead leaves. Putting his back
against the trunk of an old pine, and laying his imposing
headgear beside him, he fell asleep.

He was awoke by the fall of a pine-kernel tumbling on to
the top of his hat with a hollow clatter, denting it in and
remaining in the depression. . . .

The gendarme looked at the pine-kernel, and saw it was
green and fresh.

"Ho, ho ! a squirrel," he said to himself.

He knew that nimble animal, like the *stone-dodger* of

Maurin's fable, has a trick of twisting round stems and branches in such a way as to keep them always between itself and the sportsman's eye. So he dodged round the tree himself.

" Here he is, no ! . . . this time anyway, no !—yet I'm dead certain he moved up yonder . . . no ! . . . Mother of God ! " exclaimed Sandri suddenly, " looking for the squirrel, I've found the bird I was after, or his nest, any-way ! "

Yes, he thought he could make out, over his head, cross-bars of wood running straight and stiff athwart the sloping boughs. But if they were artificial, they had been so cleverly masked by green branches drawn in front that he was even now in doubt.

" Well, we must find out, that's all," he muttered, and taking off his uniform coat, and laying it beside his hat, he set to work to climb the tree.

This was none too easy. However, using a big boulder as a stepping-stone, he managed to reach the stump of a broken branch, and so hoisted himself by strength of wrist into the fork of the tree. There was another broken bough higher up, and another and another, forming a regular ladder, and the rest of the task was mere child's play. . . . Up he went, slowly and surely. . . .

" A platform as big as a double bed, yes, that must be it ! But, by the Lord ! " he laughed, " if the beggar sleeps up there sometimes of night, he must lash himself in, upon my word, for fear of falling ! "

Sandri was right ; there was the platform, solidly built of beams laid pretty close together, the intervals between them being stuffed with twigs and leaves. A few small pine boughs, thickly covered with foliage, had been forcibly bent into position below the construction and made it almost invisible from below.

" Now let's have a look how the confounded brigand's lair is made "—and arrived immediately underneath the platform, Sandri gripped the edge and threw his weight on his arm to try if he had a solid hold. . . .

" It might be a trap after all ? Best be prudent."

But alas ! . . . hardly had his fingers touched the nearest beam, before an unseen hand seized him by the wrist. . . .

" If you call out, Sandri, *ti fouti dabas !* I'll pitch you down ! " Maurin's voice told him in calm but peremptory tones.

Sandri, in amazement and humiliation, did not utter a sound, while the invisible hand proceeded to wind a rope round his wrist.

" Don't resist, and you'll not be hurt, I pledge you my word," said Maurin, " and before an hour's out you shall be set free."

Sandri, stunned and stupefied, thought it best to hold his tongue. What could he say ? Nothing of the smallest use ! Any sort of defence was clearly impossible.

" You're afraid, maybe, I shall shoot ? Never fear, I've just come back from a little journey to Toulon, and that's why I've no gun up here, and no dog down below to set at you. Don't be alarmed ; I'm not spiteful and I play fair ; you know that I love a *galégeade*, that's all, when the chance offers . . . as you can see for yourself now."

As he spoke he was busy tying the rope securely to the tree—the rope that was lashed round the man's wrist.

" I'd better tell you what I propose to do, to relieve your mind ; I'm going to come down and set to work to find your mate. . . . When I've got him, I shall tell him where you are. So wait for me."

Then Maurin left Sandri foaming with silent rage, and in the most ridiculous plight conceivable.

Once on terra firma, the poacher, who had seen from his tree-top the direction taken by the second gendarme, went off to meet him, repeating the same call which he had heard Sandri make use of just before.

He stopped, cut a strong, straight branch of arbutus with his knife, and used it as a walking-stick. . . . It was not long before he caught sight of the gendarme.

" Sandri has discovered my hiding-place," he accosted him ; " he's there waiting for us, gendarme."

A good-natured, simple, rather silly soul, the gendarme
felt nothing but satisfaction at the news. It did not strike
him as strange to learn from Maurin what Sandri might
naturally have been expected to come and tell him in
person, if he had been free to do as he liked.

He took things for granted for the moment. Yes, he
thought, Maurin had, no doubt, surrendered. Then he
looked so peaceable, the worthy fellow! If need be,
you would only have to clap a hand on his collar. . . . Still,
just to make things sure, the gendarme felt for his revolver
as he stepped up to Maurin. . . . At that moment he
stumbled forward, instinctively throwing out his two arms.
. . . Maurin had shoved his stick between the man's legs.
. . . A hoist of the lever . . . and the enemy lay prostrate, and Maurin was seated on top of him, his hands
already busy pinioning him!

" Villain! mind what you're doing! . . . Have a care,
you'll get into trouble! . . . We are the representatives
of the law! . . .

" Represent away," laughed Maurin, " I'm not hindering
you. Indeed, I respect you at bottom. There, that job's
done—not too tight, and yet tight enough. You've the
free use of your legs, and nothing else. Now forward,
march! . . . Man alive! you're forgetting your revolver
—there, on the ground. . . . Wait a jiffy, and I'll take
charge of it."

He took possession of the weapon and led his prisoner
on a leash, as it were, to the foot of the tree to which
Sandri was tied, high up amid the branches.

" There, look at that bird perched up yonder in the
tree-top! "

" Oh! " groaned the gendarme.

" Now listen to me. I've no grudge against you; but
I distrust you, that's all, because, you see, if I didn't,
I should most likely spend to-night in prison . . . and I'm
not a cage-bird."

" He laughs best who laughs last, eh? " suggested the
gendarme.

" Granted, granted ! . . . Now, clap your back against
that tree. Good! I'm going to lash you there with a turn
or two of rope.

" Now, the feet too—nice and tight and strong, that's it !

" A row of knots all up your legs, that's the way . . .
plenty of knots, that's what we want. . . . Now, see how
kind I am ; I put your revolver down here, within a score
of yards of you . . . there ! . . . And then, best treat of
all . . . I expect to be thanked . . . I'm going to untie
your arms. Then I shall take my departure. Having
your arms free, you can untie your legs yourself. . . . True,
it'll take you a bit of time, because there's so many knots,
and there's so many knots just to make you take a bit of
time, for I want to be far enough before you've recovered
the use of your shanks.   Once free, you can climb the tree
and set our poor Sandri at liberty ; he must be getting
tired, I expect, of sticking up there in the plight he's in."

When he had completed the lashing of the unfortunate
gendarme to his satisfaction, he stood up in front of his
prisoner and making him a deep bow :

" Hoping for the honour of another interview some day !
. . . *Adessias !* "

Then, looking up in the air :

" Good-bye, Sandri . . . don't tumble . . . till we meet
again ! "

Sandri, heroically resigned, though raging internally,
did not utter a word or even heave a sigh.

Maurin moved away, then, turning back again, while the
gendarme below was already feverishly attacking the
numerous and complicated knots that secured his legs,
and fumbling rather helplessly at them in his haste :

" Listen, friend Sandri," he said ; " you know me to
be a man of my word. If you would rather this story
didn't spread, don't say a word about it. I'm quite
aware it might get me into serious trouble, but it would
damage you both at the same time in your hopes of pro-
motion. . . . I'm a good chap, as you know. Very well,
I promise not to let on, *unless* you begin to boast."

And he marched off singing :

> J'ai rencontré ma mie
>   Lundi ;
> Elle s'en allait vendre
>   De la fumée ;
>   Lundi, fumée, tóou !
> Retourne-toi, ma mie,
> Retourne-toi, qu'il pleut !
>
> J'ai rencontré ma mie
>   Mardi ;
> Elle s'en allait vendre,
>   Du lard ;
>   Mardi, lard, lundi, fumée, tóou !
> Retourne-toi, ma mie
> Retourne-toi, qu'il pleut . . .*

And when he had finished the ditty, in seven couplets, one for each day of the week, . . . he began again at the beginning. . . .

---

* " I met my sweetheart, Monday; she was going to market to sell smoke. Monday, smoke, ho, ho ! Come back, sweetheart, come back, it's raining so !
" I met my sweetheart, Tuesday ; she was going to market to sell bacon. Monday, smoke, and Tuesday, bacon, ho, ho ! Come back, sweetheart, come back, it's raining so ! '

CHAPTER XLIV

Rari nantes in gurgite vasto.

THE Var is certainly one of the districts of France where the widest extent of unoccupied land is to be found, land uncultivated yet accessible, possessing all the charms and beauties of spots left in a state of nature.

Our woods of the Maures are wilder than anyone would suppose possible. The *maquis* of Corsica alone can give any notion of what they are like. In the Maures Mountains are to be met broad expanses of rough scrub, which the natives call the Big Woods, which it is literally impossible to penetrate.

Finding himself lost in this entanglement of thorny bushes, which form a low vault overhead, the bewildered sportsman experiences a feeling of sudden horror. There is nothing whatever to betoken his whereabouts. Which way is he to turn to discover an outlet ? He cannot tell ; the impenetrable undergrowth seems to bar all egress for ever. He hears the creatures of the wild, birds and reptiles, flying in terror at his approach ; but not a tree is within reach from which he can observe the lie of the ground. All about him is a maze of bushes with yielding boughs, but of so dense a growth that it needs a vigorous effort to push them aside and force a passage. Then they close to again behind him ; they open again before his struggles, but only to shut to again at once. They seem, somehow, endowed with a will of their own, to be enemies banded together against him. The low, crowded undergrowth seems elastic, fluid like water, like the sea that is cloven by the swimmer, yet never ceases to enclose him with an equal, uniform pressure.

Of course, this scrub is to the American forests what a pool is to the illimitable Ocean, but a drowning man does not heed the quantity of the waters that are choking him. Ocean and pool are vastly different in size, but for the perishing wretch the bitterness of death is the same.

These deep, inextricable tracts of scrub, where the broom grows tall and prickly, and so strong, when it is old, that often it cannot be bent aside, but must be turned in a series of continual zigzags—Maurin knew them all. He had studied their intricacies for years, from the vantage-ground of neighbouring heights. He would force his way into them, if need be, without fear of going astray. In such cases he would shield his legs with a " fender," a sort of divided apron tied to each leg, and made of thick sail-cloth, and don his famous " sleeves." These were an invention of his own, and were always to be found in his capacious game-bag. They consisted of two sheaths for his arms of strong sheep's-leather, two long gloves, in fact, without fingers, into which he plunged his arms up to the shoulder.

No matter how deep in the scrub, Maurin never lost his bearings. The general slope of the ground sufficed to give him the necessary sense of his whereabouts. Often he would dive suddenly into these entangled belts of under-growth in order to get ahead of the quarry he was chasing by a short cut, and reach the exact point where he could be sure of the best shot.

Many a time at a shooting party, the sportsman had sighted on a heath-clad slope the wild-boar in full flight, showing above the bushes, then disappearing again, as he bounded along, looking like a porpoise amid the waves, while on the opposite hill-side they could guess Maurin's whereabouts by the slow, regular undulations of the *maquis* as he pushed his way through it ! He was *swimming* in the scrub. . . . Then, suddenly, he would reappear, and dashing into a track, neatly cut off the animal's retreat, whip off his " sleeves " and quick as lightning unsling his gun and fire.

Thanks to these famous contrivances, Maurin was able
to follow a line very often which the wild-boar even
feared to take, though at each bound he crushes and
smashes and clears a way through the thickest of ordinary
undergrowth !

For a great part of the day Maurin and Pastouré had
been pursuing their sport together, and for more than
an hour now, ever since midday, the gendarmes had been
on their track.

" Best leave me, Pastouré.   Things are going from bad
to worse," declared Maurin.

" I mean to stick to you."

" What's the good ? you'll only ruin yourself without
helping me. . . . Away with you ! If I'm caught, you
can be of more use at liberty. I'm really a bit afraid this
time. . . . Go now, and take the dogs with you."

Pastouré obeyed . . . and Maurin disappeared into the
maquis. Presently he emerged—to find himself face to
face with a gendarme. Instantly he plunged back again,
like a diver into the sea.

The gendarme climbed a high rock, trying to see from
his elevated position whereabouts his quarry would be
likely to come out again.

" Put on your sleeves, man ! " Pastouré shouted to him
as he made off.

" No, no, not yet ! " he called back.

Then he tried a thousand tricks, showing himself every
now and then to draw his pursuers to some spot from which
he judged he could rapidly slip away, thanks to his knowledge of every accident of the ground, every slope, rock,
hollow, height, even the precise position of a tree and the
configuration of its boughs. He would swarm over high
boulders, climb veritable walls of rock, finding foothold
in tiny cracks *he* remembered, but which anyone else
might have wasted hours in looking for. He would dash
across a space he knew to be unguarded by a pathway
as fine as a thread, hidden in the heath, and used by nobody

else perhaps for years. Now he would slip along, bent double, and perfectly sheltered from sight by the leaves and branches, without stirring a twig ; then he would rise to his full height without an attempt at concealment, feeling certain that concealment was perfectly needless. Yet every time he thought he had thrown his pursuers off the track, he would catch a glimpse of one or the other of them on some pinnacle of rock, watching his movements, and cutting off his retreat—apparently. . . .

Suddenly he recognised beside Sandri the tall figure of Grondard.

" I'm done for ! " he thought. " The brute knows all the ' runs ' as well as I do. . . . I've only one resource left now—the *gros bois deis fados* (The Fairies' Wood).

This " Fairies' Wood " was the most impenetrable of all the impenetrable *maquis* of the Maures, one into which Maurin had never deemed it advisable to venture.

It was a monstrous entanglement of thorny, prickly brambles, growing thick and close, as if pressed down and squeezed together, over a broken stretch of ground, rugged and full of holes.

All Maurin's strategy was now directed to the object of drawing his enemies into a sort of broad, artificial trench, excavated by human labour, between the dense scrub on the one hand, and a pine-wood with an undergrowth of tall heath on the other. This covered way was a veritable *cul-de-sac*, ending at the foot of a wall of rock of great height.

By dint of many manœuvres, and after two hours of cunningly conceived marchings and counter-marchings, the poacher succeeded in getting near the wood whose thick covert he hoped would secure his safety.

To make surer yet of his pursuers still following where he wished, he let them come closer. . . . His enemies were fairly caught ; they really thought this time that Maurin was letting them guess the line he intended to follow.

Grondard told Sandri gleefully :

" He'll never get out again. Go after him, the rest of

you. *I*'ll go and wait for him on the other side. He can't know this particular bottom, I can see as much by the way he steers ; he's going to his undoing. You'll nab him at the end of the covered way. He's in a regular trap. . . . "

Of the two gendarmes, one followed Maurin directly up the trench, while the other hurried along under the wood to bar his flight to the right. As for the charcoal-burner, he, no doubt, was on the watch yonder, at the further limit of the scrub.

Maurin, who had fathomed their plan—for had he not suggested it himself?—was moving noiselessly forward, with his long, active stride, over the stony ground, carpeted with pine-needles.

The impenetrable brushwood stretched on his left like a woven wall, nine or ten feet high—a barrier impossible to break. . . . As he strode along, he drew his famous " sleeves " from his bag, and plunged his arms into them. His hands filled the ends of the fingerless gauntlet and he could use them quite effectively through the pliant leather. . . . On his right, yonder in the woods, he caught sight of one of the gendarmes, and wheeled round— to see Sandri catching him up from behind. . . . But he slackened his pace instead of quickening it ! . . . He reached the foot of the rocky cliff in front. . . . Where was Grondard, he wondered. . . . " Well, if *he* crosses my path and tries to stop me," he muttered— " so much the worse for him ! . . ."

" Halt, Maurin ! " cried Sandri. " You're caught at last ! "

The two gendarmes hurried up . . . a few more steps, and they would have secured their prey.

Then Maurin, his gun slung behind his back, spread his arms before his face, pointing his hands together as a diver does, and plunged into the brushwood as if it had been a great sea-wave towering in front of him. . . . His hands separated ; he opened his arms wide, pushing aside the thorny branches and shoving them behind him as if he were

swimming through the undergrowth. Then he advanced
his head into the opening; then once more he brought his
joined hands to the height of his face, and drove them a
second time like a wedge into the dense mass of the *maquis*.
. . . So he forced his way forward, stroke by stroke,
rowing, as one might say, through the bushes, cutting his
difficult way across the wood, and instantaneously lost
to the eyes of the astonished gendarmes.

Sandri uttered a cry of rage and disappointment:

"He can't go fast; let us go in after him. We shall
have him yet, we shall!"

The two minions of the law did their best to copy the
poacher's manœuvres, and threw themselves into his
wake.

The opening Maurin had left behind had not so completely
reclosed as to prevent their advancing some few paces,
but most of the branches had sprung back automatically
into their original place, and the two pursuers found themselves struggling in a perfect net of hard, spiky meshes,
which scratched and tore their hands and faces cruelly.
Bleeding and entangled they made heroic efforts for a
while to push on further, but the brambles kept catching
them continually, obliging them to halt a minute or two
at every step to get free, and tearing the stout cloth of
their military tunics. The tearing, rending noise, like a
wild-boar in flight, which Maurin made in his progress
through the scrub, soon died away in the distance. . . The
two unfortunates turned and twisted and writhed—and had
soon completely lost their bearings.

Which way were they to go now? Many a brave man
who would confront a band of foemen armed to the teeth
without a quiver, is shaken before an unknown peril,
the very strangeness of which is nerve-shattering.

"Ah! but we're in a fine fix now!" groaned Sandri.

"We haven't made twenty paces altogether!" growled
his companion.

"Well, which way are we to take now?"

"Let's follow back on our own tracks; this is the line."

" No, no, it's that."

" It's most amazing ! "

" What an infernal scamp ! "

" And it's precious hot ! "

" It seems to rain down fire in this confounded hole ! "

" Look at those bushes ; you'd think the twigs were matches, all ready to catch alight."

" It's no wonder the Maures suffer so from forest fires."

" What use are the Foresters ? "

" Now where are you off to ? "

" Best hail Grondard."

" And the other escaping all the while ! "

" My word ! can't be helped ; the first thing is to get out of this."

" Grondard ! Grondard, I say ! Halloa ! "

" I can't hear a sound."

" I can though."

" What ? "

" A sort of crackling . . . hark ! . . . like the noise a boar makes when he's snapping the twigs under him as he gallops through the woods."

" Oh ! it's Grondard coming. . . ."

" No, it's Maurin going away."

" Great God ! it's the woods on fire ! The wind's blowing this way. . . . Oh ! that Maurin, I knew he was capable of any villainy ! The scoundrel has fired the brushwood between him and us ! he's smoking us out ! We shall be roasted to death ! run for it, run ! "

Grondard, making sure the gendarmes would accuse Maurin of trying to burn them alive, had himself set fire to the inflammable scrub.

CHAPTER XLV

Shows how very readily appearances deceive men who ask nothing
better than to be deceived.

"ARE you coming with me ? " demanded Sandri.

"Yes ; lead on."

"If only we're taking the right road ! "

"The right road is to turn our back to the fire."

"Incendiary ! " growled Sandri furiously. "He shall
pay for this, with the rest of his crimes. He'll die on the
scaffold, will that blackguard ! "

"We shall never find the way out ! "

"Oh ! yes, we shall. Look, I can catch sight of the
heather clumps out in the open. . . . here we are. . . ."

"Quick, quick then ! that's the line to take."

Still pursued by the crackling of the flames, which
grew louder and louder, they reached the trench, and
followed it down hill.

When they got quite to the end :

"It's very extraordinary ! " exclaimed Sandri ; "but
the further we go from the fire the more plainly I hear it ! "

"*Parbleu !* " cried his companion, "we're not getting
further from it, we're getting nearer. . . . Curse it ! there
are two fires—one in front of us, one behind our backs !
Look . . . there, ahead of you . . . look at the smoke ! "

"Grondard ! Grondard, I say."

But nothing answered save the crackling of the short
tongues of flame that licked and consumed the tangled
brushwood, as dry as tinder after a month of midsummer
heat.

"What's to be done, Sandri ? "

"Let's try to put it out."

336

"Put it out ! why, I tell you there are two separate
fires blazing at once ! The sun has scorched up everything,
all ready for that rascal's work. The whole place will
flare up like paper. Look, look there ! it's starting in a
fresh place !."

"Shall we climb that rock ? "

"Can't be done. . . . How about that tree ? "

A tall pine stood near, the branches of which had been
cut to form steps by some sportsman. Dropping carbine
and haversack, Sandri scrambled up.

"*Three* fires, there are three ! " he shouted from his
new point of observation. "There's nothing we can do !
They've been lit at regular distances—a hundred yards,
then another at two hundred yards, ahead."

"What *shall* we do, Sandri ? "

"Make for the Forester's lodge ! Warn the Foresters,
set the semaphores working, telegraph for help. I'll go
with you, but, anyway, this time we know one of these
accursed incendiaries ! Ah ! *misère de misère !* " concluded Sandri, springing down again ; " we must run now,
but I mean to see him yet with my own eyes at work at
his devilish tricks, that damned villain . . . and then ! . . ."

"Sandri," interrupted the second gendarme, " on second
thoughts I feel sure the men at the semaphore must have
seen the smoke already. It would take me over an hour
and a half to reach the Forester's lodge. Most likely
they've signalled for help by now. Let's stop here and
keep a look out, that's the best plan, and perhaps do
something to stop the flames."

"Yes, you're right."

They turned and made for a neighbouring height, from
which they scanned carefully the surrounding country.

From the foot of several hills sheets of flame were already
rising high and sweeping towards the summits. They
were a pale yellow in the white heat of the August sunshine. . . . They mounted almost vertically ; their jagged
tops, flickering and fining off in the air, ended in a sort of
serpent's tongue that seemed to dart in and out rapidly.

z

A sharp-pointed lance of ardent heat hovered over each, while here and there the flames broke off abruptly some way short of this, and a fiery finial, like a gigantic flower torn away from its stalk, swayed and shook aloft for a moment, only to vanish almost instantly, absorbed in the rays of the burning sun. . . .

The whole landscape quivered in the reverberation of the superheated air.

The "Fairies' Wood" looked like one vast blazing faggot in a Titanic baker's oven. A mighty pyramid of smoke already hung high above, relieved against the blue sky, the top bent over in a curving plume under the influence of a current of air blowing at that great altitude.

"Look, Sandri, look yonder again! Another fire!"

"Oh! the madman! the scoundrel! the vile criminal! he's destroying the Maures!" vociferated Sandri. "If only I could see him at it, I'd send a bullet through his head, and be delighted!"

Away there, in the direction indicated by the gendarme's finger, at the foot of one of the numerous hills they could see from the height where they were perched, a fifth conflagration was beginning to roar.

"There'll be nothing more for us to see!" groaned Sandri. "The brigand will never let himself be caught in the act. Better go and meet the Foresters."

As they were making their way down the hill, they halted, listening eagerly :

"Halloa!" cried a voice a long way off, "is that you, Maurin?"

"Halloa, Pastouré, is it you?"

"Yes, where shall we find what we want now?"

"Here, close by ; so come here."

Then the voices died away in the distance.

The gendarmes had heard enough ; they knew now it was the King of the Maures who had fired his native woods. Yes, they were firmly convinced of it at any rate, so readily do appearances deceive those who wish to be deceived.

CHAPTER XLVI

An appalling, but a sublime spectacle.

FIRST the wind blew a gale, then it fell, only to begin again as hard as ever.

For two days the fight had been going on steadily against the fire, but unsuccessfully, owing to these choppings and changings of the wind, which baffled the most artfully laid plans.

A host of willing workers had gathered. Préfet, Sous-Préfet, Commandant of Gendarmerie, Head Foresters, Yeomen Foresters, wood-cutters, charcoal-burners, one and all were at their posts. Whole sections of the forest were felled in frantic haste to set a barrier of fire in the path of the conflagration; huge trenches were dug; all possible measures were concerted to combat a scourge more dreaded than an invading army.

The third day drew to a close. Thousands of acres of wood, heath, broom and pines of all sizes and ages, were flaming and smoking. Soon night fell and showed all the appalling splendour of the conflagration, which the brilliancy of the daylight had hitherto more than half concealed.

In every direction, against a background of writhing flames, could be seen countless black shapes in violent motion, men armed with picks and hatchets, running, stooping, rising again, flying to escape some intolerable blast of heat, some explosion of flaming gas shot out, as it were, from a blow-pipe, then next instant darting back to the attack.

On the morning of the third day it had seemed for a moment as if the scourge were mastered.

The Préfet and the chief military officers were stationed on a hill-top commanding a view of all the country round.

"It is at once terrible and sublime, as they always say at fires," observed the Préfet. "But how do these conflagrations begin ?"

"Mischief ! that sums it up," replied a Head Forester who was suffering from a sprain and several severe burns, and was being attended to by M. Cabissol. "Our men can show collections they have made of incendiary contrivances. We often come across them in the Crown Forests under our superintendence. The commonest is a packet of matches weighted with a small stone and hung by a bit of string from the end of a low branch in such a way that the phosphorus just scrapes a stone placed on the ground underneath. . . . The contrivance is put there in windless weather ; now let a breeze, however light, spring up, and the bough supporting the matches sways to and fro ; these rub against the stone, which is packed round with inflammable material, resinous stuff and light brushwood ; they catch alight, and the trick is done. The summer suns have made the undergrowth and trees as dry as tinder, and everything flares up in an instant. We even find—take care ; you're hurting me !—the sort of trap they call *quatre de chiffre,*—a heavy stone, you know, supported by four twigs, to one of which the bait is attached—transformed into an incendiary apparatus. . . . A fly is stuck on the end of a bit of stick, a bird comes and pecks at the bait, and so sets off the trap ; the top-stone falls, and in doing so rubs against a bundle of matches, which, in turn, set alight a fire all ready laid. A blackbird will thus fire a couple of thousand acres of wood—while the culprit, some ill-disposed gunner or wood-cutter, is snug at home a dozen leagues away."

The Préfet went to take a closer view of the volunteer workers :

"There's a fellow yonder seems to be everywhere at once . . . what a man it is ! . . . Why, yes . . . so it's you, Maurin !"

" You, is it, M. le Préfet ? We're near dead beat ; we've
not slept for three days and nights. And there's old Pastouré trotting about like a lad ! The worst is, we're doing
very little good. . . . Ah ! if I could lay hands on him,
the chap who did the mischief ! "

" Do you suspect anybody ?   Who could it be ? "

Maurin stood, his face lighted up by the tremendous
bonfire, his eyes flashing indignantly ; but he answered
circumspectly :

" I have my doubts, yes, but how to prove anything ?
. . . I've learnt my lesson,—we mustn't bring a charge
without proof to back it ! Till we meet again, M. le Préfet. . . ."

At nightfall a sinister rumour spread among the workers,
—the fire was starting afresh in several places at once
with redoubled fury.

The blaze of the conflagration made the dark immensity
of the sky seem blacker still.

The towering wall of flames left in its wake an expanse
of gigantic brands yet standing, some of which retained
their shapes as trees. The parts already blackened would
suddenly blaze out with a thousand whirling sparks, while
the glowing portions would as suddenly be extinguished,
to kindle afresh at the least puff of wind. Grim death
brooded wherever living plants had been and foliage had
covered the boughs with greenery. The wild creatures of
the woods had mostly fled, but now and again a worker
would kick his foot against the calcined carcase of some
animal. . . . Before a curtain of jagged flames, interrupted here and there by gaps of darkness, the still standing portion of the forest loomed dark and forbidding and
full of menace of future danger. The skeletons of the
biggest and oldest pines, on the contrary, over which the
fire had passed and flamed and gone out, were relieved in
weird black outlines against the golds and purples of the
conflagration. Up and down their blackened trunks ran
a fitful stream of jets of flame, devouring what was left of
branch and leaf and twinkling like a firmament of stars.

At the very top of some of them pine-cones were still alight, giving them the look of Titanic candlesticks, holding out at the end of their uneven branches a series of corpse-candles, dying tapers to light the death agonies of an expiring world. Elsewhere the flames seemed to exult in their strength, and galloping on in front rejoiced to have such noble spaces before them still left to devastate.

The great forest as yet untouched watched their approach and shuddered with panic terror. At the hour when it was wont, after the fierce heat of a summer's day, to find a cradle of repose in the calm, cool darkness, lo! there was marching to attack it a night of flame, more scorching than the sun! Everywhere was a crackling, consuming, fiery furnace, while the heated air, drawing in the fresh evening breeze, turned the valleys into roaring chimneys, with a draught powerful beyond all human calculation, an upward hurricane of air strong enough to lift a very mountain. The mere reverberation of the heat dealt death far and near around the central furnace of the conflagration. Rocks, on which the sun had already been playing all day, flew to pieces in the fervent heat.

At times the fire appeared to die down over a considerable area; all the trees seemed extinguished, and the ground grew black as the brushwood ceased to flame. . . . Suddenly a fir-cone, still glowing like the snuff of a candle at the tip of a tall bough, would burst into flame afresh, open and emit the fiery oils it was impregnated with, burst, and fly before the wind like a bomb-shell, soaring in the air and describing a long flaming parabola. . . . Still blazing fiercely, it would come down, far beyond the present range of destruction, to kindle a new and unexpected conflagration in the dry brushwood.

Then, beneath the dark canopy of this undergrowth, darting serpents of flame began to creep in search of more prey to devour. Soon these twisting snakes of fire, looking like red-hot bars of iron endowed with life and motion, would roll onwards, lift their heads, increase in length and girth, till the smallest assumed the proportions of a huge

and terrible boa-constrictor. Next they would rear themselves threateningly, and grow and grow till they seemed
some sort of huge, fantastic, nightmare hydra, with infinite
gaping jaws and a thousand forked tongues.

Finally these horrid creatures would breed others as
terrible, that writhed and rose and fell and multiplied in-
creasingly. It was a welter of appalling monsters, rolling
on in never-ending undulations—a hellish torrent, an ocean
of fire, a chaos without form and void. . . .

The world was afire—a mighty conflagration, yellow,
blue, green, white, red, under the infinite vault of night.

Now the flames would scurry back as if in flight and
terror; now they would come sweeping back bold, angry,
defiant, to the assault of all living things, which took up
the tale of panic.

A continuous roar, a tremendous diapason of sound,
boomed on and on in a minor key, a mighty noise as if the
windows of heaven were opened and the waters of the
firmament were descending in a second, a fiery deluge. . . .
Accompanying this rolling, monotonous thunder, a sharp
crackling followed each explosion, each arabesque and
caprice and embroidery of flying sparks, as they danced
out a fantastic pattern in flashing yellow beads on the
bellying cloak of the huge red flames.

Whatever had been consumed, but still retained shape and
substance, bushes yet standing and seemingly alive, though
they had exhaled their life, phantoms of tall growths of
underwood, suddenly fell together in a heap of ashes. . . .
Huge mounds of glowing cinders formed craters, veritable
volcanoes in eruption.

"The Maures are on fire! the Maures will be burnt to
ashes!" was the universal cry.

Away yonder out at sea the fishermen's boats sailed a
purple sea, over depths that seemed full of fire, reflecting
the mighty blaze from afar.

In some parts of the devoted area vast flames shot up
tall and straight, burning quietly and steadily, whenever
the wind lulled, these enormous columns of fire far over-

topping the tallest trees. . . . Then suddenly a current
of air would beat them down. The towering curtains of
smoke and fire would bend over and bow to the earth.
Then next moment the flames would shoot out again and
creep as if in stealth along the ground. They could be seen
under the network of the bushes, like nightmare monsters
behind iron bars ; but they were no prisoners ; soon they
sprang up again and climbed among the trees, setting the
boughs alight as they coiled up them hissing and sputtering ;
a whole new section of the forest, spared till then, would
take its turn to burst into flame with a roar of thunder like
a dying creature's bellow of despair.

At daybreak the beauty of the hideous sight disappeared.
The dawn seemed to send it flying in shame and confusion.
The sun's kindly blaze paled the ineffectual fires of those
flames of hate. Now the sinister expanses of blackened
earth, the great burnt skeletons of the pines, legions of
giants slain but still unfallen, became visible to men's
startled eyes. The drifting smoke from the Maures clouded
the horizons in every direction, and covered the seas to
great distances with a floating veil of mourning.

The fourth evening the *mistral* began to blow. The fire
was confined now to a definite line of march, but its fury
became insensate. . . . Fire and wind seemed one and the
same element ! Everywhere the conflagration flew like
the wind before the wind, roaring with the same frenzy,
rushing on with the same swiftness.

Fortunately the furious wind fell again after a few hours.

Meantime, several regiments of the line had been sum-
moned to fight the flames. Legions of volunteer workers
were still ceaselessly and unweariedly at work amid the
fire and smoke, but the best-conceived efforts were totally
unavailing. Then it was, and not till then, all attempts to
check the extent of the appalling disaster having failed,
that Sandri won a hearing for his formidable accusation :

" I know the incendiary. Maurin of the Maures is the
man ! "

CHAPTER XLVII

Maurin the Incendiary !

" MAURIN ! " growled a Forester, " yes, he's the incendiary,
and he's there close by ! No doubt he is making a show of
fighting the flames while he is really aiding and abetting
the fire ! . . . The *mistral* is blowing to-day, yes, but it
wasn't blowing yesterday ; yet, several times, when not a
breath of wind could be felt, fresh fires were seen to blaze
up in a moment in different directions, in rear of the
flames, so that, look you, the conflagration actually
described a great circle. It got behind its own general
line of advance, and even made progress against the
wind."

" Maurin ! . . . No, the thing's impossible ! " declared
the Préfet.

" Maurin never set fire to his beloved hills, no, not even
by accident," Cabissol affirmed with still greater emphasis.

But Sandri, on being questioned, was so clear and precise
in his accusations that a search was instituted for Maurin.
Several squads of soldiers were detailed to bring him before
the Préfet. Sandri took ten men with him for the same
purpose, not a man less !

Grondard saw him go by and hailed him :

" I'm going with you ! I know where he is ! "

They followed a half-obliterated forest path where progress in the dark night was sometimes far from easy. Right
and left was thick wood.

" Look ! " cried Grondard.

Before their eyes, a hundred and fifty yards ahead, as
close to the flames as it was possible to approach, stood
Pastouré and Maurin, surrounded by several of their

friends from Bormes, cutting, hacking, felling trees. . . .
They were laying a counter-fire.

At times a squall would beat down the flames and drive
them upon the workers, who had to fall back, turning
away their heads and throwing up their arms to guard
their faces. In their blackened hands some carried wet
rags with which they shielded their countenances from the
scorching heat. Many were dripping with water as if they
had just come out of the sea, only the water was steaming.
Here and there were men carrying away the empty buckets
and bringing them back full to put them down within
reach of the workers. These would run to them and dip
their faces and re-wet their rags in the cold water ; then,
hatchet in hand, back again to their task like patient ants,
at grips with a foe whose resources were a thousand times
greater than even their intrepidity. Maurin, while toiling
as hard as any himself, was the fugleman and guide and
leader of a whole crew of helpers.

"It's all play-acting ! " muttered Sandri—and he issued
orders in a low voice. His plan of action was simple enough
—to range his men in a half-circle that was to be gradually
drawn closer, the chord of the arc being the line of flame.

The path plunged into the very focus of the fire, and
over it the flames met, forming a vault that meant a fiery
death to any man who entered it. . . . Yes, Maurin must
inevitably be taken !

The gendarme's orders were promptly carried out, and
the cordon slowly closed upon the King of the Maures, who
was too much absorbed in his task to notice what was
toward. The men crept nearer and nearer, Sandri in
the centre of the semicircular line, on the pathway itself.
The heat grew more and more intolerable. The soldiers
paused, while the workers, undaunted, obstinate, half-
naked men, every other minute swabbing faces, arms,
hairy chests, with water, could be seen struggling like so
many demons poking or putting out the fires of hell.

Amongst them Sandri recognised Lagarrigue :

"Another bad lot, that fellow ! " he muttered.

Pastouré, happening to look round, caught sight of the gendarme. Without interrupting his work, he drew up to Maurin :

" Look out ! your gendarme is there. . . . Run for it, Maurin, I'll follow. . . . Shall we bolt to right or left, eh ? "

" Neither one nor the other," said Maurin. " They're too many for that ; take a good look."

" The deuce ! soldiers ! "

" Take a bucket," ordered Maurin. " I'll carry another ; then do exactly as I do. Trust to me and have no fear ! "

Pastouré nodded in sign of perfect obedience.

Maurin wheeled about :

" Warm work, eh, Sandri ? "

" A bit warm ! " agreed the other, glancing round to make sure his men formed a close and unbroken ring. No, there was not room between them anywhere for his captive even to attempt escape.

The others broke off their work to watch. . . . There were ten or a dozen of them there, staring in bewildered amazement ; giving back before the flames, they formed, without suspecting it, yet another obstacle to Maurin's escape, even supposing it had still been possible.

" Come, surrender, man ! " cried Sandri suddenly, in a tone of triumph.

" Come and take me ! " Maurin called back, as he plunged his feet, shod with *espadrillas*, one after the other into a bucket of water. . . . Then, crushing down repeatedly his dripping clout on his head with one hand, after plunging it again and again into the bucket he carried in the other, he darted into the hollow way, under the vaulted passage formed by the roaring flames. He dived into the fiery furnace through a portico of flame !

Pastouré followed him intrepidly, after taking the same precautions ; his cry could be heard as he disappeared :

" *Couquin dé pas Diou !* what a chap, eh ? "

Sandri could not believe his eyes. " They're both dead men, to a certainty ! " he thought to himself.

The soldiers returned *re infectâ*. The Préfet was dumb-founded ; nobody could make anything of it.

" Can it be a case of suicide ? " asked M. Cabissol with a very serious air ; " a double suicide ! Poor Maurin ; they've driven him mad amongst them ! . . ."

He thought, with good reason, he might do Maurin a service by encouraging the theory of suicide.

Every possible point of egress from the vast expanse devastated by the fire was carefully guarded.

Fresh reinforcements of soldiers had been called up from Toulon, and an effectual cordon of men watched the boundaries of the burnt, and still burning, area. In any case escape was practically impossible, and this precaution made it doubly so.

Sandri was full of self-satisfaction. " I felt certain," he said, " that one way or another I should rid the Maures of that pestilent brigand ! . . . We shall find him presently, never fear, roasted like a wild-boar, black as a coal, cooked to a turn ! . . . Then folk can sleep in their beds in peace ! "

CHAPTER XLVIII

Of the strange asylum Pastouré and Maurin found in the very heart
of the fire ; of the agreeable discourse they there enjoyed concerning the Goddess of Truth ; and how the former was moved to tell
his companion the tales of *The Oar* and *The Mariner of Calas*.

THE buckets, with which Pastouré and Maurin had had
the happy thought of providing themselves before plunging
into the fiery furnace, had been snatched up, before the fire
overwhelmed the place, near a house standing by the
roadside beside the troughs of a vast piggery, in front of
which was a well. Hither the two refugees repaired,
running over burning brands.

"Wet your shoes ! " was the cry, and they plunged their
feet in the buckets.

"Forward ! . . . *li sian !* " (here we are !).

Maurin seized a heavy balk of timber blackened by
burning and pitched it down the deep well. Pastouré
understood, and gripping another, did the same with it.
Still keeping hold of their buckets, they climbed down the
well, stepping over the still burning edge. Now they could
feel the coolness as they got lower and lower. . . . It was
high time ! A *mistral* was again rising to fan the fire in the
half-consumed woods surrounding the farm, and had set
them in a blaze again.

The two men, grasping the chain, worked their way down.
With legs wide apart, they found foothold here and there
in the numerous cracks and crevices of the walls of the
narrow well, a projecting stone also occasionally giving
handhold.

When they had almost come to the water at the bottom :

349

" Wait a bit," said the imperturbable Pastouré, " till I strike a light."

" What ! man, don't you think we've had about enough of fire by this time ? " laughed Maurin gaily.

Pastouré kindled a match. Then they looked below, and found to their delight that their plan had succeeded ; evidently the timbers touched bottom ; the tops were well out of water, and crossed each other above the surface. However deep the well, there was no fear of their drowning. . . . They climbed further down.

" It's very deep," said Maurin.

" *Coquin de sort !* it's just struck me," exclaimed Pastouré ; " yes, 'twould be a droll end, to be sure ! "

" What would ? "

" Why, to die of drowning in the middle of a fire ! "

Finally they reached the timbers where they rose above the water.

" Water's a good thing when you've just escaped fire," observed Maurin.

" Yes, this is a foot-bath, this is, comes just at the right time "—and he struck up :

En attendant que la soupe il se fait,
Anan dabas si lava'n pàou leï péds. *

" Now fill the buckets, so as to have a supply of clean water ; I foresee we shall be in this box for I don't know how long yet ! "

They filled the pails and hung them on the broken branches that stuck out here and there on the timbers.

" Can you feel the bottom with your feet ? "

" Feel the bottom ! why, these shaky old props stand six feet in the water—and it's just as well they do ! "

" If only they don't break ! "

" Each hold on to his own."

" Rest some of your weight on the stones ; there are

* " So whiles the soup's a-making, let's away down and wash our feet a bit."

several sticking out conveniently, they're like shelves made on purpose."

" Well," Maurin summed up, " we're a couple of squirrels on very poor perches ! But, anyway, we have the freedom of our arms."

" I *should* like to see Sandri's face at this minute," laughed Pastouré.

" They'll think we're dead."

" That's just what we want 'em to think."

The two men relapsed into silence for a while.

" It's a bit tiresome down here," groaned Maurin presently.

" Think of the poor devils," said Pastouré, " they used to shut up in the underground dungeons of the Bastille, and you'll feel more contented, just to remember it's been demolished ! "

After another pause of silence, he added, jokingly, as he pulled out his pipe :

" You don't mind smoke, eh ? "

" *Noum dé pas Dioû !* " cried Maurin suddenly, " I've lost mine ! "

" Well, go back and look for it ! " retorted Pastouré, laughing internally. Then he added :

" One pipe's enough. We'll take turns to smoke."

" The smoke will betray us," observed Maurin, with a grin.

" The puff from a pipe amid the smoke of a blazing mountain will hardly be noticed ! " declared Pastouré— and he proceeded to cram in the tobacco.

" Loaded ! who begins ? " he said politely.

" You first ! " said Maurin, and Pastouré lit up.

When they raised their heads, they could see a circle of sky, looking curiously black, and a fierce storm of sparks from the burning forest blowing across, between them and the quiet stars.

A considerable time wore away.

" Do you suppose they'll ever think of looking for us here ? " asked Pastouré at last.

"Oh! *we'll* take good care," laughed Maurin, "to be off before they come. . . . *Té!* I'm going aloft again a moment, to see what's going on."

He climbed to the surface and lifted his head just above the edge of the well. The stars were burning bright in the calm sky above the tract of ground, here blackened, there dotted with conflagrations, which had once been Maurin's kingdom. The fire had spread far beyond the point it had reached when he last saw it so short a while before. At the further edge of the flames through which he peered he could see the little army sent out to seize him in full retreat.

From his post of observation Maurin explained the state of things to Pastouré below :

"The fire is forcing them to retire."

"Yes, it's a good watch-dog, it is," Pastouré called back.

"Talking of dogs, what of ours ? " asked Maurin. "What's become of 'em in this general rough-and-tumble ? "

"I gave 'em to M. Cigalous yesterday to take care of, as I happened to meet him."

"Good! And now come up for a breath of fresh air. Nobody can see us at this time of night."

So Pastouré joined the other at the top of the well ; but, later on, a little before daybreak, they were afraid of being seen, and were preparing to descend again to their damp hiding-place, when Maurin said he was hungry.

"Let's collect fir-apples," suggested Pastouré. "We ought to have thought of that sooner. . . . *Té!* here's some all ready roasted."

They threw a plentiful supply down the well.

"Well, we've victuals now for a week," declared Maurin.

"And we shan't want for drink neither," laughed Pastouré.

"What's more, I've got my flat bottle full of *aiguarden* in my pocket."

So they went down again into the cool darkness. They broke open the fir-apples and ate the kernels. Then they

drank the water drawn up in the buckets. Then the pipe
was rekindled, and they smoked, taking turns one after the
other. . . .

" What are you thinking of ? " asked Pastouré.

" Of getting out of this as soon as maybe," replied
Maurin. " I'd a deal rather be anywhere else."

" Why ? " objected Pastouré. " It's very good here, in
summer-time. You know how the Russians in summer
go to the Swiss valleys. What for ? for coolness. There's
many rich folks would change places with us in the dog
days. . . . They might, with all their money. Why,
they might dig themselves wells on purpose to go down 'em
for coolness ; only they never think of it."

Up aloft, the circle of sky lost its stars. Clouds of
smoke drifted over. The day broke, first pale and wan,
then brilliantly clear.

Feet wedged against the walls, back resting on the timbers they had secured firmly in place, they were so comfortable that Maurin presently dropped off to sleep.

Pastouré, finding himself as good as alone, began to
harangue at great length, while Maurin, half opening an
eye and ear, watched him and listened in a sort of dream.

" They do say," growled Parlo-Soulet, " Truth is like
we are now, and lives at the bottom of a well. Only *she's*
stark naked. In summer, Truth should do very well,
down in the cool and damp. But if she has all about her
as many good reasons to stop her coming out as we have,
obstacles in men and obstacles in things, so many soldiers,
Préfets, Mayors, and gendarmes to confound her, then,
noum dé pas Dioû, my advice to Truth is to stay where
she is. Outside, they'd strangle her, for sure, while, if
only she keeps snug below, at least she can eat and drink
and keep life and hope in her. Now I ask you a plain
question ! They say it was Maurin fired the woods. . . .
They might as well say I did ! Maurin set fire to the
Maures ? a sportsman destroy his sporting ground ?
Roast alive—to please whom ? why, nobody !—all the
poor partridges and hares and rabbits and boars have been

2 A

burned to cinders in the last four days ? . . . Why, a man must be the biggest idiot born to think of such lunacy ! . . . But, *noum dé pas Diou*, I'm feeling chilly now. . . . The heat's all steamed away from my body, and I'm getting as cold as a water-jar. . . . *Pardi !* the place might have been made on purpose to give us the ague ! . . . Suppose we went up aloft a bit and laid out our clothes to dry ? There's fire enough for that surely, and plenty of sun too ! . . ."

" What are you saying, Parlo-Soulet ? " muttered Maurin sleepily.

" I'm saying we should be better stark naked, like Truth is, so they tell us, down a deep well such as this. . . . I'm going to put out my jacket to dry up yonder."

" Don't go out now, Pastouré, it's broad daylight. The chaps over there are on the look out for us. . . . Once you show your nose, we're caught ! "

" Yes, he's right enough there ! " grumbled Pastouré. . . . I once saw a picture of Truth, and she was quite naked. . . . She was trying to get out of the mouth of her well, but everybody, men and women, were hammering at her, and forcing her in again like a cork of oak-bark in the neck of a demijohn."

" Pastouré ! " suddenly exclaimed Maurin gleefully.

" *Òou ?* " went that worthy.

" We are saved ! "

" What, again ! "

" Yes, look behind you."

" A gallery ! "

" Yes, evidently they'd begun a *noria* here."*

" How was it we didn't see that at first ? "

" It was so dark."

" You go in first. How long is it ? "

" It has been left half finished ; but, anyway, it's over five yards long and about three feet high."

" Let's put the buckets of water in it."

* A wheel for raising water, like those in use on the banks of the Nile.

"Pass them along, then."

"Good! and here are the fir-apples to keep 'em company."

"Now," declared Maurin cheerfully, "we can wait in comfort till the danger's at an end."

"Everything comes to an end!" sighed Pastouré—"so much the worse! We're very well as we are! I don't wonder now we never meet God up there in the world, seeing He's down here at the bottom of this well. *Sian émé Diou!* we are with God!"

"*Té!* look, there's another facing yours, another gallery!"

"Let's both of us get into the same one."

"Yes, *pardi!* we shall keep each other warm better."

So they stretched themselves side by side, and after eating a meal of fir-kernels and drinking their fill, the two friends fell fast asleep, thoroughly exhausted by three sleepless nights.

On waking, they looked up as usual, and saw the friendly stars shining above them.

"Wait a little!" said Maurin, "I'm going out for news."

He ascended to the upper air, and could hear the distant shouts of the men who were stationed everywhere round the edge of the burnt area on guard. Escape was not to be thought of yet, but he made his way to the neighbouring farm, which had been hastily evacuated by the hind who occupied it at the first beginning of the disaster. The door of the house had been so warped by the heat that it had fallen off its hinges, and the way lay open.

Maurin strode in and gave a shout of joy on seeing two great loaves of bread on the kitchen table. He seized them and ran back to the well-head. Then he hauled up one end of the looped chain (from which the bucket had been detached), fastened the loaves to it, and leaning over the edge, shouted down to Pastouré:

"Halloa! here's some supper for you."

Then he followed the loaves, which his comrade had already unhooked from the chain.

"With this and our brandy, we could hold out three days yet. . . . Let's have a bit of supper."

So they took their seats at the bottom of the well, at the end of their gallery, their feet dangling to the level of the water, their loaves and flask of *aiguarden* between them. They pulled out their pocket-knives, and after a polite "at your service, may I offer you some?" they fell to.

When they had eaten heartily of the good household bread, to which the fir-kernels gave a delicious woodland flavour, they applied themselves to the flask, and elbows went up a bit too frequently.

"We're not in a situation to refuse a drop of good brandy. It warms you up, and keeps off any chance of mischief, you know."·

So free were their potations—the flask was capacious, and there was no fear of exhausting it—that Pastouré, in the congenial society of his friend Maurin, grew as talkative as if he had been all alone :

"To come back to what we were talking about—Truth, you know," he began, "who is down a well the same as we are—I wonder who was ass enough, fool enough, ignoramus enough, to go and paint her dressed like a woman, or rather undressed like a woman, for she was stark naked ? Was he such an idiot as not to know that woman and falsehood, friend Maurin, are one and the same thing. It's *falsehood* is a woman, take my word for it—and whatever's true is a man. . . . That's my notion. Never you trust women; I take this chance now you're here in a place where nobody will come to interrupt us to tell you so ; yes, I say it again : Never you trust women ! *Té !* talking of that, d'you know the story, Maurin, of the girl who didn't know what an oar was ? "

"No, tell it me," said Maurin ; "we want a bit of diversion, both of us, down here."

"I'll tell it you right enough, because I'm warm again now, and because my grandfather used to tell it me once a day regularly, and lastly, because you've never heard it !

And it surprises me you don't know it, for it's one of the good old stories they tell o' winter nights. . . . It's first-rate stuff, this liquor ! "

" You're going to get tipsy, Pastouré ! have a care ! "

" Just for once in a way, I've earned it, I do think ! . . . Well, to get to my story, one day there was a sailor wanted to get married, but as he had spent all his life in seaport towns, except when he was on the sea itself during his voyages—he had learnt one thing, that in these seaport towns women know a bit too much. While the seafarers are on the ocean, they have a way of adding to their families, *pechère !* . . . And the unmarried girls are apt to be precociously artful and just as full of tricks and lies and naughtiness as their mothers—you see what I mean ? Our sailor knew all this very well, and that's the reason, when he came to marry, he made up his mind he'd only wed a girl who had never so much as seen the sea, even at a distance, so pure and innocent a creature she couldn't tell the difference between a rudder and an oar, absolutely ignorant, in fact, of everything pertaining to the sea. ' When I've found a girl like that, I shall have got a treasure, and then I'll down anchor, straight away, and settle in the country she belongs to, feeling sure of escaping the mishaps all husbands who live in seaport towns are so liable to.' "

Pastouré broke off his narrative to ask gleefully :

" D'ye follow me, Maurin ? it's a fine beginning, eh ? "

" Go ahead, Pastouré. I'm listening. *Faï tira !* "

" So he puts an oar over his shoulder, turns his back on the sea, and away among the big hills. When he had gone a long way, right up all the way to Draguignan in the North, he came across a young girl : ' Halloa ! my pretty lass ! ' he accosted her ; ' and what's this I've got over my shoulder, eh ? d'ye know what it's called ? ' to which the girl answered quite simply : ' *Té !* sir, why, it's an oar, *pardine !* ' ' We must go further afield,' the sailor said to himself : ' Draguignan's not the place evidently to find the virtue I'm looking for ! "

" He passed by Figuanières, where he met another girl, put the same question, and received the same answer. . . . At Calas, just the same again. . . ."

" I know one, I do, about Calas," Maurin struck in, " a famous story ! "

" Shall *I* tell it you, the Calas story ? " asked Pastouré quite coolly, now more than half seas over.

" As you please ! " said Maurin, puffing solemnly at his pipe.

" At Calas," began Pastouré. . . . " But before going further, I ought to tell you that in that village the asses live on the third floor of the houses."

" Suppose you were first to finish the story of the sailor, eh ? " implored Maurin slyly. . . .

" The sailor," resumed Pastouré obediently, " travelled on and on a great way, into distant lands, far in the North, till he came to Digne. . . . There he sees a fine wench go by, a girl with a poop, my lad ! a poop like a frigate's ! and quarters, oh ! quarters like a frigate's ! ' . . . ' D'ye know, my fine lass, what I've got here ? ' ' An oar, stupid, *pardi !* ' ' It's not at Digne neither I'm to find the virtue I'm looking for,' and he pushed on further yet into the interior among the mountains. At last, a long, long way from the sea, he met another girl, as well provided as the last, with a swelling bosom of her own, and all a man need ask. She was a small woman, with fine eyes and hair and teeth—in fact, everything a wife ought to have. ' What's this I'm carrying ? ' The girl glances at him, then drops her eyes : ' That,' says she, ' my fine sir, that's a baker's shovel ! '—' *Noum dé pas Diou !* I've found the white blackbird. . . . Here's one at last is like a plum on the tree, with all its bloom untouched by anybody ! I'll marry her ! ' The sailor had been round the world again and again, and had made a pretty pile, so her parents gave him their daughter readily enough.

" So here we have the *novi* (newly married bride and bridegroom) in the nuptial chamber, he in his shirt, she already abed. He was just getting in himself when :

'Which side shall I lie, Captain, eh ? port or starboard ? '
she demanded. '*Noum dé pas Dioû!*' cried the sailor,
tearing his hair, ' she's seen an oar before now, I wager !
. . . I've tramped many a long mile in vain, it seems !
And now I'm caught tight in a sort of pitch don't melt in
the sun, oh dear ! ' . . . And he found himself, like any
other husband, just what he had tried so hard not to be."

"A very good story ! " cried Maurin, laughing heartily.

" What ! " marvelled Pastouré, " what ! had you never
heard it before ?   By God ! that's impossible ! "

"Why, of course, I've heard it before," grinned Maurin,
" if only by having listened to you telling it above a hundred
times.   But we're not here to invent new ones ; besides,
the best known are the best—because why ? because the
others get forgotten.   Now, tell me the Calas one."

" No, you tell it, since you know it."

" No, you."

" You, come," insisted Pastouré.

" I say *you*," insisted Maurin, still more emphatically.

"At Calas," proceeded Pastouré, without further pressing,
" the asses live on the third floor of the houses, because
the houses are built back to the mountain-side ; they
have their back-door on the third floor, opening on a
trackway.   So they stable the asses in the garret ; the
beasts come in by the back-door from the track, and,
staring out of the front windows, they look away south-
wards into the hills that hide the sea and the beach of
Saint-Raphaël, seven leagues away.   In some houses they
don't keep an ass, then the people occupy the third floor.
One of these, waking up one morning, looked out of window,
and saw a fog covering the Estérel and all the hill and all
the country, and coming right up to the window-ledge ;
it was a bluish-grey colour, was the fog, and very dense.

" ' Oh ! mother,' the fellow shouts—he was a young
man, ' oh ! mother, the sea's overflowed ! . . . It's come
to Calas ! . . . Quick, a boat, quick ! '   ' But we haven't
got a boat ! '   ' I know that, *parbleu !* what I mean is you
must give me the kneading-trough ! '   With his mother's

help he got the kneading-trough, which, of course, had
something the shape of a small boat, hoisted on the window-
ledge. ' Wait till I get in, and then you must launch the
boat ! '

" He got into the kneading-trough. He had taken the
shovel from the bakehouse to scull with, and when he cried
' launch ! ' his mother pushed him off, and. like an ass,
he fell from the third floor, and, plunging through the fog,
came crash ! to the ground.

" So that's the tale about Calas that you wouldn't tell
me. Yet I should have been delighted to hear it."

" The truth is, when you're tipsy, Pastouré, you tell it
better than I can. Men who have books often read 'em
through again, I'm told, when they want amusement,
whether because they're amusing, or because they're good
books, without being over and above amusing. You've
been talking like a book, you have, a book I've read before,
and I read it again when I hear you. But there, for God's
sake leave the flask alone, or you'll end by being too dread-
fully drunk."

" Never again," declared Pastouré solemnly, " never
again shall I find such an opportunity of getting tipsy
without anyone to see me. Nobody will ever believe
me, my lad ! if I tell 'em I've drunk anything better than
water at the bottom of a well. . . .

" It's no matter," he added, after a pause, " every
country has its own customs. At Calas, as you've just
been told, the asses live on the third floor of the houses,
and sometimes they tumble out of window ; while at
Saint-Tropez the folks are fond of hanging out a canary-
bird at their backs."

This last remark surprised Maurin not a little, and he
stood silent a moment or two ; then, suddenly breaking
into a great gust of laughter :

" Oh ! the backs of their houses, you mean ? "

" *Pardine !* it's not at their own backs, of course,"
grinned Pastouré, " though, 'pon my word ! it's not such
an unnatural mistake to make, after all ; one never knows

what the girls of these times may choose to wear some day ;
I remember, one while, they stuck a miniature bolster there,
and they all carry, even nowadays, a regular kitchen-
garden on their heads, cauliflowers, and artichokes, and
goodness knows what. . . . But d'ye think the time's
come to leave our well, perhaps ? "

" Wait a bit, and I'll find out and tell you," said Maurin.

" Up you go into the cross-trees, topman ! " Pastouré
shouted after him, as his comrade scrambled to the surface.

Then from aloft Maurin called down :

" Ho, Pastouré ! you can come up too."

After a minute or two, hearing nothing stirring, he hailed
again :

" Halloa, Pastouré ! I tell you, you can come up ; you
can come up."

A lamentable voice rose from the depths of the well.

" I can, can I ? that's easy to say ! but I don't feel so
sure ! Come up, yes, I should like to very much ; but I
can't. I've tried ; you come and see ! My legs won't
work. If it's not the fault of my rheumatism, why, it's
the *aïguarden's* fault, that's flat ! "

" Come, come," said Maurin, who had climbed down
again to his comrade ; " now, give me the flask ; I'm going
to take it away from you. We'll get up all right, when
you've found your head again."

" That won't be long first, old chap. But let's have a
good talk meanwhile," said Parlo-Soulet, who found the
liquor a decided stimulus to loquacity.

CHAPTER XLIX

How, by the mouth of Pastouré, Truth spake abundantly at the
bottom of a well, and discoursed to Maurin of matters the most
pleasing or the most melancholy in the world according to the
temperament and disposition of the listener, but without any
question highly profitable to the known.

PASTOURÉ, sitting at the bottom of the well beside Maurin,
was now quite drunk, and in a maudlin state.

"I shall only bring about your capture, Maurin," he
whimpered, "so go, and leave me to my unhappy fate.
I shall be all right again, one day, please God. Yes, I've
forgotten myself, Maurin. Leave me alone to drown;
it's all I deserve."

"You've taken a remedy against fatigue," Maurin com-
forted him; "only you've taken it too freely. Instead
of whimpering—for you know as well as I do I shan't
leave you in the lurch any more than you would forsake me,
give me a bit of good advice, by way of passing the time;
it'll maybe save my life, and then we'll call quits, and good
will have come out of evil. They say Truth is in wine;
then more by token, it must be in spirits. Now, ought I
to marry ? . . . Ought I to marry Tonia ? "

Pastouré never flinched—he was too drunk to fear *any*
responsibility—he answered at once :

"Truth, I told you just now, is not a woman, but a man—
and a tipsy man at that, sitting at the bottom of a well.
You'll have the truth twice over, what with the well and
what with the spirits. . . . Marry, Maurin! no, never
do anything so foolish ! Married, yes, I was married, and
all my married life I was never a free man ; I only got free
when I was a widower, and it's trying to have to long every

day for someone to die, someone you love after all, and who
is so closely bound to you !   No, Maurin, don't you marry !
One man'll tell you this, and another'll tell you that,
and a third will tell you this *and* that.   But I tell you,
don't.   It's as clear as the well-water of Truth, and the
quintessence of wine, which is spirits.   Don't marry.
Once upon a time it *was* possible, perhaps, to marry ;
now it isn't."

" And why isn't it now ? " asked Maurin.

" Because, nowadays," Pastouré expounded, " nowadays, to say nothing of the kitchen-garden they grow on
their heads, the girls have wheels ! "

" Wheels ? " grinned Maurin ;   " oh ! you're very
drunk, mate ! "

" Not so drunk as you think, Maurin.   Just you look
about you, in the streets and on the high road, and you'll
see nothing but women in breeches and women with
wheels.   They ruin their poor fathers to buy 'em, these
wheels !   Why, even in our country villages, Maurin, they
go on two wheels, the girls do, quite young girls too, to
travel faster and farther, where nobody can fellow 'em,
it they don't want to be followed, and they wear skirts
slit up the middle that are nothing better than Turcos'
trousers. . . . Thank you for nothing !   Perhaps you
might have been ready to marry a girl, when there *were*
girls, but marry a Turco, no thank you, that's not your lay.
In old days, I don't say, Maurin, in my grandfather's time,
when the women in our country places waited on their
man at table, when he came in tired from his work.   Yes,
his wife helped in his work, she did, as she ought, by staying
at home and making the soup.   He wanted good, nourish-
ing soup, and he ate it properly, sitting by himself at
table.   The wife had hers after her master was done,
and that way quarrels over meals were not so common.
Nowadays, everything's altered ! the women are a bastard
sort of men in wide trousers ; why, there's some do men's
work in the post offices and railway offices.   Everywhere
there's plenty of 'em on *òoucipèzes* (velocipedes) and

mighty few in the houses. Marry a modern woman ? No,
no, Maourin, leave that to others ! it's not the thing for us !
Never take a wife, Maurin, just when they're trying to
become voters. . . . My word ! it'll be fine times when
they are !   Ah ! I'd like to see that, and I shall, we all shall !
But never, never, while Pastouré's alive, will he let you
do anything so foolish as marry a voter !   Why, one day,
Maurin, you'd be finding yourself husband of a Deputy,
or a Senator ! Yes, there's no denying it, that's what
a man exposes himself to if he gets married these days !
If you haven't enough of politics, *I* have, without going in
for more when one's head's on the pillow !

   " Politics, politics ! we've enough of politics ! more than
enough, a hundred million times too much ! My baker
kneads 'em into his flour !   He's a Municipal Councillor,
a Radical Conservative, whatever that means, like Caboufigue, and he thinks I voted against his ticket, and that's
enough to make him give me half-baked bread, out of spite !
The wine-dealer puts 'em in his casks, these plaguy politics,
and the very man who, being a red, ought to respect the
colour of good wine, he claps in water by the bucketful,
out of spite, because I voted against his candidate who
promised him bull-fights—Spanish cow-fights, say rather !
—at Bourtoulaïgue and at Calas. . . . I never talk about
these things.   But there, I'm just bursting to out with 'em,
and out they come now, seeing we're snug and quiet at the
bottom of a well, like Truth, and drunk on *aiguarden*, my
lad, like Truth. . . . .

   " No, no, I belong to another age, Maurin, I do—an age
when the women weren't stationmasters, nor yet Turcos,
neither Senators, nor Deputies, nor lawyers, not yet
emancipated in a word !   They had emancipation enough
to get with child at the proper time, and suckle their babies
in due season, and after unswaddling one brat to get ready
for swaddling another !   That left 'em no time to run the
high roads on two wheels.   In those days they were
respected for their children ; now they're disrespected,
because they're galivanting at Antibes when their mammas

think they're at Martigues ! . . . Time ! a woman has no
time. She takes a year to bring an infant into the world
that cost *me* only a minute or two. And that's the message
I, Parlo-Soulet, proclaim to the folks of to-day from the
bottom of this well ; for in my days the women kept their
places and obeyed their husbands, the same as under the
Grand Turk. And now I'll give you a proof, Maurin, of
what I say about their obedience in former days, by telling
you the story of how and why I was born.

" My father, as was only natural, after his eldest, Victorin
died, poor chap ! wished to have a second boy. He told
my mother so, but there, she couldn't help it, you know,
and this time, instead of a man-child, she gave him a girl !
My father was very vexed, and wouldn't speak to my
mother for several days, to let her know he was not pleased
with what she had done. She understood right enough,
mate, and resolved to do better next time, Well, next
year, my father, who was waiting the event in another
room asked, ' Well ? '—' Well,' they told him, ' it's the
same as before—another girl ! ' Again, the fourth time,
the same unhappy result, which made three girls. It ended
in my ill-starred parent falling ill, for despair made him take
to drink, and he was scarce ever to be seen quite steady on
his pins, poor man—all by his wife's fault ! On this fourth
occasion, when my father was told once more it was not
a boy, but a girl, he swore by the Almighty it shouldn't
happen again, and this is what he did to prevent it. As
soon as his wife was about again, he took a *blette* (fine
switch) of hazel, and, without hurting her overmuch, just
tickled her back with it, saying over and over again :
' I want a boy ! you owe me a boy ! we must have a boy !
Now, at the fifth time of asking, if you're so unfortunate
as to give me another girl, I'll turn you out of doors, you
and your two pairs of girls, and one day you'll just find
for yourself the fools they'll want for husbands, when
they've come to an age to cheat a man ! '

" Well, 'my dear lad, my mother couldn't sleep for
thinking of it, but her obstinacy gave way ! and the fifth

time, I was born to bless my father's firmness of will, I,
Marius-César-Antoine-Auguste Pastouré, otherwise known
as Parlo-Soulet ! . . . And I can tell you the trumpets
blew and the flags flew the day I was born. . . . And that
very day, Maurin, the day I came into the world, I thought
to myself, thought I :

" ' It's quite enough to have a mother, Pastouré, my lad !
you'll never marry a wife ! ' "

" But . . . you did marry, anyway ? "

" I did," groaned Pastouré, " and that's why I can
speak as an expert of the calamity it is. Marriage is a
dark road, where a man's more like to break his head than
not. And that's the reason I tell my old friend Mòourin :
' Don't go that way, I've been there myself ! ' Well, you're
a good listener, and I give you the best advice I know.
Do as you like. If I don't give you light enough, light up
your lantern. If my words are hard, break 'em, you'll find
a good kernel inside. . . . And now you've smoked my pipe
long enough, give it me back."

Maurin did as he was bid, laughing quietly to himself.

" Té ! " Pastouré asked him, " d'ye know the tale of
The Blackbirds ? "

" Tell it me, if your legs are still too feeble to climb
up yonder to the top."

" Feeble ! they're as flabby as dead jellyfish," said
Pastouré. " Yes, I would fain keep company a bit
longer with Truth in the well."

CHAPTER L

Pastouré tells the diverting tale of the *Hen-blackbirds*, that
were cocks all the time.

" WELL, then, here's for the story of the *Hen-blackbirds*.
It's as well for you to hear it, O Mòourin, in case you should
disregard all my good advice and marry a wife—above all,
if she's one of your Tonias, the sort that are as good with
the carbine as a man. . . .

" A small farmer of our parts, a man called Sanplan, had
wedded a young woman of the Charpinois (naggers) clan.
That's a family there's plenty of to be found everywhere.

" Well, one day, Sanplan killed a couple of blackbirds
on the hill. The birds were roasted, and husband and wife
sat down to talk in the downstairs living-room of their
farmstead.

" Licking his chops preparatory to beginning, Sanplan
observed suddenly :

" ' That's a famous fine bird ! '

" ' A famous hen-bird, you mean, eh ? '

" ' No, I say what I say—a famous bird ! '

" ' Well, then, you say wrong,' retorted the wife; ' they
were hen-birds, I tell you ; the cocks aren't half so good.'

" ' Oh ! hen-birds, if you like, then ! ' grunted Sanplan,
who was a man of easy temper.

" ' Don't say, *if you like !* ' the scion of the Charpinois
snapped at him ; ' I don't choose to have you put it as
though you were doing me a favour.'

" Sanplan had only been married a few days, and, besides,
he was the sort who never make difficulties, but always
try to keep the peace instead. So, with an ingratiating
smile, he remarked :

" ' And if I do agree with you, simply and solely to please you, where's the harm, I should like to know.'

" ' So,' the woman screamed, ' you stick to it, do you? You go on saying they were cock-blackbirds ? '

" ' Not for worlds, my dear ! . . . very likely they were woodcock ! '

" ' Woodcock, woodcock ! You say that just to make fun of me ! '

" ' Well, if you will have it so, let's put it *you*'ve eaten a hen-bird, and *I* a cock. Anyway, the proof's disappeared ; you didn't taste mine, you know.'

" ' I smelt it ; and it was a hen.'

" ' Let's say no more about it ; have it the way you like.'

" ' The way I like ! have it the way I like ! ' grumbled the odious woman. ' Things are not as people like 'em, I tell you, but as they are.'

" ' Alas ! ' sighed the husband, as long-suffering as Job ; ' alas ! yes, they are as they are ! '

" But, as usual, the more unruffled remained Sanplan's temper, the more exasperated was his wife, and being no fool, she understood quite well what the unhappy fellow's sigh meant :

" ' *Aï ! las !* " she shrieked, " it's for me to sigh ! . . . my mother spoke only too true when she told me I'd soon be miserable with you ! '

" ' Bah ! your mother ! oh, yes, your mother ! '

" ' Well, and what of her—my poor mother ? You're not going to start abusing my mother now, are you ? '

" And calling the whole world to witness—there wasn't a soul anywhere near, by the by :

" ' You hear him ? you hear that, everybody ? ' she scolded ; ' he's abusing my mother now, the fellow is !, it's the last straw ! Oh ! my good, dear, darling mother ! Why, why didn't I stay in my mother's house ? '

" Sanplan was roused at last, and couldn't help saying savagely :

" ' Would God, carrion, you'd never left the hulks. there ! '

" ' That's right, now insult me ! ' yelled *Misé* Sanplan, *née* Charpinois . . . ' Go and tell everybody you married me from the hulks ! yes, and say you'll send me back there again, do ! . . . To the hulks, by God, send me to the hulks ! and why, just tell me that, why ?   Just because I won't say a hen-blackbird is a cock, and for no other reason whatsoever !   Now, isn't it right and fair to hold out that a hen isn't a cock ?   Isn't it the simple truth ? . . . A man must be mad to want to force an honest woman to say a thing that's the very opposite of common sense and plain truth ! . . . No, I was never taught to tell lies in *my* home. . . . The hulks, indeed ! . . . No, I'll not go back on my word, never ; not even to please my husband, I won't.   No, I'll never tell lies ! . . . they were *hen-birds !* HEN-BIRDS, I say ! HEN-BIRDS ! . . . They may bray me in a mortar, but they'll never make me say otherwise ! '

" The meal ended, she went on grumbling and growling in this fashion for a whole hour, knitting at a stocking the while.   Her husband didn't breathe another word. She knitted away under the lamp-light, still harping on her grievance :

" ' I'll swear they were hen-birds !   It's only fools and idiots and ignoramuses would say hen-birds were cocks ! . . . Yes, yes, hen-birds they were !   If I were at my last gasp, I'd still say the same—hen-birds they were, hen-birds they were ! '

" ' Hen-birds be it ! but God keep the cocks from such hens then ; it's their affair more than mine, anyway ! '

" ' Why, good Lord ! ' retorted the angry dame, out of all patience, ' why, you're only a silly bird yourself, a silly goose !—a fool—if you're not a knave ! '

" Thereupon Sanplan, unruffled as ever, marched out of the kitchen, pulled to the door behind him, and stumped up to bed.

" Left to herself, *Misé* Sanplan went on knitting, pulling in her thread to her in a series of little jerks. . . . When she knitted, she always let her ball of worsted roll on the

2 B

ground, this way and that, for she kept no cat or any other
domestic animal, hating them all—a dislike they one and
all fully reciprocated.

"She went on growling to herself, as before :

" ' Yes, if I were on the scaffold, I'd say it still, I would ;
the hangman wouldn't force me to say anything else.
They were hen-birds, they were !   At the Day of Judgment, I'll tell God Almighty himself the very same :
they were hen-birds ! . . . There, he's getting into his
bed now, the coward !   He's afraid to face the truth ! . . .
But if I live to be a hundred, he'll never hear anything else
from me, he won't, but : they were hen-*birds !* yes, and big,
fat *hen-birds* at that ! '

"But for all her pettishness, she took care to pull in her
thread every now and again quite gently and gingerly,
so as not to run any risk of breaking it ; for your true
grumbler never really loses her head, even at the height
of her paroxysm of ill-humour.

"Suddenly the thread refused to come. She hauled
harder, but the worsted only stretched. She looked
curiously to discover the reason, and saw that the thread
disappeared under the closed door.

" ' My man must have kicked the *cabedéou* (ball of
worsted) with his foot, the clumsy fellow, as he went out.
. . . Oh ! these men, they never notice anything ! whatever would the chap do, I wonder, if he hadn't me ! but
he has got me ! and—don't I have proofs of it every day ?—
he doesn't know his good fortune, *pauvre de moi*, not he ! '

"Then she got up, took the lamp, opened the door, and
to her great surprise observed that the thread went up
the stairs, up, up, festooned from step to step all along the
wall.

" ' Well, upon my word ! what can that mean ?   There's
some trickery in that, for sure. . . . My ball didn't go
up all of itself, I reckon ! '

"She thought no more of the blackbirds, whether cocks
or hens, at any rate she said no more about them ; for so
powerful an agent is a woman's curiosity that, to learn

a secret, the greatest chatterbox of them all will find it possible to hold her tongue a minute or two.

"The thread led her to the top of the staircase. . . . Then she saw that it penetrated, again passing under the door, into their bedroom.

"She entered, lamp in hand. She followed the thread with her eyes. . . . It climbed on to the bed, in which her husband lay asleep with one eye open, and the eye that was awake had a mischievous twinkle in it. The woman's look, following up the thread, soon arrived at the bed, where it disappeared under the clothes. She lifted the blankets and behold! the thread and ball of worsted were tied to a nice little stick, a pretty miniature cudgel, not too knotty, but a good, solid weapon for all that, with which Sanplan was in the habit of tickling up his donkey's ribs, but which for the moment seemed to be fast asleep like its master. *Misé* Sanplan never opened her lips, all her faculties being occupied with gazing at the cudgel.

" 'Now, woman,' the husband broke the silence, ' this is a first time of warning. If you persist in breaking the drum of my ears, I'll break *your* back for you. But, believe me, that's a poor plan after all ; blows never mended a quarrel yet. . . . I'm good-natured to a fault, but I mean to be respected just as much as if I were a bit ill-conditioned, you must please understand that. I'm glad to see you have the sense not to haul on a thread, if need be, to the breaking-point.

" 'When I spoke up just now and held my own, so mildly, about the blackbirds—the devil fly away with 'em ! —why did you pull so hard on the thread, eh ? The thread that ties a husband and a wife together is finer and not near so strong as your worsted, my lass, and once broken, there's neither knot nor join can ever make it as good and binding as before. If you pull too strong on the thread I speak of, it'll crack, *pechère!* and I'll just leave you to your own devices, you and your blackbirds; for I hold the good end, the ball end, tied round this stick, which represents my will and pleasure as a man. So now, get to bed, if that's your good pleasure, and leave me in peace till daylight ! '

"Whether the pestilent creature made up her mind there and then to wear worthily henceforth the name of Sanplan, and let her old one of Charpinois (nagger) fall into oblivion, I cannot say for certain," declared Pastouré, winding up his tale, " but anyway, all that night, she said no word more about blackbirds, cocks or hens, and Sanplan could sleep away like a top.

"Now six or seven hours of good, quiet sleep, when a man's married—at any rate the way Sanplan was, is always so much profit to the good. . . ."

" But you'd told me that tale, yourself, before," laughed Maurin—" like the others."

" And you'd clean forgotten you'd ever heard it from me, you heedless fellow ! "

" Not I ! it was you had forgot you'd ever told it me. . . . Come, come, all this talk with a friend has quite excited you—you, who only talk to yourself as a rule ! "

" It isn't every day a man finds himself down at the bottom of a well ! "

" Well, take a nap, and then we'll try if we can't get out of this."

But Pastouré said nothing ; he had suddenly dropped off asleep as sound as a log. This opportune drowsiness no doubt saved the two refugees, for now they lay quite still and silent, side by side in the gallery. Truth was asleep at the bottom of the well, and so she deceived the wiliest, the Sandris and Grondards.

When they came and bent over the well-head, these two, and others who were in pursuit of Maurin and Pastouré, they did not catch a sound—not even a snore.

Nor did they see anything at the bottom of the abandoned *noria*, but the flash of water down below, and floating on the surface a few fir-apples fallen from a neighbouring tree, and a couple of long, charred beams sticking out from the bottom. . . .

CHAPTER LI

In which Césariot is *forced* to admit that he owes his life to his father.

WHEN they left their hiding-place at last, they saw the herdsman approaching, the fellow who managed the piggery, the same who had lent them two loaves of bread, without knowing anything about it.

" *Òou !* it's you, Maurin ? "

The latter explained matters, winding up :

" Here's what's left of your two loaves ; we've eaten the rest. I'll pay you back when the time comes."

" You're heartily welcome to them," said the man. " But off with you, quick, to a safe place, though to tell the truth they think you're both of you dead, and it's only your carcases they're hunting for. Where d'you wish to go now ? "

" To Bormes, where I want to see someone," Maurin replied, his thoughts running on Tonia.

" Let's go by way of La Garde-Freïnet ; we have friends there will lend us a couple of nags."

It so happened they came upon a strange sight on arriving at La Garde-Freïnet. It was the feast-day of the Patron Saint, and the time-honoured game of the *Bouffés* was in full swing.

All the young men of the town and neighbourhood, armed with bellows, were chasing one another and singing in chorus :

> Sian uno bando
> De bravo jouventùro.
> Aven un grand fué qué nou brûlo.

> Si sian immagina,
> Per si lou fa passa,
> Dé prendré leïs bouffés,
> Au cùou dé si bouffa.*

Then, while they were chivying about the girls who had
come to look on to this tune, suddenly a second band of
young men would spring out, and disguised as Moorish
or negro pirates, put the first to flight, and carry off the
pretty girls under their noses ! . . .

But Maurin and Pastouré had other things to attend to.
So they quitted La Garde-Freïnet with all despatch,
mounted on the two good horses they had borrowed, having
determined to make their way along the seashore in order
to throw their pursuers off the scent. Their idea was to
follow the cornice road which climbs up and down along
the southern slopes of the Maures, above and beside the
sea-coast ; then, in case of emergency, to leave their
horses there and take sanctuary in the woods they knew
so intimately.

The fierce *mistral* had sprung up again towards four in the
afternoon, and though impeding their progress, the wind
was really favourable to their escape, because it discouraged
traffic on the roads, which were almost deserted. The
tempest roared and blustered, but in the gulf of Cavalaire,
which is like a great lake a league long, the sea in times of
mistral has little space to rise in, the coast which they were
following being protected by the Point of Camara. Further
on, however, at Saint-Tropez, the waves were rolling in on
the quay with such force and fury that again and again
they enveloped the statue of the Bailli de Suffren in
drenching clouds of spray.

When they came in view of the beach of Cavalaire, Pastouré and Maurin found themselves facing a perfect
hurricane. The trees of the plain seemed one and all
cowering in mortal terror. The sea was sweeping from

---

* "We are a band of gallant lads. We have a great bonfire which
we burn. So we are minded, that we may leap through it, to take the
bellows to blow ourselves up with behind."

the north-east, and rolling in mighty billows on the southern
shores. Vast masses of blue water were pouring in, crested
with foam, like mountains rearing their snowy tops to the
heavens. The overmastering force of the wind tore this
white spume from their summits, and drove it shorewards,
looking like great clouds, which the sea pursued savagely,
as if eager to recover its own again.

Not a boat in sight. . . . But yes, there was one, a
fishing-boat in distress yonder ! . . . She was struggling
hard against the storm, hoping to reach shelter under the
western horn of the bay of Cavalaire, and so by help of
her four oars to get safe to land—perhaps. . . . A Saint-
Tropez boat, no doubt ! . . . Without a word Maurin
spurred his horse, and Pastouré followed suit ; ten minutes
later the two were galloping round the immense curve of
the beach.

The boat had won its way by now to a place of com-
parative shelter ; but the *mistral* in its might, the *mistral*
that bends the great pines to the very earth, was even then
driving the waves furiously before it, and in this wild rush
of water the little vessel found herself carried, despite the
sheltering headland, further and further from the land.
The trees on shore seemed to be flying before the storm,
bowing and bending and cowering, like a panic-stricken
army in full flight, imitating the mad speed of the waves
themselves. Caught in this wide whirlpool, the boat
was drifting further and further from the beach. . . .
The strength of those on board was evidently exhausted.
A wave caught the poor cockleshell broadside on, and it
filled and overturned.

At the bottom of the bay, the men at the custom-house
barracks had seen the boat, and the gallant fellows were
hard at work trying to launch a row-boat, but it was a
hard job, and there was bound to be much delay.

The King of the Maures, rising in his stirrups and steady-
ing his body against the wind that blew his clothes about
wildly, kept his eyes fixed on the two shipwrecked men,
who were struggling to get a hold of the upturned boat,

showing for an instant on the top of a wave, to disappear
again next instant in the hollow between two mountainous
billows. The noise was deafening, the groaning of the
forest mingling with the roar of the ocean.

Through the din, Maurin bellowed to Pastouré :

" Wait for me, I'm off to the rescue ! "

Then the bold fellow, descendant of a long line of Saracen
pirates and Provençal fisher-folk, drove in his spurs—and
charged the sea ! . . . One moment, as the waves rolled
in, it seemed to be charging back to meet his assault,
but the next, as they retired, it fled before him. The soft
sand yielded beneath his horse's hoofs, each impress
of which was ringed with a pool of water and swirling
foam.

" I'm coming too," shouted Pastouré ; but his horse
jibbed furiously, and in three bounds unseated its ponderous
rider, and pitched him into the breaking waves. Pastouré
held on to the tail of his nag, and was safely hauled back
to terra firma, where the custom-house men picked him up
practically unhurt.

He sprang to his feet in a moment and tried to remount,
but his beast was mad with terror and excitement, and,
escaping him, dashed away at a furious gallop. So
Pastouré had to make up his mind to see Maurin attempt
the perilous adventure alone. . . . And, as his bones were
aching a bit from his fall, he allowed a young *douanier* to
go in chase of his mount.

Then all turned their eyes in fear and amazement on
the other horseman as he forced his way against the storm.
Ten times over Maurin's animal jibbed and reared, checking
in the heavy sands, which the waves left momentarily
exposed ; then the returning billows would break against
the beast's belly, as against a moving rock. The frightened
creature kept pivoting round on its hind legs, and obstinately faced the shore ; but at each of these movements,
the rider, more obstinate still, would edge his way a little
further into the sea, towards the wreck. . . . For the last
time the horse reared ; but now, just as he came down

again, he was lifted bodily by a huge wave . . . and, perforce, began to swim. . . . Maurin gripped hard with his muscular legs and sinewy knees ; he tightened the bridle, and his spurs tore the animal's flanks, which seemed to feel the bite of some unknown sea monster underneath the raging waters. Great, towering rollers swept clean over the horse's head, and looked sometimes as if they must unseat the rider ; but Maurin only bent his head and let them pass over harmlessly. . . . And all the time he was pushing farther and farther from land. . . . The onlookers could only gaze in fascinated horror—Pastouré and the six or seven custom-house men, who all stood still as statues, as if struck to stone by the very excess of suspense. . . .

The shipwrecked boatmen, clinging desperately to their upturned boat, were being driven obliquely by the force of wind and wave towards the promontory bounding the gulf to the south-east, and presently caught sight of their intrepid rescuer. . . . But Maurin swam his horse right past them, judging that the only possibility of reaching them was to take them on his way back to shore. . . . At last he wheeled about, gripped one of the men by the hair as he swung past, and yelled through the howling storm :

"Hold on tight ; hold on ! "

He dragged the fellow against his knee, and the latter, obeying instinctively, gripped it and clung.

The other saw his chance, and, being something of a swimmer, he struck out and reached the horseman's other knee.

Nothing was to be seen now on the water save the keel of the upturned boat, and this was soon swept away by the rolling waves and tempestuous wind, and disappeared. . . . The horse, seeing the land before him, made tremendous efforts to escape sea and storm, to save himself from a watery grave. . . .

"Hold on, hold on ! " Maurin kept shouting, louder than the wind and sea, every time the haggard faces of the two men emerged for a moment. His horse, free to follow its

own course, made for the shore at a spot a long way from
its starting-point ; half turning tail to the wind, the intelligent animal steered a diagonal course across the tide.
. . . Meantime, Pastouré and the customs men were
running full speed along the beach to receive them on
landing, and drag them on shore. . . .

The Lieutenant of Customs was present amongst the rest,
and the whole party, looking more than half drowned,
were hurried into the barracks, where Maurin and Pastouré
consented to stop a moment to warm themselves. Presently, when a bit recovered, they stepped up to the two
boatmen, who had had a stiff glass of *aïguarden* each, and
were beginning to regain their senses. Then :

" *Té ! té !* " cried Maurin, suddenly, in a jovial voice.
" Well, well, well ! Look, the youngster, why it's *my*
youngster ! My Césariot : . . . Well ! I *am* glad ! . . .
He can't but allow, that fellow, that he owes his life to me
. . . eh, my lad, what say you ? "

" Sir," interrupted the Lieutenant, " tell me your name,
if you please ; I want to include it in my report."

" My name, eh ? " said Maurin. " Oh ! the youngster
I've just rescued will tell you that . . . after I'm gone ! "

At that moment the young *douanier* appeared, leading
Pastouré's horse.

" Are you coming, Pastouré ? Good-bye, gentlemen !
A *mistral* and a sun like this will dry our wet clothes in
ten minutes, and our beasts' coats into the bargain !
Look you, we fear neither fire nor water, we chaps
don't ! . . ."

And the two men sprang into their saddles and rode
off at a swinging hand-gallop.

CHAPTER LII

A wolf sometimes is no match for a lamb, and the wiliest old fox may often be trapped in the simplest snare.

THEY did not enter Bormes till after nightfall, and while Pastouré kept guard on the horses, Maurin went to see M. Rinal, whom he found holding a great council of war with M. Cabissol. He explained his ideas to them, how Grondard had set fire to the woods in such a way as to lead to the belief it was he, Maurin, was the incendiary.

" I thought as much ! " was M. Cabissol's comment. . . . " Well, anyway, you are safe and sound. We shall triumph yet, sooner or later, over your enemies, never fear ! "

" It's to be hoped so, indeed, if there's any justice in the world—or else . . ." and he waved his hand in a vague gesture that was expressive of deep discouragement.

Then M. Rinal gave Maurin a report of his son's progress, which was very satisfactory—he still continued to be an excellent scholar ; after which Maurin recounted his last meetings with Sandri and Grondard.

" Keep your mind easy," M. Cabissol said finally, " I will institute an inquiry, and I guarantee it will clear matters up. We are looking, M. Rinal and myself, for a way to get you free from all these difficulties. You may count on us. And now off with you and have a good rest."

Pastouré and Maurin arranged to take a two days' rest in hiding with their friends at Bormes, and did accordingly.

On the second day Maurin engaged a little shepherd lad to go and tell Tonia, without letting her father overhear the message, that she could meet him next day, at such and such an hour, in such and such a spot ; this was at the "Oak of the Solitary," not far from Orsini's house.

But Grondard happened to run across the little shepherd boy :

" Where away, lad, so fast ? "

The lad knew Grondard, and had a wholesome terror of him. He pulled up with a very pale face, and blurted out all about his errand ; then added eagerly :

" Let me pass, sir ; I'm in such a hurry," and he darted away.

Grondard departed too, chuckling to himself, and evidently turning something over in his mind ; his lips were moving, as if he was talking to himself. . . .

It was not till the afternoon that Maurin was to see Tonia at the oak. He started away in the morning, in sportsman's rig, with his dog, which he had been to Cigalous to recover, at his heels, and he intended to break-fast at the place of rendezvous while waiting the fair Corsican's arrival. Meantime Pastouré was to bring the horses back to "La Garde Freïnet" by out-of-the-way and devious roads.

On reaching the trysting-place, Maurin was a good deal surprised to find the little shepherd-lass Fanfarnette there, seated on a big root of a tree, and watching her flock of Moorish goats feeding round her.

Like her goats, she was of a small breed, was Fanfarnette ; graceful in repose, quick in movement, she looked bright and pretty under her great hat ; her eyes had a gleam that proclaimed the wild, untamed creature she was, a look that always expressed a certain distrust, never a full, confiding friendliness.

" Halloa ! is that you, Fanfarnette ? "

" As you see, *Moussu Móourin*."

He asked himself how he was to get rid of her, and he could think of no way of managing this. It was not to save the child's blushes he wished her away—good Lord ! no, he knew her too well for that—but to escape her spiteful remarks and mocking laughter.

Pondering these matters, he stooped mechanically to examine a tiny little shoot of green, hardly formed yet, that pierced the ground at his feet. . . . Unable, so young the growth was, to remember the name of the plant he was handling, he asked himself the question out loud :

" Now, what plant is that ? "

Then he looked at Fanfarnette, and she, resting her uncertain gaze on him, answered slowly, with a smile as fresh as the young leaf he had just been fingering :

" That ? . . . oh ! it's just a plant that grows in the woods."

The answer, so full of childish ignorance, sounded delicious, putting Fanfarnette, as it were, on the level of her own silly goats, and almost persuading one of her utter and absolute innocence.

Yes, there are speeches that draw a kiss as the inevitable response, that invite the mouth like the cool freshness of a hidden spring bubbling beneath the leaves and grass.

Maurin's senses were stirred. Yet he knew the little baggage for what she was, he knew her quite well ! In the days when he was stalking the eagle for Maître Secourgeon, she had driven her flock to feed near the farm-house, the owner of the goats, a certain De la Molle, having rented a right of pasturage from the farmer.

At the time Maurin's whole thoughts had been devoted to the stalwart charms of *Misé* Secourgeon, and he had paid scant attention to little Fanfarnette, a mere child ! He was not the sort of sportsman to go after such small game. . . . At the same time he kept sundry diverting reminiscences of the little scamp of a shepherd girl, and she, we may be sure, had not forgotten.

There were other things, too, he could remember about the girl, two or three others—but not such pleasant ones, very much less so indeed !

The truth is, he had never looked at her in the same way as he did to-day, and never before had her youthful charms struck him thus. . . . " A year ago," he muttered to himself, " she was still a child ; but it is so no longer ! "

Seeing his gaze fixed on her, she broke into a merry laugh,
and Maurin, who was there expressly to meet Tonia,
abandoned all thought of sending Fanfarnette away ! . . .

He looked and looked, and, presently, sat down, not far
from her, on the trunk of a felled cork-oak. Already he
was thinking :

"Tonia is to be here presently; 'pon my word, it's a pity!"
Meanwhile Fanfarnette had sidled up to him.

" How old are you, little one ? "

" How should *I* know ? "

She must have been seventeen, but she did not look
fifteen.

Then he got up to go ; he would try to meet Tonia on
her way there and take her elsewhere. . . .

" You're going, *Moussu Móourin* ? Don't go yet ! "

So he sat down again, on the trampled heather. . . .

Then, with a spring, the child was beside him, and
stretching herself on her back, she laid her head on the
man's knees. . . . Head thrown back and face to the sky,
she looked up at him thus, with her kid-like eyes, eyes that
held no trace of emotion, but glittered with a soulless
brilliancy . . . eyes, nevertheless, that have a secret of
their own . . . the secret of animal desires and the bestial,
inevitable compulsion of physical nature.

They could hear the tinkle of the little bell carried by
the he-goat, leader of the flock, sounding among the hills
about them.

·   ·   ·   ·   ·   ·   ·   ·

His eyes lingered on Fanfarnette's fresh young face,
her thick, silky hair, and the back of her firm white neck.
. . . He still had, in front of him, before the hour of his
appointed rendezvous with Tonia, a good couple of solid
hours.

He thought of breakfast, but Fanfarnette's round little
mouth made such a childish *moue* of invitation there was no
resisting. . . .

·   ·   ·   ·   ·   ·   ·   ·

"Now," she said suddenly, "you are bound to marry me."

The words did not surprise or startle him above measure. He had heard them so often before, and so often eluded the same snare !

"Fanfarnette," he declared, "I have a present to give you, and then we'll be quits."

He drew from his game-bag a pretty, coloured silk handkerchief he had bought the day before as a gift for Tonia.

Fanfarnette laid hands on the handkerchief, unfolded it and said :

"Do you really imagine a handkerchief, even such a pretty one as this, can pay me for what I've given you ? "

Still he did not understand, and fished out of his bag a little oval mirror, framed in horn, and fitted with a cover revolving on a pivot. "Tonia," thought he, "doesn't expect them after all. . . . I can safely give 'em away."

"That's all I have," he cried. "It's for you."

Fanfarnette seized the mirror, opened it, smiled admiringly at her reflection in it, and declared with a set face of obstinate resolution :

"Yes, that's a promise of better things to come ; but you've still to pay me for what you've robbed me of ! "

"Fanfarnette," he said, " you're a sweet little thing and a darling, but, believe me ! you'll get nothing more out of me."

"You're joking ! " she answered. "Now you must marry me, I say, because you've ruined my honour."

He stood amazed for a bit ; then after a minute's thought, he was afraid !

As he knew what Fanfarnette's honour was worth, her appeal to it threw a sudden and painful light for him on the projects and intentions of the simple-minded country girl. He saw in a moment he was confronted with an enemy. His brows contracted and his look grew hard and angry, almost terrifying. She, too, realised she had a foe to face. Presently, after a moment's silence, she added, still smiling :

" If you refuse, I shall tell everybody you had me by
force, tender young thing as I am, and all men will be
against you, even your friends ; the very people who wish
you well will point the finger of scorn at you, do you see
that ?   But I'm sure you'll rather marry me, won't
you ? "

Her smile was a woman's smile. She felt sure of herself ;
something as old as the world, something formidable and
irresistible, stirred within her—the witness of our Mother
Eve !

" Fanfarnette," he said, " I'm not an easy man to be-
guile. I'm not like the red-breasts you trap when you're
keeping your flocks. I know what I know, and it's because
I know it that just now, when you drew me on with your
pretty cajoling ways, I answered you as a man does a
woman who invites him."

" *I* invited you ? "

" You did."

" Oh ! "—and she looked him boldly and defiantly
between the eyes, as she retorted :

" And what do you know of me that made you answer
me as a man does a woman ? I am only a poor, honest
girl, *pechère !* everybody will tell you that."

His brow cleared, for he was convinced that, once he had
answered her challenge in the way he had it in his power
to, the child would own to being beaten :

" What ! " he laughed, " d'you suppose I didn't see you
the other evening, down in the dell of the Darboussettes,
with little Chichourlet the shepherd lad ? "

She smiled at the recollection.

" He was gathering me blackberries," she declared.

Maurin felt his anger rising. He had seen what he had
seen.

She resumed :

" Will you marry me, or will you not ? "

" What a fool's question ! . . . No, I won't," he said
straight out ; " no, never ! "

" Well, then," she hissed between her teeth, " it'll be as

I said ; I'll make everybody believe you're a ravisher of little girls—and that's what you are ! "

He looked at the girl. He had heard tales of wizards and witches told of winter nights. In one of these an old fairy, when in her natural shape, is like an ugly dragon perched on the two legs of a *tardarasse* (buzzard), with a hooked beak, round staring eyes, and an owl's pointed ears, but when she wants to undo Christian folks she assumes the shape of a beautiful princess. . . . Beneath the childish face that smiled at him he seemed to see the monstrous beast of prey.

"Well ! " he blurted out roughly, " I don't know whether you were an honest little girl or no when I first saw you at Maître Secourgeon's farm ; but I do know that at this present in the slums of the *Casaôus* quarter there's a low pot-house where of nights all the *fénas* (good-for-nothings) of the place come to have their spree with girls. You went there one night, two months since, with a man—a man who's no longer young, and a married man ! I saw you go in . . . and, it so happened, I saw you come out again next morning."

The instant Maurin had spoken the words all Fan-farnette's prettiness vanished. . . . He looked in her face, and saw for certain what she was—a *masque* (witch) !

" What do I care what you saw ? " she cried impudently. " The man I was with is married, yes !—and that's why he'll say nothing about it ; nor yet the people of the inn, who make their living how they must—by holding their tongues. So do what you will, my man, everybody will believe me, and won't believe you ! and all the disgrace will be on your side."

He could only gaze at her, staggered and stupefied by such effrontery. At each word she said he seemed to see a venomous insect fly out of a flower. . . . Now she looked positively ugly ; her mouth was a little distorted, and her smile askance. Her eyes, the eyes of a little ill-conditioned animal, were fixed on his ; there was a sort of cloud over them, and he could catch lurking beneath their falsity a gleam of cold, calculating cruelty. The evil beast within her showed a little more plainly every moment in every feature.

Love, friendship, even sensuality had disappeared, and only cunning remained, not mere animal cunning, but the calculating cunning of base human self-interest.

Then, for the second time, a horrible feeling smote the man's heart, a thrill of fear he had never known before, for he saw a thing he had never in all his life seen before, or even believed possible, the good, gallant Maurin !

Yes, he realised the hideousness of the threat now ! And how, indeed, was he to guard himself against it ? Why should they believe him, him a strong, passionate man, against the word of this child, so young and innocent-looking ? Perhaps even M. Rinal would deem him guilty ! and Parlo-Soulet ! and Cigalous ! all his friends in fact !

" God ! is it possible ? " he groaned. " Grondard must have had some hand in this ! "

" Well ? " questioned Fanfarnette, with a look of triumphant mockery, and the grin of a wicked old fairy twisting her rosy lips, " well ? . . ."

He felt himself undone. Neither the forest-fire, nor the mad dog—nothing had ever made him tremble before ; but now he was trembling, yes, he was trembling with terror at this evil dream !

His faults and escapades—well, he gloried in them ! He knew very well a love of justice had always been his guiding-star, that men looked upon him as an honourable man in spite of all, that he walked his lonely woods surrounded by the esteem and goodwill of his people !

And lo ! overthrown by a child's lying tale, he was going to earn the reputation of a villain . . . of a Grondard ! . . . Yes, they would believe her, the artful minx, because, with women, he had always been something of a rake. . . . Everybody knew that ! And now, because of this silly child, no one would credit that he had never, never behaved treacherously to any girl ! . . . He looked at Fanfarnette, and—it was only a passing impulse, a flash no sooner kindled than extinguished—he longed to grip the little creature by the throat and beat her head against the trunk of the great oak standing there. . . . Then, horrified at his own thought, he snatched up his gun and game-bag, and fled away like a madman.

He could hear a voice calling after him :

" You know what I've told you !   You'll think it well over ! "

When he had gone half a league, he stopped ; his head was whirling, and his ideas wild and confused.   He laid down gun and game-bag under some bushes, threw himself full length on the ground, and hiding his head in his hands, burst into sobs.

Then his dog crept up softly and began to lick his hands.

CHAPTER LIII

A pretty Maid and a pretty Song.

HARDLY had Maurin left Fanfarnette before Grondard appeared. Though Maurin knew nothing of the fact, Fanfarnette was that worthy's own niece, daughter of his eldest brother, who had died years before.

"Well, little one?" he questioned, and she told him the whole story.

"Good!" muttered Grondard, "he's caught. As to his consenting to marry you, I never counted overmuch on that; all the same, if he did, I should be glad enough. It would rid me of the responsibility I feel for you."

"Why, you feel none, or next to none, uncle, not you!"

"Then it is all the same. . . . However, the great point is he's afraid. A time will come when I'll face him, and he'll just have to pay up in one way or another, in money or otherwise. . . . And then, first and foremost, I want to be revenged on him. . . . And for that, now listen here. Stay where you are for the present. You've a snack for your breakfast in your bag, eh?"

"Oh, yes!" she told him.

"Then stay here. You know Tonia? I was in hopes she would come and find you together, that scamp of a Maurin and you. . . . However, nothing's lost; she'll arrive presently. . . . Tell her how he really had you by force, and afterwards promised marriage."

"Never fear, I'll do everything just as you told me."

Then Grondard went back to his lair, while the little herdswoman breakfasted daintily. Several of her goats were very tame, and came and ate salt from her hand.

When she had finished she passed the time in weaving garlands of leaves, which she wreathed round her head, and took out her new mirror to admire the effect. Next

with twigs of rosemary she proceeded to make a tiny cage
for cicalas, singing as she worked at the top of her voice :

" Fille, tu te veux marier ?
  N'ai point d'argent à te donner."
" Qu'est cela l'argent ?   Qu'est-ce que l'argent ?
  Emprunterons à nos parents ! "
            " L'Antoine,
            Je le veux . . .
  Mariez-moi au bout de l'an :
  Je ne peux plus espèrer tant."
" Fille, tu te veux marier ?
  N'ai point de lit à te donner."
" Qu'est cela un lit ?   Pas besoin de lit !
  Se coucherons dans l'escalier. . . . "
            " L'Antoine,
            Je le veux . . .
  Mariez-moi au bout de l'an :
  Je ne veux plus espérer tant." *

She thought Tonia might perhaps hear her, and very
softly, between her teeth, she hummed another ditty :

" Qui te suivait à la fontaine,
  Morbleu, Marion ? "
" C'était une femme qui lavait,
  Mon Dieu, mon ami ! "
" Les femmes ne portent pas l'épée,
  Morbleu, Marion ! "
" C'était sa qu'nouille qu'elle avait,
  Mon Dieu, mon ami ! " †

With her keen hearing she now caught the sound of
footsteps, still a long way off, pushing through the heather.

* " You fain would marry, eh, sweetheart? But I have no pelf to
give you."—" Pelf, what of pelf? What matters that? We'll borrow
from our kin."—" Oh ! Antoine, love, I am fain, I am fain . . . e'en
marry me at the fall o' the year : I cannot go on longing so ! "
    " You fain would marry, eh, sweetheart? Nay ! I have no bed to
give you."—" Bed, what of that? What matters bed? We'll lie upon
the stairs."—" Oh ! Antoine, love, I am fain, I am fain . . . e'en
marry me at the fall o' the year : I cannot go on longing so ! "
    † " Who was't went with you to the well? tell truth, maid Marion ! "
—" It was a woman washing clothes, and that's God's truth, my
lad ! "—" Nay ! women do not wear the sword ! tell truth, maid
Marion ! "—" It was her distaff, sir, she bore ; and that's God's
truth, my lad ! "

. . . She stopped singing to listen. . . . Yes, someone was coming. . . .

When Tonia reached her and asked : " Have you been here long, Fanfarnette ? " the girl burst into tears.

" Why, what is it, child ? "

But Fanfarnette made no reply, only hiding her face in her hands. Tonia tried to draw her fingers apart to see her face, but the girl's hands instantly escaped her grasp, and were glued again over her burning cheeks.

" What is the matter, what is wrong, child ? " reiterated Tonia, who suddenly guessed something of the truth.

" *Moussu Mòourin ! Moussu Mòourin* ! " sobbed Fanfarnette. . . .

" Come, what is it ? . . . what do you mean ? . . .Why do you mention Maurin ? "

" I am ruined ! " she groaned, " I am a lost girl, *Madameïselle* Tonia ! He was here just now with me . . . and he said he would never marry me ! I know very well what the result may be ; I can't help telling you what happened. He had his will of me by force, the villain ! And he'll leave me in the lurch, who knows ? and I shall be one of those girls nobody will have, because, if they went to church, they'd be obliged to take their baby along with 'em, *pechère* ! "

Tonia was cut to the quick, He, he, Maurin, had done this ! he who had always been so straightforward with her— almost to the verge of brutality sometimes ! God ! was the thing possible ? Yet, how doubt the truth, when this innocent young thing told her it was ; crying her eyes out with shame and grief ! a defenceless child, *pechère !* an orphan !

" Good-bye ! " said Tonia abruptly. " God will punish him ! good-bye, I have things to attend to. . . . But Maurin, where is he now ? which way did he go, do you know ? "

The girl looked at the Corsican with a cold, scrutinising eye. Yes, she could give her precise information :

. " I watched him from here, as long as I could, as he pushed his way through the wood. He went by the Pas de la Masque (The Witch's Walk). Then he climbed the bushy hill-side in front. Look yonder; he's bound to be there, on the high ground where the Puits des Arbouses (Well of the Wildings) is—you know the place quite well."

" Yes, yes," panted Tonia.

" I thought I saw him sit down suddenly. No doubt he breakfasted there, and that's where he is now, you may be sure. . . ."

" Good-bye, good-bye, child ! "

Tonia was furious. She hugged the idea of avenging the poor girl ; but really and truly it was the sharp tooth of mortal jealousy that was tearing her heart.

Where was she going, running so desperately, tearing her way through briar and bramble, leaping from rock to rock, taking the shortest road, no matter what detours the path made ?

Fanfarnette watched Tonia as she went. Soon, when she saw her climbing the hill in front, she began again weaving her pretty green wreaths and humming softly :

> " Les femmes ne portent pas moustache,
>   Morbleu, Marion !
>   Les femmes ne portent pas moustache."
> " C'était des mûres qu'elle mangeait,
>   Mon Dieu, mon ami !
>   C'était des mûres qu'elle mangeait ! "
> " N'y a plus de mûres en automne,
>   Morbleu, Marion !
>   N'y a plus de mûres en automne ! "
> " C'était un' branch' qui automnait,
>   Mon Dieu, mon ami !
>   C'était un' branch' qui automnait ! "
> " . . . Eh bien, j'te couperai la tête,
>   Morbleu, Marion !
>   Eh bien, j'te couperai la tête ! " *

---

* " But women do not wear moustache ; tell truth, maid Marion ! "
—" Nay, she was eating mulberries, and that's God's truth, my
lad."—" Mulberries in Autumn time ! tell truth, maid Marion.
What ! mulberries in Autumn time ! "—" 'Twas a russet bough of
Autumn hue, and that's God's truth, my lad ! "—" . . . Ah, well !
I'll e'en cut off your head ; you can't tell truth, maid Marion ! So,
well, I'll e'en cut off your head ! "

CHAPTER LIV

Vendetta !

THE well designated by Fanfarnette lies on a minor summit of the Maures, separated from nearly all the neighbouring heights by encircling ravines. These were steep and rugged, clothed in thick brushwood, narrow, but well over a hundred and fifty feet deep. Thus from the surrounding hill-tops the well looks quite near, whereas in reality, to get there, you must descend and then climb laboriously up again at least five hundred yards of road, because of the numerous zigzags made by the mountain paths that wind through the thorny brooms and loiter and linger amid the scrub.

At his dog's loving caress Maurin had quickly recovered some degree of self-composure. Sitting up suddenly, he told himself :

"Come, come ! it's all an evil dream. Folks know me ; they'll never believe her tale. . . . Well, I must get some strength ; I shall need it all. . . ."

And opening his game-bag, he took his morning meal, giving his dog, by way of gratitude for having afforded him a little comfort in his grief, something better than mere dry bread.

"All the same," he muttered to himself, "it's an abominable business. . . . Well, well, we shall see ! "

Yes, Tonia was tracking down Maurin now ; but before beginning the chase she had gone back home, and, her fury rising higher every minute, had taken her gun.

All her love was turned to the all-absorbing hatred of savage jealousy, and she saw nothing of the road she traversed. She had slung her little carbine behind her

back, and was climbing the hill-side, helping herself with
both hands, which were soon covered with blood, as she
pushed aside the thorny boughs. The things under her
eyes, the rocks and rolling stones and knotted branches
she saw, as it were, without seeing. They passed before
the mirror of her eyes without leaving any trace in her
consciousness, like the cloud landscape, which is reflected
by the sea, but has no effect on the indifferent surfaces
of grass or sand.

In her brain was one picture, and one only—Maurin and
Fanfarnette in each other's arms!

" Oh, the scoundrel! the liar! the thief! the gallows-
bird! Oh! how right they are, keepers and gendarmes
and all, to try to arrest the villain, to hand him over to
justice. But they shan't catch him; it's my task, mine
only, to trap and kill him. It is my *vendetta*! it is for me
to end him! He has come to the end of his foul practices
—maltreating girls, and leaving bastards in every village—
ay! in every hut and cranny of the mountains and woods,
in the haunts of the foxes and martens! yes, he has come
to the end of his career of crime! It is I say so. I will
avenge all these silly wenches who were aye ready to follow
him where he would, when he would, and how he would.
He shall find out at last who'll settle his business for him!
He shall discover anyhow a man can't play false with a
maid of Corsica and go unpunished. We shall see. He
thinks he will bewitch me again, does he, with his soft
words? . . . What will he say, I wonder? . . . But there,
I am a fool! I must not go near him. I must only
cast eyes on him from a distance. . . . But oh! supposing,
even to look at him from afar, my heart were to fail me!
. . . Women are made so. You think yourself strong,
and then, lo! your senses reel, and everything is changed,
and you say abjectly, 'I am yours'—just the opposite of
what you meant to. . . . It was so before the wayside
shrine, at Notre-Dame-des-Anges; I gave myself at the
very moment when I most wanted to defend myself against
the ravisher. . . . I must never go near him then. I must

watch for him from a distance and shoot him like a mad
dog ! . . ."

She stopped in her tirade. Shoot Maurin . . . kill
him ! Suddenly the thing seemed incredible, impossible.
She could not understand how such an idea had ever
entered her head !

She unslung the carbine from her shoulder and rested
it against a bush, debating whether she had not best leave
it there. Yes, she would leave it there . . . and recover
it on her way back. Now she would run to Maurin and
seek his lips—his lips, which he gave to every woman . . .
yes, every woman ! And then that poor, innocent little
Fanfarnette, whom he had violated by sheer brute force !
. . . Yes, she must, and she would, avenge the child, she
would do justice on the wrong-doer. . . . Little Fanfarnette of all creatures ! . . .

Her head swam ; she shut her eyes . . . and saw them
together, Maurin and Fanfarnette in each other's arms !
. . . Her jealousy boiled up again. She put out her hand
to take the gun she had just put down. . . . Away, yonder,
across the ravine, on the hill of the *Puits des Arbouses*,
she had caught sight, through the branches, of Maurin,
standing and looking in her direction. . . . Did he see her ?
A fierce impulse of rage sent the blood flying through her
veins. . . . She seized the carbine . . . and raised it to her
shoulder. She was trembling so she had to rest the muzzle
in the fork of a branch. She could not steady her hand ;
she aimed, and aimed, and did not dare pull the trigger.
It seemed to beat and pulsate beneath her finger like a
human heart. She *could* not fire.

" There he stands ; yes, he is in my power, in my power,
the scoundrel ! . . . If I wanted to kill him . . . but I
don't, I can't ! . . . Ah ! if I had seen him with her . . . .
then, then I should have shot him dead . . . with her,
that Fanfarnette—or any other woman, but with her
especially, with the poor girl you pursued, pursued and
captured in spite of her resistance—coward, traitor, thief !
thief, traitor, coward ! "

Maurin moved; he was going to disappear. . . . When she could see him no longer, by an instinctive impulse, at once voluntary and involuntary, so rapid was the interplay of desire and repulsion, she pressed the trigger. . . . Besides, she hardly seemed to be firing at Maurin, now she could not see him. . . . At any rate he would feel the ball whistle by him and remember! Now too, when he was out of her sight, every other feeling but overmastering hate deserted her. . . . Besides, she was certain to miss him, though indeed—had it been in her power to do things as she wished—she would have liked to hit and wound him, not dangerously, of course, not a mortal wound, but enough to punish him . . . cruelly . . . as a Corsican should! . . . Oh! to see his blood flow! . . . and, after all, if he were to die, why not? . . . he had made her suffer too atrociously, had humiliated her too bitterly for bearing! . . Convulsively her finger tightened on the trigger.

Maurin, invisible, but with his face turned towards his enemy, saw the round puff of smoke rise above the bushes that hid his fierce Corsican sweetheart from him, and, next instant, he dropped without a sound, like a wounded boar, a bullet in his breast. . . .

CHAPTER LV

A Boar at Bay.

INSTANTLY Tonia had thrown down her weapon and uttered a loud heart-rending cry of " Maurin, Maurin ! "

She was eager to get to him with all possible speed, and as she ran she kept telling herself breathlessly : " Yes, he'll laugh finely when I tell him I tried to kill him ! "

But no answering cry had followed hers.

" He wants to make me anxious," she thought, " he's shamming dead ! he understands, and he's taking *his* revenge now ! "

She stopped for want of breath, put her hand to her heart, which was beating as if it would burst—then broke into a run again. On she ran, forced to make wide detours to avoid being hopelessly entrapped in the precipitous ravines, hurrying, stumbling, falling, scrambling to her feet again, dashing down steeps, climbing ascents, pushing a way through the thorny brooms, tearing her skirts. Legs and arms and face were soon dripping with blood under the lashes of the pliant boughs. . . . Now she would halt for a moment to listen, then start off afresh. . . .

" Oh, God ! " she ejaculated suddenly, " suppose I have killed him ! "

The terror gripped her, and she hurried along with more frantic speed than ever.

Then she paused, appalled at the vision of her lover lying bleeding, dead, perhaps disfigured . . . She seemed to see him there, at her feet, among the scrub and stones. . . .

At last her mind took in the situation clearly, in its real bearings. She had tried to kill her lover because she loved him. Dead or alive, she must get to him and nurse him—

or bury him ! Then she went straight and unhesitatingly on her way till she reached the *Puits des Arbouses*.

Maurin lay panting on the ground, his face deathly pale, his eyes shut; his dog was licking his face. There was hardly any blood to be seen ; the ball had struck the chest on the right side, below the level of the shoulder-blade ; the hæmorrhage was doubtless internal.

Tonia opened the sportsman's bag, took out the flask of brandy, poured a few drops on his lips, and moistened his temples.

"Oh, Maurin ! Maurin ! " she cried, sobbing. "Great God ! Maurin, what have I done ? Open your eyes, my poor Maurin ! . . . Maurin ! . . . Oh, God ! . . . Maurin ! . . . if only you won't die, I care nothing, nothing for the rest ! . . . You may love as many of 'em as you choose, Maurin ! I'll never be jealous again ! . . . Miserable girl that I am, what have I done to you ! No, you did *not* break your word, because you never promised. . . . I was not your wife ! you had had my love, yes—but, I can own it now, I had provoked your desires, wanted you, pursued you ! . . . Oh ! open your eyes, Maurin, speak to me ! "

She raised him gently, put the game-bag for a pillow under his head, made him drink a little more *aïguarden*.

At last he opened his eyes.

"Ah ! it's you, Tonia ? I understand it all," he faltered ; . . . "it was what you were bound to do, the girl you are ; I am not surprised ! It was my destiny."

She fell to sobbing silently.

"Forgive me, Maurin ! "

"*Eh bé*, yes, *pardi*, I forgive you ! What's in our destiny there's no avoiding for us. . . . I was fated to die this way ! "

"Die, die ! " cried Tonia in heart-broken tones. "Oh, don't die, my Maurin, my lover, my husband ! I will be yours how you will. . . . What you wish, I will say, and do—and be."

"It's a bit late now ! " said Maurin gently.

"Oh ! Maurin, for pity's sake ! forgive me," groaned

Tonia—and she bent over him, took his head in both her hands, and kissed him full on the lips, on the forehead, on the cheeks . . . on the lips again.

" *Brigand de sort !* " he laughed, " you're a fine girl, and you love me, I can see that ; but then, it hurts infernally " —and, with a shudder of pain, he went off in another faint.

When he came to himself again :

" Now," he began slowly, speaking in short, broken sentences, " my mind's clear. . . . How are you going to do ? You must get me away from here. . . . You'll want four men, at least. . . . Best tell our friends ; they'll do what's needful. . . . Four men'll be wanted, at least . . . and don't tell anybody about it. . . . I'll say my gun went off by accident . . . burn a cartridge to make 'em think so. . . . Good ! Now, off with you. . . . It'll be hard to bear, in the night ; I reckon you can't get back here again before daylight. . . ."

She drew off her underskirt, wrapped it round his legs, put her silk kerchief round his neck, fixed his felt well on his head, put the flask within his reach—made him generally as comfortable as circumstances allowed. Over his head she made a sort of penthouse roof of boughs.

" You have forgiven me, Maurin ? "

" Yes," he assured her, " but don't tease me any more."

She kissed him, and he told himself it was the last kiss he would ever receive from any woman. Then aloud :

" There's one man, Tonia," he added, " you can tell everything to, and that's M. Rinal, of Bormes—and thank him kindly from me for having taught one of my lads, little Bernard. . . . Now, away with you as fast as may be, so as to be back the sooner."

She was just going when he called her back again.

" What is it, Maurin ? "

" Don't forget to thank M. Rinal very kindly from me . . . and God bless you ! God bless you ! "

She was forced to leave him to himself ; it was necessarily a matter of hours to procure help.

By this time night had fallen. Maurin lay there on the

ground, burning with fever. A heavy drowsiness weighed on his eyelids, while his excitement sent a hundred wild dreams through his brain to struggle with the leaden oppression of sleep.

One vision kept returning again and again, clearer and more vivid than all the rest. He seemed to be changed into a wild pig, to use his own habitual form of speech—into a wounded boar. Now he could feel the blood trickling from his torn muzzle and dripping from his tusks. Now he was charging a pursuer, and then, on coming close up, he would see with a shudder the hunter was himself. . . . But he had made his spring, and was driving his (wild-boar's) fangs savagely into his own (man's) thigh, and then dashing away in flight, bound after bound, snapping the dry boughs of the undergrowth as he went.

Next the hunter, who was Maurin, would take aim, and fire, and break the animal's leg; then the brute fell on his rump, and dragged himself painfully into the covert, while distant shouts rose of "*A la barre! A la barre!*" Above all the rest he could recognise Tonia's voice . . . and afterwards Pastouré's, shouting the same cry.

The sportsmen were all hurrying up . . . and amongst them, Maurin, the most eager and determined of all. And then he himself sprang on the back of the boar, that is to say, a second himself !

After this, he could feel a twofold agonising pain, in the boar's leg, and in the man's leg, and Maurin, as hunter, was beating in the wild-boar Maurin's skull with savage blows of a sharp stone he had picked for the purpose. . . .

Reopening his eyes in the moonlight, the wounded man muttered :

" It's fever. I'm dying. Yes, it's just bad dreams, all that. . . . But why, in my dreams, did my leg hurt me so, when I'm wounded in the chest ? . . . Queer things, dreams ! . . . Well, Tonia will be back soon . . . and then they'll get me away."

It was a calm, clear night. Between the branches he could see the stars twinkling in myriads. . . . And the murmur of the great rollers reached him, resembling the sound of the pine woods, only with a regular, cadenced rhythm of its own. . . .

"Who is there I shall regret, if I'm to leave this world?" he asked himself in a momentary lull of the delirium. . . . Gendarmes? préfets? poachers? deputies? women? fur and feathers? or Tonia? my boy? My boy, M. Rinal's educating him; all's well there. . . . M. Rinal? yes, M. Rinal and no one else. . . . I shan't regret anyone else, not one. . . . Ah! yes, but I shall! . . . poor Pastouré!"

Suddenly, in his nightmare, he saw Fanfarnette and all her young, fresh, white body. . . . But as he looked in her face, lo! she had the beak of a *tardarasse* (buzzard), and she was saying over and over to him: "All the shame and disgrace will be for you, Maurin!" Then a dull, over-mastering terror fell on him; all the agonies of bodily pain bit him, all at once, like mad dogs, and with calm conviction he told himself, speaking out loud like old Pastouré: "It's good to die—to get out of view of all this. Things are best so. . . ."

A spasm of pain contracted his leg. . . . He stiffened his muscles and managed to sit up. Then he saw he was in a pool of his own blood and made a supreme effort to move away. Turning on his face, he rested his chin in his hands, and supporting his weight on his elbows, dragged himself a little way . . . the way a wild boar, whose back is broken, will still drag itself along painfully on its fore-paws. At that moment the gleam of a lantern appeared on the hill-side, visible away in front of him through the stems of the cork-oaks, which looked raw and bleeding as it were, in the crude light. He stretched himself out on his back again with a sigh and lost consciousness.

A train rushed by, with a roar and a whistle, down yonder by the sea-coast. The strident iron voice of the century drowned the dying Maurin's groan.

His dog lay at his feet and was whining pitifully.

CHAPTER LVI

M. Rinal probes Maurin's wound.

Tonia had felt sure that any really efficient help could only come from M. Rinal. She had gone to find him, therefore, had confessed everything to him, and then left him to return home to her father's.

M. Rinal sent on information to M. Cigalous, who saw to all necessary measures. A gang of bearers was needed, and a conveyance to take them promptly to the bend of the road nearest to the spot where Maurin lay. M. Cigalous could not, just at first, put his hand on four men available for this duty; but the moment he had secured them, he set out, taking them with him. M. Rinal slipped his surgical case in his pocket and accompanied M. Cigalous.

By means of a net used for making bales of hay, slung by the four corners from two wooden poles, Maurin was got down on the shoulders of the four bearers. As M. Rinal had not been equal to climbing the hill, he was waiting in the road with the carriage. On the way down Maurin had lost and regained consciousness several times.

M. Rinal had him laid on the mattress they had brought and proceeded to examine the wound. The injury did not appear fatal; the ball had made its exit below the shoulder, without, it would seem, damaging any vital organ.

M. Rinal did what he could for the moment, and bandaged his patient temporarily.

" Now," said M. Cigalous, " we must carry him to the nearest shelter."

" Where is that ? "

" At the *cantine* of Le Don."

" No, no," objected M. Rinal. . . . " Let's go to the road-

mender's rather. That's the nearest. . . . Or rather . . .
no," he hesitated, and resumed after a moment's reflection
on the charges hanging over Maurin's head, "we won't
go to the nearest, we'll go to my house"—and thither they
went.

Next day Tonia arrived, asking to see the wounded man.

"He is not to be seen," M. Rinal informed her, "least
of all by you. You must understand that; you cannot
see him just now. Besides, your visits might easily lead
to his hiding-place being discovered. Do you want to
complete his ruin ? You are not to come here again till we
send for you. Good-bye."

She bowed to his decision, and took her departure,
feeling sure the old physician could not find it in his heart
to forgive her. . . . "After all said and done, he was a
scamp who had deserved his punishment," she told herself.
She still believed, poor Tonia ! in the innocence of Fanfarnette and the guilt of Maurin !

Meantime, however, too many persons had guessed that
Maurin was at Bormes in M. Rinal's house, albeit he had
been carried there under cover of night. . . . Already M.
Rinal realised that his roof was not a sufficiently sure
refuge for the outlaw.

For the last twenty-four hours Maurin had lain in a
state of profound somnolence. On waking, his first word,
when he saw and recognised M. Rinal, was :

"You, M. Rinal, you don't believe that of me, do you ? "

M. Rinal understood what it was troubling his friend's
mind, for Fanfarnette had kept her promise. She had been
to Bormes and lodged a formal complaint against Maurin
with the Mayor !

"They laid a trap for you, my poor Maurin, and you
tumbled into it ! "

"Like a *darnagas* (shrike)," cried Maurin, trying to
smile. "Thank you, M. Rinal."

"Come, courage, all will be right yet. You'll get
well."

"I've no great wish to now ; I'm no use to anybody, and

I've had a damaging blow. . . . Oh ! I don't mean the gun-shot. . . . I'm talking of the other. Of the two women, it's the little one has killed me . . . Ah ! she's a bad one ! "

M. Rinal took his hand and pressed it.

" M. Cabissol won't believe that either, eh ? "

" No one who knows you will ; so don't get excited."

The old doctor understood but too well what was passing in the rough fellow's soul, a simple soul, after all. Maurin, for all his mocking irony, for all his biting sarcasms that spared nothing, was at heart one of those feeling natures that maintain through all the pains and pettinesses of life a great love and instinctive sympathy for mankind, and an unalterable faith in the eventual, if tardy, consummation of justice in this world. In his simplicity and ignorance, Maurin, a man of the people, a dreamer of dreams, at once a Pagan and a Christian, a Moor and a European, had, all his life long, believed in the people, hoped in the people— and, to put it in a word, in humanity.

Now both, in the person of Fanfarnette, had suddenly appeared to him fallen from their high estate, unworthy of themselves, ready for every form of treason—all for the smallest atom of self-advantage.

He had shared passionately in the mistaken belief of the genuine Sectary, which consists in a firm conviction that the mere fact of being affiliated to a certain group confers special virtues.

Behind Fanfarnette there was Grondard—yes, he could feel him, guess him, see him. It is not necessary to be able to name the precise causes of one's pain or of one's pleasure to suffer or be glad. Else what would the life of beasts be ?

Maurin, without the power to explain the reason why to himself, had come to doubt of the eventual triumph of Good over Evil. He was beginning to credit the possibility of a final victory of the Grondards over the Rinals of this world. From the exalted dream of Justice, in which he had always lived, he was falling back, heavily and painfully, into an appreciation of the Injustice of things as they' are, like the acrobat who, carried aloft by his balloon, lets go his trapeze just as he thought he was mounting to the skies—and plunges with all his weight, multiplied by the appalling rapidity of his fall, into the mud and mire below.

Hitherto he had only criticised, only seen, the defects of a machine he deemed capable of being perfected—the machine called the social state, without taking into account the perversity of human nature, without laying blame on men who are incurably self-seeking and false, and never disinterested. He supposed himself to have known and appreciated men, when, in fact, he had scrutinised them, and found fault with them only as manifested in their institutions, and not in human nature itself, that is, in the true determining factor. In one word, he had held Society to be artificially corrupt and Mankind naturally good and noble.

The generous-hearted Maurin had just fathomed the never-failing selfishness of men, inexhaustible source of every perfidy. He had never suspected the all-pervading power of self-interest, sole monarch of the world. He had a gentle, loving child's soul ; he was of those who live independent, remote from the crowd, but whose every emotion is a thought given for the general good, every impulse of indignation a revolt in favour of the mass of mankind, every protest a cry of hope for the future. In his very faults, which were all on the surface, there had never been a trace of ulterior motive, a shadow of calculation. Then, in a moment, this straightforward, simple, childish soul, dwelling in the body of a grown man, had found itself confronted with the cunning, cowardly, heartless soul of our old civilisation. . . . And this old civilisation, so corrupt and decadent, smiled at him with the lips of a girl, a mere child. . . . Was this, then, *The Truth ?* If so, what a hideous nightmare was such an awakening !

Maurin was vanquished, beaten, dead already to this world, like all idealists, those blind dreamers of dreams,

whose eyes are suddenly couched for cataract, and they
can see the whole reality of things. The crude glare of
fierce light that rouses them from their visions kills them.

This was what M. Rinal guessed. Once before he had
seen Maurin, on hearing the account of a famous trial,
then occupying the thoughts of the whole country, suddenly bite his fist till the blood came, with the anguished
cry :

" *Maï alor ? y aurïè gès dé justici !*—But, but . . . is
there no justice then at all ! "

No, no justice ! only high-hearted idealists doubt this
dismal truth. All there is, in the heart of Maurin and such
as he, is a dream of justice—a dream always disappointed,
always born afresh, admirable still, though for ever futile.
. . . Nay ! which *is* sometimes realised, but in regions
above the heads of the mass of mankind, never, alas !
within that mass itself !

No hero but feeds on his own heart, and his own heart
only. So, when the day of disillusionment comes, after
fondly imagining he was in community with all his fellows,
he finds himself face to face simply with his own petty
personality, never in presence of a God he has so yearned
after, and whom he would have loved so ardently, if He
had but revealed Himself !

" Now, d'ye see, M. Rinal, I'm good for nothing any
more but to fill a hole in the ground."

The old idealist, this Jacobin in lace ruffles, this free-
thinker who was so simple and kindly, hoped, even now,
for a reaction to a brighter outlook, and he resolved to
provoke it.

" Maurin," he began, " we are all going to put our
shoulders to the wheel, and we'll get you yet . . . a heap
of nice things."

But Maurin shook his head.

" I've been convicted," he growled, " for having stolen,
so they called it, a fool's dog. . . . Therefore they'll believe anything of me, just because I have this trifle
against me."

" Listen to me, Maurin. . . . In a month's time the election of the new President of the Republic will be held, and we will get up a bit of a report in your favour, M. Cabissol and I. Vérignon shall present it to the new President, and it will be arranged that all your offences—which all redound to your credit, are wiped out by a general amnesty. That's good hearing, eh ? "

" Yes, that will be famous ; but if it ever does come, it'll come a bit too late," sighed Maurin.

" And then—you don't know that ? Cigalous has petitioned for a life-saving medal for you, and we shall get it ! "

" All that, all that . . ." began Maurin indifferently, with a gesture as if waving something carelessly away ; but he broke off, fearing to hurt his old friend's feelings, and said instead :

" All the same, you're good and kind. You must tell my son all this, when he's grown into a man."

" Well, my good Maurin, I've sent to fetch your young-ster, Bernard, for you to kiss the little lad. Then, as you are not amnestied yet, we must get you into a safe place, out of reach of the gendarmes ; so we will get you carried elsewhere. Where would you like to go ? "

" Bernard ! " murmured Maurin. " Ah ! yes, if only *he* could see some shadow of justice in the world in days to come ! But you will train him well . . . and he will do justice, even if the world refuses it to him. As for going away from here, M. Rinal, I'm very willing ; I'm giving you overmuch trouble, I know."

" Oh ! it's not that."

" I know, I know . . . but listen here . . . we must let Pastouré know."

" He is there, in the next room. I'll go and call him in."

" Ah ! " went Maurin, with a sigh of satisfaction.

Pastouré came in at M. Rinal's summons, and after a glance at Maurin, the tender-hearted giant burst into tears :

" *Qué siès couyoun !*—what a donkey you are ! " grinned

Maurin. " Why ! I've got seventy-four wild pigs' tails at home* . . ."

" Seventy-five," corrected the colossus, crying like a child.

" *Eh bè !* " exclaimed Maurin, " we'll reach the hundred yet."

Pastouré smiled through his tears.

" And you, lad," Maurin went on, " it's true, anyway, *you* didn't believe the stuff Fanfarnette's telling ? "

" Maurin," declared Pastouré solemnly, " suppose a Maurin were on the one side, and all the women in all the whole round world on the other, and they all said the opposite of what *you* said—the weight of the whole world wouldn't kick the beam against you, in Pastouré's eyes, who knows you."

Maurin heaved a sigh, and gave his hand to his old comrade, who squeezed it fit to break the bones. . . . But the sick man was too pleased to make any complaint of the pain.

" My good, faithful Pastouré," he resumed, "listen here. You know I did a service to those *Boumians* (Bohemians, gypsies) who have built a regular village for themselves in M. de Siblas' wood, at Les Bormettes ? "

" Yes, I know," assented Pastouré.

" Well, go and see them, Explain things to them ; tell them the condition you've seen me in, and how I want to find a hiding-place in some other place than this, and to be brought away from here and carried to their friend Lagarrigues', d'ye understand ? If the gendarmes know I'm sick, they'll watch my getting well, and then nab me. I'm charged with arson and murder ! Well, when the

* In the volume entitled *The Diverting Adventures of Maurin*, the first part of the veracious chronicle of which *Maurin the Illustrious* is the sequel, the hero declares, on p. 275, that he possesses thirty-four boars' tails. This is a printer's error, which I have carefully refrained from correcting, along with several others, in order to render the *editio princeps* for ever precious to our friends the bibliophiles (Note of JEAN D'AURIOL).

time comes, I'll show up and answer my accusers, but I don't choose to be arrested and forced to speak against my will."

" I understand," said Pastouré.

" The *Boumians* will put horse to a gypsy van, and I'll ride to Lagarrigue's on my back, as I can't do it sitting up. So there, away with you ! . . . And, ah ! by the by . . . take my dog Hercules with you, leave him with our friends at Bormes, and if I die, he shall be yours ! "

M. Rinal raised no objections to this plan ; he proposed to pay his medical visits to Maurin at Lagarrigue's, that was the only difference. Pastouré had just started on his errand when little Bernard arrived.

" Ask him some question," said Maurin, " and let me hear his answer, and see if it satisfies you."

" What is the highest ideal, and the most realisable ? " asked the old professor of the lad. " Can you tell me ? We've often talked of it together."

" Yes," replied Bernard, " that everywhere the stronger owes help and protection to the weaker."

Alas ! M. Rinal was indoctrinating young Maurin with Don Quixote's madness, that strange infirmity that alone makes life endurable.

" I have always thought that without being able to put it into words," cried Maurin. . . . " Study, young one ; work hard. . . . Good-bye, *Maurin*, good-bye."

The child was led away. Then Maurin turned to M. Rinal and said :

" The stronger—look you, M. Rinal—the stronger will always be the more unjust. And the weaker only asks to replace him in order to have strength in his stead, and to turn injustice to his own profit ! The poor are socialists because they are poor ; they hold their views from interested motives, M. Rinal, from selfishness ; each for himself. But when a bourgeois who asks nothing of the people is, like you, a socialist, it is simply and solely by reason of his own good heart, since there is no self-interest involved . . . quite the contrary. And that is why I love you . . . but bourgeois like you can be counted on the fingers, you know they can ! ''

" Come, come," said M. Rinal soothingly, " don't excite yourself."

" Well," resumed Maurin after a silence, " do me the favour, M. Rinal, of getting M. Cigalous to send one of my friends from Bormes here, a man called Verdoulet, because why, I want to speak to him specially and privately . . . it will ease my mind.",

" I will go and fetch him," said M. Cabissol, who entered the room at that moment.

Verdoulet came to see Maurin the same evening, and the two were left together.

" Listen," Maurin began, " it was you killed Grondard . . . you did well. For my part, I promised you I would not, and I have not betrayed you. But I want to make sure that, on an emergency, if, for instance, the day ever comes when I am before the judges, and like to be condemned because of this business, you would speak up straight and fair in the witness-box. . . ."

Verdoulet saw Maurin was weak and ill, and was not afraid to play the coward :

" I don't know what you mean," he said—and he made hastily for the door and disappeared.

Then a great despair entered into Maurin's soul, and he said to M. Rinal, who, knowing he was alone, had come back again to talk to him, and M. Cabissol with him :

" I never thought men were so wicked and contemptible."

" I know what you mean," said M. Cabissol. " Verdoulet chooses to deny the truth. But *I* know, through his wife's incautious speeches, what he would fain hide, and which you have never spoken of."

" Ah ! " Maurin gave a sigh of relief, " then there is a good God, after all ! . . ."

CHAPTER LVII

Maurin's Last Will and Testament.

THE gypsies' van came in the night to fetch Maurin, and he was installed in the interior on a regular bed. The gendarmes who met the conveyance never for a moment dreamt that Maurin of the Maures was lying snug inside this house on wheels drawn by its half-starved horse. The driver was an old *Boumian* with close-curling hair, who sang wild, uncouth ditties, as he went along, in an unknown tongue :

> "La plaie est rouge au cœur,
> L'églantine au buisson . . .
> Prends l'églantine en fleur,
> Et prends mon cœur sanglant—
> Tirlow Tirlow !

> "L'amour est un enfant,
> Il m'a pris pas la jambe,
> Il m'a tiré à bas
> Et de cheval je suis tombé,
> Tirlow !
> Et mon front s'est ouvert
> Adieu, ma fiancée ! " *

They followed the La Molle road, which keeps along the bottom of the valley. Pastouré, whose presence beside the gypsy would have betrayed the whole secret, trotted in front, keeping a mile or so ahead, but returning from time to time in his tracks to give Maurin drink and food

---

* "The wound is red in my heart as the wild-rose on the bush . . . pluck the wild-rose in bloom and eke my bleeding heart, . . . Willow ! Willow ! Love is a boy, he has caught me by the leg and pulled me down, and dragged me from my horse, . . . Willow ! And my brow is cut open ! Good-bye, good-bye, sweetheart ! "

according to M. Rinal's instructions. Looking through
the little window of the van, Maurin could see his beloved
mountains of the Maures roll slowly past before his eyes.
As he passed by Les Campaux he heard the crack, crack
of a hammer on the stones, and knew it was old Saulnier
at work, but he did not call out to him.   What was the use ?
. . . When he was near his own hut in the plain of Cogolin,
he called a halt.

"Let's hail Pastouré to come here," he said.

"Why ?" the *Boumian* asked.

"I want to find out," Maurin told him with a smile,
"whether I have seventy-four pigs' tails or seventy-five,
as Pastouré thinks."

"'Faith!" protested the *Boumian*, "don't let's go and
compromise our safety, yours and mine, for a lot of pigs'
tails."

"You're in the right," agreed Maurin.   "So let's get
on, eh ?"

At La Foux he said :

"It was here I came across those Spanish cows !"—and
added despondently :

"Ah ! I was young then !"

Yet not above a couple of months had elapsed since
the bull-fights ; but he meant to say he had grown older
by a whole century, in himself.

When the van entered the plain of Fréjus, it finally
quitted the sea-shore to make for Roquebrune.

At the turning to Saint-Aigulf Pastouré was waiting ;
he had not dismounted.

"Maurin," he said, " I've just this moment seen Lagarrigue at this very place. He had come to say a word to
me. The place where you're to lie in hiding is the grotto
of Roquebrune. You're to go there to-night, after dark ;
meantime we'll camp where we are. A gypsy van halted
under a pine by the side of the high road won't excite anybody's suspicions."

The *Boumian* took his skinny nag out of the shafts
and hobbled it ; whereupon the hungry beast began

cropping the short grass by the roadside. Pastouré tied his mount to a tree and got into the van, where he took a seat beside Maurin's bedside. Meantime the *Boumian* lay down underneath between the four wheels, close to the savage dog that was chained there. It was four o'clock in the afternoon.

" Open the door, Pastouré, and let me see the road and the trees, and everything "—and his henchman followed his directions.

Then Maurin, from where he lay, could cast his eye through the open doorway, and follow the long white riband of the beach stretching from Saint-Aigulf to Saint-Raphaël.

Suddenly :

" Pastouré," he exclaimed, in a strange, startled voice, " I see yonder, sitting under a pine, a pretty lady, with a very pretty sunshade. . . . I *should* like to know what book it is she's so busy reading. Go and bring her here to me, will you ? "

" Are you gone mad, *Mòourin ?* "

" Go and do as I tell you. Don't you see it's my girl ? or yours, if you like it better, seeing she's married your boy ? "

Maurin was right ; it was his daughter, dressed out in very fine clothes, and trailing in the dusty roads a long fashionable skirt, the sort that has to be held up coquettishly in one hand—the whole costume and attitude being modelled upon the affectations of the middle-class dame, whom, nevertheless, the working woman hates and despises in her heart.

" What ! you here, father ? And ill ! "

" That's neither here nor there," growled Maurin. " I'm after my own business, which is no affair of yours. But yours does concern me. You were reading a book. . . . Just let me have a look at it."

She handed the volume to her father, who slowly and painfully deciphered a few lines, and then tossed it down on the bedclothes.

" I'll tell you," he resumed, " why I sent for you to come
here when I saw you ; you're too finely dressed, my girl, for
our station in life ! Besides, how comes it you're here at all,
out walking, to-day ? . . . No, don't answer. . . . You see very
well what I mean, I can guess. You're playing the grand
lady, and taking the air ! while Pastouré's lad, your husband,
is hard at work all the while ! What does it mean ?
D'you think it's right or reasonable ? You keep a servant-
girl, perhaps, eh ? It's a bit soon for that, as you've come
into nothing else that I know of but Pastouré's brother's
bit of money. Are you a flash girl a man pays, or an
honest wife, who helps her man to make his living ? The
book you're reading as you stroll to and fro under your
sunshade is a bad book. I've only read three lines of it,
and I shouldn't need to read a line more, for there's pictures
in it where you can see women showing men their garters !
D'you really think it was for this—that our girls might
read filth of that sort—that we've built so many schools ?
for it's we built 'em—we, the people—acting through our
representatives ! We were fain to teach poor, ignorant
folks—yes, but it was in order that, being taught, the lads
might know better how to follow, each his own trade,
to the best advantage, and that the girls—grown into
women—might be of most use to their husbands and
children ; and not that they might strut about by themselves in the sun, like fine ladies, reading books only meant
for loose wenches. Put your parasol away in the cupboard,
till you've done something to earn it, instead of trusting
just to your husband's weak indulgence of you, for I can
see he spoils you. My mother lived till she was eighty, and
all her life she never had anything to keep the sun and rain
off but one of those broad hats they throw back on the
shoulders when it's not raining and the sun's not too hot.
I feel certain you look down, nowadays, on your girl friends
of yesterday, for why ? because they've not made such a
grand marriage as you, though *you've* not exactly married
a ' my lord.' . . . And to think they're always like that,
these folk of the people ! Why, then, pity their misery

and help 'em to rise above it, if the moment they're a
bit better off they begin to look down upon their fellows,
and try to keep 'em at their old level ?   Look you, my girl,
men like Pastouré and me, we've all our lives been resenting
the airs many rich folks give themselves and their look
of saying : ' We're princes, we are, something higher than
the common herd ! We scorn the lower classes ! ' And yet
these haughty grandees often had good reasons—as our
officers on board ship had—for their pride, because they
possessed superior knowledge, and could sail vessels which
we uneducated fellows before the mast could only have
put right before the wind. But if this is to be all the result,
that hardly have our girls mastered their A B C at the
expense of the State before they begin flaunting their
vulgar finery and despising the apron, the working dress
their father and mother wear, why ! then, *noum dé Dioû !*
it wasn't worth our while to take such heaps of trouble
just to make poor people as idiotic as rich !   I see now, on
my death-bed, it's not politics can change men ; it's a taste
of morals is wanted. But where to find it ? . . . But now,
lass, as I'm not sure of ever seeing you again, wipe your
eyes and kiss me kindly ; but don't forget neither, that
if I wasn't sick, I'd tell you straight : ' Be off, bag and
baggage, and don't come back till you're dressed the
way your duty to your husband demands, and the
dusty road where you're walking ! ' "

She kissed him, the tears running down her cheeks,
while he was almost choking, exhausted by the long speech
he had made to relieve his feelings and satisfy his indignation.

"If I die," he added, " remember all I've said, because
why, this bit of good advice is all the inheritance I've got
to leave you, my lass. The ground my wooden hut is
built on isn't mine ; the timbers it's made of are rotten ;
there's hardly a thing inside but my Musketeer's dress,
and that's for the Musée of Arles M. Rinal told me of.
And for my boy Bernard, he'll have my seventy-four wild
pigs' tails."

" Seventy-five," corrected Pastouré, with a fine obstinacy.

" And now, good night, my girl, and don't forget my words. They'll bring you better and surer happiness than the gewgaws that dangle from a string at your belt, where my mother never carried anything but her big scissors."

When night fell, the van set out again in the bright moonlight, heading for the grotto at Roquebrune, where Lagarrigue was on the look out, stationed at the foot of the cliff. . . .

" I've taken your advice," Lagarrigue began, the moment he saw Maurin, " and given up the smuggling lay ; my chaps are only in the cave for another week. They're waiting for next pay-day, and that'll be the end."

" I'm right glad to hear it," said Maurin. " You're a fine fellow, Lagarrigue."

A system of pulleys had been contrived for hauling up the bales of tobacco into the cave, the ropes coming down from the top of the precipice to the level of the ground. A chair was adjusted to these, and Maurin seated in it with a hundred precautions. In dead silence he was hoisted in this way to the grotto, where Pastouré, with the smugglers round him, gave him a hearty welcome. Two men got hold of the ropes with a pair of gaffs and drew in the chair to the entrance of the cavern.

Then Maurin was laid on two mattresses which had been spread ready along one of the side walls, in a recess of the rock forming a sort of alcove.

" Now," laughed Pastouré, " all the gendarmes in France may search the country through and never find you. Yes, we're safe enough here at last ! . . . You've only to get well now."

" Didn't you notice, only just now," said Maurin sadly, " how along the high road, as the sun was going down, the folks don't bid each other ' Good night ; good night to you ! ' as our fathers used ? Yet it was a pleasant habit. How comes it, I wonder, that they've dropped it, if it's as they say, and men are growing more civilised as time goes on ? "

" Too many machine coaches ! " growled Pastouré with a shrug. " These bring all the world out on the roads, and it would be nothing but *good night, good night,* all the time. . . . But don't talk ; M. Rinal has given me my orders to nurse you and dress your wound till the day he's to come himself. Hold your tongue and go to sleep. . . . You've got to get well, you have ; I'm sorry enough for the poor folks, never fear, but there's only one Maurin ! "

Inside, the cave was illuminated only by the moon, which shone calm and bright, tracing a long pathway of silver across the sea that lay darkling in the distance.

CHAPTER LVIII

The Shepherds Rune.

THERE, in the smugglers' cave, among the offscourings of society, amid the acrid scent of the fresh tobacco, beneath a rugged vault of broken, uneven rock, in the cracks of which clung the knotted roots of wild, climbing plants, slept Maurin—soundly and well. For the first time in many years, he felt himself lodged in a safe and inviolable sanctuary.

At night no fire was ever lit, and all spoke in low, subdued voices.

The vast and lofty opening of the cavern mouth framed within its irregular jambs a great space of earth and sky. Far away could be descried the outline of the Alps, of the grey Maures, and the mass of Mont Vinaigre. In another direction shone the lights of Fréjus and those of Saint-Raphaël, while the steeple of the Russian church of the latter charming watering-place could be made out, and the twinkling stars of its harbour lights, and a number of fishing-craft riding at anchor.

In the plain below lakes and pools glittered in the moonlight, and the winding course of the Argens could be traced, as silvery as its name.

Beyond lay the sea, reflecting all the stars of heaven, motionless on the heaving waves, while the flash of wet stretches of sand gleamed brilliantly here and there.

At long intervals a train, speeding on its way to Paris or Nice, crossed the northern limits of the plain, a vision of smoke and flame, the hundred windows of the long moving city hurrying on to other places of light and movement—other cities.

By day the inhabitants of this strange abode cowered

in the deep and lofty tunnel of the main cave, and devoted
themselves feverishly to a hard, monotonous task-work,
which at least gave them bread to eat and a gleam of hope
amid the wretchedness of their lives.

Never-dying hope whispered in the ears of all : ' Who
knows ? forgetfulness and forgiveness always come at
last. One day, perhaps, derelicts as you are now of
society, you may return to the life of your fellows, and
walk the open streets and share in days of public rejoicing.
Then you will revisit your old haunts—markets and shops
and houses. True, there is nothing here, only lampless
gloom, the acrid smell of unripe tobacco, the weariness of
never-varying toil, seclusion—yet preferable to a prison,
because a man may sometimes persuade himself he has
chosen it voluntarily and can escape, if he choose. Is not
the rope-ladder always there, ready to one's hand ? '

All day long Maurin turned over such-like thoughts confusedly in his mind, and felt with a pang he was indeed the
brother of these outlaws. He did not scorn them ; he
shared their wretchedness, and was grateful for their
kindness, for were they not giving him all they had to
bestow, poor fellows—a refuge amongst them ?

At that moment the tobacco smugglers numbered only
five in the cave of Roquebrune—a growing lad, a very old
man, two escaped convicts from Nouméa, and, to complete
the tale, a poor, crippled, knock-kneed, partly hump-
backed man of middle age, who could never get work, and
who was the butt of unmerciful ridicule in every town he
went to. They had had to hoist him up to the cave at
night—the way horses are got on shipboard, with the
tackle they had just now used for Maurin.

The old man was called Trestournel, the lad Mignotin ;
the two convicts, the " Parisians," as their comrades called
them, answered to the nicknames of Pognon and Galette
(Tack and Tommy) respectively, the cripple to that of
Laragne. Their staple article of diet was ship's biscuit,
a pile of which was stacked in a corner under some ragged
sacks, growing mouldier and mouldier every day, varied

occasionally by a little fruit, sausage, and cheese, which
Mignotine would slip out at night to purchase at a wayside
tavern on the high road below, or which their friends outside
tied to strings to be hauled up by the hungry smugglers
with the eagerness of so many ravenous animals. On rare
occasions they indulged in wine, but they had brandy
enough, and absinthe more than enough !

Now Maurin was there, Pastouré organised a more
regular commissariat. The good-natured giant attended
personally to all details, and there was no stint of money.
The result was a very sensible improvement in the fare of
all the inhabitants of the cave. At first, in the security
of this inviolable refuge, Maurin had experienced a marked
improvement and return to strength, though his wound
still pained him badly. Alas ! what embittered all his
sufferings was the other, the moral wound—his regret for
lost illusions, his infinite disappointment and sore disgust
with human nature.

He thought overmuch in the night watches, and his old
heroic energies were slipping from him. The stain of an
odious suspicion was upon him ; he could feel it weighing
him down, burning out his vigour. His self-communings
were sad enough, but always kindly and well-meaning, for—
to use an expression frequently in the mouth of the Provençal peasantry—he was not " one of the sort who don't
know what affection is."

After nightfall a general conversation began in low tones,
while in the recesses of the cavern such as cared to smoked
a pipeful or two of all this smuggled tobacco, in constant
dread of their comrades' rebukes, for the smallest spark
of light might at any moment betray the whole band to
some traveller on the plain, or some prowling gendarme.

Then they would talk, in the intervals of gazing out at
the night through the cave-mouth, into which a bat would
sometimes flutter in with fearless unconcern.

The two convicts, " Tack " and " Tommy," would begin
a silly duet, which they repeated every night with stupid
chuckles of dismal laughter. The first would ask :

" I say, Tommy, when shall we escape from this here Liberty Hall ? "

To which the other would reply :

" When I've got my ' Tommy ' "—and the first would re-echo : " Yes, when I've got my ' Tack.' "

Then they would tell long stories of the hulks—tales to make your flesh creep—of warders felled by convicts and kicked to death, convicts shot down by warders' revolvers and then brutally manhandled, the refrain being always extraordinary, incredible escapes that were, nevertheless, true enough.

And the same squalid narratives were repeated from day to day—yesterday, to-day, to-morrow—with interminable and nauseous iteration.

" What pleasure," Maurin asked them, " can you find in telling these appalling tales ? There are so many pretty ones."

" The pretty stories don't interest us ; they have nothing to do with the like of us."

" I know one," returned Maurin, " the story of a thief, and it does as much honour to him as to the man he robbed."

" Let's hear your story, Maître Maurin."

" A poor workman—I knew the man—wanting money sorely for his wife and little ones after a long period of illness, stopped a bourgeois one night on the highway, demanding, ' your purse or your life ! '

" The bourgeois drew out his purse and tossed it to the man, and was for making off :

" ' Hold hard a bit ! ' the robber called after him. Then he opened the purse, which was full of money, extracted twenty francs, and handed back all the rest to the owner.

" ' I've no need for any more,' he told him . . . and, in his turn, began to make off with all speed.

" ' Now *you* hold hard a bit,' the bourgeois hailed him. ' Here's my name and address. I own a big factory ; come and work with my men to-morrow. . . . There's many honest folks not as honest as you ! '

"The thief accepted the offer—he told me the story himself—and he soon became the best workman and the best friend of his employer ; he used to shed tears when he spoke of him. It's a pretty story and a true one ! "

"Well, for my part," growled Tack, "I shall be sorry all my life I didn't strangle that old lady, you know, Tommy, the one they said was so rich, at Cannes."

"You may get as good a chance again yet," muttered the other.

Maurin listened in horror, his whole soul in impotent, indignant revolt.

"Mignotin's a mere lad," he burst out suddenly one time. "Don't, don't teach him these dreadful things. Give them up yourselves. Better days will dawn for you."

"For us, there'll be no better times for us," they answered surlily. "If die we must, we'll die for choice after doing for someone else. The man who perishes without a thing to lose, he wants a bit of revenge when he goes, to comfort him. Our first fault was to be wretched and starving. Yes, grub is the first virtue—tack and tommy ; that's how the world's made. I'd not have stolen the first time, if I could have paid for what I stole. What say you, old Trestournel ? "

"Trestournel's fast asleep ; he's tired out with cutting 'bacca ! " put in Mignotin.

"Trestournel's awake," protested the old peasant, now almost in his second childhood. "Trestournel," he maundered on, "can still work all day and all night too. Trestournel never sleeps ; he's thinking, thinking ! "

"Oh, ho ! and what's your thoughts, old boy, what's your thoughts ? "

Maurin, at whose bedside Pastouré was watching, attentive as a mother, was listening with a dreamy look on his pale face.

"My thoughts are old thoughts, very old," mumbled the aged peasant.

"Egad ! then, they're as old as you are ! "

" Older than I am by a hundred thousand year," piped
the patriarch.

A train went by at that moment in the distance with a
long-drawn whistle.

Trestournel said in a tone of deep seriousness :

" More by token, look at those wheels yonder . . . you
see how fast they fly, eh ? . . . Well, *I* saw the very first
wheels, the very first wheels ever made in the world ! "

So the old man said, and Maurin thought he must be
dreaming a sick man's disordered dreams, while Pastouré,
sitting by his side, kept jealous watch.

" The chaps who saw the first wheels," said one of the
convicts with a grin, " are far enough by this time, I
reckon, ah, ha ! "

" All the same, I saw 'em, such as you see me here, *I*
saw 'em, the first wheels ! "

" Tell us about it, old lad ; it'll pass the time, anyway."

" It was in our village, in the mountains far away yonder.
In my country they carried everything on mule-back.
One of our fellows, one day, went down to the town, to
Draguignan. And there he saw the first wheels ; it's
many a year since then. When he came back, he told us
all how, atop of a cross-piece, between two of these wheels,
they put a box with two long arms, and how, betwixt
the arms, a single mule harnessed in, pulled along the
wheels, that turned round and round, and how, in this
fashion, they shifted heavier loads than ever a mule can
carry. Anon, when the man had money enough to buy 'em,
these wonderful wheels, he hied back to the town again with
his mule and the *ensaris* (saddlebags of woven fibre). Then
he bought a pair of the first wheels ever were made, and
came back to our village with the wheels in his saddlebags,
one on right and one on left. And all the place ran out to
meet him ; and I and the other village children, we went
to the bottom of the hill, and came back again home,
dancing for joy before the first wheels ever reached there.
The man who'd bought 'em set 'em up on the ground
up against his house wall near the door, and everybody

for days and days came to look at 'em. But, as there was never a road in our parts to set wheels a-rolling on, there they stayed for always. Maybe they're there still, for I tell you 'twas the first wheels ever made in the world. Yes, I saw the first wheels, I did! I'm very old, I'm ninety-nine years old!"

The two convicts were holding their sides ; but Maurin did not laugh, nor did Pastouré, nor Mignotin, nor the hunchback.

"What are you grinning at?" said Maurin. "If he didn't see the first wheels, other men in other days have, and we should think of those chaps. The first wheels relieved men of a grievous load of heavy work."

"And what more have you seen, grandfather, in all these years you've lived, eh?"

"I've seen many a lot of vermin drop out, many a fine lot, every time they charmed a cow's broken horn."

"Tell us how that happens, daddy Trestournel."

"When a cow breaks off one of her horns," said the old fellow, "the vermin breed directly in the hole left in the poor beast's forehead. Then you go off to the hills and fetch an *agulancier* (briar-rose). In front of the *agulancier* you must make a deep curtsy, and at the same time trace a cross on the ground with your toe, repeating :

> " Agulancier,
> Agulancier,
> Fais-moi tomber
> Mon verminier. *

" Then you walk once round the briar-rose, make three more curtsies, and a cross with your foot after each curtsy, without ever missing one. After the fourth cross, which you mark on top of the first, you make a last bow. And then you repeat, without forgetting a word :

> " Merci, monsieur l'agulancier ;
> Tu m'as ôte mon verminier. †

* " Briar-rose, briar-rose, make my vermin swarm drop out."
† "Thank you, good sir briar-rose, you've clean cleared out my vermin swarm."

" Then you go home ; the wound is sound and clean."

" And does the horn grow again ? " asked ' Tommy ' waggishly.

" Laugh away all you who will ; but there *are* things ! " retorted the old man, in his quavering, broken voice. " Yes, there *are* things," he kept repeating, in a tone of mystery ; " some folks know .'em, and some don't. . . ."

" Trestournel," interrupted ' Tommy,' " look here, shall I tell you how I near died of laughing one day to see a man hanged—a chap I'd hanged myself, mind you ? . . . for I've not *always* used the knife, you must know."

" We should never laugh at a dying man," said Maurin rebukingly. " No, don't you tell us about your ugly triumph, my man ; you'd only be shocking the old chap here, who has never done you any harm, and who's lived so long he can't be far from the grave . . . where I shall be before him, I reckon. And then, why boast of a crime if you *have* done it ? . . . And of that I'm not so sure ; I don't want to believe it, anyway. . . . You only wanted, I suppose, when you talked like that, to poke fun at old Trestournel, because he's weak and you're strong. Would you, when your turn comes, and you're like him and me— he because he's old, and I because they've wounded me to the death—when you've no strength left, and you see your end at hand, would you like folk to come cruelly and make fun of you—eh, my lad ? . . . And don't you go saying you've done murder. Men's blood is meant to stay in their veins, out of sight ; it should never show up in the light of day. It's one of God's secrets, so to say. And that's a thing understood of folks who understand nothing else ! And if you had the misfortune to kill your fellow-man, bewail the calamity in your secret heart, and never talk of it. 'Tis a bad business you'll be sorry for on your death-bed—believe me—at the hour when the things a man has done speak in the heart, as those I've done are speaking in mine at the present moment ! But, God be thanked ! all my life through, there's none are very terrible."

The man made no answer, but hung his head in the gloom. Death is death ; and when it's Death speaks, men hold their peace.

" Maurin has said the right word," the old man declared emphatically.   " Yes, there's more things in death than in life."

The men who heard the old herdsman's voice as he uttered the words, shuddered, there in the dark cave, from which they looked out on all the mysterious world of sea and mountains, and the remote, starlit night.

Then Maurin felt a strange, inexplicable sense of sudden joy surge up within him. . . .

" And *you* know them, these things, father ? " he asked gently.

" Yes, I know them," answered the patriarch simply.

" What did you do before you came here ?   You've never told us that."

" It's true, I've never told you that. But I will tell you ; the hour is come. I had a bad son, who made my life hard. I lived overlong ; I was in his way. He wanted to take my new great-cloak off my shoulders and slip into my place with my masters. I was rich in those days ! I had ten sous a day !—ten sous and a life of freedom ! I was happy, but I had a bad son, a son who did not know the things—the things that *I* know ; and he laughed at me ! "

" What were the things, father, he did not know ? "

" The things that no man knows."

The answer set the two gaol-birds off into another guffaw of laughter.

" Don't laugh," ordered Maurin ; " there's nothing to laugh at ! . . ."

Pastouré rose to his feet, showing his gigantic stature silhouetted against the sky in the huge frame formed by the opening of the cavern.

" Anyone who don't obey Maurin " he announced quietly, " *I* will see that he does . . ."

" Oh ! you will, will you ? . . ." growled the two convicts.

" Hush, Pastouré," said Maurin soothingly ; " don't

threaten the poor fellows—you know you wouldn't hurt a
fly ! It's not anyone here they're angry with. I understand how things are ; they've been ill-treated and bullied,
and loaded with humiliations, for life is seldom just ; so
they nurse a sullen anger that's always in their hearts,
because nobody, perhaps, not even their own mother,
has ever said a soft word to them. They are not really bad
at bottom ; nobody is. We are only men, all of us."

'Tommy' was moved in spite of himself, and muttered :
" Beg pardon, Maître Maurin ! "

" There, you see, my good old Parlo-Soulet . . . he
understands I'm good for nothing now but to fill a grave,
and in face of death he grows gentle. 'Tis a good sign ;
he'll not laugh at you any more, Trestournel ! . . . Tell us
more things ! "

A silence fell on all, while the very stars seemed to wink
with a look of understanding and sympathy.

Then, softly, in the darkness, while his comrades listened
in astonishment, for as a rule he never opened his lips,
the old man began to speak again :

" Yes, I will tell you things, because this night "—here
he dropped his voice—"Death has entered in. Death is
here amongst you. You can't see his face, but I can ; it is
beautiful as a young man's."

" A drink, Pastouré, give me a drink ! " faltered Maurin,
sinking back in exhaustion.

And lo ! all there, the two convicts, Mignotin and
Laragne, all these unhappy wretches, gaol-birds, thieves
and murderers, sprang up with one impulse and pressed
round Maurin, as full of brotherly love in a moment
as Pastouré himself, offering the wounded man water,
brandy, doing whatever they could think of to make themselves useful. Those who could offer nothing else, gave
the best they could in words of consolation and farewell,
each vying with the other in such phrases as :

" How do you feel now, Maître Maurin ? . . . Does our
talking tire you ? . . . Shall we go for some wine ? . . . Do
you want to go to sleep ? "

MAURIN THE ILLUSTRIOUS   427

" No," murmured Maurin, " I love to hear the old man ;
only don't laugh at him. . . ."

" We won't laugh any more, Maître Maurin," ' Tommy '
assured him. " If everybody talked like you, man to
man like, things would go better. . . . You're a good
sort ! You're not the sort who have no love in all their
carcase—as we say in these parts—and who can give other
folks naught but anger and hate ! "

There was a long silence. Then Maurin, after drinking,
said :

" Go on again, father ; tell us all you know, Trestournel.
I won't speak another word from now."

All returned to their places, and Trestournel went on
thus :

" I know everything, yes everything ; because I've read
the Runes. I've read in the Runes, in days gone by,
with my first forbears, who are in me as the acorn of the
past is in the oak, and as the oaks of the future are in the
acorn. The future is the past."

The old man paused, and sky and plain and sea shone
outside in the calm splendour of the moonlight.

The patriarch's voice seemed to issue from some depth
of inspired mystery as it sounded in that lofty cavern,
in that strange abode looking down over the habitations
of men, where they lay below in town and village, beneath
peaceful roofs. . . . The ancient superstitions of the ages,
awakened in the hearts of these poor outlaws, amazed them
and riveted their attention. . . . They might well have
been insensible to any reasonable speech, to any common-
sense advice, but the words of this old man they called
a dotard, fascinated them—as a cadenced sound of music
such as it cannot make itself, holds a lizard momentarily
spell-bound, or the rhythmical beat of the tamer's magic
wand, ringing on the bars of their cage, will charm the
fiercest bear or tiger. For now the old herdsman's quavering voice was repeating words that had both rhythm and
rhyme :

L'ange Gabriel
Descendu du ciel
A dit à Marie :
" Mère, dormez-vous ? "
" Non, je ne dors pas ;
Je pense à l'enfant
Qui est mort en croix,
Les deux pieds cloués,
Les deux bras tendus . . .
Celui qui dira,
Le soir, le matin,
Ma douce prière,
Ne brûlera pas
Dans le feu d'enfer. *

For Maurin, the old man's words seemed to cradle his sick man's dreams — dreams of a gentle melancholy, more fateful than any violent visions. He hearkened heedfully to the old herdsman's foolish babble, as a child drinks in the fairy-tales, in which it believes, yet does not believe, thinking all the time : ' How I wish all that had really happened ! ' He was absorbed in the patriarch's memories—more than in all those of his own past life.

Already his bygone existence seemed something far away, seen from the depths and height of this cavern where all these outlaws and outcasts of society dwelt. Already he felt detached from all the passing show of life. The threads which, like rootlets, had once bound his intelligence to so many things, seemed all broken short off ; he felt it was so, but instead of being grieved he was rejoiced to know it. But he still suffered keenly whenever his memory brought suddenly back to him again the event which had produced this severance between himself and all thought and desire of living. . . . " So young a thing," he would mutter sadly, " and so false and cowardly ! . . . Ah ! poor France ! "

* " The Angel Gabriel came down from Heaven and said to Mary : ' Mary, Mother, art asleep?'—' Nay, I cannot sleep for thinking of the Child that died on the Cross, His two feet nailed, His two arms outstretched. . . . Whosoever will say, night and morning, my gentle prayer, he shall never burn in hell-fire.' "

But the old herdsman prevented the recurrence of these harrowing recollections of Maurin's by breaking into a low-voiced chant—a song of vague, half-heard, comforting words, like a mother's lullaby over her infant's cradle :

> J'ai fait un bouquet de trois fleurs
> Et les trois vierges sont mes sœurs.
> La croix de sainte Marguerite,
> Je l'ai sur ma poitrine écrite. . . . *

The old fellow lisped his words curiously, for he was singing in French that the two convicts might understand, for they did not know Provençal. But his defects of utterance did not strike even the two Parisians as strange. All were rapt in dreamland.

" Go on ! " Laragne begged in a voice of entreaty.

" Go on, go on ! " echoed Mignotin.

" Yes, I know secrets that are in the words of songs," resumed the old man slowly. . . . " And your wound, Maurin, I'll cure it, if you choose, with spells and signs. You refused once, when you first came, and I was hurt. Will you let me now, though it's a bit late, perhaps ? "

" Why not ? " agreed Maurin, to please the old fellow.

" Turn your bad side towards me.   Where is the hurt ? "

" There."

Then the old herdsman made cabalistic signs over the wound with his thumbs—signs that could not be clearly distinguished in the gloom of the cave, and chanted :

> Judas a perdu sa rougeur
> Dans le jardin des Oliviers
> Quand il trahit Notre-Seigneur. . . .†

" It's not the words only that cure," he quavered, " there's signs as well, signs as well ! three or seven, signs and figures ! . . . But maybe it's too late, too late."

---

* " I have made a posy of three flowers, and the three virgins are my sisters. The cross of St. Margaret, I have signed it on my breast. . . ."

† " Judas lost his ruddiness, in the Garden of Olives, when he betrayed Our Lord. . . ."

" If you know how to cure, why don't you cure your own wretchedness ? " asked ' Tack ' derisively.

" Yes, and ours," insisted ' Tommy.'

" I am not wretched, because I'm alive," declared the old man, " and I can see the stars, which are all men's treasure. . . . We must believe to be healed," he added mildly. " I've seen men without legs who climbed to the top of the mountains and came near to reaching the stars ; and I've seen men who had legs, and who stayed down in the dark valley. I know the secrets of things. Laragne one day will walk straight and upright, maybe. If he's twisted, is it his fault ? Yet a man makes or mars his own fortune. Yes, there's some throw spells over folks ; but the spell only touches such as are made to feel it. The wheat don't grow everywhere. In the same field one grain springs and another dies. There's secrets, yes, there's secrets ; and I know some for soldiers, I know others good against mad dogs, and others against the thunder, and to save men's souls after death. But I know never a one for those who make their own hell for themselves. . . . I knew none to save my own son from his own wickedness."

The old man could be heard sobbing in the darkness, and all hearts were stirred with pity.

" Don't cry, father," the two convicts exclaimed together, and one of them added, with a new-born feeling for others :

" You'll hurt Maître Maurin, if you do."

" Forget your grief, father ! " Maurin said. He was burning with fever, and all the things he had ever done began to pass before his eyes in a disordered dream, He marshalled in review all the incidents in his life—but he saw himself in the midst of them, as if he were a stranger to himself ; and he was surprised to behold a stranger acting in his stead, without feeling what the intruder felt. He was outside his own past life now ; yet through all these fantastic visions he could still hear all that was being said around him. . . .

" Yes," the thought kept running through his head, " yes, Pastouré must go as soon as may be and tell

M. Rinal not to put himself about to come and see me . . .
I'm dying. . . ."

"Father Trestournel," announced Mignotin by and by,
"I'm thinking of quitting here. A soldier I would be."

"Come hither, my son ; 'tis a fine trade, to defend one's
country—the good earth, that grows corn and feeds
flocks. Listen ; there's a France up in the sky as there's
one here on earth. I have the Runes and Rhymes from my
old ancient forbears. Come hither, lad."

So Mignotin stepped forward, trembling a little. The
rest saw his figure outlined as he stood all in black shadow
against the bright moonlit sky. The old man advanced
to meet the lad ; and both were in full view of all there.

"A France up in the sky, eh ? " sneered 'Tack' under
his breath.

"Nay, if you laugh at my runes, I'll not say a word.
My end is drawing near ; I must needs speak—not all the
secrets I know, but at least the things they bid me say.
Little lad, you want to be a soldier, little lad ? . . . Well
then, here's the words, and for the signs I'll make 'em on
your shoulder, and on your heart I'll do the like. And the
Virgin of France will guard you. . . . She is called Jean-
nette ; she dwells in the France that's in the sky. And
he quavered :

> France est le paradis du monde . . .
> Va combattre, je te seconde ;
> Puis tu viendras, je te le dis,
> Dans la France du Paradis. *

"Be a soldier, as *I* was a shepherd. The Shepherdess,
armed with the Sword, will know you for her own."

Mignotin resumed his seat, all overwhelmed with super-
stitious terrors. The freethinker trembled before the
wizard. All sat silent in the gloom, full of a confused
amazement at their own emotion.

* "France is the Paradise of the world ; go forth to fight, I second
you ; anon thou shalt return, I tell thee true, to the fair France of
Paradise."

Trestournel went on with his mutterings :

> Saint Martin porte un grand manteau
> Bleu comme le ciel le plus beau,
> Avec l'or du soleil pour franges,
> Comme on voit aux robes des anges . . .
> Un pauvre l'arrête en chemin
> Et le prie en tendant la main ;
> L'âge fait que le vieux tremblote,
> Le froid veut encore qu'il grelotte ;
> Alors, du haut de son cheval
> Qui foule aux pieds l'Esprit du mal,
> Le cavalier, armé du glaive,
> Ôtant son manteau, le soulève,
> Le coupe et d'un seul en fait deux :
> " Ne grelotte plus, grelotteux. . . .
> Ton manteau, comme ceux des anges,
> Avec l'or du soleil pour franges,
> Épais velours sur bleu satin,
> C'est le manteau de Saint Martin ! " *

" Ho, ho ! " laughed Pastouré, "that's a song reminds me, Maurin, of one of our drollest adventures."

But Maurin was too sad and pensive to laugh. He was pondering, no more for his own sake, but for those that should come after him, over the folly and perversity of men.

" And against mad dogs, d'ye know any charms, father ? Think you not a good stout cudgel is the best spell against a brute of that sort ? There are mad dogs too have the semblance of men."

" Yes, a cudgel is good, if you don't miss your blow. But if you do, and don't hit the brute, then try a spell on

---

* " St. Martin wears a great cloak, blue as the bluest sky, with golden sunbeams for fringes, as we see on the Angels' robes. . . . A poor man stops him by the way and begs an alms, holding out his hand ; age makes the old man tremble, and eke the cold sets him shivering ; then from his tall horse, which tramples underfoot the Spirit of Evil, the horseman, armed with his falchion, doffs his cloak, lifts it, cuts it in half, and of one makes two : " Shiver no more, thou shivering wretch . . . thy cloak, like the Angels', with golden sun-beams for fringes, thick velvet over blue satin, is the cloak of St. Martin ! "

him. For dogs there's no need of sign, and the words are
these :

> C'est le chien noir de la montagne
> Qui va tournant dans la campagne,
> Le nez soufflant, la bouche en feu,
> Et la langue aboyant à Dieu.*

" I know him," said Maurin, " I know him ! "—and in
his dim, fevered brain he saw Tonia transformed into a
howling, rabid cur. . . . But no, it was not Tonia . . . no,
it was Fanfarnette now.

Trestournel went on :

> Mais si Dieu veut que je l'arrête,
> Je mettrai le pied sur sa tête ;
> Dieu le voudra *si je le veux*,
> Car sa lumière est dans mes yeux.
> Il le voudra, si je l'en prie
> Au nom de Madame Marie
> Qui porte son petit enfant,
> Droite sur le front du serpent.
> Viens ici, grand chien de la haine !
> Dieu garde mes bêtes à laine !
> Abaisse ta férocité,
> Devant l'agneau d'humilité.
> Le vent élève ma prière
> Mais il n'éteint pas ma lumière . . .
> Gaspard, Balthazar, Melchior . . .
> Je marche avec l'étoile d'or ! †

" That's all very well, but I *should* like to know," suddenly exclaimed the irrepressible ' Tack,' " I should like

---

* " 'Tis the black dog of the mountain that goes prowling in the
plain, his muzzle panting, his mouth afire, and his tongue baying
God."

† " But if God bids me stay his course, I'll plant my foot on his foul
head ; God will wish it, *if I will it*, for His light dwells in my eyes.
He will be willing, if I beseech Him in the name of the Lady Mary,
who carries her little child in her arms, standing bold and straight on
the brow of the Serpent. Come hither, great hound of abomination !
God keep my fleecy flocks ! Abate thy ferocity before the lamb of
humility. The wind lifts my prayer heavenwards, but never quenches
my light . . . Gaspard, Balthazar, Melchior . . . I march with the
star of gold ! "

to know how to get out of here! That's what you've
got to tell, old fellow!"

"If you don't call down your own damnation on yourself, if you aren't damned by your own self to hell, why,
I have a secret for you. But if you're bent on damning
yourself wilfully, you'll only forget my words, and in the
pit of your own damnation you'll stay for ever."

Then with his low, broken voice, the tones of an old, old
man, tottering already on the brink of the tomb, where
times and seasons are no more, the old wizard began again :

> Pauvres pécheurs, le cœur me tremble,
> Comme fait la feuille du tremble,
> Comme fait l'oiseau dans son nid,
> Quand le tonnerre au ciel bruit.
> Le pont où doit passer notre âme
> Ressemble au cheveu d'une femme ;
> Dessous est un gouffre de feu,
> Au-dessus est la barbe à Dieu.
> Les deux mains vite il faut étendre,
> En la baisant il faut la prendre ;
> Et notre père, doux et bon,
> Ne secouera pas le menton.
> Tenons bien fort, quoi qu'il nous dise
> (Sauf respect de la Sainte Église),
> Et forçons-le de se baisser
> S'il veut en enfer nous chasser !
> Car dans l'éternelle géhenne,
> Pour peu que sa barbe se prenne,
> Il tirera tous les maudits
> De l'enfer dans le Paradis . . .
> Tel est, pour échappes aux flammes,
> Le secret du salut des âmes ;
> Tel est, pour entrer au saint lieu,
> Le secret de la barbe à Dieu. *

* "Poor sinners, my heart trembles as the leaf of the aspen does ;
as the bird does on its nest, when the thunder bellows in the sky.
The bridge by which our soul must pass is fine as a woman's hair,
below is a whirlpool of fire, above is God's beard. Both hands we
must outstretch, we must draw it down and grip it hard ; and our
Father, kind and good, will not shake his chin. Let us hold on well,
whate'er he say to us (saving due respect to holy Church), and force

As he finished, a loud clap of thunder shook the sky.

"Ho, ho! God A'mighty's drum!" cried Mignotin gleefully.

But next moment the old man, making the sign of the cross, stepped forward to the very edge of the precipice, whence he seemed to dominate all the land and all the sea, and standing face to the storm, he prayed :

> Sainte Barbe, la sainte fleur,
> Tient la croix de Notre-Seigneur ;
> Elle est debout sur la tourelle,
> Et répond à Dieu qui l'appelle :
> " Je reviendrai vers les élus
> Lorsque vous ne tonnerez plus ;
> Je tiens votre croix sur la terre,
> Pour en détourner le tonnerre . . .
> C'est pour cela que, nuit et jour,
> Je suis en garde sur ma tour." *

"Pastouré," cried Maurin suddenly, in an altered voice that sounded like a sob in the gloom, "help! help! I'm choking!"

All realised that a man was near his end. They came round his bed, crowding one upon the other.

"Air! more air! carry me to the mouth of the cave . . . I shall breathe easier there, and I can see all the sky too. . . ."

"Help me, everybody," said Pastouré. "Get hold of the mattress on both sides. With us five, we'll lift it easily, two on either hand, I at the head."

With the most tender care the poor fellows carried Maurin to the entrance of the cave.

him to stoop, if he is for driving us away to hell. For in the everlasting pit, if only his beard don't catch, he will draw all the accursed from hell into paradise. . . . Such then, to escape the flames, is the secret of the salvation of souls ; such, to enter the holy place, is the secret of the beard of God."

* "St. Barbe, the holy flower, holds the cross of our Lord ; she stands aloft on the turret, and answers God who calls her: 'I will come back to the elect when Thou has left off thundering ; I hold Thy cross upon the earth, to turn aside the thunder from it . . . It is for this that, night and day, I am on guard upon my tower.'"

A flash on the horizon made a zigzag cleft in the dark-blue vault, the rim of which seemed to rest away yonder on the sea. The storm was far off. The murmur of the ocean, with its countless waves, answered the rustling woods of the mountain-side on which the cavern opened.

"The world is better and more beautiful than the men that live in it ! " murmured Maurin.

All heard the words, even the aged shepherd, though he was half deaf ; he came immediately and knelt beside the dying man, to hear him and speak to him the better. . .

"You know the heavens ? " muttered the old herdsman where he knelt, pointing to the different constellations in the wide sky. " Then look, look into the depths of the heavens up yonder. . . . Look ; there are the Pleiades, like a mother partridge gathering her young ones, that peep their heads from under her wing and are happy. There are the Magi, who bring perfumes of fire and glittering gold. And there is the Star of the Shepherds. It is the finest star of all, the star of hope and love. The Shepherd's Star once guided the three kings. . . . Yes, yes . . . 'tis the shepherds lead the kings ! . . ."

Maurin was too weak now to suffer any pain. He groped for Pastouré's hand, and Pastouré, on his knees to be nearer his friend, gave it him. Maurin pressed it in his own.

Lying in the opening of the cave, he was gazing out into space. His eyes were lifted towards the blue heavens that stretched in sombre infinity above his head, and he felt as though something of himself, of his thought, rose upward with his gaze and soared aloft, far, far aloft, higher than the eagle's flight, higher than the blue air itself. . . . And this something was still himself—but himself without love, without hate, without desire. And this something that was himself was lost at last far, far aloft, light, light as a sigh, light as they say are disembodied souls.

Maurin was dead.

THE END